THE EMB*i*TTERED RUBY

✦ A DIAMOND ESTATES NOVEL ✦

NICOLE O'DELL

BARBOUR
PUBLISHING

The author is represented by MacGregor Literary.

Published by Barbour Publishing, Inc., P.O. Box 719, Uhrichsville, Ohio
44683, www.barbourbooks.com

*Our mission is to publish and distribute inspirational products offering
exceptional value and biblical encouragement to the masses.*

 Member of the
Evangelical Christian
Publishers Association

Printed in the United States of America.
Bethany Press International, Bloomington, MN, 55438; March 2012; D10003229

*Dedicated to Dawn Huffman, Chris Keaton, and Freda Calhoun
as well as the countless others who have served as counselors
in a residential setting like Diamond Estates or Teen Challenge.
Your tireless efforts with teens like Olivia, Carmen,
and me have reaped eternal rewards.*

Acknowledgments

A lot goes into the writing of a book. An author might type the words, but she could never accomplish an entire novel without the help of many people. . . .

First I'd like to thank the team at Barbour for believing in the Diamond Estates series and helping me bring it to life. Specifically Kelly McIntosh, you have supported me in big ways over the past couple of years, and I so appreciate your passion and creativity.

Literary agent extraordinaire, Chip MacGregor—thanks so much for putting up with me and helping me navigate the publishing industry.

Valerie Comer, as always, your critiques have been invaluable to me in the process of writing *The Embittered Ruby*. I thank you, and Carmen thanks you.

Kim Cash Tate, I can't write these acknowledgments without a nod to your awesome work in *More Christian than African American*. We discussed the story behind your idea for that book when I had you on Teen Talk Radio. That discussion laid the foundation for much of this story. Thanks for being you!

Writer-sisters, prayer partners, and dear friends—you all have such a huge part in everything I do, and I feel so privileged to be able to walk this journey with you.

Wil, Erik, Natalie, Emily, Logan, Megan, Ryleigh. . . Thank you for your constant support and everlasting love.

Chapter 1

"If only heaven and hell shared the same zip code," Carmen Castillo sputtered into her cell phone as she huddled on the rusty fire escape. Anything for privacy. Even if it did put her at risk of a drive-by.

"You having a tough day, C?"

"To say the least. I mean, I'm stuck here, in Hackensack, New Jersey—some weird version of hades on earth. You're still in Briarcliff Manor, New York, otherwise known as heaven." She glared down the street. "Your view is of mansions and rolling lawns; mine is of bars and nail salons." Could it get any worse?

"Let's pretend. Close those gorgeous brown eyes, and lay your pretty face on my chest. Now I'm squeezing. And even tighter. Do you feel it?"

Ah. Nate McConnell's deep, velvety voice massaged the tension from her body. Her fingers tingled as she imagined stroking the stubble on his face and then running them across his prickly blond buzz cut. Next she tried to envision her dark waves lying across his thick biceps. She couldn't quite grasp the complete visual with the horns blaring and the shop lights blinking. "It's surreal. It's like I'm watching someone else's life fall apart on a TV special. Except it's mine. All mine."

Silence.

After all, what could he say to her? Carmen knew he loved her—she'd never had a moment's doubt. They'd been together since Nate's junior year and her freshman year. Carmen had never dated anyone else, and though Nate had had a few minor relationships, he said he'd never loved anyone else. She believed him.

The big Castillo move must have hurt him, too—but obviously not like it had destroyed her. Nate still lived in luxury and kept the same address in the elite town they'd both enjoyed all their lives. At most, the distance inconvenienced him— whereas the change, and the divorce leading up to it, affected every fiber of her life. And he clearly didn't hurt enough to fight for her. But really, what did she expect him to do? Marry her? Yeah right. Like his parents would ever allow him. Judge McConnell and Hillary barely tolerated Nate dating Carmen because of her Mexican heritage—though Carmen doubted they had any idea their disdain was so obvious.

Wonder if his mom lay in bed at night and whispered, "Well, at least she's half white," as she tucked silk sheets around her feet. Then Nate's dad would turn out the light and mumble, "Yes, thank the Lord for small favors."

Little did she realize that even though Dad looked white, Grandpa Castillo had migrated right from Mexico. Where did Hillary think the Castillo name came from? And Mom. . . she was straight blue-collar Mexican. Born and raised in Hackensack. Rescued from her fate by a rich, good-looking business man and moved to upstate New York. Funny how fate has a way of rearing it's ugly head and sucking a person back into its clutches.

Nate cleared his throat. "So where's everyone else?"

"You mean you can't hear the construction racket? I can barely think over the hammering and drilling. Mom and Kimberley are in my—er, *our*—room setting up. . .get this:

bunk beds. Bunk beds? You've got to be kidding. I get to play Rock, Paper, Scissors with my little sister over who gets the top bunk. After never having shared a room for a day in my life." Laugh or cry? Punching something sounded more satisfying.

"Yeah. I bet it's a pain. I wouldn't like sharing with Charlie."

"At least your little brother is cute, and you can kind of overlook his immaturity because he's only three. He's still a baby. Kimberley, well, she's a spoiled brat. I'd almost rather share with Harper. At only eight, she falls asleep early and is still kind of cute in certain ways—though annoying in all kinds of others." Carmen peered around the cracks to peek in the window. "Speaking of the diva, there goes Kim now. Towel across her shoulder, off to take a bath in the claw-foot tub. Would you believe she sees an antique tub as an adventure? She imagines she's an art student living in Paris." Wonder if she's looked out the window yet.

"She's only thirteen. Give her a break maybe?" Nate's words sounded clipped. "Sounds like she's trying to make the best of it all."

Carmen gritted her teeth against her turbulent emotions. *Bet he's glad he called.* "I'm sorry. I'm being horrible company. I can let you go and talk to you later."

"Okay. You know I love ya. But if you want to go for now, I'll be fine." The lilt in his voice gave away his relief. "Give me a call when you feel like it."

Ending the call wasn't at all what she wanted. Carmen really wanted to discover a genie in a bottle to grant her three wishes. She'd even take just one wish. Or some ruby slippers. *There's no place like home.* But if she couldn't have her ultimate dream of putting things back the way they were, she'd at least take time with her boyfriend. Was even that small a favor too much to ask the universe? Carmen stared at the lifeless phone in her hand. Apparently.

How would she see Nate anymore? Maybe she could talk her parents into letting her live with Dad. A shudder rippled from head to toe. No matter how bad things got in Hackensack, it couldn't be as bad as being around Cheerleader Barbie and her pom-poms. Tiffany, who turned simple, everyday tasks into a cheer. "The coffee's. . .ready? Okay!" *Rah, rah. Gag.* But Tiffany wouldn't be around forever. No way. At least not if Carmen could help it. And Carmen intended to help it.

Not ready to go back inside, Carmen closed her eyes. Maybe if she could imagine hard enough, she'd be able to teleport herself back home, taking a dip in the pool or soaking in the hot tub. She breathed air deep into her lungs, somehow expecting the familiar smell of the cedar planks in the sauna. Instead exhaust fumes from the buses and grease from the diner across the street attacked her senses.

No use.

Carmen slipped her phone into the pocket of her jeans and pried herself from the stucco wall she'd been leaning against. Crumbling plaster pelted the metal grid of the fire escape and rained onto the street below.

A whistle pierced the din of traffic.

Shielding her eyes against the sun, Carmen squinted up the neighborhood. Nothing there but two old men on a bus-stop bench outside the drugstore. Down the road, little kids played on the uneven sidewalk. Where had the whistle come from? Finally her gaze settled on four menacing teens leaning on the lamppost across the street. One dark pair of eyes drew hers like magnets. He cocked his head and stared holes into Carmen's flaming cheeks.

Shirtless, he touched the black-and-gold bandana tied around his bulging bicep. Then he shifted position, and Carmen saw the largest tattoo she'd ever seen in person. A huge lion with a five-pointed crown on its head was inked on his right side, starting at his ribs and winding around to the middle of his back.

Carmen's eyes roved to take in the garb of the others. All black and gold. The tattoos among them too numerous to count. Latin Kings.

Did they carry. . . ? Oh, yep. Right in plain view. A polished handle stuck out of the waistband of the tallest of the group. How many of the others had guns?

Great. Now she crouched alone on a narrow fire escape, in a place God had forgotten about, being leered at by a gang. Carmen wanted to be safe inside, cocooned on her bunk bed or better yet on the queen four-poster she'd left behind in New York, but she had frozen under their sneers. Too scared to move—too afraid to appear nervous or show any sign of weakness. What were they doing there outside her apartment? More importantly, why were they staring at her?

The leader snapped his fingers, and a cigarette appeared at his lips. Another pair of hands flicked a lighter, and it sparked to life. He took a long drag and blew out the smoke in slow motion. Then he winked one dark eye at her and ran his tongue along his lips.

Carmen shivered as goose bumps speckled her body from head to toe. She flung the sliding door to the side and scurried back through the opening. She slid it shut, latched the lock, and lowered the bar until it clicked into place.

Don't look. Don't even turn around. Keep moving, and don't look back.

She could feel their laser-sharp stares burning holes between her shoulder blades as she moved though the family room. A quick right and she stood in the hallway. Three more steps to her room. Was she safe there? Were any of them?

Those jerks were going to be trouble. Just what she'd expected when she moved to New Jersey.

Chapter 2

Main Street, Hackensack, New Jersey. Great place to take a sightseeing tour if someone wanted pictures of rundown buildings and homeless people. Carmen scuffed along the sidewalk, careful to avoid the side of the street where those gang members had been standing and ogling her the day before. "There used to be a market near Main Street," Mom had said. Should have been easy enough. People in Hackensack cooked, right?

Pangs of longing struck Carmen's gut as she remembered the decadent aisles of the Whole Foods in White Plains. Wandering the rows of culinary perfection hour upon hour several times a week, Carmen invented recipes and special treats using the polished produce and pungent herbs. Would the salesclerks forget her name if she'd only be there once a month, or even less?

Carmen shuffled past a run-down library. The grease odor from several hole-in-the-wall restaurants seemed to follow her down the street. And the gym boasted a life-size mural of a steroid junkie punching a bag.

Definitely no shortage of nail salons, barbershops, pawn shops, convenience stores, and lawyers' offices. But a market? Maybe she could ask someone for directions. She lifted her eyes just enough to peek around for a friendly looking pedestrian, but from the looks of things she'd better explore on her own. Carmen slipped her hand in her pocket and gripped her cell phone. . .just in case.

Ah. There across the street with a wide green awning, GIANT FARMERS' MARKET. Sounded like a store made especially for her. Carmen waited for a gold Monte Carlo with bass pumping from the speakers to pass and then jogged to the other side. Her head down, she pulled the glass door open and stepped inside. As her eyes adjusted to the fluorescent lighting, she glanced around the store.

Now this place had hope. Fresh. Bright. Almost happy.

Piles of colorful produce. Artichokes, guava, pomegranate. Some things even she didn't recognize. Shocker. Should probably learn the place before making selections. She wandered up and down the aisles, touching the bags and reading labels. The Latin aisle alone boasted rows and rows of bottles Carmen had never seen. Ethnic oddities, rare herbs and. . .um. . .pig ears? Those might have to wait for another time. Mom sent her on a milk, eggs, and bread kind of shopping trip. But maybe, for lack of anything better to do in Hackensack, she'd be able to practice for culinary school with some of the specialty things in here.

Thirty minutes later, Carmen hurried back to the apartment. Her bags banged against her legs and twisted as she walked. The plastic dug into her wrists, cutting off the circulation. She'd had enough culture for one day. Odd though, no one glanced at her the whole way home—at least not that she'd seen. Didn't she stand out at all? Couldn't they tell she didn't belong there—that her home existed far away? Probably a good thing she blended in, though. Not like Kimberley, who had luscious blond hair like their dad. Wonder if things would be more difficult for her?

Dead bolt. Lock. Second lock. The door swung open three inches then jerked. She shoved her face into the opening to see into the room. "Hey. Can someone come take the chain off the door so I can get in? These bags are heavy."

Little Harper cartwheeled across the room, her tongue poking through the space where her tooth had once been. "Coming." She closed the door and slid the chain off before skipping toward the kitchen.

Eight-year-olds never just walked. Or was Harper the only one who bounced everywhere she went?

Carmen rushed through the door, reached her foot back to nudge it shut, then hurried to the galley kitchen. She heaved her packages onto the gold-flecked countertop and freed her wrists from the bags. Red rings remained where they'd indented her skin. "Phew. I almost lost the whole load. Where's Mom?"

"In your room." Harper flashed a dimpled smile and bounded down the short hallway.

Carmen took a deep breath before entering her bedroom. She'd been a real grump lately. Maybe surprising everyone with a nice dinner would help make up for some of her bad attitude. "Hey. I'm back." She stepped over the tools and packing material strewn across the stained and tattered carpet. After all, it wasn't Mom's fault they'd had to move into the dingy apartment. Which was probably rat infested. And should be condemned.

Mom probably shouldn't have told Carmen about the money battles she was embroiled in between Dad and the lawyers—but at least Carmen could sort of understand why they were in the situation they were. At least for now.

Well. . .not entirely Mom's fault, anyway. There had to have been a place across the river they could have rented, right? Yeah, yeah. They needed to be close to Mom's new job at the dentist office. Affordable. Close to public transportation. Carmen had heard it all. But did she buy it? She just hoped they hadn't been dragged out to the end of the earth just to make Dad feel guilty for taking his lawyer's advice and withholding money until the court settled the divorce. It sure didn't look like he suffered under the weight of regret.

"You're still at it, huh?" Carmen sank to the floor and picked up the instructions. French? She flipped the paper over. "Want some help?"

Mom swiped at the hair strands that escaped from her ponytail then went back to wrestling with a screwdriver. "I think I'm almost done. Finally. How'd the shopping go?"

"I found this neat market—they have lots of fun cooking stuff. I'm going to make a surprise dinner tonight."

"Okay, but remember, even though God's sure been faithful to us, we don't have extra money for you to buy all kinds of exotic foods to play chef with. At least not now."

Carmen took a deep breath. The God stuff again. "I know, Mom. Just trying to do something nice. Besides, I don't *play* chef." Change the subject. "But hey. Since the bunk beds aren't finished, how about we just separate them and put one on each side of the room? Or better yet, put Kimberley's in the living room."

The hammer clanged as Mom dropped the screwdriver on top of it. "We've been over this. We have no choice, Carmen. You've got to share a room with Kimberley, and trying to squeeze two separate beds in here is silly. It would take up way too much room, and there'd be no place to put all your books. Unless, of course, you want to give up some of your bookshelves."

Over Carmen's dead body. "You can't be serious. My books?" The cookbooks alone would fill two shelves.

"I didn't think so. Then that's all there is to it." She sat back on her heels. "You know, it's not like I'm thrilled to share with

Harper. At my age, I didn't expect to be roommates with an eight-year-old."

"But. . ." Oh, what was the point in arguing? Stop thinking about her big bedroom at home. . .er. . .at Dad's. The good life wasn't her life anymore—at least it stood waiting for her to visit two weekends a month. Carmen looked around the tiny space. Up at the water spots on the ceiling then down at their mirror images on the carpet—one pair of them reminded her of elephants with their trunks raised in salute to each other. Her new home—whether she liked it or not. But she didn't like it one bit. "Why can't I at least commute to my old school from here? I mean, I could take the bus. Nate and I Googled it."

Mom pressed her fingers into her temples until her knuckles turned white. "You Googled *what* exactly?" She thrust out each word with what seemed a huge effort.

Oh no. Mom appeared done in. Why hadn't Carmen waited to bring this up after dinner? Too late, though. "Um, the bus schedule. All I'd have to do is catch the one-sixty-five a block away at State Street. Then hop on the number seven subway at Times Square. A quick ride to Grand Central, and then I'd get on the Metro-North Hudson Line to Ossining, and then I'm basically there."

"Right. And what time is the first bus at State Street? Four a.m.?" Mom shook her head. "You're talking to a native New Yorker. I know full well what you just described is at least two hours' traveling time each way."

Two and a half actually. But admitting the actual travel times to Mom sure wouldn't help Carmen's cause at all. Besides, Carmen didn't pick Hackensack. They could have moved closer to home if only Dr. Miller from Mom's church hadn't offered her a receptionist job in his Hacker location. "I don't mind the travel. Really. I can do homework, read, or even nap."

"No way, Carmen. Walking around outside this apartment while it's still dark in the morning and then not getting home until after dark? I don't think so. It's just not safe to have you traipsing all over two states twice a day."

It had to be safer than going to school in Hackensack. But Mom wouldn't like to hear that at all.

"Plus what about your sisters—how are they supposed to get to school, and who will be here for them after? I'll be working at the dentist office during the day and hopefully doing Mary Kay facials at night."

But why was it Carmen's responsibility to be the parent?

Mom slapped her hands on her thighs and pulled herself up, her knees creaking the whole way. "I have an idea, though. If you and Nate want to be together so much, why doesn't he do the daily bus pilgrimage and transfer to college in New Jersey to be with you? How about trying the chivalrous thing for once, rather than expecting you to do all the work."

"Right, like his parents are going to let Nate McConnell, heir to the throne of their political empire, slum it in Hackensack, New Jersey." Carmen wrinkled her nose and gazed out the tiny window at the billboards and barred store windows below them. He wouldn't do it anyway. No way. "Just forget about it. Besides, it's a lot harder to transfer colleges, and he's been in classes for a month now. And since I already started the year at my old school, I could skip the whole transfer process completely and just keep going to my school."

Mom ignored her. She grunted and leaned back at her hips, rotating her upper body. "I'm getting too old for this," she muttered.

"You're thirty-three. That's so not old." They'd had the same discussion before. Mom, still young and pretty, could lose a few pounds, sure, but who couldn't really? Maybe if she did, maybe if she bought some new clothes and got a trendy haircut, then maybe Dad would want her back and they could all go home.

And makeup. Hopefully Mom's new Mary Kay venture would add a little color to her own face. Maybe they'd teach her to get rid of those dark circles and bags under her eyes. She'd never be as young and, um, perky, as Tiffany. . .but she could be a better version of herself without even trying very hard. Mom had better step it up if she wanted Dad back. But how could Carmen convince her without hurting her feelings? Especially when she didn't seem to want him back.

"Hey guys, what's up?" A tiny blur of flowing black hair bounded across the room and rolled onto the bottom bunk. Harper rested her elbows on the bare mattress and propped her chin in her hands.

"Get off my bed." Carmen swatted her little sister down and fitted the bottom sheet onto the bed.

"Um. You might want to know, Kim says she gets the bottom." Harper shrugged. "Just giving you a fair warning."

"Hah. I don't think so. Kimberley's in for a rude awakening if she thinks I'm climbing to the top bunk every day. Ain't happening."

"Well, I'm going to leave you two to battle it out on your own." Mom plugged her ears as she left the room.

Yeah. Not going to be a battle. Dad always said to choose her fights carefully and select which hills she would die on. Possession of the bottom bunk was a war she'd fight to the death.

Carmen marched into the family room where Kimberley was painting her nails bright blue. "First of all, your nails look moldy. Secondly, I get the bottom bunk."

Kimberley glanced up. "Fine."

Did she say fine? Wait. Had the whole thing been a setup? Had Kim sent Harper in there on a reverse-psychology mission?

Harper giggled in the corner.

Carmen's hands balled into fists. They were lucky Mom was home. Little sisters were so annoying. One day. . .one day she'd be free of them.

Mom scooted sideways down the hallway, her arms stacked with cardboard and trash from her construction project. She dumped it all into a pile by the front door. "Kim and Harper, I need you two to haul this stuff down to the Dumpster." She turned to Carmen. "I have a facial party tonight. So you'll be in charge, of course."

Thanks for asking. Not like she had a life anyway. Don't suppose it's a paid gig? "Okay. Are you going to let them go to the Dumpster by themselves?"

Mom looked confused. "They're old enough to throw away the trash."

"You can't let them run around here like they did at home. It's just not safe, remember?" Hadn't Mom heard her own lecture? "I'll go with them." Carmen shrugged on a sweater and grabbed an armful.

Two trips down the back stairs, and they were finished. Carmen stomped back to her room without a word. *Don't follow. Please don't follow.* She had stuff to take care of and needed complete privacy. Once in her room, she pulled the door shut and locked it.

No such luck. She sensed them on the other side of the door before she heard the knock. Why couldn't she get even a moment to herself? "What do you want?"

"I just wanted to say sorry for tricking you about the bed. And thanks for helping with the trash." Kimberley spoke through the door. At least she didn't ask to come in.

"Me, too." Harper giggled. "But it was funny."

Carmen opened the door a crack. "Thanks for the apologies.

Now can I just have like fifteen minutes alone? Please?"

"Okie doke." Harper grabbed Kim's hand and scurried away, pulling the door shut behind her.

Finally. Carmen ran to her dresser and rummaged through the drawers then turned to the closet and dug through the three unpacked boxes of books. Not there. She pulled her purple nylon tennis bag from under her bed and plowed through the deodorant, granola bars, hairspray, and extra socks. Not there either. Where were they? She'd already missed two of her birth-control pills, and they were still nowhere to be found. In an entire year of taking them, these were the first ones she'd missed. If she found them, she'd just double up for two days— no problem.

But if she couldn't find them, then what would she do?

Carmen rubbed her chin and turned in a circle, looking at everything in her room. Had she said something to Nate about where she put them? But she couldn't ask him—then he'd know she'd missed some, and they were supposed to get together after tennis practice tomorrow. He had a special evening all planned while his parents were away, and then he intended to stay over with her at Dad's. Carmen sure didn't want to mess everything up.

Where were those pills? *Think. Think.*

Chapter 3

Eggplant parmigiana. Their third dinner in Hackensack. If they couldn't live like rich New Yorkers, they could at least eat like them. Once in a while. Carmen blew on the steaming sauce before slurping a sample from the spoon. She kissed her fingertips. *Perfecto.*

The oven timer dinged. Carmen pulled open the squeaky door and slid out the tray of garlic bread, the cheese brown and bubbly. "It's ready, you guys."

Harper slid into the kitchen on her socks and skidded to a stop just before slamming into the countertop peninsula. "Mmm. Bread!" She reached for the least-brown piece.

"Harper." Carmen reached a plate under the bread to catch the cheese about to ooze to the floor. She placed a serving fork in the salad and tossed it with the Caesar dressing just as Mom came in.

"I smelled it all the way in my room—hoped that's what you made. This'll be great." She picked up a plate and served herself.

Kimberley strolled into the room, bouncing her head to the tunes on her iPod. "Just salad for me. I'm watching my weight."

Hah. Little did she know, the Caesar salad with dressing, cheese, and croutons was about as bad as the full dinner.

Kim added a hunk of cheesy garlic toast to her plate.

"Uh, Kim. So much for watching your weight."

Kim shrugged and sashayed from the kitchen, right past Mom, to sit cross-legged on the couch—her Juicy sweats most likely riding too low in back like they always did.

Harper sat on the floor near Kim and put her plate on the coffee table. She picked up the remote as she chewed her first bite.

They would never have gotten away with skipping a family dinner at. . .home. Carmen glanced at Mom, eating alone at the dining-room table as she thumbed through the pages of her latest Mary Kay catalog. Sure didn't look lonely or depressed.

Fine. Carmen had no plans to stick around and force family togetherness if no one else wanted it. She grabbed her dinner and a Coke then went to her room. No one said a word to stop her.

She shut the door and slid to the floor with her back against the edge of the bed, drew her knees up, and rested her plate on them. She forked a bite of cheesy eggplant and twisted it until the molten strands gave out. After letting it cool for a couple of seconds, she scraped the bite from the fork with her teeth. Ouch! She shuffled it around on her tongue and huffed air to cool it more. Delicious. Carmen didn't need anyone else to confirm it for her to know the truth.

Her pocket vibrated. She wiped her hands on the carpet and dug for her phone. A text message from Dad?

Traveling. I'll pick u guys up in the morning instead of tonight.

What? Didn't such a major change of plans at least warrant a phone call? Carmen touched and held the number Five button then pressed the phone to her ear. It rang one time.

"You've reached Daniel Castillo. . ."

Voice mail? But he'd sent a text message only seconds ago, so his phone must have been on. How could he send his own daughter straight to voice mail on purpose? And what's worse, how could he miss the first night of the first weekend of visitation?

"Kim!" Carmen shouted down the hall. "Did you get a text from Dad?"

"Let me check," Kim yelled back. "No. Why?"

Great. He expected Carmen to do his dirty work.

๖

Nate's evening class ended at eight. What time was it anyway? Carmen touched the display on her phone to bring it to life. Nine o'clock already? He'd been out for an hour and hadn't called or texted. What could he be doing? Was he avoiding her? Could she really blame him considering her attitude lately? She sure hadn't been the picture of pleasantry during the past week since the move.

Should she call him? Maybe he was staring at his phone wondering why she hadn't called him. It wasn't 1950; girls were allowed to call boys. Carmen pressed the number Two speed-dial button and waited for him to answer.

"Hey. I was just thinking about you. You excited about tomorrow night?"

Carmen breathed a sigh of relief. He sounded normal. She eased the door closed and sank onto her bed. She nestled her head between the four extra-fluffy pillows. "You kidding? Of course I am. Any time with you is awesome."

"Mmm-hmm. Where's everyone tonight?"

Carmen imagined Nate sprawled on the floor cushions in front of the TV in his room. Too bad he wasn't curled up there with her. "Mom's out at a Mary Kay thing at an old friend's house. I'm babysitting—the girls are watching a movie."

"If only I lived closer. I'd be over." Nate's hypnotic voice lulled Carmen into a dream state.

"I know. It's going to be impossible to get used to this. Two weekends a month?" Carmen sighed. Even though they'd be together more than many couples, four days a month wasn't nearly enough for them.

"How's it going to work exactly? Your dad is going to come pick you up on Fridays, right?

Hadn't they been over this a ton of times? "Yeah, every other Friday. He'll pick us up at four o'clock. Then on the off weeks, Mom will bring me up for my tennis lesson on Saturday mornings. But I'll have to come right back home with her after."

"Hmm. If you can get your mom to let me stay overnight like your dad does, I could bring you back home from your Saturday tennis lessons on those in-between weekends and then spend the night. But I don't see her agreeing to that."

No way Mom would ever let Nate stay overnight. Besides, where would he sleep? Top bunk? Not likely. The rickety flea-market sofa with the duct tape holding the back together? Hardly. "I'll see what I can do. Not promising anything, though."

"Yeah. I get it. Never know, though."

"Plus, don't forget, this weekend could have been longer if Dad hadn't blown us off for tonight. He was supposed to pick us up today, but he said his trip went long." She didn't fully believe him, though it was difficult to get the details from nothing but a text message. "So he's not coming for us until it's time for me to get to tennis in the morning." If he made her miss tennis. . . Carmen shuddered. The team was already frustrated enough that she couldn't be there during the week and could only come for the Saturday lessons. She was lucky to still be on the team. If she weren't a good player, she'd have gotten kicked off for sure. Hopes of a college scholarship for tennis were probably out the window. But at least she could still play.

"Right. But hey, let's focus on the good news. We have

tomorrow night all to ourselves." Like convincing a child it's an okay thing there's no Santa. "Oh, and in other good news, you'll have lots more to tell Nosy Nellie with all those people you'll be meeting."

"Hey. You leave my journal alone. And she's just Nellie. Not *Nosy* Nellie." Carmen laughed.

"Someday you're going to have to let me see her."

Carmen loved to hear him call her journal a *her* just like she did. "What's funny is Mom made me start writing my thoughts about other people to Nellie as a way to break my obsession with gossip. All it did though is make me really, really good at it. Now I can pick out the worst in anyone just so I have something to tell her."

"Okay. Now I really want to see your jour—Nellie. What have you written in there about your horrible boyfriend?"

"Oh, you know. It's just girl talk between me and Nellie. She thinks I should dump you after all I've told her about you."

"Hey. No fair. I'm going to start my own journal."

Oh, the threats. "Ha. Then maybe your gossip journal can date my gossip journal."

"Right. Then we'd have no secrets anymore."

"Yeah. Scratch that idea." Nate would be horrified if he saw her journal. Not about him—he was perfect as far as boyfriends go. But everyone else was fair game. Especially his mother.

"Hey. What secrets are you keeping?"

"Oh, that's for me and Nellie to know and you never to find out." Carmen laughed.

"It's great to hear you laugh, C."

Should Carmen tell him about the gang members who had taken up residence on the street outside her apartment? What about the recent fact she'd lost her birth-control pills and had missed four doses already? Hah. Carmen wondered which of those two bits of information would be worse news to her boyfriend. Who was she kidding? She knew the answer.

Speaking of which, where had her packet of pills disappeared to? If she didn't want to tell Nate she'd missed some, and if she didn't want to upset him by avoiding him all weekend, she might have to stay home tomorrow night after all. How did it even work when a person missed birth control for several days in a row? Surely people did it all the time. She'd have to Google it when she got off the phone. Couldn't very well ask Mom what to do about it since she didn't even know Carmen took them—it was against her religion. One which she believed Carmen at least sort of shared.

Banging came from the family room, followed by a loud crash. Footsteps pounded down the hallway and stopped right outside Carmen's room before the door flung open, the doorknob banging on the wall, fitting right into the hole a previous renter had left behind from an apparent fit of rage.

"She won't stop throwing the pillows at my head." Kimberley shoved her finger in Harper's face.

"Well she's making fun of my movie." Harper whopped Kimberley with a bed pillow.

"Only babies watch *Finding Nemo*."

Great. "Hang on, Nate." Carmen covered the phone receiver and glared. "You two better get out of here right now. I'm dead serious."

"Or what? This is my room, too, you know." Kimberley jutted out one hip and put her hands on her waist. "In fact. Come on, Harper. Let's play a game up here." She climbed onto the top bunk and reached down.

Harper dropped the pillow and tossed her teddy bear up onto the bed then clasped Kim's hand and scrambled to get onto the bunk, suddenly united with her sister in joint purpose to torment Carmen.

Wonderful. "Nate, I'm going to have to go. The urchins have made their move."

"Okay. Call me before you go to bed if you want to."

Their tradition. Carmen loved the sultry, raspy whispers into her cell phone under the covers before she drifted off each night. But everything had changed. "It depends if Kim falls asleep before I do or not." Carmen couldn't have those conversations with Nate with her sister listening in from three feet above her.

"True dat. I'll be around if she does."

For now, but how long would his patience last? Gorgeous college hunks didn't have to deal with all the hassles of dating someone younger. One day even Nate would tire of it.

"Love you."

"Love you, too." Carmen clicked the phone off and pried herself off her pillows. She didn't want to hang around in there with the two stooges.

"Ooh. Love you, snookum." Kim smooched the air.

"Love you, too, pumpkin." Harper kissed her teddy bear.

"You two need to grow up." Carmen slammed the door behind her, not quite sealing off the giggles.

She grabbed a Coke from the ancient gold refrigerator—used to industrial-size stainless steel appliances, Carmen hadn't seen one so old except on reruns of *The Brady Bunch*—and settled on the sofa with her computer. The sounds from the bedroom had diminished to a semi-ignorable roar, so Carmen flipped open her laptop and went right to Google.

What happens if I miss four birth-control pills? While she waited for the page to load—thank you dial-up—she walked to the window. But wait. . .she felt crampy in her lower abdomen. Come to think of it, she'd had dull cramps for a few hours. But her period wasn't due for another couple of weeks yet. Could the missed pills have started her cycle early?

A trip to the bathroom to confirm her suspicions and a Google search later, Carmen had a plan. According to the online birth-control gods, she could stop looking for the old pack, wait a couple of days, and just start a brand-new one. Which was perfect timing. She'd pick up her new pack from the Value Drugs in Briarcliff Manor and then start it on Monday night. The articles said she and Nate would have to be extra careful for the whole month—which meant she'd have to tell him. Small price to pay for relief, though.

Phew. Definitely a crisis averted—though Nate might not see it quite the same way after all of his careful planning for their special romantic night tomorrow. But what if she'd gotten pregnant? A pregnancy would be horrible under the current circumstances. Having a baby with Nate one day sounded wonderful—but not anytime soon. He'd just have to get over the disappointment.

Carmen thought back to the day Dad took her to the clinic to get The Pill. She'd been trying to work up the nerve to ask for months. But one day, totally out of nowhere, he approached her and said, "I'm not stupid, Carmen. I know you're going to have sex. I'm sure you and Nate already are. So we're going to keep you safe." She'd been so afraid he'd ask her to confirm his suspicions, but he never had.

Ugh. He did proceed to talk to her about STDs and how the pill didn't prevent those. Duh. Sex Ed and a bit of logic taught her that. Still, she had to listen to his spiel if she wanted him to follow through with the promise to get her on the pill.

Uncomfortable conversation, to say the least. But she had her protection.

Mom would have a stroke if she found out her daughter was on the pill and had been for a long time. Well, she couldn't find out. Simple.

Carmen snaked an arm from under the covers and fumbled for the alarm clock she'd placed on the floor near her bed. The SNOOZE button did its job for the third time. She'd better make it the last one or Dad would have to park and come up to the apartment to wait for them.

Hey, maybe that wasn't such a bad idea. If he came up, Mom would have to talk to him, and he'd be forced to see where his daughters had been sentenced to live while he played lawyer games. But what if Mom wore her ratty navy-blue bathrobe and had bed head? That kind of disaster might set the cause back even further. Besides, Carmen didn't want to miss her tennis lesson.

What would Kim and Harper do while Carmen played at the country club? Mid-September was way too cold to swim, and they hated golf. They'd be stuck home alone with Dad and his bimbo. Carmen lifted a leg, pressed her foot into the springs, and jiggled the top bunk. "Yo, Kim. Want to stay and hang out with me at the courts today?" Her little sister used to beg for the privilege, and it had to be better than going to Dad's, where Tiffany reigned as queen. Anything beat being around her.

"What? And watch you flounce around the tennis court like Captain Jack Sparrow? I'll pass." Kimberley leaned over the top bunk. "Besides, Tiff is going to show me some cheer moves and let me try on her Eagles uniform."

"Tiff? Since when do you call that. . .that. . .oh, whatever." Gross. If her little sister wanted to kiss up to their own private home-wrecker, she would have to do it alone. Carmen wanted no part of it. "And when did you make these plans? Have you talked to *her*?"

"Tiffany? Sure I've talked to her. We text. Jealous much?" Kimberley laughed. "Oh, and I'm pretty sure I'm going to beat you to the bathroom." She flung her legs over and lowered herself until her toes touched the carpet.

"Fine," Carmen muttered into her pillow. "I'm going to beat you to the front seat." Why did she let Kimberley bring out the immature brat in her every single time? Carmen had had it. She climbed from her bed with her sights set on forty-five minutes in a car with Dad sans Tiffany. That woman. . .needed to get lost, and Mom and Dad had to get back together. But how?

An idea began to take shape. Carmen loped the few steps down the hall to the room Mom shared with Harper. "Hey. Dad's picking us up in about an hour, and I have a date with Nate tonight. Any chance you could show me how to use your makeup? Maybe demonstrate on yourself so I can do it to myself later?"

Mom's tired eyes perked up. "Really? You hardly ever want to wear makeup. How exciting. Let me get my cases."

Brilliant. The ruse would get Mom all pretty before Dad got there. But then how to get him up to the apartment? Carmen flipped open her phone and texted Dad: CAN U COME UP WHEN U GET HERE? HAVE LOTS TO CARRY.

Perfect. Now to deal with Mom's clothes.

Fifty minutes later, expertly made-up and unknowingly dressed to accentuate her curves, Mom went to make coffee.

Dad had never texted back to say no, so Carmen's plan was a go.

Carmen selected a black tennis skirt and a red hoodie from the pile near the tiny closet and slipped into it. She looked dressed for the club. Well, kind of. She smirked into the mirror. No pink, green, or navy for her, country-club rebel that she was. She grabbed her racquet, tennis duffel, and overnight bag and hurried to the hall.

Harper looked all ready to go, backpack and all. She perched on the couch with her Nintendo DS, thumbs going like crazy.

Kimberley came from the bathroom dressed in an outfit no doubt intended to please *Tiff*, and Mom peeked out the window to the street below. Looked like no one wanted a confrontation. Little did they know Carmen had already asked Dad to come up.

"Girls," Mom called from the window as she looked down onto the street "Time to go." "Your da—um. . .your ride is here."

Chapter 4

Uh-oh. Why had mom sounded so strange? Carmen tripped over Harper's unicorn Pillow Pal as she hurried to the open window and peered down to her biggest nightmare.

A sleek, black convertible BMW decked out in chrome everything sat roaring its money and power for all of Hackensack to see. . .and hear. Tiffany flipped her blond waves from under the collar of her white leather jacket then slid her chunky black sunglasses up her forehead and back over the top of her head. How was it Tiffany managed to create a halo of perfectly highlighted gold framing her face, but whenever Carmen tried that move, she had hair sticking up in every direction? Tiffany must practice it in the mirror. Or maybe grace came naturally to people like her.

Bracelets slid to her slender elbow as Tiffany's long arm reached up through the open roof to wave. Judging by the people leaning out their windows, Tiffany's shiny black convertible drew more attention than Dad's car would have. Or was it Tiffany herself who commanded the stares of the onlookers? Either way, the combo was unstoppable.

"Your dad said you needed help with your things. But I just got my nails done. Mind making two trips?" Tiffany spoke barely loud enough for Carmen to hear, then pulled her hand close to scrutinize her nails.

"I get shotgun." Kimberley darted past Carmen and bounded down the stairway to the street.

I'd like a shotgun.

Mom's ruby-painted lips parted slightly as she watched her middle daughter run from the apartment without even a backward glance.

Harper slipped on her Selena Gomez hoodie and reached up to hug Mom.

Mom stooped down and clutched Harper's tiny shoulders. "You be good."

"We'll be back tomorrow, Mommy. Don't be lonely, okay?" Harper's wise green eyes glistened.

"I'm going to be fine, little bug. You go have a good time." Mom squeezed Harper and then patted her behind as she scampered out the door.

Carmen gazed into her mom's eyes. It must be torture to watch as her daughters climbed into the car with the woman who destroyed her marriage. . .the woman who now lived in Mom's home and slept in her bed. Carmen took a deep breath. Why hadn't she even considered Mom's feelings before? The situation was difficult for Carmen, sure. But what about her mother? She'd lost even more than Carmen had. "Mom. I'm sorry I've been so selfish. This can't be easy for you."

Her mother gulped back a sob and nodded. "Thanks for thinking of me—it means a lot. Now really, put all the sad stuff out of your head, and try to have a good time with your father."

Well, Dad was a no-show apparently, and having fun with Tiffany was out of the question. But at least Nate was a sure thing. Unless. . . Did Mom need her to stay behind for the weekend? "You positive? I don't have to go. We could hang out and stuff. Maybe explore the town." Mom would say no—she had to. But if she didn't, if Mom needed Carmen's company this weekend, she'd stay. Nate would probably hate her, but she could—

"No, no. You go on. I really appreciate the offer." Mom rolled her shoulders back a few inches like she always harped on Carmen to do. "I'm going to be just fine. Now scoot."

Carmen hid her relief as best she could. "As long as you're sure."

A horn blared.

The back of Carmen's neck bristled, and she gritted her teeth. Tiffany had just honked at her? Seriously? Who did she think she was?

Backpack. Laptop. Cell phone. Carmen gathered her things as slowly as possible. Kissed her mom on the cheek and sauntered down the stairs. She wouldn't hurry for Tiffany, no matter what.

Tiffany drummed her fingernails on the dashboard.

Nails suddenly dry, Tiff? Or were they never wet and just some excuse she gave so she didn't have to move? "Careful, you'll mess up your nails."

Frowning, Tiffany pulled her hand closer and inspected them.

Kimberley leaned forward and flipped the seat up so Carmen could climb into the back. For once, no argument from Carmen. Kim could sit in the passenger's seat.

"How's it going?" Tiffany flashed her best rah-rah grin.

"Fine. Where's my dad?" Carmen had no intention of making this easy for her.

Tiffany flinched. "His trip ran a little long. I'm going to drop you at tennis. He should be home by the time you're done."

Carmen crossed her arms and gazed out the window. "He'd planned to fly in last night and be here this morning."

Tiffany shrugged. "Things change. You know how it goes."

"It had already been changed from the original plan," Carmen muttered as she slouched below the gust of pollution swarming the car as they sped along the streets of New Jersey. Maybe if she pretended she was asleep they would all leave her alone.

Harper, bless her, snoozed peacefully against the window. Oh, to be so innocent and trusting. Not a care in the world. Little did she know.

The road sounds blended with Kimberley's incessant chatter about makeup and clothes. Tiffany lapped up the chance to spew her wisdom. "With those big blue eyes of yours, you should use a little bit of eyeliner. But if you do. . ."

Carmen opened her eyes, and they were already crossing the Tappan Zee Bridge. About twenty more minutes to the Sleepy Hollow Country Club and her handsome tennis pro, Zach Stafford. Was there any such thing as an ugly tennis pro? Carmen chuckled.

Nate harbored a little jealousy toward Zach even though he'd never admit it. How could he not? Gorgeous and athletic, Zach was a force on and off the courts. But his beautiful wife and two kids put him a bit out of reach for Carmen. Not to mention he was like twenty-something, maybe even close to thirty. Nate had nothing to worry about.

"You awake, Carm?"

Carm? No one ever called her that, and the last person she wanted a nickname from was Tiffany. She refused to dignify her weak attempt at relating with a response until Tiffany used her full name.

"Carmen?" Tiffany's voice dropped from proud lioness to plaintive kitten.

"Hmm?"

Tiffany flashed a hesitant grin into the rearview mirror. "Hey, I was just thinking. We should work out together sometime. You know, go for a run, whatever. Seeing as how we're both athletes and all."

Athletes? Cheerleaders bounced around in short skirts and posed for a calendar once a year. "Don't you think there's a little difference between what we do? I mean, tennis is a real sport. With sweat and everything."

Tiffany's eyes narrowed. "I know you think pro cheerleaders are idiots, but we work really hard. You have no idea. And it's highly competitive."

"Oh, I know. I've seen the Dallas Cowboy Cheerleader reality show. No body fat, great highlights, cute in the uniform. Sounds like a sport to me. Besides, aren't you retired?"

"Cut it out." Kimberley shot a glare toward the backseat.

Good. Carmen had gotten to her, too.

Tiffany took a deep breath, her fingers gripping the steering wheel. "I'm not retired from everything. It's not like I sit home every day eating doughnuts and watching soap operas. I left the Philadelphia Eagles cheerleading squad to move on to other things."

Yeah, my dad. "I'm sure it does take a lot of work to get your hair and makeup just right every day." Carmen's gut twinged with a touch of guilt at her snark—but not enough to apologize. "Oh look. We're here."

They drove between the stone columns and through the massive iron gates at Sleepy Hollow Country Club. Like right through the pearly gates straight into heaven. Only three nights in Hackensack and already her home away from home in New York felt like a distant dream.

Did she even belong there anymore, or was she nothing more than a temporary guest? A visitor in her own home? An alien in her old life? Only time would tell.

Carmen climbed out from the backseat and hurried past the golf-course entrance. She passed through the locker-room doors, blazed past the attendant at the sink, ignored the ladies gossiping by the lockers, and exited right onto the courts. Her tennis racquet bounced against her knee as she jogged out to her position.

"I see we're skipping the small talk today?" Zach chuckled. *Love you, but not in the mood.* "Yeah, let's just play."

Zach threw a ball into the air, reared back his racquet, and skimmed the ball right over the net in a perfect serve.

WHAP!

WHOP!

Carmen returned volley after volley with a vengeance. She raised her arm high above her head in a serve so powerful it lifted both her feet off the ground.

"Wow, girl. Go easy on an old man, will you?" Zach rubbed his face with a towel and guzzled some water. "What's gotten into you today? You're playing like you have something to prove."

More like someone to destroy. "I don't know. Just getting out some frustrations. Feels good." Carmen hunched down and shifted from side to side, spinning her racquet in her hands.

"We'll have to get you worked up more often. Before tournaments, if possible."

"The way my life's been going, it shouldn't be a problem."

A fifty-something club employee in a sharply creased uniform stepped onto the court with a clipboard in hand. "Excuse me. Are you Carmen Castillo?" She overpronounced the Spanish accent, and her upturned nose gave away her distaste.

What does she want? "Yeah. That's me. What's up?"

"I'm Corelle, the membership manager." The woman's nose twitched. "I just wondered if your father has signed you in as a guest for today. I don't have record of it."

"What are you talking about? I don't have to sign in. We're members here." Carmen's heart began to thud. Pretty clear where the conversation headed.

She lowered her glasses and peered over the rims. "Young lady, your father is a member. Your mother moved away, and she has changed the residency of you and your sisters. . . ."

How could that she-devil Nazi have such private information? Someone had to have turned it in. Tiffany maybe?

". . .which, of course, means you can't be listed on the membership. Your father may bring you as a guest as often as he'd like though—at the standard guest rates. And of course, you do lose your member pricing on lessons and other amenities."

"Of course I do." Carmen looked up at the gymnasium's fluorescent lighting, hoping it would dry her eyes before she gave Cruella. . .um. . .Corelle the satisfaction of an emotional response. "Don't you think this is a conversation you should have with my dad?"

"I'd love to, but he's not here. Which, since you're no longer a member, means you're trespassing." Corelle pushed her glasses back in place. "We'll make an exception today, but in the future you'll only be allowed to use the club if you're accompanied by a member." The country-club Nazi turned on her heels and strode away.

How typical. If it could go wrong for Carmen, it would. She faced Zach. "You wanted me worked up so I'd be powerful on the courts? I guess it can't get any better than right now. Oh, but it won't do us any good; I have to leave." She spun around toward the locker room. Hold the tears until the shower. Don't cry in front of Zach.

Zach reached out a hand and clutched Carmen's wrist.

"Surely your Dad will work things out for you. It'll be okay. You'll see."

She shook her hand free. "Don't count on it."

⑤

Dear Nellie,

Sigh. I've talked to you about Tiffany before. I really shouldn't give her the brain power it takes to even write this entry. But she's got me so angry! Surprise, surpise. I know. But you'll never believe what she did. Well, at least what I think she did. She told the country club I'm not living here anymore, so now I can't play tennis there. Can you even believe she'd do such a thing? I don't even think Dad will or can do a thing about it. There goes tennis.

And she picked us up today in her fancy car. People were leaning out their windows to look at her. Gross. I think I'm going to spike her drinks with something to make her fat. Then I can sit back and watch her head spin when Dad drops her.

She needs to go back to Philadelphia, or there's no hope of Mom and Dad getting back together. How can I get rid of her?

Love,
Carmen

⑤

Carmen snuggled in her favorite deck chair wrapped in the well-worn wedding-ring quilt Grandma had made when Carmen was a baby. The pool spread out before her. Carmen watched as the tranquil water flowed over the rocks and into the hot tub. The rushing of the falls soothed her rattled nerves. Where was Nate? She needed to see him. How could he be late when they hadn't seen each other in days?

The french doors off the sunroom opened, and an angel

stepped out. Carmen's breath caught as she saw Nate standing across the pool. The midmorning sun shone behind him, and his reflection reached across the water and almost touched her on the other side.

He leaned on the doorframe and stared at her. His eyes went right into her heart and soul. Like he read her from the inside out.

He seemed so far away though. Separated by a world of water. In the moment and in life. *Come closer.* But at least her pool. . .um, *Dad's* pool. . .wasn't the Hudson River, which divided their states. If she closed her eyes, maybe she could freeze-frame the image of Nate filling the doorway looking at her.

SPLASH!

Carmen raised her arms to shield against the wave rising from the deep end like a tsunami. It rained down a torrent big enough to almost reach her spot on the deck. Had Nate jumped in? No. There he stood, stunned and drenched, in the same spot he'd been before Carmen blinked. Carmen glared at the surface of the water and waited until the intruder came up for air. Who was it? A flash of red appeared in the water near her, and then Kimberley's head broke the surface.

"What's your boyfriend doing just standing there? It's creepy."

Argh. Kim. Carmen rolled her eyes at Nate. "Can you believe this?"

He grinned.

"What are you doing swimming in that icy water? It might still technically be summer, but it's freezing out here." Carmen stood and reached a towel toward her sister.

Kimberley waved away the towel. "I'm going in the hot tub. Want to come? Or are you two going to go make out somewhere?"

"Like it's any of your business."

⑤

"Where are my girls?" a voice boomed through the house and ricocheted off the walls and bounced off the high ceilings.

Carmen heard feet scamper down the hall and then slide across the slick wood toward the top of the stairs. Had to be the all-forgiving Harper. "What time is it?"

Nate swiped his finger across his cell phone screen to bring it to life. "Um. . .three thirty."

"Oh, he's only about forty-four hours late. Not bad. Must have been some meeting." She unfurled from the warm nest she'd built beside Nate on her bed and stretched her arms far over her head. "Want to pause the movie?"

Nate scowled and pointed the remote at the plasma TV, freezing Natalie Portman midword. "You've seen this like a hundred times."

"One hundred and one should probably do it." Carmen winked at Nate then sauntered toward the stairs. No way she'd go bounding toward her long-lost daddy who'd finally graced them with his presence. Nah. He could wait a minute for her this time.

"Hey, Carmen." Dad looked up the stairs and watched her descend the last four steps into the foyer.

Carmen crossed her arms and held his gaze with a challenging stare. "Hi."

He blinked twice then looked down at Harper tucked in the crook of his arm. "How are my girls?"

"We missed you, Daddy, and then you didn't come for us. Why didn't you?"

Way to go, Harper. If Carmen had said it, he'd have thought she was being difficult. But impish Harper could get away with it.

"I'm sorry, sweet pea. I had some problems come up at the account I had to take care of in LA. I had to stay until the problem resolved." Dad smiled. "You wouldn't want Daddy to lose his job, would you?"

Not that his job did his children a whole lot of good anymore. Carmen bit her lip. Best to change the subject before she said something she'd regret. "There's a problem at the country club—they won't let me keep coming since I don't live here anymore."

"An oversight, I'm sure. I'll see what I can do about it on Monday."

"I'm not sure it's going to be as easy as you think. The membership Nazi was dead serious about me not coming back."

"Okay. I said I'd look into it. But come on—I just got home. . .no shop talk. What do you say we all go get a soda from the kitchen and catch up?"

"Cool." Kimberley came around the corner with her beach towel slung over her shoulder.

"I can't. Nate's over. We're watching a movie." Carmen put her foot up on the step behind her, ready to bolt.

"I haven't seen you in two weeks."

Eww. She hated it when he whined. "Well, last night and today was supposed to be our time. I kept myself free and available. But. . .what can I say?" Carmen shrugged and turned away.

Dad exhaled.

Carmen cringed, waiting for him to tell her to come back, but no words came. She won, and her point had been made. Now to get back to her bedroom. She hurried down the hall, dove into the bed, and tried to re-create her pillow cloud beside Nate.

"Since your dad's home, where am I going to sleep? Will it still be okay to sleep in your room?" Nate twisted a lock of Carmen's hair between his fingers.

"Of course you can. It's just, well, you know how it is. You'll have to keep your hands to yourself. . .um. . .for other reasons." She squirmed. "You know."

Nate scowled. "The weekend gets better and better."

Carmen raised one eyebrow. "What? My company isn't enough for you?"

"Of course your company is enough. It's. . .I haven't seen you in a while. It'll be even longer this next time and every time after, since we'll have to wait the whole two weeks. And we were planning a special night. What am I supposed to do?"

Wait. You're supposed to wait. Like Carmen should have made him do from the start. "I guess we'll find out if it's true. What's the old saying? Absence makes the heart grow stronger?"

"Fonder." Judging by his sulk, it didn't look like he bought it.

Would Nate pass the test? Oh, he'd make it through the night all right; it was long-term Carmen worried about.

Chapter 5

Night and day. Fire and ice. Happy and sad. The extremes pelted Carmen's consciousness as she floated ghostlike through the front doors, past the security guard, and into her new school for the first day of her junior year. She looked ahead but watched everything in her periphery. Lockers lining the wall, people walking by, couples kissing in the doorways, students talking on cell phones, sports jerseys, books. Everything existed as it had at her old school, but they looked different: cracked, faded, worn, old. Briarcliff High School had been so. . .sparkly. And so not. . .scary.

Nate had suggested she search for some things about Hackensack she liked better than Briarcliff. But did he really believe she could come up with things, or was he just trying to make her feel better? Because, at first glance, the quest for positive at Hackensack didn't look promising.

Wham!

Carmen hit a brick wall. Her books slid from her arms and smacked the worn tile around her feet. Loose-leaf paper scattered in every direction. Her eyes traveled up slowly—then up even more—until they locked with the dark pair belonging to the guy from the street outside her apartment. He'd looked much shorter from the fire escape. And why did he always stare at her with that same creepy laser-like glare?

Act cool. Be confident. "What? No apology?" Carmen broke the lock of his intense gaze as she bent to scoop up her books and papers. Good thing the school hadn't issued her a laptop like at Briarcliff.

He grunted and stepped over Carmen's hunched body and let his foot scuff over the top of the books she'd just stacked, spreading them back along the hallway. He sauntered away, shrugging his shoulder toward his friends, who immediately followed.

Tears sprang to her eyes. Why? What had she done to him? Would everyone act rude and cold toward her like that jerk? She tried to gather her things into a bundle so she could at least get out of the middle of the hallway, but papers and workbooks kept slipping from her grip. *Don't cry.* She blinked her eyes hard against the impending flood.

Two hands reached from behind her and grabbed her books. Carmen stood and whirled around. "What's your problem?"

A guy about her own age reached the neatened stack out to her. "Simma down, chica. Be easy. I'm just tryin' to help a girl out."

Carmen read the tattoo that curved around the front of his neck. "Diego? Is that your name?"

"What? You think I inked someone else's handle on my throat? That'd be dumb."

He had a point. Then again, anyone who would lay still and let someone else jab needles in his jugular couldn't be playing with a full deck. But what did he want with her? Carmen took her books and rested them on her hip and waited.

Diego gestured down the hall. "Do you know those dudes?"

What did he care? "No. I've seen them before though."

His eyes narrowed. "Where?"

"Outside my apart—wait. Why do you want to know?"

She had to be more careful. *Don't think we're in Kansas anymore, Toto.*

"Look. You know what's happening here, don't you?"

"What do you mean? Nothing's happening here. I'm just trying to get to class."

"Oh great." Diego sighed. "Listen, newbie. You're going to have to wise up real fast. You're being scoped out. They're going to try to claim you for their gang. The leader, Marco, he prolly wants you for his girl."

"His girl?" Carmen laughed. "He's never even spoken to me. He doesn't know me at all."

Diego let his eyes rove up and down Carmen's body. "Oh, chica. He knows you plenty."

Carmen shivered. "Gross."

"You really don't get how this works, do you?"

"And I suppose you're going to teach me?" Carmen squared her shoulders. Time to toughen up. "I'll probably find out you're in it with Marco. Whatever 'it' is."

"Look. I can't be late for class, or I'll get suspended again. But I'm telling you. Stay away from Marco. He ain't no good for nothin'."

"Don't worry about it. I already have a boyfriend anyway." When they found out about Nate, they'd leave her alone.

"Here? At this school? Then where is he?" Diego glanced both ways down the hallway.

"No, he goes to NYU." That bit of info should get them to back off.

Diego stared, unblinking for a few seconds, then burst into laughter. "Listen. If Marco bugs you, tell him *I'm* your boyfriend. Leave any talk of college boy out of it. Trust me."

Yeah right. "I don't think so." Like she would pretend she had some gangbanger for a boyfriend. "Besides, aren't you afraid of Marco getting mad at you?"

"Mad at me?" Diego shook his head. "No. Marco don't mess with me. You don't believe me now, but you'll see. You be calling on Diego's name within the week."

⑤

Where on earth was Mr. Hastings' office? Furthermore, why did the guidance counselor want to see Carmen on her first day of school? Unlikely they were going to plan out her future on day one. The student monitor said two hallways down, take a right, and it's the last door on the right. Carmen put her hand on a doorknob. Something looked funny. This couldn't be the office.

She pressed the door open a crack and peeked inside. Mops, brooms, buckets, and the unmistakable scent of those wood chips they pile on top of vomit for some reason no one knows. No guidance counselor.

Great. So even the hall monitor had it in for her. Like an unspoken rule: devour the new girl. No matter. Carmen squared her shoulders and turned away from the maintenance closet. She'd never let them get to her.

The door to her left led outside. If she opened it and ran, would an alarm go off? How far could she get before they caught up with her?

No point in even trying. Her life belonged to everyone else, and she just had to play along.

After wandering for a bit, she finally found the office in the exact opposite direction she'd been sent. Nice. *Little Miss Hall Monitor, your dreaded misdirection tactic—while stealthy and effective—won't break me.*

Carmen knocked on the window and poked her head into the office. "Mr. Hastings? I'm Carmen Castillo. You wanted to see me?"

"It's wonderful to meet you. Welcome to Hackensack High

School." He beamed like he welcomed her to the White House.

"Uh, thanks." What was he so happy about?

"Have a seat." Mr. Hastings gathered some papers together. "How is your day going so far?"

Carmen shrugged. "It's okay. Just figuring things out."

"Great. Well, I just wanted to discuss a few things with you. I know it's your first day, but one of the items on my list is rather time sensitive." He slid a blue sheet of paper across the desk.

Carmen read it as she pulled it toward her. "College fair? Tonight?" The first day of school was hard enough. Carmen didn't want to come back to school later the same day—or anytime she didn't have to.

"Yes. As a junior, it's time to start thinking about college possibilities. Judging by your grades, I'm assuming you plan to go to college."

Was that a question or a statement? College had always been the plan. But now, who knew? Better yet, who cared?

"Well, it's really important to keep your options open. The fair gives you an opportunity to explore the offerings of various colleges and universities. You can even bring your parents."

No way was she going to—wait. Had he said parents? An idea crept into Carmen's brain. College night might be a good way to get Mom and Dad together. And Mom would probably dress up, with makeup and everything, since it would be her time meeting Carmen's teachers. Getting Mom there would be no problem, and Dad stayed in town all week, but would he come all the way to New Jersey just because she asked?

Only time would tell.

§

Dear Nellie,

First day of school today. Assaulted by Marco and rescued by Diego. Diego is an interesting guy. He wants me to pretend he's my boyfriend so Marco and the other bangers will leave me alone. What if he's the one playing games and I just cause myself more problems by going along with his plan? And why would he care about me in the first place? Something feels fishy. Oh, and why doesn't he already have his own girlfriend if he has so much power?

Diego's a really cool-looking dude. He's got tats all over his body. They had to hurt. So either he has a high tolerance for pain, or he's some kind of weird pain seeker. Either way, he's intriguing. I probably should stay away from him though. Something tells me Diego's as much trouble as the dude he's trying to protect me from.

Love,
Carmen

ॐ

Carmen had no idea how exhausting it was to mess with people's minds until she'd spent the afternoon working magic to get both her parents to come to the college fair without knowing the other would be there. Couldn't she skip the event and crawl into bed?

Was it even worth the effort? A college fair wasn't necessary to find a culinary school—there were only a few perfect choices. But she'd heard the hope laced in both Mom's and Dad's words when they assumed attendance at the fair meant Carmen might be exploring other options. Fine with her. They could think whatever they wanted to. As long as it got them together in the same room.

The drive to school passed too quickly. It would probably be even more awkward walking into the school with her mother by her side than all alone as the new girl earlier. At least Mom looked pretty hot—for a middle-aged woman anyway. She'd dropped a few pounds, had on skinny jeans and some great boots she'd bought a few years ago but had never even worn. A flowy brown top, some gold bangles skimming her slimmer wrists, and her hair loose and wavy—she almost looked like a student rather than a parent. Would Dad notice? Or was it too late for him to see good in his ex-wife? Then again, he would be comparing her mother to a professional cheerleader. As good as Mom looked, who could compete with someone like Tiffany? If a person liked that kind of perky perfection. Ewww. No thanks.

As they approached the school, Carmen spotted her dad waving from the steps at the front door, still dressed in his business suit. Handsome. Grinning. He tipped his head down to speak to a blond student beside him who turned and waved at Carmen.

Who was th—?

Tiffany?

Carmen's heart sank. What was *she* doing there? Impossible. There was no way her father had brought his bimbo to his own daughter's college night at school. How could her dad have so little class? How would Mom feel about coming face-to-face with her home-wrecker so soon?

Mom gasped, and her steps slowed.

Carmen wanted to sneak a peek at her but was afraid to look.

She grabbed Carmen's hand and pulled until they both stopped moving. Her grip tightened.

Carmen looked at her mother's chalky, lifeless face.

What had she done? It was Carmen's fault they were all here. If she had known just how clueless Dad really was, she'd never have arranged this. So much for trying to get Mom and Dad back together. Her scheming had done nothing more than drive the knife deeper into Mom's back.

Mom let go of Carmen's hand. "I'm leaving. I'll pick you up after."

"You can't, Mom. Please." But Carmen didn't even want to be around that adulteress, so how could she blame her mom for wanting to bolt?

"You know I'd do anything you ask me to, honey. But don't you think this is asking a bit too much?" Mom rubbed her temples. "I'd really like to disappear before I have to talk to them." Her glance darted toward Dad and Tiffany, who had started their approach.

"All right. I understand. Let's get out of here." No way she'd let Mom leave by herself. Carmen grabbed her mother's elbow and ushered her back toward the car.

Footsteps drew closer behind them.

"Pamela, Carmen. How's it going? I'm so glad you let us know about tonight. Tiff and I wouldn't have missed it for the world."

Carmen whirled around and glared at her oblivious father. Could he really be so stupid? How could Carmen never have seen hints of this level of insensitivity before? A person didn't turn into a cruel monster overnight. There had to have been evidence all along. It was like she'd never known the man. Then again, what did she expect from him? A solid, loving dad and husband didn't kick his family out so he could move *Barbie* into her dream house at their expense.

She shifted her gaze to Tiffany, gloating by his side.

Her eyes sparkled with power. "Well, hello there, Carmen. Nice to see you again so soon. It's such a shame we can only have you stay over four nights a month."

Stay over? While the four days might be factual, she clearly meant the phrasing to bite. It had been Carmen's house first. And if Carmen had her way, it would be her house long after Dad disposed of Tiffany, as he would once he tired of her, too. She was nothing compared to Mom, so she didn't stand a chance.

Tiffany inspected her claws, a smile tugging at the corners of her mouth.

"Turns out we have to go. I'll give you a call later, Dad." Carmen reached for Mom's rigid arm.

"You're leaving? We came all this way. . . ." His eyes appealed to Tiffany to do something—which made perfect sense, since he was apparently helpless to do anything for himself.

Tiffany waved him off. "Oh, it's okay, Daniel. If they need to run, it'll be fine. I have a lot of closet organization to plan anyway."

Dad's eyes flashed, and he shot Tiffany a look demanding—no, it was unmistakable, begging—she not say any more.

Hmm. There was something going on. Something Dad didn't want her to find out about. Carmen would accept the challenge, thank you very much. "Closet organizing?"

"Oh yeah, I had a top designer come and design me a dream one—more like a dressing room—right off our bedroom. Construction started today." Tiffany's eyes flickered to Mom's mottled face.

Carmen should let it go—if for no other reason than Mom shouldn't have to be subjected to this torture. Carmen tried to ignore her intuition, which told her Tiffany was up to no good. If only she could resist taking the bait. But she was helpless—like watching a fight—not fun to witness, but impossible to look away. "Off my parents' bedroom? What do you mean? There's no space to build. . .unless. . ."

Tiffany studied Carmen's face and said nothing as she let the truth sink in.

She had to be joking. Carmen clenched her jaw to keep her composure. "You punched a hole between my parents' room and mine and you're turning *my* bedroom into your private dressing room. Is that what you're trying to tell me?"

Tiffany tickled her French-manicured nails up and down Dad's arm. "Oh no, dear. That's not what happened at all. You see, I contracted some construction on *my* house. You're only there four days a month. Hardly enough time to stake a claim on any certain part of it—especially a main bedroom. You and Harper can share a room. Or you can have one of the bedrooms in the basement if you insist on your own space when you're visiting."

Carmen's jaw dropped. *When I'm visiting?* She squinted at her dad. Was he hearing this? And Kimberley got to keep her own room? Carmen's hand clenched into a fist. Guess it paid to suck up. Well, add bedroom to the list of losses. Things just got better and better.

Dad stared at the ground. He didn't flinch when Tiffany intertwined her fingers in his. He hadn't protested when Tiffany opened her big mouth. Didn't try to intervene when she said her hurtful words. What a weak-willed jerk. Plain and simple.

Mom deserved better.

꩜

Industrial landscape flew by the car window as they hurled toward home past street construction and office buildings. "You okay, Mom?"

"Yeah. I'm fine." She gripped the steering wheel, her thumbnail scratching marks into the black rubber. "I'm reminded. That's all."

"Reminded?"

"Yep. Of why we're divorced. That man—your father?" Her knuckles turned white from her grip. "I don't even know him. Apparently never did. Marrying him has proven to be the biggest mistake of my life."

All my fault. Mom would have never made the choice to marry Dad if she hadn't been pregnant. And really, it was right he'd married her—not every guy would have come through in such a big way—and they did have some good years together, and they were a happy family, or at least Carmen had thought so. Why couldn't Dad have been more like Nate? Now there was one to hold on to. If Mom had had a guy like Nate, she wouldn't be in this predicament.

But Nate was all Carmen's. Wait just a second. Maybe she'd stumbled upon the answer. Carmen and Nate should get married, get a place to live, start a family of their own—just the two of them. Do it right. Forever.

Nate would never marry her right now though. He had college to finish then law school. He'd never want to get saddled with a family at this point in his life, even though other people sixteen and eighteen did it all the time—all throughout history. Even in the Bible.

He would if he had to trade places with Carmen and live her new life. He'd want out just as badly as she did. Dad married Mom at exactly Nate's age, and Mom had been Carmen's, so why couldn't she and Nate get married, too? But Mom and Dad hadn't decided to marry for no reason. Mom had been pregnant, so Dad probably felt like he didn't have a choice.

Those words played in Carmen's mind again. Dad hadn't had a choice.

She had her solution.

Carmen could get pregnant.

The words hung in her brain as if suspended in a cartoon thought bubble.

Then Nate would be forced to take her in, marry her, be with her forever. No more Hackensack. No more stupid high school. No more smelly apartment over a nail salon. She'd miss her sisters and her mom—but not enough to stick around the mess Carmen had no part in creating. No more loneliness.

But what if Nate wouldn't do it? What if he pushed for an abortion?

No, he'd never ask Carmen to even consider terminating the pregnancy. His family would want him to face his responsibilities. Judge McConnell's political career and upcoming senate race couldn't withstand the scandal of abortion or Nate having an illegitimate child out there he didn't take care of.

They'd get married. They'd be a family. How great would it be to have a real family with Nate?

Mom and Dad had been happy for a long time. They had built all of the good stuff that comes with being a family because of a baby. So could she.

Nate would do the same thing if he were in her shoes. Wouldn't he? If he really knew what she endured, if he really got it, he would have thought of this already. So she'd just be helping him along a little bit. Every guy wanted to be a knight in shining armor or a Prince Charming. Right? A little prodding couldn't do anything but help him out.

"Earth to Carmen. We're home, sleepyhead."

Making no effort to correct her mom's assumptions, Carmen floated from the parked car to the apartment entrance and then up the stairs, eager to get to her bedroom so she could think. The street noises provided background music to mask her thundering heart.

Could she actually do something so treacherous? Would it make her the worst girlfriend on the planet? Did people actually do this kind of thing? Technically it would be starting their marriage, their family, on a lie. But Nate would never have to know. He'd fall in love with their baby, and how it came about would never even be a question. But the big question was if Carmen could live with herself if she did such a thing. She'd be costing Nate a shot at a great future just so she could have what she wanted. He could still go to college. It didn't have to change everything—just some things. Right?

Carmen reached in her top drawer and pulled the brand-new pill pack from beneath her balled-up socks and stared at the circle of pills. She was due to take her first one of the month that night. And the month was already compromised because of missing so many in the last cycle. If she was actually going to do this, the timing couldn't be better. But maybe she should wait and think about things for another month. Carmen's heart sank at the prospect of waiting. The sooner, the better. Before she changed her mind.

She pressed the first tiny pill through its foil backing and held it in her palm as she carried it to the bathroom. Final decision time. What would it be? Take the pills as prescribed, or plan for a baby—a family—with Nate.

The tiny pill rolled on her palm as she shifted from foot to foot. Oblivious to just how much power it possessed. She knew what she wanted to do—but once she made up her mind, either way, she'd be propelled forward. . .no going back. Carmen gripped the pill in her fist and held it over the toilet. This was crazy!

Last chance to change her mind.

She pressed the lever with her empty hand, and the water began to swirl in the bowl like an upside-down tornado. "I'm sorry, Nate," Carmen whispered. She opened her hand and let the pill drop into the tempestuous water just before it got sucked down the pipes.

Decision made.

Chapter 6

"There's a letter for you on the table from Sleepy Hollow Country Club." Mom stuck her head out of the bathroom door as she pulled on a pair of rubber gloves.

Cleaning day. Great. Carmen's backpack slid from her shoulder to the floor. *Thud.*

"Ooh, what is it?" Harper ran to the table and grabbed the letter.

Kimberley snatched it from Harper's grasp. "Let's take a look and see." She inserted her finger into the slot and made a tiny tear, eyes twinkling with mischief.

"Don't you dare." Carmen's heart pounded. "I'm serious, Kim. You're committing a federal offense called mail tampering."

Carmen tugged on Kim's sweater sleeve, the knit threatening to unravel. She had to get her hands on that letter . . .her sister had no right playing keep-away with her mail.

"Yeah, what are you going to do about it?" Kim danced around the room, holding the mail out of Carmen's reach. "Besides, why the fuss? Unless. . ." Kimberley's eyes widened. "Is this a love letter from Zach?" She hopped up on a dining chair and lifted the envelope in the air as she tore it open.

"Oh come on. It's not a love—" Carmen vowed to kill her little sister.

"Dear Ms. Castillo," Kim grinned. "I guess that's you, Carmen."

Carmen's shoulders slumped. Kim intended to read the letter. Why didn't Mom stop her?

"This letter is to inform you all future tennis lessons with Zach Stafford have been canceled, and your standing in the competition rotation has been. . ."—Kim glanced at Carmen— "forfeited due to nonmembership." Her mouth dropped open, and she gaped at Carmen. "What is this? Are they serious?"

"You'll have to ask your father."

Carmen spun on her heels but froze when she heard footsteps behind her. "Do *not* follow me. Don't even think about it." Hurrying to her room, thankful her sisters left her alone for once, Carmen gulped back sobs until she slammed her door, and then she slumped on the floor and let them flow.

"Hey, baby." A tattooed arm snaked around Carmen's shoulders and pulled her away from her locker into the mass of students milling in the hallway.

Marco.

"I'm not your baby." *Act cool. Be confident. Don't let him see you shake.* Carmen tried the pep talk, positive she failed miserably.

"Oh?" Marco chuckled. "S'what you think, chica. Everyone wants to be Marco's girl."

Carmen slammed her locker door, spun the combination lock, and faced him. "Sorry. Not this chica."

His eyes flashed with momentary anger—a glimpse into his soul. She'd gone too far.

"Listen, we can do this the hard way or the easy way. Your call."

This? What did he mean? "No offense, Marco. Really."

"Better." His face softened, and then he reached his arm around her back and pulled her close.

"No." She shrugged his touch off her body. "I didn't mean any offense, but I did mean it. You've got the wrong girl."

Carmen took one step back, ready to flee.

Marco snapped his finger. "Shooter. José."

Shoot her, José? Carmen's head whipped wildly around as she searched for a gunman.

Two of Marco's comrades appeared from nowhere. They crossed their leather-clad arms and planted their expensive shoes right in her way. *Oh.* Shooter was his name, not a direct order. He had been the one with the gun by the lamppost the other day.

Carmen glanced in every direction, looking for any way to go that promised escape or even refuge. In one direction a door led to the outside—but the padlock assured its impassibility. Another direction led straight into a dead end. Marco and company blocked her only way out, which also happened to be the way to the front office.

"More and more I'm sure I have the right girl. I like 'em feisty." Marco pressed her against the lockers and put one arm to each side of her head. He leaned close and licked his lips. "Face it, baby, you're all mine."

Carmen ducked under his outstretched arm and pulled away from the cluster.

José hooted. "You gonna let her get away with that?"

This had gone way too far. "Look, you guys. No offense, really. It's just. . .I have a boyfriend." *Please let it go.*

They snickered.

Shooter smacked Marco's back. "Guess she's taken, Marco."

Marco grinned, flashing a mouthful of silver caps. "Oh, well in that case. . .you tell yo' boyfriend, from wherever you came from, you moved on. Believe me, baby, he has, too. Right?" Marco raised his eyebrows at his buddies. "You fine, but no girl is worth waiting around for."

"I know that's right." José bumped his knuckles with Marco and then Shooter.

What a bunch of jerks! Carmen had to get away from them, no matter what.

Another arm crept around Carmen's shoulders and squeezed her tight. She jumped and glanced back to find out the identity of her newest attacker.

Diego. What a relief. Or was it?

"Whachu doin' messin' with my girl, Marco?" Diego flipped the toothpick in his mouth end over end while he stared Marco down.

Marco dissolved. "Your girl? I didn't know." He scowled at Carmen. "Why didn't you say so, little chica? Save us all some trouble." He looked up at Diego. "I didn't mean nothin' by it, man."

"I'll let it go this time, but don't let me see you talking to her again. Got it?"

Marco nodded then flashed his gaze toward Carmen and held her eye contact. There was no mistaking—he wasn't finished with her yet. He snapped his fingers at his boys, and they swaggered away.

Carmen's shoulders sagged, and she exhaled the breath she'd been holding for far too long. "Thanks for coming to my rescue. We can have a public breakup in a few days."

"Oh, I don't know. By the looks of things, you need Diego as much as Diego needs himself a piece of arm candy with no strings attached." He shrugged. "We'll see how it goes."

Why? Why did Diego want to help her? Why did Marco fear him? And why did he always refer to himself in third person? Ah, the mysteries of life.

But at least she'd made it through one more day.

⟲

"I missed you a ton this week." Carmen poured orange juice for Nate. "Our first full two-week spread between visitation weekends. Which I know you know as well as I do."

"It sure was a long two weeks. Three total if you count since the day of the move."

Kimberley peeked into the kitchen, squinting as the morning sun hit her face. "Oooh, I missed you, too, snookum." She smooched the air.

Nate's eyes twinkled.

"Kim, get out of here! You need to stop spying."

"Spying? Um, last I checked I live here, too. Just coming in for breakfast. But with the way you two carry on, I've lost my appetite." She stomped from the room.

"You should go a little easier on her. She only wants you to like her. She looks up to you so much."

"But she's *always* there. I need space. We need space."

"We had some space last night." Nate winked and pulled her onto his lap.

Carmen giggled.

Harper rounded the corner into the kitchen. "Oh gross!" She stuck her finger in her mouth and made gagging noises. "Do you two ever let up? I'm never going to have a boyfriend if I have to act like you two. Ick."

"You'll change your mind. Won't she, babe?" Nate wiggled his eyebrows.

"Without a doubt. Come on. Let's get out of here." Carmen grabbed Nate's hand and tugged him into the backyard, where they settled on deck chairs.

"Hey, it's Saturday. Why aren't you going to tennis?"

Carmen eyed him. "It's over. Dad won't pay for me to be an out-of-resident member. Mom can't afford it, of course. Dad could take me as a guest, but I couldn't be a regular on Zach's schedule or in competition if I'm only a guest. So, there you go." She crossed her arms and waited for a reaction.

Nate blinked. "You're losing tennis, too? I don't see how your dad could let that happen to you along with everything else."

"Hi, guys!" Tiffany sashayed toward them in skin-tight white jeans and a zebra-print silk top.

"That's how." Carmen jerked her head at Tiffany.

"Your dad and I are going furniture shopping. Want to come?"

Do I want to take a bullet to my brain? "No. I don't think so. We're going over to Nate's."

"Furniture for what?" Nate asked.

"Mainly for my dressing room. I need a vanity and an armoire. Plus maybe some office furniture for your dad. Depends if I'm feeling generous." She winked at Carmen.

It's his *money!* Carmen wanted to shout. How dare she talk about being generous.

Nate stood up and put on his best politician smile. "Hey, Tiffany. Mind if I ask you something?"

Oh no, Nate. Don't do it. Please. It won't help. She'll only take pleasure in knowing it got to me.

"Sure." Tiffany batted her long eyelashes.

"What's the deal with Carmen's tennis? I mean, does she really have to quit completely? Isn't there some way you could talk to her dad and work things out since she loves it so much?"

"Oh, believe me, we've talked about it at length. It's probably better this way since he's not home a lot. The club says it's not fair to the others on the team since Carmen can only show up on the weekends anyway. So they're happy to have her spot open for someone more regular." Tiffany pivoted toward the house. "Gotta run. The stores are waiting."

Like her attendance was her fault. And she was still way better than any of the others even if she could only make it on the weekends.

Nate shrugged at Carmen. "Sorry, babe."

"At least you tried. Appreciate the effort—lost cause though. Tiffany gets what Tiffany wants, and I rank somewhere near the bottom on her list of concerns apparently." Above garbage men but below furry animals—which didn't say a whole lot considering the mink and chinchilla coats hanging in her brand-new dressing room.

"I just can't believe you're not going to play tennis anymore. You're so good at it—and you love it." Nate sank back into the chair he'd vacated.

"Mom says to pray about it. Anything can change." If Nate worried so much about it now, maybe he would get her a membership once they got married. Or after the baby came.

"Yeah. Maybe."

"What? I thought you believed in prayer and God and all that stuff." Carmen flipped onto her stomach with a balled-up towel beneath her cheek.

"Yeah. I mean, I guess so. You know how it is. We go to church sometimes, but mostly not. I went through the classes and made my first communion. That's about the extent of it." He intertwined his fingers with Carmen's.

If he didn't really know God even though he had everything going for him, how could she ever trust the theory that some divine being watched out for *her* from up above? Nope. No doubt about it. She was on her own.

"But really, if you think praying will help you get over losing tennis. . .and everything else, by all means, go for it." Nate's eyes softened as he gazed at Carmen. "I don't know how you can be so calm."

Because I have a plan.

Chapter 7

Consuelo is still scrubbing the kitchen floor, so don't go in there, okay?" Mrs. McConnell called from some deep recess of the McMansion.

"Uh. Hi, Mom." Nate winked at Carmen.

The blond suburban queen came around the corner, drying her hands on a monogramed dish towel. "Hi, son. Hey, Carmen." She finished drying her hands on her khaki pants and pulled her white sweater closed around a black blouse. Hillary McConnell's cleaning outfit.

Did her smile waver, or had Carmen only imagined the kink in Hillary's steely armor?

"What are you two doing today?"

"Just hanging out. Nothing special." Nate gestured toward the kitchen. "She almost finished? We're starved."

"I think so, but who knows?" Mrs. McConnell turned to Carmen. "Hey, maybe you could ask her how long she'll be. You speak her language, right?"

Oh great. This should be fun. *Her language* happens to be Spanish. And yes, Carmen spoke it. Carmen glanced at the ceramic tile, imported from Spain, no doubt. Maybe it would open up and swallow her whole before she had to humiliate herself. Carmen's body moved toward the arched entrance to the kitchen as though propelled by some unseen force. Stop moving, feet. Once she arrived at the kitchen, Carmen would have to open her mouth and widen the gulf between herself and Nate's family. Maybe it had been Mrs. McConnell's plan all along to point out to Nate that his girlfriend was no better than a cleaning lady.

Why couldn't they have shown up at Nate's just thirty minutes later? The last thing she needed was to have her ethnicity pointed out to Mrs. McConnell in all its Mexican glory. Nate's parents had a hard enough time tolerating their son dating a rich Mexican girl from down the street. But now. . .now she was a poor Mexican girl from Hackensack, New Jersey. . .in a single-parent home. . .living in an apartment. . . . Carmen could only begin to imagine the way they felt about her. This little interaction with the cleaning lady sure wouldn't help.

Deep breath. "*Cuantos tiempo?*" Carmen's voice croaked out in barely a whisper.

The maid scooted back on her knees and continued to scrub and hum.

A little louder. "Cuantos tiempo *mas?*"

Still nothing? Seriously?

Consuelo shifted position on the floor again, and Carmen noticed the wires hanging down from her ears. Of course. An iPod. Carmen stepped in a little farther and said with force, "How much longer? Cuantos tiempo *mas?*"

Consuelo's head jerked up as though she'd been slapped— the surprise smoothed out the deep lines on her face. They reappeared as her grin spread from ear to ear. "Carmen. *Mi chica. Es bueno verte!*" She clambered to her feet, smoothed down her light gray skirt and white apron, and pulled Carmen into a tight embrace. "*Como esta tu familia? Estoy orando para tu.*"

Just ignore Mrs. McConnell's raised eyebrows. Fraternizing with the help was bad enough, but doing it in Spanish? Carmen doubted she'd recover from this in Nate's parents' eyes. Not that she held out much hope before. She should have ignored Consuelo. But the cleaning lady had said she'd been praying for Carmen's family. Carmen couldn't snub her.

"*Mas o menos.*" Carmen held up one hand and twisted it. What could she say? Of course her family wasn't fine. But poor Consuelo with her four kids to feed and family back home waiting for her paycheck to arrive every month had it as bad as Carmen. Worse? Probably not. At least as bad. Wouldn't it be harder to move from the lap of luxury to a bunk bed in Hackensack than to have always lived that way?

Hillary McConnell cleared her throat, and Nate shifted his feet.

Oh, right. "Consuelo, cuantos tiempo mas?" Carmen gestured at the expansive floor.

Consuelo looked at her chunky plastic watch. "Eh. *Quince minutos. . .aproxidament.*"

"She said fifteen more minutes." Carmen locked eyes with Nate's mom.

"Thank you, dear. That'll be fine." She patted Carmen's arm as she strode from the room.

Realization doused Carmen. Of course Mrs. McConnell understood basic Spanish. She had to be able to communicate with her own employee—if she couldn't, she'd have hired someone else.

No matter. Carmen would have her moment of revenge. Wonder if Nate's mom understood Spanish for *she's having my baby*?

Chapter 8

"A single mom with three girls? They are so going to pounce on us at church." Carmen slumped on Mom's bed and pulled the rumpled covers over her already-dressed body. She'd managed to keep the subject of church off the table in the weeks since their move by claiming illness, too much homework, or whatever else she could think of. But Mom sure looked determined to drag them all out for their public disgrace that morning.

"What are you talking about?" Mom finished brushing on some gloss and smacked her lips together.

"Oh, they're going to see us as their next project. You know, those poor Castillo girls—like we're in need." Not that they weren't.

"Well, aren't we?"

"Not from a bunch of strangers trying to make some convert quota." Carmen bit the corner of her nail too short then squeezed it tight until blood surfaced. She stared at the pooling blood like a bug squirming under a microscope. The sting reminded her she was, indeed, alive. It didn't prove she mattered, but alive was a start.

"Just give them a chance. That's all I ask." Mom slipped into her heels and tightened the slingback around her slender ankles. "You might be surprised. This church comes highly recommended. A lot of my old friends go here."

As Carmen sat in the front seat waiting for Mom to start the car, she tried to think of a way out. Get sick? Just say no. Hide. No, she was stuck. The ten-minute drive to the church on the better side of town would be nowhere near long enough. Carmen hadn't been to her old church in a couple of years, but at least the longer drive to that one had been green and plush. Now, the drab gray of the scenery out Carmen's window depressed her. And the bars on some of the store windows weren't very inviting.

"She's touching me," Harper whined, and scuffle noises ensued.

"Girls, please don't fight. You'll mess up your dresses," Mom begged.

Maybe they would rip each other's clothes. Then they'd have to go home. Carmen would make them a consolation lunch, and they could watch old movies all afternoon.

"Speaking of dresses"—Mom looked Carmen over head to toe—"couldn't you have worn something other than jeans today?"

Carmen shrugged. "I like my jeans, and I doubt God cares." Or notices.

The car turned into the parking lot of Hackensack First Christian. Oh boy. No more stalling.

Carmen followed Mom into the church, averting her eyes from any potential recognition from classmates. Probably the children of Mom's old classmates. Same people, different outfits. These people wouldn't understand her. Tears stung her eyes. Why was she acting like such a baby? She'd never been a loner before, but now she wanted to hide in her room all day. She missed the old happy, outgoing Carmen she'd once been, but that girl had disappeared. The girl without a care in the world.

The one who mattered. Carmen dug her fingernails into her palm. The pain was good for a moment's relief.

"Look, girls. There're tons of kids over there." Mom gestured to the section at the front left where three rows were filled with teens and younger youth. "Do you want to go sit with them?"

What, like a play date? No thanks.

"We do!" Kimberley grabbed Harper's hand and yanked her toward the front.

"Uh. I'll pass." Carmen slid into a chair next to her mom and slouched, for once wishing Kim and Harper were less friendly.

The music started. *Ugh. Here we go.* Carmen rose from her chair after she made sure everyone else had stood. Once upon a time, she'd loved this stuff. Until logic made her almost positive God didn't exist except as the higher power people could find deep within themselves. He was a good idea for people to lean on when they were in trouble. But God or no God, Carmen's life had gone up and down, been happy or sad, subject to everyone else's whims and stupid decisions. None of it seemed to depend on an unseen force of nature, so it made more sense to accept that He wasn't real.

The woven fabric on the seat back in front of her prickled under her fingernail as she picked at the loose threads. Ten. Ten lighting fixtures hung low from the ceiling. Three. Three men in suits occupied thrones—okay, seats—on the stage. Or they'd probably call it a platform. Whatever.

Why did people have to raise their hands when they sang? Maybe they wanted to be the best little worshipper to convince everyone around them they were closest to God. Didn't the Bible say people should be private when they prayed and stuff? Carmen could swear she'd heard that somewhere.

Where were the doors? Carmen shifted her feet and glanced around the room for an escape route. Could she leave to go to the bathroom? No. Everyone would look at her, and she'd make a spectacle of herself. What if she just sat down? Was there some rule against sitting if you weren't pushing a walker? She could check her text messages to pass the time. Surely Nate had written. He'd better have—not one message yesterday. First time he'd missed a day in the history of their relationship. Hopefully the last time.

"Thank you, worship team and band. You can all be seated." The silver-haired pastor held his hands out in front of him and gestured downward.

Finally.

"I'm privileged to introduce our guests to you today. They've come all the way from Colorado to share the ways God has touched them and is now touching lives through them. I could ramble on and on. . ."

I'm sure you could.

". . .save as much time as possible for our guests to share with you. I'd first like to welcome Ben Bradley, director of Diamond Estates."

A wavy-haired guy in a shiny gray suit took four steps— more like leaps—and bounded onto the stage. He pumped the pastor's hand and flashed a full set of sparkly whites at the congregation. Oh boy—one of those.

"Before I begin, let's put first things first and pray." He lifted his arms toward the ceiling and looked up. "Father, I come before You surrendered as Your servant. Please grant me the words to say to reveal Your heart to these precious people, and please open their hearts and minds to Your touch. Amen."

Hmm. Figured he'd be more wordy.

Ben ran his fingers through the silver-peppered hair above

each ear then looked out at the audience with kind eyes. "Today's teens are hurting. Sometimes so much so the only way to get them grounded in faith and teach them how to make good decisions is to pluck them out of their current environment completely. We'll call it a reboot."

Several people laughed—not sure what was funny. Carmen felt like her life had been rebooted already, and it hadn't been fun at all. What was this guy trying to sell? Whatever it was, Carmen wasn't buying.

"At Diamond Estates we work to uncover God's most precious gems from the deepest mire. Teen girls come to Diamond Estates and live there for approximately a year. They're immersed in Bible study, prayer, worship, service, and everything else that goes into a well-rounded faith walk. Plus they participate in several counseling sessions every week— personally, in a group setting, and by Skype with their families. The goal is for the girls to return home with a new faith, vigorously ready to walk with Jesus and face the world with a family prepared to support her."

Quite a lofty goal.

The congregation broke into applause.

"These girls come to us with all sorts of issues: promiscuity, drug and alcohol abuse, sexual abuse, and anything else you can imagine. You're going to get the opportunity to hear from two of those girls today. One of them is already a graduate of Diamond Estates and lives in Colorado. The other is one of our longer-term residents who is about to graduate and go home to her family. I'll let them tell you their stories themselves."

He smiled and nodded at a girl in the front row. "First, I'd like to welcome Julia Hernandez to the stage." A tiny Mexican girl popped out from among the group of teens. She'd fit right in—like she'd belonged there. Well maybe she could take

Carmen's place. Maybe they could trade.

"Hi. I'm Julia. Peeps call me Ju-Ju. I'm going to start by telling you a little bit about my background. This part is always the hardest. So I hope you understand if I stumble around a little." Her hands shook as she tucked her wild curls behind her ear.

"The story starts before I was born—don't they all? I mean, we're all born into trouble of some kind, no? But for me, my life consisted of gangs and a 'hood full of violence."

Much like Carmen's new home, probably.

"My mom tried really hard to shield me and my brother from everything, and we did pretty good until. . .well, until I turned twelve." Ju-Ju's knuckles turned white on the sides of the podium.

"Mom and Scotty were shot in a drive-by while watching TV in our apartment." She took a ragged breath. "I was in my room asleep when it all went down. I woke up and—you know how it can take awhile for you to figure out what the noise you heard while you were sleeping actually was?" She raised her eyebrows until some people nodded.

"Well, that's not at all how it went for me. I knew right away what had happened, but I stayed in my room, shaking, too scared to come out. I huddled under my covers, trembling for over an hour before I could bring myself to go out there. I kept imagining the scene, and I didn't want to see it because I knew there'd be no going back once I did. But no matter what I pictured in my head, the real sight was worse."

Ju-Ju gripped the podium. "I often wonder to this day if they'd be alive if I'd been strong enough to get them help sooner instead of huddling in there like a coward." She wiped a tear from her cheek. "But there I was, facing my new reality of being all alone in the great big scary world. I knew they'd come for me and send me to some foster home, and I couldn't let it happen 'cause I'd heard stories. So I ran." She shrugged as though the weight of her decision wasn't a big deal. Like it had been the most natural thing in the world for her to do.

Alone on the streets at twelve? No family at all? And Carmen thought *she* had it bad. She glanced at some of the faces in the audience. Several men shook their heads in disbelief, and a few women in hats dabbed their eyes with a tissue. She moved her gaze to the teens in the front few rows, expecting them to be mocking and smirking, but they were riveted.

"So, over the next year, I kind of scrambled for food and begged for money. I found places to sleep wherever I could—benches, doorways, alleys, and sometimes a shelter had room, but I couldn't stay too long or someone would call family services, and I'd get hauled off to foster care."

She shrugged. "Eventually I figured out that big-city businessmen would let me stay in their nice warm hotel rooms and send me off with money the next morning if I gave them some company. So I did."

Had Carmen heard that right? Was Ju-Ju talking about prostitution? Carmen leaned forward just a bit.

"Over time it got easier and easier, and I forgot what life was supposed to be like." The young speaker gasped for breath. She'd let those words roll out so fast—probably wanted that part of her speech over as soon as possible.

Vibration in her pocket jolted Carmen out of the story. Would it be rude to check her messages? Of course it would. But she had to know if Nate had texted.

"Drugs, alcohol, prostitution. Who'd have thought all of that just by looking at me?" Julia shook her head. "I can hardly believe it myself sometimes. But the worst part? The decisions that stick with me to this day—the ones that will haunt me for the rest of my life—are the ones in which I chose to take the lives of my unborn babies." She held up two fingers and wiped a tear from her cheek. "This is the hardest part to talk about, and I'm not going to stay on this for too long, but I do want to say one thing." She made eye contact with the teens in front.

"Never, ever, ever is life so hard or is your situation so bad you have to resort to sin to get out of it. Ben will teach about that from the Bible in a minute. But it's a promise from God in First Corinthians chapter ten that He'll always make a way for you to not have to choose sin. I made the wrong choice, and I'll regret it forever."

Carmen glanced at her mom. Her makeup looked perfect, except one penciled-in eyebrow had smudged when she wiped away a tear. She still hadn't gotten used to her new look and how to maintain it. But she sure did seem to be enjoying the guest speakers.

"But!"

Carmen gasped and jolted in her seat along with the rest of the congregation as Ju-Ju shouted, her face all lit up with joy.

"One day I wandered through the streets like I did every day, looking for a meal or a companion for the night. I passed over a few guys who gave me the creeps and then got hired for the entire night by an out-of-towner. An all-nighter was considered a cherry job because it usually meant a few hours of good sleep and a warm shower in the morning."

Ju-Ju smiled. "The dude turned out to be an angel. Or at least the next best thing. Mark Stapleton happened to be a Chicago police officer serving as a short-term missionary in New York who posed as a john."

On a mission trip and he hires a prostitute? What a hypocrite.

"He paid me well and then spent every minute he paid

for telling me about Jesus. By morning I was lugging all of my possessions in one carry-on bag as I boarded a plane for Colorado. I moved into Diamond Estates and haven't looked back since."

Julia gazed out at the audience and locked eyes with several teens in the front then moved her gaze to Carmen. "Officer Mark Stapleton led me to Christ, but being at Diamond Estates has allowed me to learn and grow in my relationship with God. I've been healed, forgiven, and fully restored."

The church broke into applause as Ju-Ju walked across the stage.

Wow. Quite a story. How would Carmen have handled the same situation? Could she have been so strong?

Ben jumped from his seat to assist Julia down the stairs.

Perfect timing. Carmen slipped her phone from her pocket to the empty seat beside her. With one finger she swiped it open to her most recent text.

C, CELL BATTERY DIED AND I COULDN'T FIND MY PHONE. CHARGING NOW. WILL CALL U LATER.

Carmen fought the urge to squeal. He'd been concerned about worrying her. Phew. Should she sneak a quick reply? Nah. Waiting and wondering wouldn't hurt him a bit. She slid the phone back into place and raised her eyes to listen to the speaker.

Grinning, Ben had taken the microphone again. "Ju-Ju graduated from our program about two months ago, and she lives with a local family serving in the church and the community. God radically changed her life." He looked down at his companions and smiled.

"Next, I'm going to welcome Tricia to the stage." He nodded to a statuesque African American who glided toward the front like she walked on air. Was it arrogance? No, not arrogance. She just had grace. Elegance bubbling up from deep within. Something Carmen would never have.

"Tricia came from a life of modeling. It's very difficult for an insecure girl—even one from a large, happy, loving family—to thrive in a world demanding perfection. As a result, Tricia searched for love in all the wrong places, to quote an old song. She looked for identity and approval in the attention she got from boys. Tricia's identity search eventually led her to Diamond Estates, where we've worked to teach her how Jesus sees her. Tricia's going to talk a bit more about life at the center."

That kind of made sense. Nate sure did fill Carmen's soul. When he looked at her just right, she felt like the most beautiful woman on the planet. When he paid a lot of attention to her, she felt valuable. Then again, when he didn't. . .

"Hi. I'm Tricia. Like Ben said, I'm going to graduate from Diamond Estates in about six months. Quite a long while after I should have." Her lip twitched, and her bracelet clinked against the microphone as she gripped it with white-knuckled fingers. "This is the first time I'm telling my story to strangers, so bear with me. I'm a little nervous."

What did she have to be nervous about? She could rival any of the contestants on those reality runway shows. Her presence captivated Carmen at first glance.

"I've been in modeling since I was a little girl. Maybe it all sounds glamorous to you, but it's not."

Right. Poor girl. Carmen didn't want to hear the horrors of long photo shoots and other catastrophes of the lucky elite.

Tricia chuckled. "I see some of you are skeptical. I understand. I really I do. The thing is, being a model doesn't change a girl into something better; it just highlights something meaningless and makes it the most important thing about her. In other words, my looks should be the least important thing about who I am. Yet, through the industry I was in, my looks defined me. Worth, potential, income, and ability rest solely on appearance. The pressure to be what's expected and to conform in both looks and actions is so high."

She twisted a ring on her finger. "But at Diamond Estates I was able to leave it all behind me. You see, if I had stayed in my hometown, surrounded by my old friends, I'd have never been able to pull myself away from their expectations and from my own reputation. It was like by entering Diamond Estates, I got a do-over. I tried really hard to change my thinking right away. I knew who I wanted to be, and I did everything I could to force myself into that mold. But old habits die hard. Eventually the same old physical issues snuck in, and I found myself back in a life of binging and purging in futile efforts to be rail thin. I spent all my time worried about my weight and fighting so hard to be skinny it almost killed me. It wasn't until I hit rock bottom that I could identify my misplaced dependency. I needed to stop focusing on myself and turn my focus on God."

Cue the God stuff.

"Once I did, everything became clear. I finally saw myself the way He sees me. I finally knew what it meant to be secure. I no longer needed the attention or approval of a boy or employment with a modeling agency. I was me, and that was enough. No matter what."

Carmen's head swam with confusion. What did it all mean? Focus on God? Dependency on Him? It didn't make any sense. How could she have faith in someone who had proven to be completely uninterested in her life? In what hurt her. In what she lost. In what she wanted. It made no sense to think she should put blind trust in a being who hadn't intervened a single time in the mess her parents had created. The last straw was tennis. How hard would it have been for God, supposedly the Creator of the universe, to work it out so she could keep playing? It was almost as though He wanted to watch her suffer. Like using the rays of the sun to burn a bug with a magnifying glass.

Nate, on the other hand, made her feel alive. He reached her soul and soothed the wrinkles away. He made everything good. Beside him, Carmen felt safe. Like she had worth and mattered to someone. If she had to choose between God or Nate, it was no contest. Mom would be horrified if she heard Carmen say all that. But it was true.

Mr. Bradley gripped the front of the wooden podium and pulled himself forward. His eyes gleamed like he wanted to bore his truth into the souls of the congregation.

Oops, Carmen had missed most of what he'd said. Probably for the best anyway.

"If you're here today and you don't have Jesus, you have a life-controlling problem. It's out of hand. Some of you might deal with alcoholism, some with drugs, some with sexual sins or any number of things. For some of you, it may be simple unbelief controlling your life."

Unbelief? Well, that described Carmen. But she was fine with it. Her unbelief made more sense to her than the blind devotion she witnessed all around her.

"He can take your pain, your sin, even your unbelief and heal it right here. . . ."

Yeah. No thanks. That's where Carmen checked out. That's where she clicked her ruby slippers and went to the place in her head with the Briarcliff Manor zip code. The place that had been taken from her. Where it was warm and solid like Nate's arms. The place she felt whole.

There's no place like home.

Chapter 9

Pink hand towels to match the pink soaps and new wastebasket. Looked like Mom had been taking a few too many sips of the Mary Kay Kool-Aid. At least she seemed happy. And she looked like a million bucks.

Carmen gripped the doorknob leading from the bathroom, a room she'd become more familiar with than her own these recent weeks. She took a deep breath, opened the door and stepped through. Walking down the hallway, she avoided the pink area rugs that had been strewn along the floor in the short time since she'd closed the door. How long had she been in the bathroom? Pink roses now towered on the hallway table.

The scent of cherry blossoms wafted through the air. Carmen clutched her churning abdomen. Where was that smell coming from? Oh. The new pink air freshener plugged into the outlet. She swallowed hard. "Mom, don't you think this pink stuff is going a little too f—"

What on earth?

Mom stood in the center of the family room in front of an easel, wearing a pink business suit, lecturing an empty love seat about its responsibility to treat its Mary Kay career like a business.

"Uh, Mom. Did you convert the couch?"

"Ahh!" Mom tossed her pen in the air and waved her hands

in front of her face like she was swatting away a swarm of bees. Carmen watched the pen flip end over end until it landed on the top of Mom's pink pump.

If she weren't about to throw up again, Carmen would have cracked up. Mom had been a fun one to startle ever since Carmen could remember. Recently Carmen and Daddy had started sneaking up on Mom from different angles and recording her reactions with the voice recorder app on their iPhones. Mom hated it when they posted her screams on Facebook. They couldn't help themselves though. How had things gotten so far from those not-so-very-long-ago days when they could all have fun together—often at Mom's expense?

"You okay?" Carmen squelched a giggle at Mom's blanched expression.

"You guys have got to stop doing that. I'm going to have a heart attack one of these days." She fanned herself with the cable guide. "You feeling okay?" Mom hurried to Carmen's side and pressed a hand to her forehead.

Carmen stepped back from the hand. "I'm fine. Just ate something that didn't agree with me." How long would Carmen be able to sell that story? "What's going on around here? It looks like this place is a stop on the Candy Land game board."

"I'm having my girls over tonight for team training. It's my first, so I'm a little nervous." She flipped a page over to the back of the easel, revealing a glossy pie chart with numbers and percentages about women and makeup.

"What are you training? And who are your girls?" Great. People in the apartment. Would Mom expect Carmen to stick around and entertain them?

"You know. The consultants I've signed under me. They're my team. So I have to train them if I ever hope to quit my day job." She shrugged. "It's no big deal—should be fun."

No big deal, huh? Then why the high-pitched squeal and clipped words? Totally nervous. "Your ankles are trembling, Mom. Better have some more pink Kool-Aid before they get here."

§

Dear Nellie,

Those girls in church today, did you see them? Whoa. Talk about two sick tickets. What messed-up lives. I mean, it's all good they got themselves together and are in a better place, but I think they could have done it all without leaning on God as a crutch. It just takes some willpower and motivation.

Take Ju-Ju for example. She's so tiny and looks so young—anyone who would hire her as a prostitute would have to be like a pedophile or something. She risked her life every night just for a place to sleep? That's crazy. Anyone would know there's a better way with or without God. If she were smart—not saying she's not, but we have to look at the evidence—she'd have tried out the foster program and then run away if it didn't work out. It would sure have been worth a shot anyway.

Then look at Tricia. Oh, come on. She wants us to believe she had it so rough? I don't think so. That's just crazy. She's gorgeous, graceful, and elegant. She comes from a good home. Her parents are still together. Puh-leeze. Binging and purging? I'm not buying it. Sounds like someone is an attention hog and just wasn't getting enough in front of the camera. Or maybe it's all just a publicity stunt. That's probably it.

Whatever. Just goes to show you, Nellie, people are all kinds of crazy, and they'll stop at nothing to get what they want.

Love,
Carmen

ᕲ

"So what's your story?" Theresa Martinez, the girl who sat behind her in Home Ec, waited at Carmen's locker.

"My story?" Sigh. Carmen simply wanted to get through the school day—no more, no less. She didn't want to make small talk. Even more, she didn't want to make friends. She lived on borrowed time in Hackensack. . .on her way out.

Kayla Ortega stepped up. "Yeah, your story. You know: Why are you here? Where did you come from? How do you know Diego? Trust me, you want to tell us because they're already making up stories about you."

"Who is? What kind of stories?"

"Oh, everyone. And Marco. Some of them have you pegged as a Narc. Others think you're just crazy."

A Narc? Like an informer to the cops? Hilarious. Maybe she should play that angle up a bit. "And you? What do you think?"

"I think you're sad." Kayla shrugged. "Theresa, not so much. She figures you're probably on the run."

"Yep. You found me out. I'm a mob princess from Chicago in the witness protection program." Carmen slammed her locker door. "Tell them that story. Let 'em chew on it for a while."

"You probably want to get your truth out. Trust us." Kayla leaned in. "The more you try to keep yourself above us, the harder it's going to be for you."

"I'm not trying to be better than you. I don't think I am." Carmen didn't think it—she knew it. She wasn't supposed to live here.

Kayla rolled her eyes. "It shows in everything you do. Even the way you move through the halls. But whatever, you tell yourself whatever you want to believe." She shrugged. "It really makes no difference to me—I don't care what you do. You should know, though, some of us heard you have a fancy college boyfriend, but you're with Diego. So that doesn't make sense. If you're two-timing Diego, he won't be happy. You don't want Diego unhappy with you, trust me."

Carmen looked at Theresa, who'd remained silent through the exchange and tipped her chin up. "What do you think?"

Theresa held her stare for a few heartbeats. "I think you're in over your head."

Someone finally talked some sense. In more ways than one.

ⓢ

"Happy birthday to you. Happy birthday, dear Carmen! Happy birthday to you!"

"Now make a wish." Nate grinned.

Carmen leaned over the dining table to reach the German chocolate cake with homemade pecan-coconut frosting she'd made herself earlier that day. Mom would have made it, but Carmen couldn't stand the thought of cake mix from a box.

She glanced at Nate and smiled as she inhaled. *I wish for a new life with Nate.* She blew out the seventeen candles in two tries. Not that she expected the wish to come true. She could hope though.

Nate passed a corner piece to Harper. What did he think of the apartment? If only she could have witnessed the horror on his face as his Camaro brought him closer and closer to her side of the universe.

Carmen couldn't wait for a moment alone so she could ask him. She'd bring him out on the fire escape later—oh no! She couldn't bring him out there. What if Marco and his pals were hanging out across the street? Word of Nate would travel around the school so fast. It would confirm the rumors of her college boyfriend. Then everyone would expect her to endure public scorn—or worse—from Diego. She'd have to keep Nate hidden. If anyone asked about the Camaro, she could say she had no idea. Or maybe that he was her cousin visiting from upstate.

"Time for presents." Harper bounced at Carmen's right elbow. "Open mine. Open mine."

Carmen grinned at the infectious glee before she could help herself. She tore off the balloon wrapping paper to find a long slender box. She lifted the top to reveal a plastic necklace. A cross necklace.

Harper's smile went from ear to ear. "Don't you love it?"

"It's beautiful, Harp. Thank you." Carmen pulled her close for a hug.

"Here, let me put it on." Harper took the box from Carmen and readied the chain to fasten around Carmen's neck.

She lifted her thick waves and felt the necklace fall into place. The cross heavy on her chest. She'd wear it when Harper was around, but not to school.

"Mine next." Mom handed Carmen a small, heavy box with a card on top.

She tore open the card. Slow down. Don't let them see the rush. All she wanted was some time alone with Nate. Away from prying eyes seeking her approval, waiting for her to smile and laugh. It was so difficult to find something to laugh about lately. Carmen read the words of the card out loud but didn't register a single one of them. Go through the paces; that was the best she could do. A plastic card fell from the envelope onto the floor.

"Wow. Thirty dollars for iTunes? Awesome, Mom. Thank you." There'd been a day not very long ago that would have been a hundred, but those days were long gone. "I know just what I'm going to download."

"There's something in the box, but I thought the iTunes would help with the sting." Her eyes twinkled.

Sting? "Oh great. What is it, underwear and socks?" Carmen laughed and tore off the same balloon paper to find a Bible engraved with her name. Seriously? What would she do with a personalized Bible?

"I know you're not into reading the Bible right now, Carmen. But the Lord has promised He's begun a work in you, so I'm just making sure you have access to Him whenever you might want it."

"Thanks, Mom. Really." Mom loved her. She meant well and even held back when she'd prefer to push Carmen toward God. It had to be difficult for Mom, who had such a strong faith. Carmen would cherish the Bible. One of her first grown-up gifts ever. Carmen thought of the children's picture-book Bible she had on her shelf and the family Bibles in Mom's room. But this one was special because it was all hers; maybe one day she'd even read it.

"Well, I can't possibly top that. But here's my gift." Nate lifted a small box.

It felt a shame to tear off the professional wrapping.

"What?" Carmen turned the box over in her hands. "Is this the newest iPhone? I didn't even think these were out yet."

"My dad pulled a few strings." Nate grinned. "You like?"

"I love!" She threw her arms around his neck and squeezed. He loved her and wanted to make her happy. Carmen just knew he'd embrace the idea of being together as a family forever. She couldn't wait.

"Well." Mom cleared her throat and twisted her watch around her wrist to read it. "I hate to rush off, but I have a facial to give down the street." She raised one expertly sculpted eyebrow at Carmen and Nate. "You two behave yourselves, you hear?"

"We'll be fine. As long as they leave us alone." Carmen

jerked her head toward her little sisters.

"Girls. . ." Mom gave them her stern look. The look she thought powerful enough to speak volumes but that was actually ignored the moment she turned her back.

"We'll be good, Mom." Kimberley winked at Carmen when Mom turned to leave.

"Oh great." Carmen rolled her eyes at Nate, who laughed.

"Would you like me to walk you to your party, Mrs. Castillo?"

There. Carmen had known it all along. He did think they were slumming it and needed protection. He was right.

"Oh, you're sweet. I'll be fine though." She bent to pick up her pink cases. "Here. If you could just slip this up to my shoulder, that would be great."

"You sure, Mom? You look kind of like a Pepto-Bismol beacon walking down the street. You sure you'll be okay? You can't run fast in those stilettos."

"They aren't stilettos, and I'll be fine. Lock up behind me." Mom kissed the air once for each of them. "Oh, and take care of the dishes, okay?"

Happy birthday to me. "Sure, Mom."

Carmen slid the chain into place and then rushed through the dishes. She'd have done them in half the time with the dishwasher at home. Sigh.

Dishes done, Carmen dried her hands and led Nate to the couch. She slid a movie into the Blu-ray player she'd pilfered from Dad's house and sat down beside him. She played with his hand before raising her eyes to his face. "It's bad, isn't it?"

"What? This?" He gestured to the apartment.

"Yeah. In here. Out there." She cocked her head toward the street. "All of it."

"Well, it's not Briarcliff, but we both knew it wouldn't be.

I don't think it's nearly as bad as you described." Nate looked around. "It could be way worse. And at least we have each other."

Very true. Carmen nestled into his embrace and settled in to watch the movie. Exactly how it would be every night when they were married. Except when they went out to dinner. They'd go out a lot so Carmen could try out other chefs' work. Maybe she could even graduate early and start culinary school ahead of time. Get a jump on their future.

The credits ended and still no sign of the girls. Maybe Mom had a talk with them and they intended to leave Nate and Carmen alone. Hah. The bliss wouldn't last long. They were probably off scheming something at that very moment. But Carmen would enjoy the peace and quiet as long as it lasted.

Bang. Bang. Bang.

What? Who? Carmen jumped from the couch. She looked at Nate. His eyes were wide with shock, too. What had caused that banging?

Knock. Knock.

"This is the police. I need you to open up."

Carmen gasped. The police? She reached for the handle.

"Hold it." Nate stepped between her and the door. "Show me some identification, please." Nate waited, his eye locked on the peephole. After a moment he nodded and opened the door. It jerked when the chain caught, so he shut it, removed the chain, and tried again.

Come on already. What's going on?

The door swung open. Carmen stared at her mother, rumpled, ragged, and short of breath.

"Mom!" Carmen pulled her mom into the apartment. "What happened to you?" She lifted the straps of one of the Mary Kay suitcases off her mom's shoulder. Where had the other one gone?

Nate looked at the police officer.

The cop cleared his throat. "She was mugged. She's okay, just shaken up. I'm going to have to take her statement, but maybe you'd like to make her a cup of tea."

"Come sit down. Are you hurt?" Carmen led her mother to the dining-room table.

Mom shook her head. "Not really. I twisted my ankle when my shoe broke. And my arm hurts from where he yanked my bag off. But that's about it." She chuckled. "Guess I should have let Nate walk me, huh?"

"Yeah, Mrs. Castillo." The cop shook his head. "What were you thinking? This isn't the kind of neighborhood you want to be walking through in high heels in the dark. You were kind of asking for trouble."

"Oh? So it's her fault she was assaulted and robbed?" Carmen shrieked. "What if she'd been raped? Would you say a rape was her fault, too?"

"Simmer down, hot sauce. I'm not the enemy here."

Carmen's mouth clamped shut. He should be reported for rudeness. She stomped off to the kitchen to make the tea. At least she could still hear and see everything going on.

"Let's show some respect to the ladies here, sir. Okay?" Nate handed Mom a cool compress for her forehead and squatted down beside her while the cop asked his questions.

Carmen brought her the steaming mug.

Mom held it with two trembling hands and let the steam bathe her face.

"Do you need to go to the hospital, Mrs. Castillo?" Nate looked at Carmen. "I'll take you right now."

"Oh no. I don't think so." She rotated her ankle and flexed her arm. "No. I'll be sore, but nothing's broken."

"Okay. I think I've got all the info I need, but I may be

calling if I think of something else. Here's my card." The cop placed his hat on his head. "I'll be in touch if we need something more or if we find the guy."

But don't hold your breath. Carmen held out zero hope they'd catch the jerk. But at least Mom was okay.

Harper skipped into the family room. "Hey. Mom's home. Cool. Let's all play a game together." She looked from one face to the next. "Wait. Did something happen?"

"No, sweetie." Mom patted Harper's back. "Everything's fine. Go ahead and pick out a game."

Harper bounded off, oblivious to the dark world around her. Must be nice.

৯

"Hey, you. What are you doing out here?" Nate rolled so he faced forward on the couch.

"Shh." Carmen lifted the quilt. "Scoot over and let me in."

Nate shifted a few inches and lifted the blanket.

Carmen slid her legs in between his and nestled in against him.

"You're going to get us in trouble if we get caught out here sleeping together," Nate whispered. "Your Mom will never let me stay again. You sure that's such a good idea?"

"I'll go back soon. I'm not going to fall asleep. Don't worry. Besides, after the day she had, there's no way Mom is going to wake up."

Someday, maybe someday soon, they'd have their own couch in their own apartment, maybe even with a fireplace, where they could cuddle and fall asleep every night. One of them would wake up to find the fire fizzled to embers and lead the other to bed. So grown up. So happy. Family.

Chapter 10

They expected her to do *what* on that stick? Eww. What if she got some on her hands? Carmen pinched the pregnancy test between her fingers, her gaze traveling from the cotton end to the toilet seat. She tipped the box over and shook it. Were there gloves in there somewhere? Nothing. It was her, the stick, and the toilet.

Well, the test wasn't going to take itself. She placed the plastic end between her teeth while she shimmied her jeans to a heap on the floor. Now or never.

Okay. Now what? Three minutes until she could read an accurate result. Carmen capped the end, put the test down on the sink, and perched on the edge of the cold porcelain tub, which she'd yet to use in the five weeks they'd lived there, preferring the shower down the hall. She set an alarm on her new iPhone to go off in three minutes. Carmen didn't want to stare at the stick and watch for the digital display to read PREGNANT or NOT PREGNANT. She just wanted one big reveal after the allotted three minutes had passed. But, as with all important things, the waiting was the hardest part. Three minutes stretched in front of her and blended into eternity.

Carmen hoped she was pregnant. . .didn't she? Hadn't a baby been the goal? Then why was she shaking? So much rested on Nate's reaction to the news. If he didn't man up, Carmen's whole plan would backfire, and she'd be left to handle it on her own. Then what would she do? Did they still make those teen mom TV shows? She could get on one of those. The McConnells would want to crawl into a hole. It would almost be worth it just to hear Hillary's reaction.

Was it too late to back out? Carmen tapped her foot and bit her nail. Hadn't three minutes passed yet? Didn't they make those morning-after pills for people who forgot to use protection the night before? What about two-week-after pills? No, even she knew she'd passed the time for measures like that.

If she truly was pregnant, she had only a few options. Have it or don't. Easy choice between those. She drew the line well before abortion. Ideally, she'd marry Nate and have the baby. If only it were solely her choice to make. She couldn't force him, and the fact Carmen could end up doing it alone remained a viable possibility. She probably should have thought all the possibilities through before the three-minute clock of doom started ticktocking its way into her future. As though it were the clock's fault. It had to be someone's fault—anyone's but hers.

She didn't feel pregnant. If she truly were, wouldn't she be throwing up or something? Then again, she kind of had been constantly nauseous the past couple of weeks And she was definitely late. . .and she was never late.

BUZZ.

The cell phone vibrated as the alarm sounded its annoyance. Carmen clutched it as she turned it off. Too bad someone else wasn't there who could look at the results for her. Did it really matter though? She knew what the test would show. But once she confirmed it, there was no going back. . .ever. She'd be changed for the rest of her life. No matter the outcome. Nate could slough it off. He could walk away. But she couldn't run from this one.

Cheeks puffed as she exhaled, Carmen reached across the countertop, her bangles clinking on the gold-flecked laminate, and picked up the test with a tissue. She turned it over slowly and closed her eyes for a brief moment before looking.

The tiny window with its plastic shield had so much power. It revealed the fruition of the dreams of countless couples every day, and it dashed the hopes of countless others. In that tiny space the answer to one of life's biggest questions lay immutable, unchangeable. Once Carmen read the results, she couldn't ever be restored to her prior self. She would be changed with the truth, or rather, with the knowledge of the truth.

Suspended in her unknown reality, Carmen blinked at the test.

PREGNANT.

Carmen slid from the edge of the bathtub to the floor with a thud. Pregnant. She'd hoped for it, expected it, even wanted it. Then why did a lump settle in her stomach warning of things to come? Why didn't her spirit soar with the thrill? Stuck with her choice now, for better or worse, she'd have to take some time to get used to it. Carmen would probably deserve it if her diabolical plan backfired on her, yet she clung to threads of hope and visions of a family far, far away from there.

Should she tell Nate right away or wait a few weeks to make sure it stuck? What would he say? Should she call him?

No. She'd have to have this conversation in person, for sure.

Or. . .maybe not in person. She could send an e-mail—or even a text. Facebook status update?

No. None of that would do. She'd have to face him as soon as possible and hope he didn't see right through her. What if he suspected she'd done this on purpose? But he had no reason to. She'd always been the one to be paranoid about her pills. He never even asked if she'd been taking them. Because he trusted her. Ugh.

Carmen pried herself from the floor and collected the empty box, wrapper, and instructions. She folded everything together as compact as she could get it then shoved it back into the drug-store sack. She'd bury it at the bottom of the kitchen garbage, under the contents of the yet-unwashed breakfast dishes and a pile of coffee grounds.

Her eyes moved up to the mirror in front of her. Who stared back at her? She barely recognized her as the little privileged girl who'd had everything.

A human being grew inside her at that very moment. A tiny little baby who would depend on her for everything. What had she done? How could she ever pull this off?

Nate had to come through for her. He just had to. If he did, everything would be okay. But if he didn't. . .

"Carmen. *She's* downstairs waiting for you. You okay?" Mom gave the door a few light knocks.

"Yeah. I'm fine, Mom. Be right out." Carmen flushed then ran the water to buy herself a few more moments and shoved the trash into her back pocket. Once she opened the door, she'd be entering a whole new world. A world in which she was somebody's mother.

Hand on the doorknob, she took a deep breath, opened it, then stepped through.

"You'd better get down there. She's honked a few times." Mom handed Carmen her overnight bag and ushered her to the door. The last thing she'd probably want would be to have Tiffany come knocking.

"I never did the dishes though." How could Carmen throw away the garbage if she couldn't get to the kitchen?

"I'll take care of it. Don't worry about anything; just go have fun. I love you."

"Love you, Mom. See you in a couple of days." Carmen

leaned on her mom for a hug then left the apartment, pulling the door closed behind her. She waited until she heard the chain lock slide into place then dropped her bag onto the floor and zipped it open. She stashed the bag of contraband into the armhole of her favorite NYU sweatshirt then followed another long bleat of the car horn down the stairs.

"What took you so long?" Tiffany scowled as Kimberley leaned forward and pulled the seat against her back so Carmen could climb into the rear.

Carmen ignored her.

"Hey, you." Nate pulled her close and kissed her neck. "I missed you. I've been counting the days until Saturday morning when I could see my girl."

"Mmm. Me, too." Carmen slid her arms around his neck and clasped her elbows. She breathed in his scent, letting it intoxicate her senses.

"Sorry I couldn't see you last night. My stupid cousin had to go and get married." Nate scowled.

"I know. It's fine." Her voice sounded strange even to her own ears.

Nate reached behind his head and tugged her arms free then pulled back to peer into her eyes. "You okay?"

"Do you think we could go for a drive or go somewhere private?" They sure couldn't talk in her basement bedroom and risk being interrupted. If Kim and Harper found out Nate was in the house, they wouldn't give up until they found him. He had to quit being so nice to them so they'd leave him alone.

Kimberley occupied the theater room, watching a movie with Tiffany, and Dad was due home any minute and would enter through the garage, so that ruled out the kitchen. If they were going to talk, they had to get out of the house pronto.

"Mmm-hmm. I like the way you think." Nate licked his lips.

Carmen giggled. "No. Not for that kind of privacy. I just. . . We need to talk." She wiped her sweaty palms on her jeans.

"Everything okay?" Nate's eyebrows knitted together.

"Yeah, don't worry. We just need some privacy where no one can interrupt us."

Nate set his jaw with determination. He grabbed her hand and pulled Carmen through the house, out the front door, and into his Camaro parked right outside. He stared at the road and drove in complete silence until they were well away from the property. "Are you about to break up with me?" His eyes darted toward the passenger seat and then back to the traffic.

"Oh no!" Carmen clutched his hand with both of hers. "Nothing like that. In fact, the opposite is more like it."

Obvious relief flooded his face. "I'm not sure what you mean. But I'm glad it's not what I was afraid of."

Nice development. Great to know he feared her dumping him. Maybe things would go better than she'd hoped when she dropped the bomb.

The Camaro sailed into an empty parking space at the nature preserve. "Want to walk?" Nate tipped his head toward the winding path.

Carmen nodded and pulled herself from the deep bucket seat. From all she'd seen and heard about being pregnant, in a few months climbing out of his car would be much more difficult. She glanced at the backseat. Was there room back there for an infant car seat?

Nate hurried toward the walking trail then slowed so Carmen could fall in with his steps. "Okay. You're scaring me. What's up?"

"I have to tell you something, but I'm afraid you're going to get mad." Carmen bit the inside of her lower lip until she tasted blood. How could she say this to him? "Just promise you'll listen until I'm thr—"

He stopped dead on the trail and turned to face Carmen. "Did you cheat on me? Is that what this is about? Because if you did. . .I don't even know what to say. That's like the worst thing you could tell me. I can't believe you'd—"

"I'm pregnant, Nate."

Chapter 11

Carmen watched as Nate's face turned white then sort of gray. His expression was blank—his eyes didn't even twitch. Was he going to pass out? What would she do if he collapsed?

"Say something." Please. Please.

"I. What? Us?" Nate blanched. "You can't be serious. How?" He strode away from her toward the trees lining the path.

This was nowhere near the reaction she'd hoped for. Well, what had she expected really? Cartwheels and hugs? Carmen needed to give him time to adjust. He would come around. He'd have to. Right?

Carmen stayed in the center of the path where he'd left her. Walkers and runners stepped around her. Several shot her glares, but she stood rooted to her spot. Staring. Waiting.

Nate hunched over, his hands on his knees, shoulders shaking. Was he crying? Should she go to him?

A few moments later, he wiped his face with his sleeve, pulled his shoulders back, took a deep breath, and slowly turned, searching. His eyes found their target and rested on Carmen's face.

She gasped. His face was drawn. His eyes scared. She'd put that pain on his face, the fear in his heart. It was her fault.

Nate stared at her for several long moments. Not blinking. She stared at his chest, looking for evidence of breathing.

What was he thinking? Did he hate her? Did he know what she'd done? *Say something, Nate.* Why didn't he speak?

He shook his head like a duck shaking water off his back, and then he jogged to her side. "I'm so sorry about my reaction, Carmen. Really. I don't know what came over me. Shock, I guess." Nate grabbed her shoulders. "Don't you worry about a thing. We're in this together. We'll get through it together. You and me."

Ah. Together. The word she'd been waiting for.

"So, how soon can we take care of it? Does anyone else know? How much will it cost?" Nate's eyes danced with hope. He'd taken charge.

"What are you talking about? You're not suggesting an abortion, are you?" Horror filled her gut. Not at all the direction she'd wanted this conversation to go.

Nate reeled back. "Well, we can't have a baby, Carmen. You know that."

He looked so hopeful. His future rested in her hands, and he knew it. Maybe he was right. Maybe she should consider an abortion. . . . No! She needed to focus on the goal. "We *are* having a baby, so apparently we *can*." Carmen crossed her arms and narrowed her gaze. "Abortion's not an option, Nate."

He stared at her for several long seconds then slowly nodded. "You're right. I'm sorry. I don't know what came over me. Of course we can't abort our baby."

Our baby. Magical words, those. She took his hand and pulled him from the path. They sank onto the grass, flat on their backs, and stared into the sun.

Put the situation in his hands now. Let him rescue her. Carmen rolled to her side and rested her cheek on the crook of his arm. "So what do we do then?" *This is when you ask me to marry you, Nate.*

"I'm going to need a little time to process. I need to think this through. You've had a lot more time to sort this out than I have."

"That's totally fair." Carmen shrugged and pulled herself up from the grass. "Why don't you take me back to my dad's and spend the afternoon figuring things out. We can talk tonight."

Nate nodded.

Silence thundered in Carmen's ears on the drive back to the house. What was Nate thinking at that moment? Was he scared? Sad? Mad? Happy? She stole sideways glances at him every few seconds, hoping for a clue, but his stoic face gave nothing away. He looked fragile. Carmen didn't dare touch him lest he shatter into a million pieces.

Like his future.

No. She had to stop worrying. It would be fine. Great even. Eye on the prize—this was what she'd wanted. These first hours of realization and then acceptance would be the most difficult. Afterward things would get easier. At least she hoped they would. They had to.

When the car stopped in the driveway, Nate shifted it into PARK. He kept his eyes forward.

Carmen climbed out and plodded toward the house, desperate to flop on her bed and cry or sleep for hours. Spent.

The window buzzed down. "Hey."

Carmen turned back to the car.

Nate's hand reached through the open window, his fingers waiting for her contact.

She raised hers to grip his. Electricity shot through her at the warm touch.

"Tell me, C. What do you want to see happen here?"

Carmen locked eyes with him and blinked twice. "I want us to be a family." She shrugged.

Nate held her gaze then nodded.

"Carmen, Nate's here for you."

Carmen opened one eye to the darkened room. What time was it? She peered at the clock on the bedside table. Six o'clock. She'd slept for five hours? How could that be? She hadn't napped like a baby in years. Maybe a decade. She pulled herself from her bed, ran her fingers through her hair, hoping it wasn't too much of a mess, then opened the door. "Send him down."

She rushed into the bathroom and swished a mouthful of mouthwash. What would Nate tell her? Hopefully he'd reached some kind of decision. But was it the right one?

"Hey. You in here?" Nate poked his head in, his eyes smiling.

She'd take his expression as a good sign. "Over here. I took a nap—give me just a sec to pull myself together."

"I remember Mom always felt exhausted when she was pregnant with Charlie. Do you think that's what's happening to you, too?"

"I hadn't thought of it being pregnancy related. Maybe. I kind of thought I was just emotional and needed a break from it all. Probably a little bit of both." So far, so good. He was thinking about pregnancy and smiling.

"Makes sense." Nate nodded. "Hey, c'mere. Where's my kiss?" He pulled her close.

Carmen sank into his embrace, and they fell back into the sofa, swallowed by the red cushions. If only they could stay tucked in the clouds forever. But they had to get up. She wanted to hear what he had to say. . .but then again, maybe she didn't.

"Okay, Carmen, let's talk." Nate helped her sit up. He smiled and tugged on the dark braid hanging in front of her right shoulder. "Listen, I know this is all a big shock to us."

Carmen nodded. Not really a shock, but okay—she'd go with it.

"It isn't at all what we'd planned. But when two people love each other and have a relationship, this can happen sometimes—it's part of the risk we took when we got physical with each other, you know?"

She nodded. The Birds and the Bees 101.

"So, the question now is what we do about it." He turned her hand over and compared their palms as though he were a fortune-teller.

Quit stalling, Nate. What does the future say? It's in your hands.

"We ruled out abortion earlier. So we have three options left as I see it."

Carmen leaned forward. This is where her fate would be decided. "Number one?"

Nate stared at the floor. "We have the baby and give it up for adoption."

Don't think so. "Number two?"

"We have the baby and stay together—do our best to share in raising it. See what happens."

Uh-huh. Closer. "Number three?"

Nate took a deep breath and raised his eyes to meet hers. "We get married."

Way more like it. "Which of those sounds best to you?"

"Honestly, adoption would be awful. I can't imagine having a baby and then giving it away. Then to spend the rest of our lives knowing it's out there somewhere." He shuddered.

"I agree. So we have one option off the table?"

"Yeah." Nate shrugged. "For now, at least. I think number two would be okay. I mean, we'd both take care of the baby as much as possible. It just seems unlikely things would work out for us for very long."

"So we're left with. . ."

Nate cleared his throat and slipped from the couch to the floor on one knee and clasped her hand. "That leaves us here. Will you marry me, Carmen? I love you, and I love our baby. I want us to be together. A family."

"Really?" Carmen fought against her grin. He couldn't mean it. Her plan actually worked?

"Yes, really." Nate's smile faded. "It's not going to be easy—a lot's going to change. I can't imagine my parents will help much. They're going to be devastated. . . . In fact, this will probably mess up my dad's senate race."

"Does it have to though? I mean it's not like we aren't going to handle everything ourselves."

"Face it, C. There are a lot of reasons—right or wrong—that our marriage and baby will be a problem for them." Nate shrugged. "But I can't live my life making decisions based on what's best for my parents. You and our baby, that's what's most important now."

Carmen tugged Nate from the floor to the couch beside her and nestled under the protective wing of his strong arm. "I love you, Nater."

"I love you, too." He rubbed her belly. "And I love this little guy. Or girl."

And all felt right in the world.

Chapter 12

Hey, baby." Diego sidled up to Carmen as she applied lip gloss at her locker. He leaned in close until his nicotine breath left fog on her mirror.

"Must you do that?" she hissed through her teeth with a fake smile planted on her face. People were surely watching the supposedly happy couple.

"Oh, believe me. I must." He wiggled his eyebrows.

Just ignore the flirting. "Tell me something. How'd you get the reputation you have for being such a tough guy?"

"Oh, you kill a rival gang member or two, and people start to leave you alone." He popped a toothpick between his teeth and watched for her reaction.

Carmen gasped. "Are you serious? Did you kill someone? Is that true?" What was she doing hanging around with a murderer?

Diego's eyes twinkled. "I don't know, is it?"

Why couldn't he be straight with her? She'd have to find out his story as soon as possible. Or get out of there. Abandoning him by leaving was a much better idea. If she could get herself back home, enrolled in her old school, none of this would matter. She and Nate had better make some plans fast.

"I still don't understand what you're getting out of this weird relationship we have—if you'd even call it that. More like a one-sided arrangement. I hope you know, I'm not going to date you for real." Was he really acting out of the kindness of his purportedly murderous heart? Or was he attracted to her? Hard to say which was less believable, or which was worse. Wonder what he'd do when he found out she was pregnant?

"Diego knows the score, baby. Trust me. He's just worried about you." He gave her a quizzical gaze then narrowed his eyes. "But you'd better start being a little nicer to me or people are going to wonder." Diego flipped his toothpick end over end between his teeth, his Adam's apple bouncing beneath his tattoo.

"I'll try." Carmen laughed. "But trust me. I doubt people are going to wonder why I'm being rude to you. You're not so bad though."

"Let's leave the details alone, and be glad I can protect you, okay?" Diego slipped his arm across her shoulders and pulled Carmen close for a hug then slunk away in the other direction.

She was engaged. Nate would have a fit if he knew about Diego. What was she thinking letting some other guy touch her mere days after she'd gotten engaged—with or without a ring—though he promised one was coming. Would she dare wear it to school?

But Carmen had reason to be afraid. She stuck out in New Jersey and had already been under the scrutiny of some scary people. In a lot of ways she felt lucky to have Diego on her side. But on the other hand, what if he was just the flipside of the same coin and not really any safer than the others? Carmen had to hope he was being straight with her though. She had no other choice.

Nate wouldn't understand that she felt she had no options. How could he? He existed in a different world than the one Carmen now inhabited—one she'd barely known existed a few short months ago. But it wouldn't be long before he rescued her from this landfill she now called home.

Although, what if they couldn't afford a place back home in Briarcliff? What if they wound up living in a dingier apartment than the one she had now? What if they had to drop out of school and get jobs? What if they couldn't raise a baby right? She probably should have thought some of the challenges through before she followed through with The Plan. But it was too late now. She'd have to handle whatever came her way.

She didn't have to face it alone though. Nate would take care of everything. He wouldn't let anything bad happen to them.

"What are you doing hangin' with homeboy? He's trouble, you know?" Theresa stepped in line with Carmen on the way to Home Ec.

Kayla stepped up to the other side. "No, he isn't. Diego's a pussycat."

"How can you say that?" Theresa shook her head, her black braids whipping her face. "He's been busted for two murders." She rolled her eyes and shook her head. "Unbelievable you want to pretend stuff never happened."

What stuff? Carmen looked back and forth between the girls. Say more.

"Busted, but not convicted. He said one was self-defense and the other was to defend his girlfriend. In my book, that makes him all right." Kayla crossed her arms on her chest.

Could Carmen ask the girls questions? Or maybe they'd share more info if she didn't interrupt.

"A gangbanger. A murderer. An addict." Theresa scoffed. "Yeah, a real good guy."

"He's none of those things. How can you say that? There is no proof to any of it."

"Yeah, if you don't consider the murder weapon and bloody hands proof."

Murder weapon? Blood? What had she gotten herself into?

Kayla shrugged a shoulder and tipped her head. "Besides. Find me one guy here who isn't any of those things."

"There are some. But you're right—not many. Diego is special to me. I even hang with him sometimes, but I keep to myself so I can stay outta trouble." Theresa nodded at Carmen. "Which is exactly what you need to be doing, girl."

Kayla stepped between them. "Just don't be dissing Diego, T. He never hurt you. He wouldn't hurt a fly if he didn't have to."

"Look, Kayla, just because you've been crushing on him since second grade don't mean it's fair not to tell homegirl here the truth. She has the right to know what's she's getting into."

"I can take care of myself." Carmen's voice croaked. She cleared her throat. "Thanks though. I appreciate the concern."

Kayla and Theresa locked eyes and burst into laughter. "If you think you can take care of yourself, girlfriend, you really do need Diego. You're in over your head, sista. Consider yourself warned."

🌀

Beep. Beep. Beep.

Waves crashed onto the deck. The boat rocked. Carmen gripped the sides, sure she'd get washed overboard with the next swell.

Beep. Beep. Beep.

The roller coaster rounded the bend and climbed the steep hill slowly. It perched at the top, the front end tipping over the edge, teasing. . .taunting. . .

What? Carmen forced her body upright. She threw the covers off her body and stumbled to the bathroom. Her stomach revolted against the movement. She wanted to lie down and wait for it to pass, but she knew what was coming. She grabbed the door and pulled herself into the restroom, slamming the door behind her. In one motion, she fell to her knees in front of the toilet and flung the handle to turn the bathtub on as a barrier to the evidence of her retching.

The gushing of water from the bathtub faucet masked the sound of her heaves. Deep breaths and calm thoughts came nowhere near to soothing her churning gut. How long would this go on? She'd already thrown up more in the three weeks since her pregnancy test than she had in her entire life put together. If this didn't end soon, she'd waste away to nothing. At eight weeks pregnant, the websites said she had about four more weeks of morning sickness, and then the second trimester should be easier unless she had it rougher than most. At this rate it would be tough to keep the baby a secret much longer.

Carmen reached across the edge of the tub and into the flow. She cupped her hands and splashed her face. The cool water felt like life. Refreshing, forgiving. Carmen pressed a plush towel into her face and held it there for a moment. Would she ever feel human again? It was like an alien had taken over her body and she had no control over what happened to her. She folded the towel back into place and stepped from the bathroom.

"Ahh!" Carmen reared back at the site of someone leaning against the wall opposite the door, waiting with arms crossed.

Tiffany. Her ponytail, perfect white jeans, and fitted tee made her appear around Carmen's own age. Yet her eyes held understanding Carmen hadn't seen before.

"When are you due?" If someone didn't know her better, Tiffany's blue eyes might have been mistaken for sympathetic.

How did she know? Should Carmen deny it? "Due? What are you talking about? I'm just. . . I have the flu. I'm not—"

"Oh come on. I know the signs. I'm an aunt. I have friends who are moms. Trust me. Plus. . ." Tiffany reached a hand to touch Carmen's arm. "I found your pregnancy test when I was putting away laundry. The positive result was pretty telling."

"You found what? You have no right to go through my things. Besides, the test wasn't even mine." Good one, Carmen. Only a fool would believe that.

"You expect me to believe a friend of yours took a pregnancy test, which came out positive, and then asked you to hold on to the dirty pee stick for her?" Tiffany raised her eyebrows. "Come on. Really?"

Carmen folded her arms on her chest. She didn't have to deny or confirm anything. Tiffany had no proof. Well, at least if she didn't count the positive pregnancy test as proof.

"Look, you need to let us help you. Your dad and I will get you through this. You only need to talk to us. Let us in."

Who did she think she was, swooping in like some BFF? "I'm not talking to you about anything. Even if there were something to talk about." Carmen tried to shove past. She had to get out of the hallway before the walls closed in on her.

Tiffany planted her pedicured bare feet shoulder-width apart, blocking Carmen's exit. "Listen. I know we got off to a bad start. And I get why—I really do. But I'm here. I'm part of your dad's life; I'm part of your life. And I'm not going anywhere." She smiled gently, barely setting off the dimple in her right cheek.

Like the friendly approach softened the blow. Nice try.

"Look, I know your secret, and I'm able to help you out. Think about it." Tiffany touched Carmen's arm again. "You need someone who's on your side."

Carmen fought against the impulse to flinch under the contact. She almost won. Why did it have to be Tiffany who became Carmen's first confidant? Anyone but her.

Tiffany held Carmen's gaze with eyes that held no judgment

then turned to walk away.

"Tiffany?"

She flipped around, eyes dancing with hope. "Yes?"

"You won't say anything to anyone, will you?"

"Your secret is safe with me. For now." Tiffany offered a bigger smile. "But eventually—soon, actually—you're going to have to face this. You can't avoid it forever."

Sooner or later. Preferably later.

Chapter 13

"Nate, we shouldn't tell your parents anything yet." No way. He was begging for trouble before they needed it. They'd never support them; Hillary would make sure of it. Nate just couldn't see the truth about his mom. Or he didn't want to see it.

"They deserve to know." Nate steered his car onto the long driveway and crept to the middle of the U until they were idling in front of the main entrance. "My dad's going to have to do some political damage control, so I owe him the time to do it before it all goes public."

Since when did the kid have to watch out for the dad's career? "I don't see why you think his political career has anything to do with us. This is your life—and mine." The more Carmen thought about things, the more convinced she became. If they told his parents, they'd want her to have an abortion. They'd probably offer to pay for it and then help them sweep it under the rug. After the trauma passed, they'd find a way to separate Nate and Carmen. And that would be it.

She had to keep Nate from letting such a thing happen to them.

"Nate, you don't understand how this thing works. If we wait until the second trimester, which is only one more month away, they'd be less likely to push me to abort the baby because it's even more frowned upon that late in the pregnancy. Some doctors won't even do it, so I'd have to go to a slimy clinic, and even your mom couldn't expect me to do that." And even if they tried to convince Nate to do it, their reasoning would have no effect on him by then. At least Carmen could hope she was right.

"My parents wouldn't try to get us to terminate the pregnancy—they don't believe in abortion. My dad's pretty much built his career on being pro-life. But even if they did try to get us to abort, it wouldn't mean we would. We have to do what's right for us. We're not going to kill our baby." Nate patted Carmen's leg. "That option's off the table."

She tried to smile then turned her gaze to the flower beds and landscaping out the car window. Nate underestimated his mother's power. He'd soon learn.

"It'll be okay, babe. You'll be glad when this part is over."

"We'll see, I guess." Carmen took a deep breath and opened the car door. "Here goes nothing."

Like a lamb to the slaughter, she dragged one lead foot in front of the other and approached the house. "We can still change our minds."

"Come on." Nate grabbed Carmen's hand and barreled through the front door like he was charging toward an end zone. "Mom. Dad," he called through the house then paused with his ear cocked toward the staircase. "Where are you guys?"

"We're on our way down." Mr. McConnell's voice came from far away.

A far-off door closed, and footsteps sounded on the hardwood upstairs hallway. The steps grew louder as they clicked down the stairs then into the dining room.

"So what's the big emergency?" Judge McConnell pushed his glasses up an inch so they rested against his forehead above his eyes. Now there was a true *four-eyes*. "We've been so worried ever since we got your call."

"Yeah. Why all the mystery?" Mrs. McConnell walked right past Carmen and kissed Nate's cheek.

"Why don't we sit down?" Nate gestured toward the dining room, his hand on his mom's elbow.

Hillary gave a hollow laugh. "Why am I so nervous? I can't remember the last time you called a *family* meeting, Nate." Her eyes darted to Carmen with an unspoken question.

Little did she know soon Carmen would be included in every family meeting and function. Even political ones. Oh, it was going to make Hillary crazy. That fact shouldn't make Carmen happy. . .and it didn't. Much.

The judge sat at the head of the table, his wife to his right. Nate occupied the chair opposite his dad, leaving Carmen to sit beside Hillary. Within choking distance.

Carmen scooted her chair a few inches closer to Nate. Better, but not close enough.

The antique grandfather clock in the foyer bellowed its somber cry three times. Like a death knell.

"Can we get to the point here, son? I have work I need to return to ASAP." Nate's dad checked his iPhone.

Nate covered Carmen's cold hand with his warm one. A flush peeked out from the collar of his shirt and tinged his ears. So he *was* embarrassed or nervous. . .or something. Carmen relaxed under the strange consolation of the evidence of Nate's human emotions. At least he had some awareness of the magnitude of what he was about to tell his parents. His bravado must have been for her sake.

He cleared his throat and squeezed Carmen's hand.

Here we go. Carmen's fingertips turned white under Nate's grip. The silence dragged on. *Spit it out, Nate.*

"We're having a baby."

Time stood still as the words took hold.

The cell phone slipped from the judge's fingers and banged on the table like a gavel pronouncing them both guilty then bounced to the floor.

"You're what?" Hillary's jaw dropped, and she raised her hands to the sides of her face. She turned to Carmen. "How dare you?"

"It takes two, Hillary." Nate's dad put his head in his hands.

"Don't be stupid, Michael. Do you have any idea what this means?"

"Yes. I know exactly what this means. Our son committed a felony by having sex with a minor."

Ouch.

"That's not what I meant, and you know it."

Back and forth, like watching a tennis volley. Hillary whopping the balls with her anger, Michael barely getting them back over the net in his sadness.

Mr. McConnell shook his head in disbelief and turned his tired gaze onto Nate. "How did this happen?"

"Seriously, Michael? You need to know how this happened? I'll tell you. That little tramp threw herself at our son, and now his life is ruined."

"Mother. Don't call Carmen names. This was not her fault."

"Of course it was. She trapped you. Now she probably wants you to marry her, doesn't she? Smart girl. Anything to leave the slums and crawl her way back to the good life." Hillary glared at Carmen—once a minor annoyance, now a major adversary who threatened to upset everything the McConnell Empire held dear.

Wow. Hillary was even cleverer than Carmen had given her credit for. Then again, it took a manipulative woman to know one.

"Don't say anything like that again, Mother." Nate stood up and paced to the picture windows. "In fact, it would probably be best if you spoke directly to me and left Carmen out of this for now."

"What are your plans?" Mr. McConnell's glasses slipped to the center of his nose, where they sat crooked. He made no move to reposition them.

Nate took a deep breath. The veins in his neck throbbed. His eyelashes fell heavy with each blink—as though even blinking his eyes drew from too many resources under the mounting pressure. "We're going to get married."

Hillary's face morphed through denial, fear, sadness, then anger. It stopped on anger. "Over my dead white body."

White body? Who said that kind of thing? "People are people. Why would you qualify your body with a color as though it were something special because of it?" The words had rushed out of Carmen before she could stop them.

Nate pressed hard into his closed eyes, as though relieving the pressure.

"Hill, you need to get a hold of yourself before you say something you regret. Something we all regret." Judge McConnell locked eyes with her.

"You worried about protecting your career, Michael? It's a little late for damage control." She jerked her head at Nate. "His tramp destroyed any hope of winning your election."

Nate grabbed Carmen's hand. "I've had it. Mother, I'm taking Carmen out of here. She doesn't deserve to be treated like this. I think you need time to consider how you're acting—it's embarrassing. I can't talk to you right now." He pulled Carmen toward the door. "Know this. We are getting married as soon as possible, and there's nothing you can do to stop us. Get on board, or don't. Your choice. It's happening with or without you."

My hero.

They made it out to the porch before Carmen turned her watery eyes onto Nate. "I'm so sorry." The tears began to fall. She really did love Nate, and she did want to marry him and have his baby. But he should have had more say in the matter. Not that she could tell him so now.

"You have nothing to be sorry for." He pulled her close and rubbed her shoulder blades. "We're in this together. For better or worse."

⟳

Dear Nellie,

Hillary McConnell makes me so mad. . . . I'd honestly love to hit her or pull her hair. That's how mad she makes me. First of all, she's a racist. She puts me and Consuelo on the same level and makes it clear that we're far beneath her status. I wish you could have seen her face when we told her I was pregnant. Her head almost spun around in circles she was so angry. The whole baby thing is almost worth it just to put her through that.

She's evil.

Love,
Carmen

⟳

"Where's my dad?" Carmen reached behind Tiffany's back for the coffeepot.

"He had a meeting this morning." Tiffany cracked an egg into a sizzling skillet. "You know, you shouldn't be drinking caffeine."

"So I've heard. I guess it just doesn't seem real to me yet." What did Tiffany care anyway?

"Well, it will in a few hours. I'm taking you to the doctor." She glanced up at Carmen as though measuring her reaction.

Don't think so. At least not yet. Carmen needed more time. "But—"

"Nope. You can't make me party to putting yourself and the baby in danger." Tiffany put her hands on her hips. "There won't be any argument about this. You have to be nearing your second trimester by now. You see a doctor, or I tell everyone what's going on. We leave in an hour. Be in the car, or I start making calls."

Of course Tiffany was right. And if Carmen were being honest, she'd have to admit that Tiffany's move was impressive. But once Carmen saw someone, the bliss of la-la land would be over. She'd have to face facts. But she supposed it was past time. "All right. What will we tell the girls?"

"Oh, easy. I'll tell them you and I want to have some alone time." Tiffany wiped the countertop. "I'll drop them at the mall with fifty bucks each to burn."

"That should do it." In fact, it sounded way more fun than a sterile examination room and the judgmental stares of the other moms-to-be.

Oh boy. Carmen couldn't wait.

"I'm going to shower. I'll meet you down here in an hour." Why today? Why couldn't this have waited?

And shouldn't Nate go along? Should she call him and ask him to go with her? But it might be humiliating to have to answer all those questions about periods, sex, and due dates. Yeah. Now that she thought about it—it would be mortifying. Maybe she'd be better off doing the first appointment alone. Nate could come to the next one.

Seventy minutes later, Carmen couldn't stall another second. She plastered a smile on her face and met the rest of the girls at the car. Tucked into the corner of the backseat, Carmen tried to snooze, hoping to avoid questions. She needn't have worried.

"I have more than you," Harper taunted and waved her bills at Kimberley.

Kim snorted. "No you don't. I have two twenties and a ten."

"I have ten fives." Harper waved her wad of bills.

"That's the same amount, dummy."

"I don't care. It feels like more."

The car stopped in front of the mall's food-court entrance, and Kimberley and Harper hopped out. Finally. "Thanks, Tiff. Bye, Carmen." Harper blew a kiss as Tiffany pulled away from the curb.

Carmen watched the world pass by as the car sped her toward the moment when she'd trade in her youth for a medical chart that proved she'd entered the adult world. Even though she'd asked for it, it was surreal.

What would little Harper say about Carmen moving out, getting married, and having a baby? Her big sister sure hadn't set a very good example for her. How about Kim? She kept her problems bottled up—there was no way to know for sure how Kim felt about things. Carmen feared she'd take it the hardest.

"Here we are." Tiffany sounded way too cheery for the occasion.

Duh. "I can see that."

Tiffany steered the car into the parking space with the stork sign for expectant moms. "Might as well use the perks that come with your condition." She turned the ignition and slipped the keys into her purse.

Lighten up on the cheer, Tiffany. It's so annoying. Carmen made no move to get out of the car until Tiffany knocked on her window. "Coming?"

Sigh. Carmen opened her door and put one foot on the pavement. Then the other. Her legs felt like lead. She really just needed to get this over with, but it was so hard to move.

"Come on, pick up your feet. Shuffling along just draws attention to yourself. Be confident." Tiffany poked Carmen in the ribs.

Carmen didn't laugh. Though Tiffany had a point—hmm, twice in one day. If Carmen acted like she shouldn't be there, then people would assume she shouldn't. But how did they know how old she was, really? And there'd be no way they could know she was there because she was pregnant. She could be getting her annual exam or might have an infection of some kind. Oh, right, like an STD? Yeah, there was a better option.

With only three people waiting in chairs and one person standing at the desk, the office wasn't nearly as packed as Carmen had expected. Not so bad. She could do this.

Eww. Carmen nudged Tiffany. "Look at that lady. Three o'clock."

Tiffany inched around. "Carmen. Shh. She's just very pregnant. You'll look just like her one day soon."

"Gross."

The grandmother type in front of them scooted out of the way, still using the countertop to rest her purse while tucking her insurance card into her wallet.

"Go on. Tell her your name." Tiffany gave a gentle push on Carmen's arm.

Couldn't Tiff have done it? Carmen stepped forward. "I have an appointment. Carmen Castillo." Hopefully her whisper sounded confident enough.

"Well hello, dear. This is your first time with us?" The bubbly nurse in the rubber-ducky scrubs at the front desk grinned and slid a clipboard beneath the sliding-glass partition. Why glass? In case some rogue pregnant mafia bride went postal on them?

Moving toward the waiting area, Carmen flipped through

the papers and reached for the pen dangling by a two-foot length of fuzzy green yarn.

"Just fill those out as best you can, dear. Be sure to calculate the first day of your last period correctly so we can give you an accurate due date." The nurse bit back the smile that tugged at the corners of her mouth but shot a quick glance out at the few patients in the waiting room.

The whale-like woman gasped and clutched her stomach.

Carmen froze. Had that nurse actually done that on purpose just to get a response out of the other patients? Wasn't there some kind of patient confidentiality law that she just broke? Maybe Carmen could sue after she got over her humiliation. If she ever did.

The card fluttered from the old lady's hand and landed on the floor. She clucked her lips and shook her head as she stooped to pick it up. "Ridiculous," she muttered and glared at Carmen.

"I know, can you believe it?" Tiffany sighed at the elderly woman. She touched the woman's arm like they were coconspirators witnessing some kind of teen tragedy.

What? Carmen thought Tiffany was on *her* side. In a weird sort of way, anyway.

Tiffany gave the horrified woman an I've-got-a-secret grin. "Years of fertility treatments, and the poor girl is finally talking due dates."

The woman clucked her tongue and shook her head, the disapproval oozing from her wrinkles.

Did she say fertil—? Ha! *Nice one, Tiff.* Carmen giggled then glanced at the nurse who'd been watching from behind the glass.

The disapproval sailed from the nurse's face, and her eyes twinkled. Humor won out over disapproval.

Carmen filled out her papers—what she could answer

anyway. That was where a bio mom would have come in handy over the home-wrecker girlfriend. Tossing aside the issues of *Fit Pregnancy* and *Parents* from the stack of magazines on the side table, Carmen settled back into a chair with a copy of *Cosmo Bride*. Time enough for the mom stuff later. She had a wedding to plan.

A nurse in panda scrubs opened the door to the inner sanctum. She wrinkled her nose at the chart in her hand. "Carmen Castillo?"

Castee-yo. Not Cas-till-oh. Come on. Did people really not get the double *L* pronunciation? "That's me." She gathered her things and followed.

"Want me to come or stay here?" Tiffany rose from her chair.

Did Carmen want to go alone? Not really. But was this experience something she wanted to share with Tiffany? Not really. Still, alone was worse. "Yeah, come on if it's okay."

Tiffany nodded. "Right behind you."

The carpet was brown. That's all Carmen could think about on the long walk past the women in the waiting room and the nurses at the bustling nurses' station. She couldn't possibly look them in the eye. Better to stare at the ground and just follow the feet in front of her. One day soon she'd be waddling behind that same nurse like a duck on steroids.

The feet stopped at an intersection where the nurse stood in front of a scale with a digital readout hanging on the wall.

"Okay. Hop on. Shoes on or off—doesn't matter. Just do it the same way next time." She held the chart with her pen poised to record the info.

A public weigh-in? Horrifying. Carmen stepped on the platform. The digital display began flashing numbers. What was this, *The Biggest Loser*? Yep. *That's me.*

"Okay. Looks like you're at 124."

Seriously? "What, the flashing neon lights weren't enough, so you had to announce it to the world?"

"Huh?" The nurse's eyebrows furrowed.

Tiffany nudged Carmen with her elbow. "Be nice."

The nurse frowned. "This way." She stopped in front of the restroom. "We'll need a urine sample. You can use this cup and then slide it into the little cubby there behind the toilet."

"Oh. A pregnancy test won't be necessary. I know for sure I'm pregnant." The positive EPT, the morning sickness, the expanding belly. . .proof enough for Carmen.

Nurse Panda looked down her nose. "I'm quite sure you do, dear. That's not what we're testing for. Just leave your sample there. We'll collect a new one at each visit."

Lovely.

Carmen pulled the door closed. Would have been nice if they explained what they were looking for before just expecting her to follow orders. Maybe she should have said no.

"We're waiting right outside."

Perfect.

Urinating on plastic seemed to have become a habit of Carmen's lately. At least this time she didn't have to wait three minutes for the results. Screwing the cap on tightly, Carmen followed instructions and set the cup in the proper place. She washed her hands and opened the door. Tiffany and Nurse Panda were leaning against the wall waiting for her.

"Right this way." She gestured into a small examination room. "Go ahead and undress completely. Put the gown on with the opening in back and then have a seat on the exam table. The doctor will be right in."

Naked in a paper dress, Carmen tried to hold the back closed as she got onto the table like climbing onto an amusement-park ride. She could almost hear the announcer.

"Buckle your seat belts, and get ready for the next ride at The Most Humiliating Day in History."

Tiffany smiled. "Seafoam green is definitely your color."

"Oh? You like?"

"Belt that thing, and you could wear it to the prom."

"Funny. But now you're pushing it." The prom. Would Carmen ever get to go to the prom now? She would have gone with Nate last year, but she'd been sick with pneumonia. The year before, she couldn't go because the school didn't allow freshmen to attend even with a date who qualified. This was supposed to have been her year.

If the online due-date calculators were accurate, the baby would come in the middle of June. No prom for Carmen.

Nurse Panda opened the door and pushed a metal cart into the room. "I'm going to take some measurements, and then the doctor will come talk to you."

Blood pressure. Temperature. Pulse. "Okay, now lay back on the table and lift your gown. I'm going to measure the height of your fundus."

My what? I don't think so. "Uh, can I have a sheet or something before I lift my gown?"

The nurse sighed and yanked open a drawer. She handed Carmen a sheet and waited.

Sorry to bother you, lady.

Tiffany cleared her throat. "You know, I think I need to speak up here. Is there someone else who could take over? Your disdain for Carmen is clear, and it's making us both uncomfortable."

Go, Tiffany!

"You're saying you'd like to have a different nurse?" Panda's eyes were wide.

"I think that would be best."

"Fine. One will be in shortly." The nurse huffed from the exam room without bothering to close the door.

"I have a feeling we'll be waiting for a long time." Tiffany checked her watch.

A light knock sounded on the door frame. A young nurse flashed deep dimples as she soared into the room. "Hey. I'm Shelly. Glad to meet you." She shook Carmen's hand. "I feel like I need to apologize for Carol. Please don't be offended. It's especially hard for her to deal with teen pregnancies for. . .personal reasons. But I think you and I are going to get along great."

Shelly helped Carmen lay back on the table then lifted her paper gown, careful to cover her with the sheet. "Let me get a quick measurement." She stretched the tape from Carmen's pubic bone to a spot on her stomach. "This tells us if your uterus is the size it should be at this point in your pregnancy." She consulted a chart. "Yep. You're eleven weeks pregnant and measuring at ten weeks. That's well within range. Especially since it's a bit early for these measurements anyway."

"Let me help you sit up." She grasped Carmen's hand and pulled. "Okay, now the fun stuff."

Prenatal vitamins. Do this. Don't do that. Weight gain. Movement. Sure hope Tiffany was taking notes. Next time Carmen would bring Nate to the visit. Wonder when they'd hear the heartbeat? Can't ask the nurse because she probably already said it. Carmen could Google it later. So far Google had been as helpful as the medical professionals.

"So if there are no more questions, I'll send the doctor in for your exam, and then you'll be free to go grow a baby."

Sounded easy enough.

⑤

"I wanted you to know I'm going to have a talk with my mom after dinner tomorrow night." Nate's voice had a hopeful ring.

"I don't care if you do talk to your mom. It's not like you're going to convince her we're doing the right thing." Carmen gripped the cell phone. Sunday nights after leaving him to come back to Hackensack were always the hardest.

Nate sighed. "Listen, I know you're not a big fan of hers. And I get why—I'm not a huge supporter right now either. Just. . .um. . .just try to be a little more forgiving. She's a good person, deep down. She only wants the best for me. And she's my mom. We're stuck with her."

"Honestly, I just don't think it's worth trying to open her eyes right now." Lest she get to Nate in the process. "I want to make sure we're good and aren't going to be swayed by her words."

"Us? No way. We're fine. I'm just trying to give her the time she needs to come around."

"Something tells me you'll be waiting past the time this baby starts kindergarten."

Nate sighed. "She's my mom."

"I understand. But I think we could be married for twenty years and have four kids and she'd still see me as the Mexican girl from the slums." Carmen swiped away a tear. *Don't cry— or at least don't let him know you're crying.* "I'll never be good enough for her, Nate."

"No one would. Trust me."

He hadn't denied what she'd said though. Carmen had no hope of ever meeting Hillary McConnell's approval. At least the judge didn't seem as opposed to Carmen as his wife was. If only Hillary didn't have so much influence over him, it might not be so bad.

"Hey, I have a surprise for you this weekend—it will prove to you just how solid we are."

Now he was talking. "A surprise? What is it?"

"Yeah. I'm going to tell you. I can see that happening. You'll just have to wait. But I promise it'll be worth it."

The lilt in Nate's voice conjured his smiling face in Carmen's imagination. Now there was the Nate she'd known all these years. Phew. "It's a deal. I can't wait." *Cosmo* said to end phone calls on a high note. "I have to go now. . .dinner's about to burn."

Chapter 14

MEET ME AT THE CORNER OF MAIN AND EAST CAMDEN AT NOON TODAY.

Carmen stood at the kitchen counter and spooned Cheerios into her mouth. She read the text message from Hillary McConnell for what had to be the hundredth time. It wasn't even a question. More like a direct order. Who did that woman think she was to order Carmen around? If she weren't so curious about what Hillary had to say, Carmen wouldn't even consider going.

Would Nate know what was going on? And if he did know, why hadn't he clued her in last night? Carmen looked at the time on her cell phone display. Oh man. She couldn't even ask Nate about what his mother was up to because he was in class until two o'clock. Six more hours until she had any hope of speaking with him. And the meeting would be long past.

Had Hillary timed it to coincide with Nate's schedule on purpose, knowing he was unreachable during class time? Or was it a lucky coincidence? Knowing her, it was no accident. She calculated every move she made. And she always came out on top. That meant Nate had no idea what his mother was doing. She was up to no good.

Carmen's stomach rolled. More morning sickness, or pure dread? Probably both. She hurried to the bathroom and pulled the door closed. How many hours had she logged in there that month? Carmen perched in her usual spot on the edge of the tub. Too bad Mom hadn't left for work already so Carmen could stay there until the meeting if she had to.

She didn't have far to walk. Hillary could have picked an address on the other side of the tracks where the neighborhoods weren't quite as dicey. But instead she'd chosen a location too close to where Carmen lived for it to have been a fluke. Hey, where had Hillary gotten Carmen's address anyway? Hillary would come face-to-face with the truth about Carmen's new life. She'd prove her worst suspicions to be fact.

Now Carmen had to decide if she'd show up or not. It would require ditching school, but school didn't matter much to Carmen anymore. They couldn't do anything to her now. She'd probably go meet Hillary out of simple curiosity—she had to know what Hillary wanted. But Carmen would have to be on guard. Hillary McConnell didn't do anything without a well-orchestrated plan that resulted in her coming out on top. And she was the type who would stop at nothing to get what she wanted. Carmen couldn't let that happen.

A light rap on the bathroom door jolted Carmen from her thoughts. "You okay in there? You're going to be late for school if you don't get moving."

Carmen flushed the toilet and stood up from her posture of worship at the throne of morning sickness. "I'll be right out." She flipped on the water and scrubbed her hands then reached for her toothbrush and toothpaste. Yuck. Barfing every morning was sure getting old.

As she brushed, Carmen inspected her splotchy face in the mirror. She'd have to raid Mom's Mary Kay bins before she left the apartment so small children didn't shy away in horror at her ghostlike appearance. Maybe it was time to ask for her own set of the good makeup—not that cheap stuff she sometimes used. Mom would jump at the chance to see Carmen all glammed out.

Poking her head out the doorway, Carmen looked both ways. Best to avoid Mom if at all possible because, unless Carmen was imagining things, Mom had been looking at her funny lately.

Now, where was Mom?

Click. Click. Click. The stove's gas flame must have caught. Someone flipped on the faucet in the kitchen and let the water run. Sounded like Mom was bustling in there, which meant Carmen could sneak out of the bathroom without any conversation. She slipped from her spot in the doorway and hurried into Mom's bedroom then jogged to the dresser where Mom put on her face every day.

Falling to her knees, Carmen lifted the lid on a Rubbermaid bin and fumbled through more bottles of promise and tubes of hope than any one person could use in a lifetime. Got to love the Mary Kay discount. Carmen knocked over the one tub missing a lid, and a cloud of powder puffed to her face. Sputtering, she swiped the plume away and reached for the foundation. Where were those little wedge spongy things?

Ah-ha. Carmen reached into a Ziploc bag, pushed aside the gunky used sponges, and grabbed a clean one. She tried to squirt the makeup onto the edge, just like she'd seen Mom do, but nothing came out of the almost-empty tube. Carmen rolled the end like a tube of toothpaste and held the hole up as she squeezed.

In a quick spurt, the makeup shot out over the wedge, dripped down to the avocado countertop, and splattered on the gold rug.

Oh no. Not now. Nothing ever went smoothly for her.

Carmen grabbed a handful of cotton balls to tackle the oily stains on the rug. No. She'd have to deal with the mess later.

Sopping the sticky makeup off the Rubbermaid lid with one hand, she shoved the tubes back into the bin.

Perfection was way too much work. It didn't matter. Nate liked her better without a lot makeup anyway. But he hadn't seen her in a while. Would he still feel the same now that she'd taken on that pregnancy glow—which didn't seem as *lovely* as people always claimed it was? What about when she got all fat? Would he still think she was beautiful?

ॐ

On the street in front of the nail salon below their apartment, Carmen glanced in both directions. She could turn right and walk toward Giant Farmers' Market, or she could turn left and make her way toward the assigned meeting location to scope it out.

She had no money for food, so the market would be depressing. She felt through the pockets and crevasses in her Gucci bag. Her fingers closed on a handful of coins. Plenty for a cappuccino at Java's Brewin'. Should she even drink stuff like that right now? Wasn't there some rule about pregnant women not drinking caffeine? Well, one cup couldn't hurt anything. Could it? Besides, a lot of girls didn't even find out they were pregnant until they were much further along. Surely they had coffee and did all sorts of things before they knew.

The cracks in the sidewalk passed by under her feet, and Carmen took no care to avoid them. It wasn't like she wanted to break her mother's back or anything, but those days of reciting rhymes and thinking some silly move would affect some sort of big change in someone else's life were long over. Took more than stepping on a crack to get anyone's attention these days.

Carmen spoke into her phone, "Call Nate." Argh. Right to voice mail. He must still be in class. "Hey, I need to ask you something. If you get this between classes, call me, okay? All I need is a minute, and it really can't wait. Thanks. Love you. Bye."

Cool. Carmen spied an ornate stone structure across the street. Johnson Public Library. Cool-looking building, but it probably survived on nothing but castaway books from other libraries—like the one in Briarcliff. At least she could get books there though. She could always hang out in there if she needed to kill more time after her coffee. But for now the JAVA'S BREWIN' sign beckoned to her from the next block.

Minutes later, with her sugar-free, french-vanilla cappuccino in hand, all Carmen needed was a quiet place to figure some things out. Ah, a chair by the window. Perfect. She'd hang there for a while.

Tucking her feet under her, Carmen settled in and looked at the time on her phone. Her classmates were in second period by now. She'd have been in biology if she were in school. This was way better than school any day.

Carmen gripped her iPhone and touched the Safari icon. *Yes!* Free Wi-Fi. She dug through her bag until she found the iTunes card she'd gotten for her birthday. That was about to come in really handy. She scrolled to the icon for the app store. In the search bar, she typed *voice recorder* then waited for it to do its magic. Several free apps popped up, but the one for $1.99 had much better ratings. Plus, if it wasn't a better app, they wouldn't make you pay for it, right? The experiment had to work on the first try. Carmen couldn't take any chances.

ॐ

Attorney at Law? Carmen scrolled to double-check the address in the text message. Why did Hillary want to meet at a lawyer's office? The woman was up to no good, as usual. But what could she have cooked up this time? Poor Judge McConnell—smart man, but wouldn't have gone anywhere politically without Hillary's games. She was a master manipulator who always got her way. Always. It even embarrassed Nate sometimes, though he rarely admitted it. Hmm. Wonder if Hillary had finally met her match.

Should Carmen go in or wait outside? She didn't know for sure they were meeting in the office with the attorney. Maybe Hillary wanted to grab a bench and talk outside. Carmen would just hang out for a while. If Hillary didn't show up in a few minutes, Carmen could text her.

Carmen's eye roved the busy street around her. Equal parts shoppers and homeless people. A few cars parked near the sidewalk. One looked like it had been there for weeks with a shattered back window and a parking ticket under the wiper blades. This wasn't the worst part of town, but a definite far cry from the landscape Hillary McConnell was used to observing from her car window.

Stepping over a wad of smeared gum, Carmen wandered to a bus-stop bench and perched on the edge, careful not to lean on the black smudges toward the back.

A haggard woman wearing two winter coats over purple pajama pants and bright red clogs pushed a metal cart past the bench. Everything she owned in the whole world all fit in that one little cart. She glared at Carmen with sad eyes, which, judging by the clear-blue brightness and long lashes, had once been pretty. Did she sense Carmen's disdain, or did the bag lady simply hate Carmen for her designer clothes and purse?

Don't worry, lady. There won't be more luxuries where these came from. Carmen's designer days were over. She'd thought she might get something cool from Dad for her birthday—the iTunes card from Mom wasn't a bad gift, but it didn't do much to keep her wardrobe replenished. Not that she'd be able to fit into her couture clothes much longer anyway.

Carmen smiled at the old woman, who grunted and

shuffled away. *Click your red heels together, lady. Maybe you'll find your way out of your mess.*

She slid the lock to the right to toggle her phone display to life. Twenty minutes late. How long did Her Highness expect Carmen to sit and wait for her? Should she text Hillary?

No. Carmen hadn't called this meeting, yet she was on time. It wasn't her job to hunt Hillary down. Five more minutes, and she'd leave. Maybe she'd hide around the corner so she could see Hillary's face when she arrived only to find Carmen had left.

Four minutes later, a silver Bentley slid to the curb, its driver inching in, careful not to get too close. A tuxedoed chauffeur stepped from the driver's side and walked around to Hillary's door.

She hired a chauffeur? She didn't normally use one. What nerve. How could she pull into Hackensack like the Queen of England? Way to relate to the common folks, Hill. I'm sure the senate candidate's constituents will appreciate it.

The chauffeur reached a gloved hand down to help Mrs. McConnell to the sidewalk.

Tiptoeing as though through molten lava in shoes made of gold, Hillary grimaced at her surroundings and headed for her destination.

Give me a break. Carmen pretended to read her text messages. No way she'd give Hillary the satisfaction of reacting to her display or even appearing to notice. One last swipe of her finger to turn the recorder on, and Carmen slipped her phone into her loose jacket pocket, where there'd be no risk of it being bumped or jostled off. "Oh, hello, Mrs. McConnell. I was just about to leave—figured I had the wrong time or something."

"I'm glad you were able to meet me. Though I assume you skipped school to do it." Hillary turned her nose up.

There was just no pleasing her. "I didn't choose the time."

Carmen steeled herself against Hillary.

"Our appointment is right in here." Mrs. McConnell lifted her chin and led the way into the brick building. Once inside, they climbed a wooden staircase to the second floor, where a placard on a wooden door read HORACE C. BROWNING, ATTORNEY AT LAW.

Carmen didn't like the idea of going in there with no preparation. "Excuse me. I'd like to know why we're here before we go in." Was she being sued or arrested? No, lawyers didn't arrest people. But whatever Hillary had planned for the meeting couldn't be good. And how had she set it up so quickly?

"You'll find out soon enough." Hillary used a handkerchief to open the heavy door then deposited the soiled cloth in the trash. "Shall we?" She gestured for Carmen to lead the way.

What, was Hillary afraid Carmen would bolt? Not like she hadn't considered the option.

Too late. A bald man with horn-rimmed glasses stretched his hand across his desk. "I'm Horace Browning. Pleased to meet you."

"Carmen Castillo. What's this all about?"

He startled at Carmen's brusque reply and raised a bushy eyebrow. "Just take a seat for a moment. Would you like some coffee or a soda?" He riffled through some papers.

Get on with it already. "No, thank you." Carmen drummed the nubs of her fingernails on his desk. Another minute and she was out of here.

Mr. Browning spread his legs to allow his stomach to settle between them, giving him more room to scoot his chair in. Gross.

He wiped his shiny head with a tissue then looked at Carmen. "Miss Castillo, I'm going to get right to it."

Carmen would believe it when she saw it.

"My client has an offer for you." Horace tipped his head toward Hillary.

Here we go.

"I have an affidavit here for you to look over and sign." He slid a single page across the desk. Did she read disapproval on Horace's face?

Carmen's eyes skimmed the paper and took in several key phrases. *Paternity. No claim. No rights.* "Let me get this straight." She glared at Hillary. "You want me to sign this document stating Nate isn't the father of our baby and promise I will never seek proof that he is? You want me to release Nate from all parental rights and responsibilities to his own child? Am I understanding this document correctly?"

"Exactly. Ideally, I'd like for you to have an abortion, but this is a good-enough second best."

How could Hillary McConnell live with herself? "I'm completely speechless. I cannot fathom what made you think I'd sign this."

Horace cleared his throat. "Well, we want you to sign it if it's true. And"—he coughed—"Mrs. McConnell feels terrible about your situation, so she's prepared to help out with your needs." He slid a folded check across the desk. He hesitated a brief moment before letting go.

Hillary was bribing her? Carmen didn't want to touch the nasty thing. But she had to know. She unfolded it with one finger, but didn't pick it up.

Twenty-five thousand dollars? Say it out loud for the recording. "Twenty-five thousand dollars? Am I reading this check correctly?"

"That's right. Just a token to get you started." Hillary beamed like she knew she had Carmen right where she wanted her.

"Are you kidding me?" Carmen glared into Hillary's eyes.

"You want to buy me out of your son's life?" She turned her gaze to Horace. "Is she serious about this? I feel like I'm in some bad made-for-TV movie."

"No. Don't read into this too much, young lady. Mrs. Mc-Connell simply wishes to help you with some expenses because you're going to be facing your. . .um. . .predicament alone."

What a crock. "Um. No, I'm not. This isn't even up for discussion. There's no way I'm signing that paper or cashing your check."

Mr. Browning picked up the affidavit and slid the check back into his file folder. "I suspected not. Thank you for your—"

Hillary jumped to her feet. Her chair crashed to the floor behind her.

Carmen raised her arms in front of her face. Who knew what that woman was capable of?

"Now you listen here, girlie." Hillary jabbed her finger at the breath coming from Carmen's nose. "You will sign this paper if for no other reason than you do love my son."

Carmen glanced at Horace. "If she lays one gnarled finger on me, you call 911 immediately."

He nodded. "Please sit down, Mrs. McConnell. You're not helping your cause right now."

Hillary exhaled as though cleansing her body in one of her yoga classes. Keeping her steely eyes locked on Carmen's, she reached a hand down to right the chair she'd upended. Lowering her body, she perched on the edge of her seat and allowed the corners of her mouth to turn up in a wavering smile.

She was crazier than Carmen had ever imagined.

"Listen, Nate has a bright future ahead of him, and you're destroying it. A baby will ruin everything for him. College. Law school. Politics. Everything. Dating a Mexican was enough of a liability when you were rich, but now. . .and with a baby? You're destroying my son, and he's too stupid to see it."

Horace shook his head. Looked like Hillary had gone too far even for a slimy attorney.

Carmen stared her down. How dare she put voice to such ridiculous prejudices? Carmen had always suspected Hillary had harbored hatred in her heart, but to speak it out, to say it as though her thoughts were the most natural and expected thing . . .an evil woman. Pure despicable evil.

Hillary's face softened with mock concern. She grasped Carmen's hand and looked into her eyes—one mother to another. "Just let him go."

Chapter 15

Maybe Hillary was right, though Carmen had no intention of letting her know that—which was why she'd fled the office. And she certainly wasn't right about everything— probably not even about most things. But maybe Nate should be free if he wanted to be. He should have some say in his future. If he didn't, if Nate got stuck in a life-changing situation because of Carmen's manipulations, then Carmen was no better than his mother.

She stepped over a crack in the sidewalk and shoved her hands deep into her pockets. Nate would never walk away. He was too honorable of a man. She could always dump him and tell him the baby wasn't his. But he'd never believe her. He'd probably want a paternity test to prove he was the father. Carmen chuckled. Most guys wanted a paternity test to prove the opposite.

What had she done?

No! Carmen shook off the guilt and doubt pelting her heart. She wanted Nate. This whole thing was because she needed a family and so did he, whether he knew it or not. They'd be happy together, and their son or daughter would be adorable.

They'd have a baby shower—but not until after the little one came so people could see how cute it was. They'd name it something trendy but unique like McKennedy—oh that would

sound stupid. McKennedy McConnell. Carmen laughed. How
about just Kennedy for a girl? Maybe Elijah for a boy? They
could go have family pictures taken for Christmas cards. Their
voice mail would say something adorable like, "You've reached
the McConnell's. We're here; we're just busy playing with the
baby. Leave a message, and we'll call you right back." We. The
"we" was the part Carmen ached for.

The cell phone vibrated in her pocket. Nate. What should
she say to him? Should she come right out and tell him what his
mother had done? Would it turn him against his mom, or could
it backfire and make him think twice about Carmen? Really,
she needed to think this through. His mom had been willing
to fork out twenty-five grand to get rid of Carmen. Maybe if
Nate knew how serious Hillary was, he'd be willing to listen to
his mother's reasoning about Carmen, the baby, and everything
else. The phone beeped as it accepted a voice-mail message.
She'd check it later, after she figured out what to do.

"Hey, chica. How come you're not in school?"

Carmen's breath caught in her throat. Why hadn't she taken
self-defense? She spun around expecting to fend off an attacker.
"Diego." Her shoulders slumped in relief as the air whooshed
from her lungs. "You scared me, man."

"You need to open your eyes. I've been following you since
you left that lawyer's office. Did you really not know I was back
there?"

Were there others? Carmen whipped her head around and
glanced back down the street. Cars and busses whizzed by, but
nothing looked strange. "You followed me? Why?" Was she
wrong for trusting him? He looked sincere, but how could she
know for sure?

"I wanted to make sure you were okay. You need to wise
up. Diego ain't always going to be around." He wiggled his

eyebrows. "Unless you want him to be."

"Very funny." A good friend, even sort of cute in many ways, but definitely not someone Carmen would date even if Nate weren't in the picture.

Diego slipped his arm over her shoulders and pulled her close. "If Marco could see us now."

Carmen laughed. "He'd probably come so unglued the silver would fall off his teeth."

"But reality check, chica. You was pretty clueless walking down this street. You better be more careful."

"I'll be fine. I was just thinking. . . . Lost track of where I was."

"A deadly mistake." Diego squeezed her again then let her go as he stepped backward. "We need to keep you safe. Diego's reputation is at stake now. Word on the street is Marco ain't too happy. You need to watch your back."

ᔆ

Dear Nellie,
Hillary McConnell is the devil incarnate.
Love,
Carmen

Chapter 16

"God knows your secrets and sees right into your heart."
Carmen looked down at her hands and picked at her fingernail. Avoid eye contact at all costs. That pastor up there could probably read her mind, which screamed, *Get me out of here!*

Finally. Mom rose for the closing song. Harper sat three rows ahead with her new friend from school. Carmen scanned the rows one by one. Kimberley was supposedly sitting with a group of teens she knew, but Carmen couldn't find her anywhere. What could she be up to? Didn't Mom notice Kim was missing? Carmen would have to pay a little closer attention to Kim while she still could. No sense letting her head down a rough road if Carmen could help her avoid it. Carmen knew firsthand the types of things a desperate girl was capable of doing.

"Amen." The pastor smiled down at the people. "May the Lord bless you and keep you. May He make His face shine down upon you and give you peace."

The people began to file out of the sanctuary, creating a bottleneck at the doors to the lobby as they stopped to shake the pastor's hand.

"Hey, Carmen." A hand reached through the line, grabbed her sleeve, and pulled back.

"Theresa. Hey. I didn't know you went here." Great. Blend

the lines between school and church.

"Yep. My dad's the pastor, actually."

You mean the mind reader? "Cool." How did Carmen not know that?

"So anyway, several of us are going out to lunch and then to hang out at the mall. Come with us?" Theresa actually looked hopeful. Why did she want Carmen around? Because of Diego, probably. Maybe Theresa assumed Diego would come.

It sounded kind of fun. But who were the "several of us" Theresa had mentioned? Carmen couldn't ask and then back out if she didn't like what she heard. That would be rude. Best if she just begged off now. "I can't. Mom has plans for us today."

"Okay, then next week—you have plenty of warning now." Theresa grinned and held up one long finger. "I won't take no for an answer."

Great. A BFF in Hackensack. Just what she'd always wanted.

৬

> *Dear Nellie,*
> *You wouldn't believe this girl Theresa. She's nice enough for a PK, but she's kind of a hypocrite. She hangs out with gangbangers and then gets all spiritual at church. She's kind of pretty, even though she's clearly a Jersey girl with the big hair and hoop earrings to her shoulders. She means well, I think. In fact, I think she wants to be my friend. A friend. . . hmm. . .suppose anything's possible.*
> *Nah. . .*
>
> *Love,*
> *Carmen*

৬

"Aren't you scared?" Nate rubbed his temples and glanced out the window of their favorite burger joint. "I mean, aren't you at all worried about the future and how we'll provide for this baby?"

Carmen twirled the straw in her glass, the ice cubes tinkling on the sides. She moved her food around on her plate, but couldn't stomach the thought of actually taking a bite. "Scared? Not really. I mean, there are a lot of unknowns, but we can handle them. If other people do, we can." *Don't go weak now, Nate.*

"I'm not so sure about that anymore." He stirred his ketchup with a french fry and popped it in his mouth.

His mother had gotten to him. She must have been working overtime. Dread filled the pit of Carmen's stomach like lava at the bottom of a volcano. She searched her brain for the perfect words. "Look. We're in this. It is what it is. We can't back out now. At least I can't. I suppose you could run away, but I sure can't." Play the guilt card. Nate was a sucker for that one.

The guilt clouded his eyes just as she'd planned. He'd never leave her to handle it all on her own.

"I'm not suggesting abortion—but maybe we should consider adoption. You know, at least talk about it." Nate kept his face down, but raised hopeful eyes to hers.

"Are you kidding me? I'd actually rather talk abortion even though that's not happening. I could never have a baby out there and not even know what it looked like." Carmen shuddered. "I can't stand the thought of someone else raising my baby."

Nate shrugged. "At this point it shouldn't really be about us, should it?"

Ugh. That struck like a sucker punch. True, she'd been pretty selfish. And true, the baby wasn't being considered very much. But that would change as soon as they figured out their own future. They had time to work the baby into it. Didn't they? "It's all part of the process, Nate. We have to get ourselves organized before we can really think about the baby. Pretty soon it will all be about the baby."

He pushed his half-eaten cheeseburger and pile of soggy

fries to the edge of the table. "That's the thing. What if we can't figure things out? What if we're throwing all of our goals and dreams away under the pretense of giving the baby a family, but in the end we destroy us all?"

The words hung in the air then settled around them like ash after a volcano erupted. What then? Could he be right? If that happened, if they weren't a happy family like Carmen envisioned, then they'd be worse off than before this whole fiasco started. And there would be one more person who'd have to suffer the fallout. But it was too late. Wasn't it?

"Fact is, Nate, I'm pregnant. I'm having the baby. You're in, or you're out. I'm sorry if you feel like you don't have a lot of control over this situation, but you do have choices." Carmen folded her straw wrapper into tiny triangles.

"The only choice I have is whether or not I marry you and parent this baby, or I don't. That doesn't seem like a lot of options."

"You have more than I do."

"Not the way I see it." Nate turned his face to the side and stared out the window. His chiseled face and furrowed brow reflected back on top of the dark, snowy scene outside. "Okay. Thing is, I love you. That hasn't changed. Nothing has changed really. I'm probably just having cold feet. I suspect it won't be the last time." He turned back to Carmen and took her hands. "I'm not bailing on you or on our baby. I promise."

She squeezed his hands and nodded. For now anyway.

🌀

"We have a date tonight." Diego peered beyond the chain holding the apartment door closed.

Pretty nervy. "We do, huh?" He showed up without warning and thought he could order her around?

"Yep. Diego thinks we need to light a fire in this

relationship." He wiggled his eyebrows.

"Uh-huh." That boy was too full of himself. But people might start getting suspicious about their fake relationship if they didn't make some public appearances. "It's probably not a bad idea to get out and let people see us together."

"S'all I been sayin'."

"But why didn't you call first?"

"I didn't have your number. Besides, that's not how Diego rolls. This way's more fun." Diego gestured at the lock. "This convo is becoming a drag. You comin' or what?"

"Right now?" She raised the leg of her frog pajama pant. "I'm not really dressed for public viewing."

"Okay. Five minutes. Meet us downstairs." He pulled the door shut.

Who's *us*?

"Mom. I'm going to go out with some kids from school for a while. Okay?"

"Okay. No walking the street. Keep your cell phone on you at all times. I'm glad you're making friends. Just don't stay out too late, and be careful."

She still had no clue. Why didn't she want to know the details? Who Carmen would be with. Where they were going. What time she'd be home. Mom had been super strict in New York, but then totally let go of boundaries when they moved to New Jersey? Made no sense. Probably the guilt factor.

What to wear? If only Carmen knew where they were going. It didn't really matter though. Denim worked fine no matter what. Not like they'd be going to a fancy dinner or a show on Broadway. Carmen dug in her closet for her favorite pair of jeans. Bummer. They'd been washed so they needed to be broken in again. Should only take an hour or so to get them comfy. She stepped out of her pajamas and pulled her jeans over her hips.

She had to tug a little harder than normal to fit the button through the hole. The Great Expansion had begun.

Already? It seemed early. The books said most pregnant women could stay in their regular clothes until well past the start of the second trimester. Carmen still had three weeks until then. She'd have to think about investing in a new pair of jeans. She dug in her closet for her favorite sweatshirt. Hope she wasn't supposed to dress up.

One day not very far down the road, she'd pop out, and people would start noticing her bump. What would they say about her when word started getting around? They'd all think the baby was Deigo's. Could she blame them, though? Carmen would have jumped all over that gossip herself if it were someone else in her shoes.

Carmen hurried down the stairs to the Chevy beater rumbling at the curb. Diego sat in the front seat with an open one beside him. Carmen peered into the back window. Theresa? So, did she run with these guys or not? She was tough to figure out. Carmen would have to keep her eye on Theresa.

Who was the dude next to her? He wore all black and stared out the side window. He didn't move a muscle when Carmen slid into the front seat. She waited for an introduction. None came. Alrighty then.

They drove for fewer than five minutes and squealed to a stop in someone's front yard. Right in their grass. Carmen chuckled at the thought of someone parking on her dad's lawn. He'd come unglued.

"Why'd you park on the lawn?"

Diego grinned. "Easier to make a quick getaway."

Of course it was. How silly of her.

Throngs of people her own age and much, much older milled around the battered house. So, it was a party. Why couldn't Diego have just told her ahead of time? Always so mysterious. And the guy in the back? Who was he, and why was he with them? Even more, why didn't Diego introduce them? He seemed to want to pretend the mystery guy wasn't even there. What was that about?

They climbed out of the car, and Carmen stumbled to keep up with Diego. He seemed to be looking for someone. . .or maybe something. He went through the front door, leaving her alone outside. Should she follow or wait?

Theresa sidled up to her as they pursued Diego. "Listen, you don't want to be here. Trust me."

"Why not?"

"Drugs. Lots of drugs. And probably some fighting. Maybe a gunshot or two. Still think you're in for a fun little high-school party? Remember, sugar, you're far from Kansas now."

"I'm just minding my own business, hanging out with my boyfriend." Carmen shrugged. "Thanks for the warning though." It couldn't be as bad as Theresa made it out to be. Maybe she was jealous of Carmen's relationship with Diego. Maybe Theresa secretly had a thing for him.

Theresa shook her head. "You just don't get it, do you? This isn't a game. This is real life, and it ain't something you want to mess around with."

Carmen planted her hands on her hips. "What about you? Why are you here if it's so dangerous?"

"I'm stuck with this life. It's mine. There ain't no way out of it for me. Plus, Diego's my cousin, and we're friends."

Cousin? Hadn't seen that one coming.

"Deep down, he's a good guy. He just. . ." Theresa rubbed her forehead then locked eyes with Carmen. "Let me tell you this. I have God on my side. I pray every day that He keeps me safe and even that He keeps Diego safe—but I don't know if God protects my cousin anymore. Not after he killed people."

So the killings were real? How could Carmen find out if they were in self-defense or not? "Nothing I've seen tells me that he's violent. I think he's a decent guy."

"He is. But look, he's going to watch his own back first, and where Diego goes, trouble always shows up on its own. And you bring him an extra layer of conflict he doesn't need. . . . Marco."

Ah. That's what she was upset about. Marco. "Diego is a big boy. He can decide who his friends are without your help, T."

"Where's my girl?" Diego poked his head out and squinted into the dark.

"I'm over here." Carmen jogged over to the porch. Diego slipped his arm around her shoulders. "What's going on?"

"Oh, not much."

"Why did you leave me out here though? I felt really weird."

"There's nothing for you in there, pretty girl. Diego thinks you'll be just fine out here."

Should she protest? Carmen wanted to see what was going on inside the house, but maybe it was best she stay unaware. "So who was that guy in the backseat by Theresa?"

"Nobody. A ghost."

Chapter 17

A glossy sheet of photo paper floated onto the dining-room table in front of Nate like a leaf wafting from a tree.

Carmen jolted at the intrusion and glanced up. Hillary. With her hands on her hips. Watching Nate. Waiting. Oh no, it couldn't be good, whatever it was. Carmen let her eyes sneak over to Nate's face, white as a sheet, then down to the picture he held.

Diego's gold tooth flashed as he stood with his arm around a laughing Carmen, walking somewhere down the street from Horace Browning's law office the day she'd skipped school.

Hillary towered over Nate to look at the picture. As if she hadn't studied it enough. "What do you have to say for yourself, young lady?"

"To you? Nothing." Carmen jerked her head at Nate. "If he wants to talk about it, fine. But I don't owe you an explanation about this or anything."

Nate gasped and dropped the picture onto the table. "How can you talk to my mom like that?"

Things were going to get ugly. But it was past time Nate knew the truth about his mom. "You don't even know the half of it. And this picture is not at all what it seems."

"It looks pretty incriminating, young lady." Hillary spat her words like they were bitter on her tongue.

"Would you please stop calling me 'young lady'?" And if she wanted to talk about incriminating. . .

Hillary held up the photo. "Who is this dirtbag? Why is he touching you? Why are you laughing? And what kind of damage control am I going to have to do?"

"What part of 'none of your business' do you not understand?" Carmen needed to hold her ground. If she weakened or wavered, it would be all over. She wouldn't give Hillary McConnell the satisfaction.

Hillary reared back like she'd been slapped.

Nice innocent act, lady.

"Carmen." Nate jumped to his feet. "She's my mom. You can't talk to her like that."

"Just sit down for a second. I promise you'll be glad you did. She thinks she had evidence to incriminate me, but her picture means absolutely nothing. Why don't you ask her what she was doing just before it was taken?"

He turned to his mother. "What is she talking about?"

"I wasn't doing anything other than finding out what little miss was up to. Looks like my suspicions were right on target."

Carmen rolled her eyes. If it weren't so tragic, it would almost be fun to see Hillary's face when the recording started playing. "She tried to buy me off, Nate."

His eyes whipped between Carmen and Hillary. The infamous in-law tug-of-war. Bet he hadn't expected to deal with that so soon in his life. "What are you talking about? No." Nate held up a hand to Carmen. "Let me ask Mom. What is Carmen talking about?"

"Oh, don't listen to her. She just wants you to turn on me so you won't question her about that photo. Which, by the way, isn't the only one."

Nate squeezed his eyes shut. "One thing at a time, Mom.

What did you do?"

At least the heat was off Carmen for a moment. Not forever though. How would she ever explain about Diego? Nate wouldn't understand. And she sure didn't want to have the conversation about the danger where she lived in front of Mrs. McConnell. Then again, Nate knew. He'd seen what happened to Mom.

Well? Wasn't Hillary going to say something? No? Fine. "I'll tell you what she did. She made me ditch school and meet her at a lawyer's office, where she tried to get me to sign a paper saying you weren't the father of the baby, and she wanted me to take twenty-five grand to disappear from your life."

Nate turned his pale, open-mouthed expression to his mother. "Is this true?"

"That's not at all how it happened, son. Don't listen to her." Hillary waved her hand. "I was just worried about my boy. Sue me."

Nodding, Nate turned puppy-dog eyes to Carmen. "Please. She's just scared. Have a little compassion. This is bad for her and for my dad. Give them some time."

"Twenty-five thousand dollars, Nate. To get me out of your life. To take your baby far away—or worse, to kill it. You can somehow make excuses for her? Really?"

Hillary sobbed.

A sudden prick of the old conscience, huh? Nice try.

Mrs. McConnell blew her nose. "If that was how it happened, then you'd be right. I'd be a monster. But that wasn't at all the case. I was trying to help. I care about you both. I love you both."

Carmen fought against the bile rising in her stomach. "Oh? Is that a fact? Well, since you seem to be all about proof, I've got some of my own." Carmen brought her phone's display to life and found the app. She pushed PLAY on the recorded file.

"You want me to sign this document stating Nate isn't the father of our baby and promise I will never seek proof that he is? You want me to release Nate from all parental rights and responsibilities to his own child? Am I understanding this document correctly?"

"Exactly. Ideally, I'd like for you to have an abortion, but this is a good-enough second best."

Hillary turned on Carmen with wild eyes. "I will be contacting my attorney. It can't possibly be legal to record someone without their knowledge."

"That's enough." Nate swiped the phone from Carmen and pressed STOP. He rested his head in his hands and leaned his elbows on the table. "How could you?"

Who did he mean?

"How could you do that, Mother? That's the ultimate betrayal. I don't know how I can forgive you."

Hillary cleared her throat. "I was just looking out for you. You'll have to realize that sooner or later. But speaking of betrayal, you seem to be forgetting that picture right there. What does she have to say for herself?"

"That's none of your business, Mother. I'll have that discussion with Carmen privately."

"I have the right to hear this conversation. She's carrying my grandchild."

"You gave up that right when you tried to pay to have the baby murdered. You're an assassin."

Technically, no. Carmen would be the assassin if she'd taken money for murder. But at least he was on the right track with the accusations.

"Fine. Ruin your life. I'm washing my hands of the whole thing." She huffed toward the kitchen then turned in the doorway, the reflection from the chandelier twinkling on her blond waves like a mirror ball. "Just know, Nate. If you move forward with this, you're going to have to do it on your own. Your father and I aren't going to support this ridiculousness." She strode from the room and never looked back.

Carmen's turn to face the music.

Nate stared at the picture in his hands. He lifted it up to his eyes and peered closely at it. "Does his neck say 'Diego'?"

Carmen nodded. How could she convince him that nothing was going on between her and Diego? It would have been way better if she'd told him a long time ago that she needed protection. Maybe he and Diego could even have been friends.

"What's the deal with this joker? He looks like a gang-banger." Nate sounded more curious than mad.

"He's just a friend. He. . .um. . .protects me." Carmen stared at her hands.

"Protects you from what?"

"From other gangbangers mainly." Carmen stood and paced. "Look, until you've walked a mile in my shoes, don't think you know what it's like. My new school is scary; the gangbangers are terrifying. Right off the bat I got tagged by this one guy and his gang friends. Diego saw I was in trouble and told them I was his girl so they'd leave me alone. He was a lifesaver. Nothing has ever happened between us, nor will it."

Nate nodded as the words sank in. "But why didn't you tell me this before now?"

"It's so hard to know what to do. I wasn't sure if you'd laugh at me for being scared, plus I felt like I was being such a drag for complaining all the time."

"That's pretty stupid, Carmen. I mean, now my mom has these pictures and people think you're messing with this guy." Nate rocked back in his chair and stared into her eyes like he was trying to read her soul.

So that was how criminals felt while waiting for the jury to come back with a verdict. Completely out of control of their own lives.

Nate let the front legs of his chair thud on the tile floor. "That settles it."

Oh no. He was about to dump her. What would she do? Alone. Pregnant. In Hackensack, New Jersey. The worst of the worst-case scenarios.

"We're moving out. I found us a little place to rent—the guesthouse of some family friends—but I couldn't decide if it was smart to jump right into things. But we might as well. We'll have to get jobs, but I want you out of Hackensack, and I want us to be together."

No way! "Really?" Carmen squealed and threw her arms around his neck. She squeezed and bounced. She was coming back home. She could go to her old school, at least for a few months. She'd be with Nate all the time. "I'm so excited." There was a little thing called a baby they'd have to worry about, but it was a small price to pay.

"Yeah, well, there's still a lot to think about." He reached behind his head and pulled her arms down. "We need to make some plans. Plus you've got to get permission in writing. I'm an adult, and you're still a minor. We can't forget that."

Hmm. Good point. How would she ever get permission from Mom? She'd never agree to this scheme. Even asking her was the surest way to throw a big roadblock in their path. Would Dad give the permission? Maybe he was her best shot. At least he wouldn't have as many things to react to as Mom would since he's the one who got Carmen on the pill. Guess it was time to tell him. Mom would have to find out the hard way—after it was too late to do anything to stop them.

༄

"Mr. Castillo, I'd like to marry your daughter." Nate stood with his chin raised and his shoulders squared. Proud. Manly. He glanced at Tiffany on the couch on the other side of the room.

Tiffany nodded. She seemed to approve, but why not? This would get Carmen even more out of her way.

Dad's eyebrows shot up. "What? Now? Why?" His gaze darted from Carmen to Nate and back to Carmen. "Are you. . . pregnant?" He glared at Nate.

"Yes, Dad. I am." It wasn't like he didn't know they were sexually active. Birth control wasn't for kissing.

"Wow. This is quite a shock." He slumped back into his recliner. "Just give me a minute to let it sink in."

They waited.

"A grandpa. I'm going to be a grandfather?" He didn't exactly smile. He just tried on the label.

Carmen nodded.

"I didn't see that one coming." Dad exhaled. "What does your mom say?"

Defining moment. "We haven't told her."

If Dad got self-righteous now, he'd make Carmen tell her mom.

"What? Why? She's going to have a fit that you told me first."

Tiffany cleared her throat.

"Wait. Tiff knew?" Dad chuckled. "Your poor mom is going to go apoplectic. Let's just keep that bit of info to ourselves, okay?"

Everyone nodded.

"Now, what are your plans?"

Nate sat in the chair across from Dad. "I've found us a place to rent, and we want to move in right away so I can get Carmen back in New York, where she belongs. We'll both get jobs, and then we want to get married as soon as possible."

"You sound like you've thought things through. I just have to wonder if you really know what you're in for though. Marriage is hard work. Raising a child is hard work. That's true even when you're thirty. You guys are so young."

What did he know about marriage and hard work?

"We know, sir. It's. . .it's what we think is best." Nate looked down at the floor.

"You know all of your options though? I mean, you've looked into abortion, adoption, even simply waiting awhile to get married?"

"We have, Dad. None of those are possible." He was being cooler about this than Carmen had expected.

"Sounds to me like you guys are handling things well." Tiffany's eyes held a ray of hope.

Sorry, Tiff. There won't be any bonding experiences today.

"The thing is, sir." Nate coughed. "We, uh, need your permission. In writing."

Dad rubbed his chin. "Yeah. I saw that coming. You want me to allow this to happen before your mom even knows any of this is going on?"

Carmen nodded. "You know Mom. She's strict. She doesn't even know that we're. . .that we. . ."

Dad held up his hand. "I get it. I wish I didn't know either." He closed his eyes for a brief moment and looked five years older when he opened them again. "What do I need to sign?"

༄

"Mom, can we talk?" Carmen leaned on the doorframe to the bathroom Mom shared with Harper. From the looks of things, Mom had about ten more minutes of makeup to apply.

"Sure. You talk while I finish up. I have a facial to do in Edgewater at eight tonight. Should be some good money, but I need to leave in the next fifteen minutes if I have any hope of making it there on time."

Carmen nodded. This was such a bad time to tell her. She probably wouldn't go do her party once she got the news. Or she'd storm out mad and drive like a maniac and get in an accident. "Never mind then. We'll talk later."

"No, no. I want to talk now. I've been worried about you, and I want to know what's going on."

She asked for it. Do it like taking off a Band-Aid. "Okay. I'm moving out."

"Funny. You are so *not* moving out." Mom continued to apply lip liner.

"I really am. Nate and I have rented a place, and I'm going. Tonight."

Hair held back with a purple headband, lips lined with dark liner, eyes wild with surprise, Mom looked like a crazy person. "You'd need my permission for that, and there's no way I'm going to allow such a thing."

Oh man. This would sting. "I have Dad's permission in writing. I'm sorry." Carmen cringed. The last thing she wanted was to be the cause of another blow to Mom.

She sank onto the toilet, her face pale beneath her makeup. "You're serious?"

"Yeah." Carmen leaned against the wall, careful not to let her stomach stick out. Was it possible to get out of the house with Mom not even asking about the possibility of pregnancy? She didn't know Carmen was sexually active, so maybe it wouldn't occur to her.

"I know you hate it here in New Jersey. I know this move has been hard on you most of all, but don't you think this is a drastic step?"

"It's what I have to do." Don't crumble under the pressure of pleasing Mom.

"What about your sisters? What kind of message are you sending them?" A tear escaped and left a track through the makeup.

"It's not like I'm abandoning Harper and Kim. It's just a choice I'm making for my own life." Carmen raised her shoulders. "This won't be the last time a choice I make affects them." She offered Mom a tissue.

"When is this happening? You said tonight?" She shook her head. "No. We need more time to talk about this." Mom blew her nose and blotted her eyes.

"I am leaving tonight. After I pack enough for a few days. I'll get the rest this weekend." Carmen folded her arms across her chest. Don't back down.

Mom shook her head. "Oh no. You leave this house against my wishes, you do it with nothing but what you can fit in your backpack or wear on your body. You're not hauling boxes and boxes from this home without my blessing, and I certainly can't offer it with nothing but a five-minute conversation."

She couldn't be serious. "What about all my other stuff like my books?"

"Everything stays here. I'm not going to argue or negotiate about this, Carmen." Mom rubbed her temples like she always did at the beginning of a migraine. "You can hang around for a few days, talk it over with me, give me more time—and see what we come up with. But if you leave tonight, you're going to do it on your own."

She could probably have backed down and waited a couple of days. But Carmen wanted nothing more than to escape her apartment and hop a train to New York. To Nate. "Fine. There's nothing I need that I can't fit in my bag. I'm out of here. Call me if you come to your senses. And my phone *is* going with me. Nate bought it." She'd have to get on his plan right away. From the sounds of things, Mom probably wouldn't keep paying for her package. "It didn't have to be this way, Mom."

Carmen turned her back on her crying mother and stormed into her bedroom. She shoved as much as she could fit into her backpack and purse. Tied her favorite sweatshirts around her waist, grabbed her phone charger and hair dryer, and left. Carmen would have to call Harper and Kimberley when Mom was out later.

She jogged down the stairs and turned toward the bus stop, tears raining onto the sidewalk below her feet. Why did it have to be so difficult? She only wanted a good life. Why was that such a bad thing?

Hard to believe Mom never asked why this was all happening. It never crossed her mind Carmen might be pregnant or that there might be some reason other than general unhappiness? Would knowing the whole truth have changed things? Maybe Carmen should have led with the whole story. Would things have turned out differently if she had?

She leaned against the lamppost to wait for the right bus to show up.

Mom would come around. She had to. It had been just too big of a shock for her to deal with so quickly. Too much to process. It probably wasn't fair of Carmen to throw it at her and expect her to adapt within the space of a few minutes. Mom didn't deserve that kind of treatment. But what was Carmen to do? She had to think about herself. . .her new life. . .Nate. . . the baby.

Carmen shrieked as a hand gripped her elbow. She felt hot breath on her neck.

"Does your boyfriend know you're out alone at night?" a voice growled just inches from her ear. "Big mistake, chica. Big mistake."

Chapter 18

Marco flashed a sinister grin full of silver teeth.
Why hadn't she listened to Diego and been more careful? Her last night in Hackensack and she was going to get murdered on the street. Or worse. So close to freedom, yet so far away.

Who knew where she was? Mom and Nate. Mom wouldn't be calling Nate tonight—that much Carmen knew for sure. Nate wouldn't know Carmen was missing until sometime after ten o'clock when the train would arrive at the station and she wouldn't be on it.

Another glint of silver sparked the space in front of Carmen's face. This time from Marco's hand. In a whoosh, she felt something cold press against the front of her neck as he spun her around. Did Marco have a real knife against her throat? He couldn't be serious.

"Just start walking. Turn right at the corner."

She started to move, numb from head to toe. Was she in shock? How was it that she was being dragged through the streets of New Jersey, pregnant, with a gang leader's knife pressed to her throat? What a far cry from her old life.

"Marco. What are you doing? Don't be dumb." Carmen wriggled and tried to pull herself free. She clawed at the dragon tattoo on his forearm. If only she could reach his face with her fingers.

A sharp lash stung her throat. The knife! Was she bleeding? It didn't feel deep, but how could she know without actually seeing it? Her heart thundered in her chest. This might be her last night alive. There was still so much she wanted to do with her life. Marry Nate. Have their baby. Maybe buy a house.

"Don't you be an idiot, chica. Wake up and realize I'm in charge. Diego is nowhere to be found. Tonight you're mine." Marco laughed.

Think, Carmen. Be smart. Wasn't Marco afraid of Diego? "But tomorrow Diego will come after you. Why would you want to make him mad?"

"Why do I want to make him mad? So he'll come after me, stupid. Hopefully tonight. . .tomorrow might be too late for you." Marco shoved her forward. "Get in there."

Carmen stumbled toward the doorway of an abandoned building. "What are you going to do to me?" Every horror film she'd ever seen came rushing into Carmen's consciousness. Why had she watched those stupid slasher movies with Dad? Her heart was about to pound out of her chest.

"Just get in there." He kicked at the back of her legs.

Carmen fell forward through the doorway onto her face. Pain shot through her nose and radiated into the back of her head.

"Well, well. Whatchu got there, Marco?"

Oh no. José. He was worse than Marco, and he always had a gun on him. And when José was around, Shooter was never far away—judging by his name, he'd have a gun, too. If only she could see. Carmen lifted her cheek from the cool concrete and squinted against the darkness.

A match struck across the cavernous space, and when the flame met the cigarette, Carmen spied Shooter's glowing eyes staring down at her.

A light came on in a room somewhere behind her. At least

she could make out shadows and enough of their faces to know who was who and where they were. Except, who was back there? Who turned the light on?

"If you guys let me go, I won't tell anyone. I promise." *God, please.*

"You think that's some sort of prize? Your silence?" Marco laughed. "You still don't know how this works, do you? Let me spell it out crystal clear for you." He flicked his cigarette to the ground and smashed it into the dirty warehouse floor. "Here's the simple version even you can understand. Diego, he our enemy. We want to fight him. I hear you're having his baby."

What? Where had he heard about the baby? How had word gotten around? She'd told no one in Jersey. Not even her own family. How could she convince him it wasn't true? "I'm not—"

"Save it, sister." José high-fived Shooter.

"You having his baby. So we get to you; we get to him. It's simple."

But Carmen couldn't stand not knowing. How had they found out she was pregnant? Naturally they assumed it was Diego's, but no one knew. Diego didn't even know.

There had to be a way out of this mess. Carmen searched the space for something, anything. She couldn't fight off three guys. Especially when one had a knife to her throat and at least one of the others had a gun. And there was some unidentified presence elsewhere on the premises. What would they do to her? What would they do to her baby? Shame it took the gravest situation possible for Carmen to feel the first inklings of maternal feelings toward the life inside her. She wanted nothing more than to protect her baby, but the situation looked grim.

God, please help me out of this mess.

José shoved Carmen into a rickety chair. "Sit there and don't get any crazy ideas."

She waited for a rope to appear around her body or her wrists, but none came. At least they hadn't killed her right off. Every moment she kept it together was another chance of getting out of there alive.

A cell phone rang. "Where is he?" Marco's voice growled into the dim room. "Let me know when he's two minutes away."

Silence.

They waited. For what? Who else was coming? Carmen squinted. If only she could see through the dark better.

Minutes that felt like hours passed.

"He's here, Marco." José laughed. "He's got company."

"Figured as much. You be lookout at the window. Shooter, you watch the door. I'm going out."

Carmen strained to hear.

"Well, if it isn't my old pal Diego. Whachu comin' 'round here for?"

Should Carmen yell to let him know she was in here? If she didn't tell him, how would he know?

"You got my girl in there? You tell me."

Oh, Diego already knew. Of course. Dangling her safety was how they got him here. Carmen's deceptions had put another life at risk.

God. . .

No, praying was silly. No one was up there to hear the prayers, but if there were some deity, some creator of the universe, He'd never waste time with her. She'd already blown it, big-time. But it wasn't fair that so many other people would go down because of her. He should save Diego at least. And the baby. *Please, God, save the baby.*

"I want yo money and power."

"Why'd you think Diego could give you either?"

"You been made in the deal that went down yesterday.

I want the cash. And, as for power, you just need to make it known. La chica is my girl."

"Ain't happenin'."

"Oh? Has Diego gone soft on a girl? First time for everything."

"You don't want her. She too backpack for you."

"Sayin' it like a true baby daddy."

"I'm not a baby da—put the gun away, Marco."

"Nah. I'm about up to the rims with you. I think it's time we say good-bye."

Bang!

Bang!

"Marco got plugged. Get out there, Shooter."

"They both down." José crouched at the window and clicked something on his gun. "Let's go. Diego gots two more gunners out there."

Shooter and José crept through the door, staying low to the ground. Had they forgotten about her, or did they expect her to stay put? Not happening. She had to move while she had the chance. But who was that person who'd turned the light on earlier? Would she come face-to-face with her worst nightmare the minute she stepped outside? A risk she had to take.

Her heart pounded so loud, she was surprised they didn't hear it and come running back to secure their prize. She crossed the warehouse floor and made it to the back door, away from the action outside. Through the door and into the fresh air. No problem.

Run. She ran and ran as far away from there as she could get. Her backpack bounced against her lower back as her legs pumped like pistons.

Move, legs. Move. Carmen's thighs burned, and her lungs were about to explode. She couldn't run another step if her life depended on it. Oh, it did, actually. *Keep going. Keep going.*

She looked back down the street. The deserted warehouse was now a dot in the distance. No one had followed her—that she knew of anyway. She'd never claim to have the best street smarts. She spied a pay phone hanging from the brick wall of the drug store. *Please work.* She didn't want to call from her cell, which they could easily trace.

"911. What's your emergency?" a cheery female voice answered the phone.

"I need to report a gunshot. The victim is injured—I think unconscious." Carmen gasped for air.

"What's the address?"

Breathe, Carmen. She gave the street name and an approximation of the building number. *Breathe.*

"Your name?"

"Um. . .this is an anonymous call." Would they take the info and act on it if Carmen didn't say who she was?

The sigh came through the phone wires. "Fine. Care to share any more information?"

"There are other men there; some have guns. I saw at least three guns. But there might be a fourth." Would she ever find out who the secret man was in the back?

"Anything else?"

"Only that you should hurry." Carmen hung up the pay phone and hurried into the night without looking back.

🌀

Carmen took deep breaths and let them out slowly, trying to calm the trembling reverberating deep in her bones. The train squealed to a stop, and the doors slid open at Grand Central Station. She lifted her bag and made her way to the station platform. How would she ever pull off keeping Nate unaware of the night's events? She should just tell him what happened.

No. If she did, he'd make her talk to the police. She'd have to go back there. She'd have to see those people. Carmen would be in the news. And Hillary would find out about what happened. Nope. Way better to leave it all behind and move on with her new life. But if that was how she was going to play it, she'd better pull herself together.

Carmen weaved her way through the maze of travelers and Salvation Army Santas ringing their holiday bells. They started earlier and earlier every year it seemed. Here they were, still more than a week from Thanksgiving, and they were at it already. Santa hats and all.

Finally she had to maneuver past a street band with an open guitar case sprinkled with coins before she could step into the restroom. She splashed some cool water onto her face and gazed into the mirror.

Who was that person? Virtually unrecognizable, inside and out.

Out in the main corridor, Carmen checked the arrival and departure displays. Twenty minutes until the train for Ossining. She should call the hospital to find out about Diego while she waited. But would they tell her anything if she didn't give her name? They probably wouldn't talk to her even if she did tell them who she was because she wasn't family. And what if they had a way to trace the call? She wanted nothing to do with this situation.

Diego had risked his life—maybe given it—for her, and she abandoned him. Just walked away like nothing had happened. But what could she have done? If she'd stayed, she'd probably have been shot, or worse. Plus, the last thing she wanted was to be on the evening news somehow connected to those gangs. Hillary would have loved it, and it just might have pushed Nate over the edge, too. This way Carmen could just move on.

Maybe she'd be able to visit Diego in a few days—if he were alive. If she thought she wouldn't get caught.

Her train squealed into the station, and the doors opened. She climbed in and settled in a seat. Head back on the headrest, Carmen closed her eyes and begged for sleep to come. Anything to forget.

Bang. Bang. Bang. The sound of the gunshots replayed in her mind over and over. Who shot whom first? It had sounded like Diego had taken the first bullet. But there was no way to tell. She'd probably find out on the news later that night.

What if he died for her? Was it her fault? She didn't deserve such a good friend.

🌀

"Hi, honey. I'm home." Carmen breezed through the door and let her bags slide to the ceramic tile floor in the entryway.

"I know, silly. I just picked you up from the train station."

Carmen giggled. "Oh, humor me. I've always wanted to say that."

"Come here, you." Nate rushed to her and pulled her into a tight embrace. "I'm glad you're here. Can you believe it?"

Every few minutes Carmen managed to put the events of the evening out of her head and revel in the excitement of moving in with Nate. "No, I can't believe it at all. It can't get any better than this."

But then it all came rushing back into her consciousness. *Be calm.* It would be okay if she could just make it through the night without breaking down. Everything hinged on her being able to keep control.

"Yep. It can. Come on over here and have a seat." Nate pulled Carmen's hand to the floral couch. "Be right back. One sec." He tore off down the hallway toward the two bedrooms in back.

Thankfully the place was furnished, even though the floral was a bit much for her taste. Almost like they'd expected a gardener to live there. Oh, maybe that's what the house was meant for. Either way, at least Carmen and Nate didn't have to worry about furniture.

Nate returned and sat beside her. He took Carmen's hand and slipped off the sofa, down to one knee. He whipped a small blue box out of his NYU sweatshirt pocket with his free hand. "I love you, and I love the idea of our family. I can't wait to spend my life with you. So, will you marry me?" He flipped the top open to reveal a round solitaire in a white-gold vintage setting.

Carmen gasped. The ring he'd chosen looked like a cross between all the ones she'd circled in *Cosmo Bride* during the past week. It had to be at least a full carat. Wonder where he'd gotten the money to buy it. "It's gorgeous. I can't even believe it's mine. How can you afford this?"

Nate plucked the ring from its velvet nest and slipped it on Carmen's finger. "Don't you worry about it. I have some money. We'll talk about all that another time. Let's just enjoy the moment."

Carmen sank back into the cushions and held her hand in front of her face. She twisted it in every direction to see the rainbows of light twinkle off the diamond. "It's amazing. I'm so excited." She grabbed Nate's hands and squeezed. "I couldn't be happier."

"You still haven't answered yet. Will you marry me?"

"Of course I will!" She threw her arms around his neck and pulled him close. "I already told you that before." Carmen giggled.

"I know, but the ring makes it official. And since you said yes, I have another surprise for you."

Carmen pulled back. "Really? What could it be? You've

already given me everything I wanted."

"Not quite." He handed Carmen a legal-sized envelope.

"What is this?" She turned it over in her hands.

"Just open it. You'll see." Nate sat back with a smug grin on his face.

Carmen slid her finger under the seal and popped the flap open. She pulled out a packet of papers. "This looks like a contract." She unfolded it and stared at the Sleepy Hollow Country Club centennial crest logo at the top of the page. "Is this what I think it is?"

"You're now a member in good standing, and Zach will meet you on the indoor courts tomorrow at nine o'clock."

Carmen's eyes filled with tears. All she'd wanted was to feel loved, cared for, protected. And here Nate was giving her all of those things and way more. "I don't know how to thank you. This night means so much to me. I love you."

"I love you, too."

"Bad timing, I know. But I have to go to the bathroom. Bad. Part of pregnancy, I guess." Carmen stood up. "Don't go anywhere though."

Nate stretched out on the couch and reached for the remote. He winked. "I'm not going anywhere."

At least the nausea seemed to have passed during the last week. The constant need to visit the bathroom wasn't so bad when it didn't involve vomiting. Carmen lowered her jeans and stepped over to the toilet. What was that? She bent to look closer. A spot of bright-red blood on her princess frog panties. Blood was never good while pregnant, was it? Did it always mean tragedy, or was there such a thing as normal blood? Why hadn't she listened when the nurse was rattling off the instructions?

Should she call someone for help? The spot was only about the size of a quarter. Carmen huddled on the toilet and pulled out her phone. In the Google search bar, she typed *bleeding at ten weeks pregnant*.

Hundreds of things came up on the results page.

Might be nothing.

Might be something.

Probably nothing.

Unless more blood showed up, she'd go with the probably nothing angle. The explanation for the potential causes seemed viable. Stretching cervix. Changing body. Infection. All reasonable and not really dangerous to her or the baby. Well, infection wasn't great, but it could be treated. She'd keep her eye on things and follow the advice.

Now to decide whether or not to tell Nate.

Nah. Why start now with honesty and openness?

Chapter 19

Carmen pulled the blanket up to her chin and nuzzled into the bed. What rubbed against her foot? She opened one eye, and memories flooded in with the sunlight. She was in her new home, sleeping beside Nate. "Mmm. What a nice way to wake up. Let's just stay like this all day."

Nate pulled her close. "I'm all for it."

Tennis. Carmen sat up. "What time is it? I have lessons today." She jumped from the bed and searched for her backpack. So much for playing house.

"Hah. My gift came back to bite me already. I should have scheduled your lesson for two o'clock in the afternoon."

"Yeah. That'll teach you." Carmen winked.

"Oh, hey. If you're wondering what to wear, check the closet."

Carmen rushed to the mirrored bifold and pulled it open. Six or seven hangers held various clothing items she'd have to check out later. But right now her eyes zeroed in on two tennis dresses. A white one and a black one. "You're spoiling me, Nater."

"I fully intend to keep doing it." He rolled over. "But right now I'm going back to sleep. Let me know when it's five minutes from time to go." Nate pulled the maroon-and-navy-striped comforter over his head.

"Deal."

How was it that just last week she was a seventeen-year-old

high school junior, and now she was building a family with the man she loved? Exactly where she wanted to be. And it was almost Thanksgiving. Would she and Nate have their very first Christmas tree in a couple of weeks? What a dream come true.

Now, which dress to choose. Memory of the blood from last night twinged at her gut. She'd wear the black one, just in case. Maybe she shouldn't even play tennis right now. Should she call the doctor? She would at least tell Zach she needed to take it easy. He might even notice why. The tennis dress didn't look like it would conceal her tiny round baby bump.

Hair in a ponytail, she nudged Nate. "Hey, you. I'm about ready to go. You coming, too?"

"Of course. We have big plans today." He rolled from the bed and stumbled to the bathroom. The door clicked shut, and the shower gushed.

Great. He'd never be ready in five minutes. Why did men always do that? Allow only a fraction of the time it actually took to get ready and then wonder why they're always late? Oh well. Carmen sat down at the computer and typed, *Is it okay to play sports while pregnant?*

She scanned article after article that all seemed to say a pregnant woman was perfectly able to do whatever her body was used to doing before the pregnancy. Don't start any new sports or activities, but keep right on doing the familiar. It said some people even ran marathons while pregnant if their body had been conditioned for it before.

What if it had been a couple of months though? Carmen hadn't played in a while, but she felt positive her body was still conditioned for it. So, according to the articles, it was okay to play tennis. Should she maybe not do it though? It had only been a few hours since she'd had the bleeding incident. And the day before had been pretty traumatic for her. Maybe it would be best to sit out one more week. If she explained why, Nate and Zach would understand.

But then Nate would make her go to the doctor. Unless maybe she showed him the articles. If he read the bleeding could be absolutely nothing, maybe he'd not jump to crazy and get all worried. No. Who was she kidding? That wasn't her Nater. He'd go ballistic. And he'd be mad she didn't tell him right when it happened. What to do?

Nate opened the bathroom door wearing nothing but a towel, his blond hair glistening from his shower. He looked her over and grinned. "I can't wait to see you on the courts looking all hot and sweaty in that tennis dress."

Yeah. It was settled. She was playing.

৯

"Zach!" Carmen jogged out onto one of the indoor courts and hugged her instructor. "I've missed you, and I've desperately missed playing so much."

"Ah, so the tennis gets a *desperately*, but me just a little? I see how I rate." Zach winked a clear-blue eye that had brought many girls to swoon. "Seriously though, I've missed you, too, girl. Bird on the wire says a lot's been going on with you these days." Zach held her out at arm's length and looked right at her belly. "You sure you're okay to play?"

Guess he knew already. "Of course. Should take it a bit easier than I used to. But I'm good." She jogged over to her serving position.

Carmen twirled her tennis racquet in her hands then rotated her shoulders to loosen up. She threw the ball up in the air, reared the racquet back, and let go with a smash that surprised even her.

Zach saw it coming and didn't bother to try returning it. "That's not what I'd call taking it easy."

"I know. Just getting it out of my system. It feels great to let loose a little."

They settled into a comfortable cadence of volleys that echoed off the walls and reminded Carmen why she loved the game so much.

"Hey. It's been thirty minutes. Shouldn't you take a water break?"

Carmen nodded. "Good idea." She took her water and sat on the edge of the bottom bleacher. She emptied the bottle in two long drinks.

"Um. Carmen, I'm not liking how you look right now. You're kind of pale, sort of ashy." Zach squatted down and looked into her eyes. "You okay?"

"I think so. I am a little crampy though. Maybe I should rest awhile." Things felt a little funny. Zach looked kind of fuzzy.

Zach eyed her for a moment.

"What? I'm okay."

He nodded. "I'll be right back." He jogged over to a locker-room attendant who was picking up towels in the bleachers. Zach must have told him to do something because he took off running from the gym.

What was happening to her? Carmen's thoughts grew a bit fuzzy.

"It's going to be okay."

"Nater? You're here?" What was the warm feeling between her legs? "I think I might have wet myself. Can you help me?"

Nate nodded and squeezed her. "Help is on the way. You're going to be okay."

Her stomach clenched, and it felt like her back was ripping in half. "My stomach hurts really bad." What did it mean? Was the baby okay? Was she dying?

"I know. I know. Just hold on."

✿

"Stop scratching, sweetie."

Who was that woman talking to her? Why were they holding her hands so tight? "It itches. What's going on?" *Make it stop.*

"She's waking up." The same woman spoke again.

"Hey, babe. Can you hear me?"

Nate's voice. He was there.

"Why do I itch so bad?" She tried to open her eyes, but the room was so bright.

"You had an allergic reaction to the morphine. The itching should start to go away soon. We gave you some Benadryl."

Morphine? Carmen looked up at the nurse. "What happened?"

The nurse looked beyond Carmen and nodded to Nate.

He stepped to the bedside and took Carmen's hand. "You. . . had an accident. You started bleeding. You were. . .very sick. We. . ." He begged the nurse with his eyes.

If Nate couldn't bring himself to tell her, then her worst fears were confirmed. "The baby?"

Nate shook his head.

"Sweetheart, you were hemorrhaging. You could have died. There was nothing we could do at that point." The nurse patted Carmen's arm just below the IV.

Carmen placed her hand on her lower abdomen where she'd only recently noticed the changes signaling the growing life. "Is it. . . Did you. . . Will I. . . ?" How could she ask some stranger to confirm her dead baby was no longer inside her? But she already knew.

"It's all over, sweetie. You're going to be sore for a few days. And you're going to stay here at least overnight to receive fluid and possibly more blood. But the hard part is over."

That's what she thought. Carmen nodded and rolled to her side.

Nate came around to the other side of the bed and crouched down to Carmen's eye level.

No. Not now. She couldn't deal with Nate being sweet to her right then. Not after all she'd put him through. She needed peace and blessed sleep. She fluttered her eyes and pretended to drift off.

"Poor dear. She's had a tough time of it." The nurse reached over Carmen's head from behind her and dimmed the overhead lights.

"Yes, she sure has." Nate sighed. "Do you think she'll sleep for a while?"

"Oh yes. Morphine was enough to knock her out, but then the Benadryl to fight the allergy will do an even better job of it."

"Okay, I'm going to go get something to eat. I'll be back in a few minutes."

"You take your time, honey. She'll be out for hours."

Not likely. Carmen's guilt pummeled her brain. If she could ever manage to fall asleep, it would be sweet relief from the pain she felt and the pain she'd caused. But there was no way her body would. . .

Carmen's eyes blinked open.

Darkness filled the room.

She let her eyes flutter closed again. What time was it? Had she actually slept? It felt like someone was in the room with her, but she didn't want to move. The peaceful quiet felt too good to destroy.

"You awake?"

Mom. What did she know? Had she been told about the baby? Carmen opened her eyes and searched for her mom.

They locked eyes.

Carmen swallowed. "I don't know what to say."

"Neither do I." Mom smiled softly and tightened her skirt against the back of her legs then sat on the edge of the bed. "I hadn't seen this coming at all. I sort of feel like a fool. I'm so sorry I wasn't there for you—I was so clueless." Mom's face morphed as her emotions went through the spectrum.

"It's not your fault, Mom. I'm sorry that you were blindsided by all of this. It really wasn't fair to you."

"No. It wasn't fair." Mom smoothed her pink suit lapel. "I have to ask you some things, Carmen. I'm sorry to throw this at you in the middle of all you're going through. But the police came to see me twice, I spoke with your father and Tiffany on the phone, and I've pieced some things together myself. All I need from you are some yes or no answers, okay?"

"K." If it weren't for the sound of her heartbeat, Carmen would swear time stood still.

"Were you involved in a gang fight yesterday?"

Carmen nodded. What must Mom think of her?

"Did you place an anonymous emergency call to report the shooting?"

Carmen nodded. How could she have abandoned Diego?

"Did you get pregnant on purpose so Nate would marry you and you could move out?"

Carmen brought her hands to her face and sobbed. This was the worst one. "Yes. But please don't tell Nate. Please. He'll never forgive me."

Mom's face turned white.

A throat cleared on the far side of the room.

Nate stepped from the shadows. "Too late."

☙

"Hi, pumpkin." Dad stroked Carmen's head as she woke from a nap.

Tiffany, Kim, and Harper stood in front of her hospital bed, each holding two helium-filled balloons shaped like a different animal.

"What's the big celebration?" Carmen jerked her head toward the balloons. "I don't feel much like a party."

"Just trying to make you feel better. Balloons always make me happy." Harper reached her arms around her sister. "Are you okay?"

"Physically, I'm going to be fine, the doctors say. We'll talk about the other stuff later."

Dad looked at Mom. "Where's Nate?"

She shrugged. "He left awhile ago."

"He won't be back." Carmen pulled a pillow over her face. Why didn't they all just leave? Couldn't they see that the last thing she wanted to do was make conversation? She needed time to think. Cry. Pray.

Yes, pray. It was probably past time for praying. She had sure made a big mess of things trying to go it alone. She had no one to blame but herself. At least if she'd been praying all along, she and God would have had a share in the blame.

Mom slipped the strap of her purse over her shoulder. "I'm going to get some air and leave you all to your little party. But I have a few things I want to say first, and I want every one of you to hear it."

She took a deep breath. "I'm sickened—disgusted, actually—that you people did all of this behind my back. I'm so angry that you"—she jabbed her finger at Dad and Tiffany— "didn't respect my position as her mother enough to include me on something as grave as a pregnancy."

Dad nodded and looked down. "You're right. I'm really sorry, Pam."

Mom turned to Carmen. "And I'm furious you would visit

a doctor and discuss details about your pregnancy with *her*"—
another poke at Tiffany—"instead of me. I'm angry, and I'm
crushed. But most of all, I'm terrified at what's happened to the
people I've given my life to love. How you all could make the
choices you've made lately"—she looked pointedly at Dad—"is
beyond me." She spun from the room and slammed the door
behind her.

Say something. Someone. Anyone. The silence in the room
was too much.

Hot tears squeezed from Carmen's eyes and fell to the pillow
in big droplets. "Can you guys just go? I'm not feeling very
good." *Please, just leave. Don't talk. No hugs. No lengthy good-
byes.* Carmen didn't open her eyes, but heard lots of movement
going on around her. When she peeked, the door was closing.
They were gone.

Carmen closed her eyes.

A slight rap sounded on the door. *They've got to be kidding.
What now?* "Come in." *Just make it quick.*

Nate. *Oh, Nate. He came.* Carmen reached a hand toward
him. "Nate, I. . .I'm so sorry."

"Save it." He ignored her hand. "Listen. I am so angry and
hurt, I don't even know why I'm back here, where I waited
hours for you to wake up because I was so worried about you,
only to find out. . ." Nate whipped his head from side to side as
though trying to reset an Etch A Sketch.

Should Carmen speak? *Maybe it would be better to stay silent.*

"I loved you. I loved you so much I chose you over my
family. I thought we'd grow old together—I wanted that. I
thought you did, too."

"I did. More than anything." Carmen's stomach was hollow
from the life ripped from within and from the dashed hope
standing right before her.

"Not enough. Not enough to trust me. Not enough to let me decide for myself. You wanted things your way at any cost. And it wound up costing us everything."

"Can you ever forgive me?" *Please say yes. Please say we can keep trying. Please make another miracle happen.*

"I believe one day I will forgive you enough not to hate you. But I will never be able to love you like I once did. Never." He wiped his eyes as the tears fell.

Carmen squeezed her eyes closed. So much pain.

"I just came here to say my piece and to ask for the ring back. It's only right."

Oh no. She had to take off the ring. So final. Carmen lifted it in front of her face and stared at it to burn its facets into her memory. Proof she'd once been truly loved. She slipped the ring off her finger and reached it out to him. *Please let our skin touch one more time.* She only wanted to feel that electricity one more time.

Nate held his hand below hers and waited for her to let it fall.

Okay. Have it your way. She released the ring and watched his strong hand swallow it whole.

Done.

He gazed into her eyes for one brief moment then spun away and left. Forever.

Carmen's throat constricted around sobs that bellowed to the surface. When they finally popped through, they wracked her body like aliens. She shook from head to toe. The only thing that offered comfort was the moans. They started in her belly and flew past her heart, escaping with some sliver of the pain on their wings.

Maybe one day they'd carry it all away.

Chapter 20

I'm sorry, Carmen, but you can't come back home."
Her mother stood in Carmen's living room for the first time ever. The same room she was meant to share with Nate. The one to which he'd never return.

"Mom. You can't be serious." Carmen's stomach churned. "What do you mean I can't come back home?" How could a mother do such a thing to her own daughter after all that had happened? Carmen couldn't stay here. Not where she and Nate had meant to be a family. She couldn't afford the rent anyway. Was she going to have to live with Dad and Tiffany?

"Listen, I'd like nothing more than to go back to the way things were before all of this garbage of the past few months. But we can't pretend it didn't happen." She shook her head. "I'm worried about you, and there are more important things at stake than just having you back at home like nothing's changed."

"What are you talking about?" Carmen's heart threatened to jump out of her chest. She'd never live with Tiffany. Carmen couldn't do it. Mom wouldn't expect her to, would she? Was this because she was angry? Jealous?

"There are deeper issues at stake, and I can't pretend these things didn't happen. The reprehensible choices you've made. . . You were so desperate for a way out, you tricked your boyfriend into getting you pregnant. You moved out of our home and into an apartment with him. You've been involved in gang activity. People almost died. A baby did die." Her knuckles popped one at a time as she ticked the list off on her fingers. "Not to mention all you've been through personally this year: a divorce, a move, a new school, a pregnancy, a miscarriage, a breakup. . . the list goes on and on." Mom swiped at a stream of tears marking cracks in her foundation.

"You think I don't know all of that?" Carmen jumped up; her chair banged on the linoleum in the dinette where she'd been sitting. "Don't forget to add rejected by my mom to the list." How could she? "I lose my baby, my fiancé, and my mother in the same week? Just months after I lost my dad? How could you do this to me? I thought, of everyone, you'd be the one to stand by my side."

"I'm not rejecting you, sweetheart. I'm getting you the help you need, if you'll take it."

"What are you talking about? Counseling?" Carmen saw herself spending hours during the next months—make that years—camped out on a shrink's couch.

"I'm sure counseling will be part of it. But there has to be more. Remember the group of girls who came to church awhile back?"

Alarm bells rang in Carmen's ears. She crossed her arms on her chest. "Which girls?"

"Come on, you know exactly what I'm talking about. The group from Diamond Estates. They gave their testimonies the first week we visited the church."

"What about them? Didn't you think they were a little wacko?" Anything to keep the conversation from arriving at its predictable destination.

"No, actually. I thought those girls had been through a lot and had found God's grace and mercy on the other side. Exactly what I want for you."

"So you're saying I have to go there?"

"What I'm saying is, if you want to come home to live, you can only do it if you get help first. Right now Diamond Estates is the best way I can see how." She stared at Carmen. "Or you can reject the help you need and go live with your dad."

"Yeah, well, that's not happening." Not as long as Tiffany lived there.

Mom reached out a business card. "Here's the phone number to Diamond Estates. I've spoken with Ben Bradley, the director. He's happy to talk with you, but asked for you to be the one to call him."

Ben Bradley, Director. Diamond Estates. Where the finest gems are pulled from the deepest roughs. She couldn't go to a place like that. What would people say? How would she explain it to Kim and Harper? What about Dad? Would he think she was crazy? Or maybe he already did.

Then again, the idea of getting away held some appeal. Living far away from the whole mess. Starting over. Figuring out how to get through all the junk life had thrown at her. Help. Peace. Forgiveness. All things she desperately needed. But could she find them at Diamond Estates? Did they even exist?

"You have to be out of this apartment when?" Mom whispered.

"Thursday." How had her life gotten so messed up?

"Thanksgiving? Well, you're welcome at the apartment for Thanksgiving dinner, and you can spend the night if you have somewhere to be on Friday. I'll borrow a car and drive you to the airport even. I suggest you do some thinking and praying. I'll help you in any way I can, but ultimately, the choice has to be yours."

⚜

"Diamond Estates, Ben Bradley speaking."

Hang up. Just hang up. Forget the whole thing. This was sheer lunacy.

"Hello? Is anyone there?" His voice grew a bit impatient.

Now or never. "Mr. Bradley?"

"This is he. How can I help you?"

It was only a conversation. It didn't require a commitment to anything. Speak.

"Hi. I'm Carmen Castillo. You don't know me, but I think you spoke with my mom recently."

"Hi, Carmen. I'm glad you called. May I just say something to you before we start talking?"

"Uh. Sure." That was odd. She'd expected to have to carry the conversation, even to have to beg to be let into the program.

"Jesus loves you."

The words hit her body like a warm, enveloping hug. If it had been anyone else who'd spoken those words, at any other moment in her life, she'd have laughed at the cliché. But it was time for her to hear them, even if she couldn't quite believe them.

"Why don't you fill me in on all that's been going on, Carmen? Let's see if we can't figure something out."

Carmen poured out every detail, every kernel of dirty truth, and every bit of her shame. She laid it bare on those phone wires to Diamond Estates. She sensed they soared through Ben Bradley's heart and landed at the feet of Jesus as though carried on a prayer. How did she know? Carmen had no idea. It made no sense, yet it felt real.

"That's it. The end of the story." Broken and spilled out, Carmen exhaled.

"Ah. But you're so wrong. No, not the end of the story. The end of the nightmare. This part is when Jesus comes in and turns the weeping into laughing. The sadness into joy. And the emptiness into fullness."

Did he always talk like a poet? It sounded great right then. But it might be weird when life was normal. Then again, would life ever be normal again? Was it ever before? Maybe it was time to create a new normal.

"All right. So let's see what we can do about getting you here as soon as possible."

"I'm homeless as of Thursday. I'd like to spend Thanksgiving with my mom and sisters. So I could leave Friday. If that's too soon, I could probably stay with my dad until you are ready for me to come if I have to."

"Nope. Friday is a good day. We'll book you a flight and get the information to you. Will you be able to get to the airport, or do you need us to arrange for transportation?"

"I think I'll have a ride. Can I call you back if I don't?" Mom might have trouble borrowing a car the day after Thanksgiving. She could ask Dad. . .but. . .

"Absolutely. Can I pray for you?"

Here we go.

※

"I can't believe you're actually doing it. You're moving away? To Colorado? I thought it was all a big joke or something." Harper's lower lids filled with tears. "How can you leave us?" She sank to her knees on the carpet in front of the couch.

Mom clicked off the television.

"I have to go so I can come back and be the big sister you need me to be." Carmen thought her heart would break at Harper's sad little face. She'd let her sisters down at such a critical stage in their lives.

"Kim. Stay strong, okay? Don't do something stupid like I did. Promise me." Would Kim finally speak to her? It had been days. Thanksgiving dinner was silent. "It's so hard to know you hate me. I love you, Kim." Carmen turned to leave the room.

"I don't hate you." Kim pounded her fists on the coffee table. "I just. . . I don't understand any of it. And I'm scared. And I'm mad. You were supposed to be the strong one. The smart one. Now what am I supposed to do? I needed you!"

"I know. I don't have a lot of answers for you yet. But I'm going to get them. Can you wait? Will you keep yourself safe and out of trouble until I get back and can help you through all of this?"

Kimberley nodded.

"Do you promise me?"

Kim locked eyes with her big sister. "I mean, yeah. Fine. I'll be good. Is that what you want to hear? I just think it's selfish and wrong that it has to be this way."

"It's totally fair to feel like that, sis—to be angry. I wish it could be different. It's just. . . Oh man, I've messed up my whole life, and I need a fresh start. Can you find a way to pray for me and want the best for me?"

"Of course I want the best for you, you big dummy. I just can't figure out what happened to you. I guess you're right. Maybe you do need to do this." Kim shook her head. "I know I could never do it. No way."

Kim was stronger than she knew. She wouldn't have to do this because she'd never find herself in such a predicament. "Trust me. It's not easy. But I think it may be my only chance."

"I think I understand."

Carmen's shoulders sank as tension flooded away. An unfamiliar tugging of a smile tickled her face as she embraced Kim.

Harper scooted over on her knees and joined the huddle.

How long had it been since Carmen felt freedom from guilt and regret? Was that a permanent possibility, or was she sentenced to a lifetime of mourning?

ॶ

Carmen pushed open a door exactly like the one she'd stared

at during her own days in the hospital last week. "So when are they busting you out of here?" Would Diego be allowed to go home, or would they haul him off to jail right away?

"Hey! It's my girlfriend. Come sit by Diego. He could use some company."

That made two of them. Carmen slid onto the bed beside Diego and leaned her head on his shoulder. How had their friendship become so close? It seemed sort of ridiculous. Like they needed each other to get through the junk. "Seriously, though, when do you get out?"

"Oh, believe me, I'm not in any big hurry to leave the hospital. I'll be going from here to jail. And then probably prison."

"Yeah, I thought that might be the case." Why did he talk normal when he wasn't around his friends? Who was he pretending for? Her or them?

"So, it's fine if they want to keep me around. The food's better here. The nurses are way hotter than the guards." Diego shrugged.

"Typical male." Carmen's nervous laugh croaked out more like a cackle.

They watched a string of dust wave from the ceiling vent across the room.

She'd been a complete stranger to him, yet he'd sacrificed so much for her and asked nothing in return. Carmen grabbed his hand. "I'm really sorry."

"You got nothing to apologize for. If I didn't get busted now, it would have been soon. And the next one mighta killed me."

Carmen nodded. Probably very true.

"Okay. So what now? What happens to us?" Was there an *us*? Would they stay in touch and remain friends? Would Carmen have a pen pal in prison? Or should they cut their losses and say good-bye? How did something like this work?

"What happens now is you go get your life back together. You live a good one. Have a family when the time is right. Be the person you were meant to be, which is someone pretty special." Diego smiled.

Carmen poked at a hole in the thin blanket. "What about you?"

"Me? It'll be awhile before I have that chance, but I'd like to think it'll come one day."

"Diego?"

"Hmm?"

"I think you're a big phony. I think you're the best gangbanger *actor* there is, but it's not you." Carmen slid from the bed and took his hands. She looked into his eyes. "Listen to me. No matter what other people tell you, you are a special person. You have a lot of great qualities, and my life wouldn't have been the same without you in it. Take that with you. Make it a part of who you are. You define who you are. Don't let other people do it for you."

"Word." His eyes twinkled. "Diego gets it."

Carmen kissed him on the cheek. "Some things never change."

⟳

"Do you have everything you need?" Mom stood beside the open trunk of the car she'd borrowed from a Mary Kay friend to take Carmen to the airport.

"Now don't go getting all maternal, Mom. You'll start crying if you do." Carmen didn't think she could take looking at her mom's cheeks lined with tears another time.

"Oh, I'm going to cry, you'd better believe it." She looked down at Carmen's luggage being wheeled away for curbside check-in. "Are you sure I shouldn't be going with you to help you get settled and, you know, check things out?"

She was the one who had forced Carmen's hand out of love. Now she was waffling for the same reason. "Nope. I need to do this on my own. You know what they say, I got myself into this mess. . . ."

Mom nodded. "Yeah, I can see why you'd feel that way, but it's still hard to let go." She grabbed Carmen's chin. "You know I don't want you to leave. I want you where you belong, sleeping down the hall from me every night. But circumstances being what they are, I believe this is the best way to get that back." She peered into Carmen's eyes. "You understand what I'm saying, right?"

"Yes. I do." Oh no. The tears stung behind her eyelids. Carmen took a deep breath. "Let's make it short and sweet. I'm going to go through security and get on my plane. You're going to go home. I'll call you when I get there before I have to turn in my phone and then after that as often as I can. Have faith in God and in me. Okay?"

"You got it. I love you." She grabbed her daughter and pulled her close.

"I love you, too." Carmen stepped away from the hug and backed toward the automatic doors. Once they closed in front of her, Carmen gave a little wave and turned away from her mom. She stepped toward the line to security. *Don't cry.* She'd made it this far. *Don't lose it now.* The tears burned. Rapid blinks helped some. *Think of something else. Anything.*

No! Not Nate. Don't go there. What else? Theresa. She was someone safe to think about. Carmen should have given her more of a chance. She probably could have used a friend, and it was pretty obvious Theresa had conflict in her life. Wonder if she'd have been interested in a friendship with Carmen? What would it have been like to be raised by a pastor? The line inched forward as Carmen compared her life to the one she assumed Theresa had. She'd always seemed happy enough though.

"Ticket and photo ID please." The TSA agent glared at Carmen.

Relax, lady. Wonder what would happen if Carmen said *bomb.* Not shouted it, just whispered the word. Would they arrest her?

"Okay, you're clear. Step over there."

Carmen got in line behind the other sock-footed travelers and shuffled her belongings through the line. She'd never traveled alone before. Was she crazy for doing this? Was this too extreme? Maybe she was ready to face her past and deal with it on her own. She felt different. . .maybe different was enough. It was a lot to ask for a girl her age to leave everything she knew, get on a plane, and fly to the complete unknown in search of something she'd never experienced, with no real guarantees she'd find it. What was it that compelled her to get on that plane waiting at the gate even then? What propelled her to put one foot in front of the other and walk through the security checkpoint, submitting to the stares of strangers?

Blind faith. . .or pure stupidity?

Chapter 21

Where would the plane fly off to next? Carmen could just sit in her seat and soar to some island getaway. Maybe she'd luck out and find she'd booked herself on a plane destined for Aruba after it dropped its load in Denver. She'd just catch a ride to where the family had vacationed the summer before Carmen turned fifteen. Such a happy time. Had the trip really only been two and a half years ago? How did a lifetime's worth of experiences fit into the space of two short years?

Following the lead of the other passengers, Carmen gathered her bag and iPhone and shuffled through the plane's exit door. What did they call the corridor leading from the plane to the airport? The gangway? Felt more like a gangplank. Like the pilot was a pirate and the airplane was a ship. Carmen, forced to walk to the end of the plank and fall into the raging sea to face certain death, moved forward as if compelled by an unseen force.

Oh, come on, Carmen. Get a grip and quit with the extreme drama. Going to Diamond Estates was her own choice because she'd messed up. No one had tied her up and stowed her on that plane, and no one would force her to stay there if she didn't want to. And the people there weren't out to get her. In fact, they wanted to help her.

Okay. Pep talk helped some.

Now, where to find her luggage? The overhead signs pointed to the escalator for baggage claim. She strode to the one closest to her and walked out onto the top step. Carmen searched the floor below, hoping for some sign of where she needed to go once she reached the bottom. Dad had always said to act confident and never let people see if she was confused or out of her league. First rule of sales, he said. Navigating an airport and meeting up with a stranger wasn't exactly a sales meeting—but, then again, all of life required selling something, whether a tangible product or an intangible ideal to someone.

Was Ben over there leaning on the Dollar Rent A Car counter? Couldn't be. That guy looked too relaxed and casual. A Broncos sweatshirt and jeans? Ben was more high strung than the dude over there—more glitzy. If it was him, he sure was a far cry from the shiny gray suit he'd worn to church when his group visited. The man checked his iPhone. Smiled. Typed something out on the display. Turned his face just a bit as the escalator completed its descent. Yep, it was Ben all right.

Carmen's stomach flipped. Why so nervous now? Ben looked like a normal-enough guy. But maybe that was part of the problem. The whole situation began to feel a little too real for Carmen's comfort. In just a moment, when she ran out of escalator floor beneath her feet, she'd have to communicate with Ben Bradley and would then be connected to him and to a place she'd once thought was crazy. Three more steps. Two. One. And, the end.

Act confident. Carmen stepped onto the carpet, repositioned the straps of her bag on her shoulder, flipped her hair back, and plowed over to Ben. She put out her hand. "Ben Bradley?"

He startled but took her hand in the same moment. "Carmen?"

She nodded. "In the flesh."

His smile broadened as he pumped her hand. "I'm so glad you've arrived. I'm sorry if I seem caught off guard. I thought your plane had a few more minutes before it landed. Welcome to Denver."

Awkward. "Thanks." Carmen looked beyond the people milling around them. "I'm, uh, going to go get my stuff." She stepped in the direction of the baggage carousel.

"Will you be able to manage it on your own? I'm waiting for one other person and want to make sure I don't miss her."

"Oh, sure. I can handle it fine." Wonder who he was waiting for? Another new girl or someone else? Hopefully it would be another new girl—sharing the arrival with someone else would take some of the focus off Carmen. Unless the girl was annoying. Come to think of it, what would it be like to share a house with twenty or more girls? If it was anything like living with her sisters. . .oh no. The bags sailed by on the conveyor belt. Carmen searched for the polka-dotted Kate Spade knockoffs. Couldn't miss them.

The smaller of her two bags approached on the belt. Carmen yanked it to the floor beside her. There came the second one. What if she let it pass and make another round through the airport on the baggage system? It would buy her a few minutes before having to reunite with Ben for more awkwardness.

No real point. Might as well face the day. *Act confident.* Maybe if she kept telling herself that, the confidence would ooze through her pores. Carmen grabbed her suitcase handle and pulled it off the runner, knocking the smaller one to the floor. She righted it, turned them to face the same direction, grabbed on, and pulled them toward where Ben had stood just minutes before.

He was gone. Great. Now what? She scanned the area. Tons of Broncos sweatshirts. It was Denver during football season after all. But no familiar face. Where could he be?

A touch on her elbow sent shivers up her arm. Carmen whirled around.

"Hey, sorry to startle you. Are you ready? Leila's already in the van outside. Her luggage came in on the other carousel." Ben nodded his head toward the sliding doors.

"Ready as I'll ever be." Carmen turned to find her bags to pull, but Ben had already grabbed them and was striding toward the van with the magnetic DIAMOND ESTATES sign on the side.

Carmen tried to peer into the smoky glass. Who would she find on the other side of it? She pulled open the door to find the only occupant sleeping—or pretending to sleep, smart girl—right behind the driver's seat with her head on the window beside her. Interesting development. Well, at least it would give Carmen time to study up on the details while Ben drove.

Making her way past the first bench, Carmen was carful not to bump it. Let the girl sleep. She passed the second bench and settled into the back one. Hopefully Ben wouldn't find her seating choice rude, but at this point, he couldn't possibly have a stellar opinion of her anyway.

He settled into his seat, waved into the rearview mirror, and pulled away from the curb. He turned on some light music.

Even better. Carmen slipped in her earbuds. It felt like time for some Usher. She leaned back to watch the scenery float by. Even she had to admit it was pretty exciting to know she'd be up in the mountains very soon. So different to actually be living there than taking a week-long vacation like the ski trips the family took most years. Not anymore.

Would she get to ski while she was in Denver—the ski capital of America? Maybe Dad could send her stuff.

What was the deal with the girl up there? She seemed kind

of plain. Cute maybe—in an isn't-my-guinea-pig-cute? sort of way—chubby definitely. Her curly hair, parted in the middle, hung in frizzy ringlets past her shoulders. From the looks of the outgrowth, the highlights had to be six months old. So did she not care enough to get the highlights updated, or was she broke? But really, how much could a box of Clairol cost? And the glasses. Ugh. They sat crooked across the bridge of her freckled nose. Ah, maybe not. Looked like part freckles, part zits.

What could she have done to land her in Diamond Estates? She sure didn't look like the kind of girl who got messed up with boys. Or rather, the kind of girl boys noticed. Maybe her issue was a drug thing.

It would sure be interesting to find out the stories of all the girls. Nellie was in for a real treat.

Carmen gripped the headrest in front of her to keep from toppling over as the van hung a sharp right.

Ben pulled up to a gas pump, turned the ignition, and pulled out the keys. "I'm going to get some gas. Why don't you move up here and chat with me, Carmen?" He gestured to the passenger seat beside him. "We can let Leila sleep." He climbed down from the van and approached the pump.

Oh great. Small talk with Ben Bradley. Just what she'd had in mind. There was probably no appropriate way to get out of it. Carmen sighed and stepped past the middle bench. She hesitated before moving past the one where Leila slept. If she tripped and fell into the seat back, Leila would wake up and have to share in the misery. But what if she was annoying, too? Carmen eased past and climbed between the captain's chairs into the passenger's seat.

Ben grinned and opened the door. "Good. I've got company for the ride up the mountain."

Oh goody.

Better take charge before he started asking a bunch of questions. Carmen was sure that would come later. "So how did you get involved with Diamond Estates?" That should keep him talking.

"When I was a teenager, I could have used a place like this. So could my wife, Alicia." Ben smiled. "We were high school sweethearts. So in love."

Just like Carmen and Nate.

"But we made some bad choices our senior year, and Alicia got pregnant. We got married, had our son, Justin, and set off to find the truth."

That simple, huh? "Wow. So why a place like this, and why did you choose to work with girls?"

"Diamond Estates was an idea the Lord birthed in our hearts when Alicia and I looked back over our struggle. We realized that staying in the midst of our situations while we were trying to change had made it much more difficult than it needed to be." He glanced at Carmen. "The Lord showed me how sometimes teens need to be plucked out of their environment so they can focus on getting healthy."

Actually made a little sense. "I can see what you mean. But why girls?"

"Ask God." Ben shrugged. "It's what Alicia and I both felt called to do."

Carmen searched her brain for something else to ask Ben so he wouldn't turn the questions to her. "You said you had a son, Justin. Any others?"

"Nope." Ben's eyes darkened for an instant. "Justin's an only child."

Hmm. There was a story there.

The van turned into a clearing and passed under some low

branches that scraped the top.

Leila sat up and rubbed the sleep from her eyes. Guess some of the snoozing had been real. Probably not all though.

Ben glanced at Carmen and then back at Leila and said, "Welcome home, girls."

Carmen stared out the window at a grand stone mansion. She could almost reach back in time and hear the monks chanting. Beyond the main house stood a barn with a wide pasture behind it that curved around the mountain. Horses nuzzled at the dusting of snow to uncover the still-green grass.

Curlicue reached her fingers beneath her glasses and rubbed her eyes. "Was I asleep the whole ride?"

Ben laughed. "I guess that's what thirteen hours of travel will do to you." He looked at Carmen. "Leila and Carmen. You two will have lots of time to get acquainted as we go through the orientation procedures today."

"Great!" Leila turned and flashed a silver smile at Carmen.

Leila looked like a needy puppy dog with those thick glasses and braces—the kind of girl who wanted you to be her *best friend forever and ever.* Carmen didn't do the whole BFF thing—Leila would find out soon enough. Where was she from anyway? Thirteen hours of travel. Did he mean straight flying or with layovers? It was like a big mystery. Time to put on her CSI hat.

❧

"This is a perfect time for me to give you a tour since the house is empty with everyone out skiing for the day."

Carmen's ears perked up. "Oh? They get to ski?"

"You bet. We have an agreement with Beaver Creek. We go up there once a month to clean the grounds, and they let us ski for free."

Carmen nodded. Beaver Creek? Didn't Dad have clients there? Maybe she could ask for some free passes and skip the cleaning.

They entered through the tallest door Carmen had ever seen. She waited for it to swing shut behind her and lock itself like in horror movies.

Ben pulled the door closed and left it unlocked.

Had she expected it to be like jail? Metal gates shutting the girls into eight-by-eight cells? Not exactly, but. . . Well, maybe that is what she expected subconsciously. This was at least better than the prison she'd imagined.

Carmen let her gaze travel the expansive foyer. Candles flickering in sconces shone an eerie glow onto the buttery walls. The wooden staircase spiraled up to the unknown. Several entryways led from the foyer.

"Where are the bedrooms? Or is it one big dorm like in *Little Orphan Annie*?" Carmen searched her surroundings.

Ben laughed. "In no way is it like *Annie,* unless you like to make up song and dance numbers."

Uh. No.

"It's four to a room. We'll go up there and get you settled a little later. Let's finish the tour of the downstairs and then have a little chat in my office before the rest of the house gets home."

Leila pranced along at Ben's feet. Lapping up every word he said on the tour. At least with her around, Carmen could hang back and not be expected to respond to every single thing he said. It gave her a chance to check things out.

Ben took a few long strides toward the arched opening nearest the front door. "Come right through here. This is my favorite room in the house." He stood back to let them pass.

"Those windows are amazing." Leila turned in a full circle, her mouth open wide with awe. She reached a hand to touch the one closest to her. A stained-glass depiction of the resurrection of Christ.

Eww. Gross. If Leila chewed her fingernails any shorter,

she'd hit the bone. That aside, she was right. The windows lining the room really were a work of art. "They're pretty cool." Neat how they did the nativity scene with baby Jesus in gold so it looked like he glowed.

"This room is my favorite because I feel like I'm surrounded with history—with *the* story." Ben's eyes grew misty. "These windows tell the story of God's love and passionate pursuit of His beloved throughout all of time."

"I can see what you mean." Leila let her fingers trail over the yellow glass where the sunlight radiated on the tomb where Jesus had lain.

Carmen surveyed the space. "What's this room for?" A stage? Clusters of pillows on the floor, but no real furniture of any kind? Weird.

"This is the prayer room. We meet in here every single morning for quiet time with God. Some people spend the time alone. Others like to pray in groups."

Prayer time, she'd expected. But. . . "The stage?"

"Oh, we don't use that anymore. There was a time when we had our own church services here, but now we drive down the mountain to attend a local congregation."

Carmen nodded. What had she gotten herself into? She'd be expected to go to church every week. . .hopefully only once. She'd probably have to pray. Not out loud. No way would she pray out loud. And they'd make her study her Bible. At least she had her personalized one from Mom.

"Moving on." Ben strode from the room then turned left down a hallway lined with doors. He touched the first one on his right. "This is the women's restroom."

Leila pushed the door open a crack and peeked inside. "Smells good. Like powder." She smiled.

"Alicia, my wife, likes to keep things feminine around here."

He poked his head in and smiled. "She says if I had my way there'd be plaid wallpaper with deer antlers and a bear-skin rug in every room. She's probably right."

Good thing Alicia decorated.

Ben stopped in front of a swinging door with a window. "We're about to enter the kitchen. Marilyn is getting things ready for dinner, so we won't bother her too long." He held the door back and let the girls pass him.

"Hey, Marilyn. What's for dinner?"

With the ground beef up to Marilyn's elbows and the piles of potatoes beside her jiggly belly, Carmen took a guess. "Mmm. Meatloaf and mashed potatoes."

"That's right." Marilyn grinned, her cheeks pink. "You going to introduce us, Ben?" She rolled her eyes at the girls like a coconspirator.

Could it be? A normal person? Had she found an ally among the staff? Carmen smiled back.

"Marilyn, these two young ladies are Leila and Carmen. They're moving in today."

Carmen wished he'd stop saying that. "Well, I'm staying here for a while. I wouldn't exactly say moving in." A temporary arrangement.

Marilyn's eyes sparkled. "I get it, honey. The idea takes some getting used to. But trust me. When you get a taste of this meatloaf, you'll change your address right quick."

Ben held up his cell phone. "I'll be in the hallway for just a moment. You three can get to know each other for a minute."

So much for not bothering Marilyn. Carmen took inventory of the industrial kitchen with all the latest appliances. "Do you ever let people cook with you?"

"*Let?* Hah. It's more of a requirement." Marilyn's jowls wobbled when she laughed. "The girls all take turns."

"I love to cook. Since I was little I always wanted to be a chef."
Carmen let her gaze travel to the floor.

"And now?" Marilyn stared so intently, Carmen felt compelled
to raise her eyes.

Carmen shrugged. "Now? Oh, who knows? I'm just hoping
to make it through this program. Then I guess I'll think about
what I want to be when I grow up."

Marilyn nodded and shifted her gaze to Leila. "How about
you? What are your plans?"

Lelia shrugged. "I'd like to be an adoption lawyer or an
international adoption liaison."

Where had that come from? The chubby girl with braces
must be smart. And why adoption? Usually people with sordid
pasts wanted to be social workers or psychologists. The adoption
angle must play into Leila's history somehow.

When she got her hands on a notebook, she needed to fill
Nellie in. Page one: Ben Bradley. Page two: Leila. . . ? "Hey,
what's your last name anyway?"

Leila blinked. "Wong." She turned her back to them and
seemed to take in the rest of the room.

Wong? Carmen mouthed to Marilyn.

Marilyn shrugged.

Carmen nodded. There was a story there.

Chapter 22

This was a joke, right? Carmen stared at the list of Diamond Estates rules and regulations. It went on for pages and pages.

"I know it must seem like a lot. In fact, we've recently revised this list, and the line items more than tripled when we did the revisions. We found that by keeping things simple as we had in the past left too much room for confusion—too many things left open to interpretation." Ben rocked back in his swivel chair and clasped his hands behind his head. "This way we all know what to expect from each other."

Carmen flipped through the booklet. Rule twenty-two said there could be no communication or exchange of personal information with non-DE people off campus. Number twenty-three focused on makeup. Twenty-four was skirt length. "Can I speak frankly?"

"Sure. We encourage openness here, Carmen. As long as you're respectful."

Carmen's head shook side to side like a bobblehead with Parkinson's. Not that her protest would do a bit of good. "Respectfully, I think this is a crock."

Leila gasped, and her chin about hit the floor.

Ben's eyebrows rose, but he said nothing as he waited for Carmen to go on.

"I mean, you can force me into the mold of a perfect girl,

but that doesn't make it true. Is it a real change if I'm only acting a certain way because of your rules? Shouldn't it be because it's what I want to do?"

"You've actually just keyed into an important aspect of the idea of free will—a very basic tenet of the Christian faith. We'll be covering free will in great detail during the coming weeks, but in essence, what you're saying is true."

Right on. He agreed with her. Carmen could get used to that.

"I can't force you to be a follower of Christ. But I can make you function as someone who won't be a stumbling block to others and who won't allow worldly stuff to get in the way of the movement of the Holy Spirit—at least while you're here."

What could she say in response? In a weird voodoo sort of way, it made sense. "I just don't know if I can remember all these rules, let alone follow them." Carmen turned to Leila and gestured at the packet. "What about you? What do you think about all this?"

Leila shrugged, looked away, and gave a wavering smile. "I'll do whatever they want me to do. I don't have any problem following rules."

Then what *was* her problem? Was she always so totally agreeable? A people pleaser.

Had Leila made eye contact with anyone even once? Maybe with Marilyn. Carmen searched her memory but couldn't conjure the image.

Leila had pretty eyes behind those thick glasses, but she needed to learn how to use them. And, though she was ready with a silvery smile at all times, Leila needed to grow a backbone before she'd have any hope of making it in a place like this. Surely the girls at Diamond Estates would be tough as nails and out for blood. Maybe Carmen could watch out for her like Diego had looked out for Carmen—well, not exactly the same way. But first she had to find out what Leila was in for.

🌀

Ben approached a closed door and pulled a ring of keys out of his pocket. "The bedrooms are all at the top of these stairs."

"It's locked?" Even though it might be fancier than jail, being locked away in a tower like Rapunzel had much the same feel to it.

"Sure, when no one is home or not supposed to be up there. The lock doesn't work from the reverse. You can always get out. The fire marshal wouldn't appreciate it if we trapped you all in your second-floor rooms." Ben laughed like he was a one-man comedy show. At least Carmen wouldn't be triggering some latent fear of confined spaces. She'd never been claustrophobic before, but being locked in could definitely have done it.

"What's the deal with the graffiti?" Lelia ran her hand along the graphic walls of the stairway.

"Oh, isn't that fun? A few months ago we decided to let the girls choose a section of wall space to decorate however they'd like."

"You got some girls with some mad art skillz." Carmen heard the Hackensack in her dialect. She couldn't help it in the face of the territorial designs. Did Ben understand the paintings for what they were? She stopped in front of an upside-down crown with *Latin Kings* written across it. Beside it was a glowing crown with *King of Kings* scripted across its center. Hmm. Signaling someone's transformation? "Who painted this one?"

"Oh, that section is Ju-Ju's. She graduated about a few months ago. You'll meet her soon—you'll have to ask her about her design. It's a beautiful story."

"I remember her from my church."

Ju-Ju's words came flooding back to Carmen. She'd had it rough—to take care of herself all alone she had to be strong. Was she stronger than Carmen?

What would Carmen paint on the wall if she had the opportunity? Right now? A black hole. Hopefully one day soon she'd have a different picture in mind.

"And here we are." Ben opened a door and gestured for them to enter the bedroom. "This is your room."

"Both of us?" Carmen took in the two sets of bunk beds. No way. Bunk beds? Not again.

"Yep. I've got both of you in here with two girls who have been here awhile. They'll help you get through the basics and figure things out here at Diamond."

"Awesome." Leila looked at Carmen with those hopeful BFF eyes.

Oh boy.

Ben looked around the room. "I see your belongings have already been brought up for you. So unless you have any other questions right now, I'll leave you to get settled." He backed out the doorway. "There's a phone out here on the wall. It calls 911 or rings in the staff quarters. Feel free to call on us if you have any problems or needs. We'll see you downstairs for dinner at five thirty."

Ben left, taking *the force* with him. His energy had filled this space, and now it seemed hollow.

Carmen stepped across the room to a closed doorway. "Ah, a bathroom. It's pretty nice. Double sink. Separate shower. Cool." Time to unpack. She turned back to the room.

Leila hadn't moved an inch. "Where do you want to sleep?" She nodded at the unoccupied bunk bed. "Top or bottom?"

If Carmen had been her, she'd have snatched her top choice immediately. "What do you prefer?" Would the top bunk even hold Leila's weight?

"I don't care; you pick."

Carmen would never have chosen the top under different

circumstances, but fear of being crushed to death made a person do crazy things. "Okay then. I'm going with the top."

Lelia nodded like she'd assumed the top would be Carmen's choice.

Crawling from end to end on her bunk as she tugged the fitted sheet into place, Carmen felt a twinge of nostalgia. She'd had these sheets for years. As she smoothed her favorite blanket out, the sense of longing for home grew heightened in this strange place.

The room was silent except for the zippers of their suitcases and the sliding of drawers. *Say something.* Hardly ever at a loss for words, even though she often chose not to use them, Carmen searched for something to say.

So, what brings you to. . . No. That was rude.

Do you miss home? No. Why rub her nose in it?

What do you really think of this place? No. Leila would be all sunshine and roses.

"So, meatloaf for dinner?" Leila's words intruded the silence.

That's what she picked as a conversation opener? Meatloaf. "Yeah. Smelled like it might be good." Carmen shrugged. Who cared?

"I didn't know it would be like this. It looked like the tables in there were set up like a restaurant. Want to sit with me at dinner?" Leila looked down at her hands and pulled at a Claddagh ring stuck around her middle finger. The ring didn't move.

"Why not? No one wants to eat alone, right?"

Leila nodded. "That's like my biggest fear—that I'd have to sit there at a table by myself like every day in school."

Carmen's heart sank. Poor girl. "Well, as far as I'm concerned, you can eat with me every day." Not like offers were beating down Carmen's door. But maybe soon they would be.

But. . .oh no. What if some cooler girls wanted Carmen to

join them, but now she'd promised Leila? How would she break her promise? Well, she'd have to face that dilemma when it happened. At least for now she wouldn't be eating alone.

"Is your finger okay?" The puffiness probably didn't matter, but the red looked menacing.

Leila grimaced. "My ring is stuck. I'm not sure how to get it off. I should have never put it on, but I wanted to wear it."

"Come with me. We'll get it off." Carmen gestured toward the bathroom, where she ran Leila's hand under cool water and squirted some soap from the wall dispenser right onto the ring. It grew slippery, and Carmen shimmied it off Leila's hand.

"Oh, great. I had no idea what I was going to do. Thanks." Leila rubbed her sore knuckle.

Carmen rinsed the ring and then inspected it. "It's an Irish thing, isn't it? What's it called?"

"It's a Claddagh ring. There are a few legends about what it means, but yeah, it's Irish."

"Cool." Carmen handed it back to her. Her fingers rubbed the spot where her engagement ring had been.

Lelia glanced in the mirror, pulled the sleeves of her white Maui sweatshirt down past her wrists, and gripped them in her fists. She left the bathroom, climbed into the lower bunk, and pulled a paperback from her carry-on.

Looked like social time was over.

What was Carmen supposed to do? Could she go explore the grounds by herself? Or was she expected to stay in her room and wait? She probably wasn't free to inspect outside, but maybe they weren't even allowed to wander the house alone. Surprisingly there wasn't anything like that in the rules, except where it said she had to keep to the schedule at all times. As far as she knew, she had nowhere to go, and wandering didn't seem to be breaking the rules. Like Dad always said, it's a lot easier to ask forgiveness than permission.

Carmen looked at her watch. The rest of the girls wouldn't be back for more than an hour still.

A snore came from the bottom bunk.

That settled it. Carmen reached for her cell phone—oh right, confiscated—and bolted from the room before she changed her mind.

She walked down the hallway, sure no one would be around, then crept down the stairs, hoping they wouldn't squeak. At the bottom of the stairs, she opened the door one inch at a time. What was she so afraid of? It's not like Ben could fault her. She wasn't told where to be or what to do.

A right turn and a short walk led her to a door she hadn't seen yet. Probably locked. Carmen put her hand on the ancient knob. *Please don't open to Ben Bradley on the toilet.* Maybe she should knock. But that would give her presence away to anyone nearby. She turned the handle as slowly as the second hand of a clock. It opened easily. Was the lock broken?

She peered through the doorway and waited as her eyes adjusted to the dim light. A dirt-and-stone stairway looking like it had been carved right into the mountainside led down to cavernous darkness. Now what? She'd come this far. But how could she walk down the stairs in such a creepy place and enter a room or, whatever, blindly? Was she crazy?

A foot lowered onto the first step. Apparently she was.

Another step.

Carmen waited for a creak. Of course none came. The earth itself didn't make scary noises.

Toes reached below for another step.

Seventeen stairs later, Carmen felt both feet on a landing of some sort. She patted the earth around where she stood. Why was there no light? Something tickled her face, and she squelched a scream. She waved her hands in front of her face in case it was a spider. But if not a spider, what?

There. Carmen grasped a string of some kind and pulled. Light flooded the narrow space. She stood inches from a wooden door. Of course she would open it. She hadn't come so far to turn back without knowing where the journey would have ended. She wriggled to the side, but the space was too small to open the door while she stood beside it, so Carmen backed up three steps, reached forward, and swung it open.

Cool air blasted her face. Was she outside? Carmen peered through the doorway. Another hallway? No, more like a passageway.

She stepped through, leaving her sanity somewhere on the stairs behind her. Was she starring in some weird horror movie?

The lower ceiling forced Carmen to hunch over, and she crept along the dark tunnel that smelled of minerals and musty earth. The scent reminded her of family trips to Meramec Cavern in Missouri. Exploring the caves and running her fingers across the stalactites and stalagmites—one went up and one went down. Carmen could never remember which was which. . .but Dad always knew.

She plodded on and on in that weird half-hunched position. When would she reach the end? What would be there when she did? And what if the door was locked when she got back? Nah. One thing at a time. No sense letting her nerves get the best of her.

Wham! The top of her head banged into something solid. Carmen rubbed her skull then patted the object with both hands. It was cool like metal, but smooth and flat like a door. Where was the handle? Ah. There it was. A little lower than where it should have been.

Locked.

Carmen felt the dirt wall on both sides of her body. Her hand brushed against something—a key! She carefully placed her hand over it and closed her fist around it so she wouldn't knock it down. It would be difficult to bend over and search the confined area in the dark.

The key slipped easily into the lock, and Carmen readied herself to move through. It opened without a squeak or moan. Carmen leaned forward into the mountain air. Outside. She was outside, beyond the house quite a ways. Behind the horse barn? It hadn't felt like she'd walked that far, but she must have.

This had to be against the rules. She'd better get back before she got caught.

Maybe she should tell someone about how easy it was for her to get out.

Or maybe she'd keep that tidbit of info to herself. At least for now.

Feeling her way back along the passage, Carmen tripped over her feet and stumbled forward, planting her face in the dirt. She sputtered and spat, flecks of mud flying from her teeth. Gross. She stood as high as she could and brushed the front of her pants. Why had she worn her light jeans that day?

Her back throbbing from being bent over for so long, Carmen hurried on. The slight chance that the door would be locked and she'd never be found niggled at her and hurried her along.

Finally back at the doorway to the stairs that would take her up to the main house, Carmen stepped through and pulled her body fully upright. She stretched her arms up and lengthened her spine then pulled the cord, dousing the light. Seventeen stairs back to the top.

Carmen's shoulder bumped into the closed door at the top. She reached for the door handle, prepared to turn it slowly so as not to alert anyone to her presence. Hopefully she could make it back to her room, change, and maybe even shower before anyone realized she'd been gone.

Her wrist turned the knob. Nothing happened. She tried again. The handle didn't move even a fraction of an inch.

Locked.

Chapter 23

Who would have locked it without looking to see if someone was in there? Unless it was like the bedrooms and locked automatically. Which would make sense for security purposes, but made things really tricky for Carmen.

Carmen needed a moment to figure things out, so she sat on the top step.

She had to get out of there. What could she do? No matter how she did it, she'd be in trouble. If she pounded away on the door, someone would come, but it might be Ben. If not him, maybe a staff member or one of the girls, and then word would get around that she'd been prowling around outside. If she went back through the passage and tried to use the front entrance, which Ben hadn't locked, she'd almost surely bump into him.

Carmen had no choice. She'd have to knock and face whatever happened.

Tap. Tap. If it were possible to whisper a knock, Carmen managed to do it several times. But no one came. Maybe no one was out there. She'd wait until she heard voices or footsteps.

Minutes went by and turned into what felt like hours.

Was that laughter? Carmen pressed her ear against the door and wished for supersonic hearing. Yes. The sound was definitely laughing.

She carefully knocked loud enough that they would hear

her, but quietly enough that hopefully no one else would.

"Did you hear that?"

"I think so. Was it knocking?"

"Do you think?"

"We could look."

Yes. Great idea. Look. Carmen knocked two more times a bit harder.

"Here, help me open it." Sounded like feet scrambling on the floor just outside.

Should she talk to them? They hadn't spoken to her. Kind of odd the girls weren't worried about who they were letting in.

The space opened up to bright light shining around two smiling faces. Carmen's rescuers. She recognized one as the beautiful black goddess who'd visited her church. What was her name?

The other girl—compact like a gymnast and blond—was a complete stranger. "Carmen, I presume? What on earth are you doing out here?"

"Um. . .just checking things out?" Carmen shrugged. Would these girls turn her in?

"Hey. I'm Tricia, this is Kira."

Carmen let her eye adjust to the light. Ah. Tricia. That was it.

Carmen dusted a hand off on her already-soiled jeans and reached it out. "Carmen."

The girls nodded, a smile tugging at the corners of their mouths. "We're your new roommates."

Laughter bubbled to the surface and spewed over.

Kira's ponytail bobbed. "Yeah, it's a really odd predicament to get yourself in on your first day here. Whatever possessed you to go in there?"

Carmen shrugged. "Just adventurous, I guess."

"Well, you'd better get back up to the room and clean up

before someone finds out." Tricia fought against the laughter.

"You mean they don't know?" But would they soon? "Nah. Kira and I got back from skiing and found one girl sleeping on the bottom bunk and the other nowhere to be found. That's almost never a good sign." She chuckled. "Can't say I've ever found someone out here. Finding and using the phone is the typical new-girl scheme." Tricia began to walk toward the bedroom stairs.

Carmen followed closely. She might actually get away with her foolishness. "So you're my roommates?" Great first impression. She'd have to be a lot more careful from now on.

"In the flesh." Kira flashed a million-dollar smile. "We'll get along fine, I'm sure. Only. . ."

"Only what?" What could Carmen have done already? Well, besides the obvious.

Kira looked at Tricia and jerked her head back toward Carmen. "Ask her."

"That girl sleeping up in the room right now, have you heard her snoring? It's like a train rumble." Tricia grimaced. "I mean, I don't want to gossip or be mean, but I've got to get my sleep."

"We'll figure something out." Kira smiled and nodded as a girl passed them looking horrified at Carmen's appearance. "In the meantime, we need to get her back to the room so she can pay the shower a nice long visit before dinner."

"Oh, and about dinner." Tricia grinned as she held open the door to the staircase up to the dorms. "You can sit with us."

Oh great.

⑤

"Feel better?" Tricia looked up from her magazine when Carmen let the steam out of the bathroom.

"Yeah. I was pretty grimy."

"I'll bet you were." Kira winked.

Carmen slicked as much moisture from her long, thick hair as possible. There was no way it would dry before dinner, even if she pulled out the blow dryer. She twisted it into a knot and secured it with a giant claw clip.

Leila bustled around her dresser and bed area, still wearing her travel clothes. Come to think of it, her sleeping clothes, too. And where were all her bags? Was that why she made it to the van so fast? No suitcase?

"Looking pretty homey over here." Carmen touched the plastic flower leis hanging from the drawer handles and picked up what she assumed was a family photo. She squinted at the faces—no way those super tiny, gorgeous Koreans were Leila's family. The black-haired woman and two teenage girls wore bikinis—and deserved to—and the man was muscular and tanned. They held absolutely no resemblance to Leila at all. "Who are these people? Friends from Hawaii?"

"Let me see." Kira plucked the frame out of Carmen's hand.

"Uh. No. That's my mom, dad, and sisters." Leila busied herself arranging her pillows.

Kira's eyebrows rose two inches as she lifted the picture closer to her face.

Ah. Wong. Adopted. That made sense. But how could Carmen ask for more info? Everything she thought to say came off potentially offensive.

> Carmen: *Are you adopted?*
> Leila: *Why, do I look adopted?*
> Or, Carmen: *Wow, your family is really beautiful.*
> Leila: *Most of us.*
> Or, Carmen: *Want to talk about it?*
> Leila: *Talk about what? How imperfect I am in a*
>   *perfect family?*

Probably best to let Leila bring up whatever she wanted to talk about and then leave the rest alone. Though that did nothing to quell Carmen's curiosity.

An awkward silence blanketed the space. What was a safe topic? "So I hear we're having meatloaf tonight."

Leila shot Carmen a quizzical look.

Tricia nodded. "I can take a hint. Ready for dinner?"

Okay, now what to do about the seating arrangements?

"We can all sit together." Kira practically bounced to the door. "Let's go."

Leila grinned. "Sounds good."

They followed half a dozen other girls down the stairs toward the dining room. Conversations and laughter filled the hallways. Everyone seemed so happy. If the staff handed each of the girls a little paper cup filled with pills, Carmen would know what was up. Happy pills. She wasn't about to get medicated like that. Hopefully that wasn't the case. But there had to be an explanation for why everyone was so cheery.

Oh, except for that girl up ahead. Carmen watched the lone figure slough along to dinner, looking down the whole way. She picked up a tray, set it on the metal bars in front of the serving counter, and slid it past the main course, past the veggies and potatoes, past the drinks, and stopped in front of the pudding and Jell-O. Her black, stringy hair hung in front of her eyes as she selected two red Jell-Os and two vanilla puddings. Without making eye contact with anyone, she selected a seat in the back of the room and sat alone with her back to the rest of the room.

Carmen pushed her tray along the rails and accepted portions of each item offered. Marilyn's famous meatloaf? Carmen would be the judge of that. Unless she'd cracked some eggs in there, dumped in mounds of bread crumbs, and added hunks of onion and green pepper, its only hope was moderate.

But time would tell.

The dessert offerings were amazing. They rivaled the selection at any Old Country Buffet. Carmen chose a frosted brownie then pulled the middle handle on the ice-cream machine for some swirl.

"Isn't that cool? It's new." Tricia bypassed the desserts completely.

"Yeah, it's awesome. I'll have to watch it though. These desserts will be my downfall."

Tricia led the way to a table by the windows. "Oh, trust me, I know."

Oh right. Tricia was the model with the eating disorder. "But you're so thin. You can't possibly struggle with weight."

"I go up and down like everyone else. I've had a really hard time with it over the months and years, but I believe I've finally gotten it under control."

Kira and Leila slid into the seats opposite Carmen and Tricia.

"The ice-cream machine was a donation from a friend of mine—Olivia. I'll have to tell you about her. She graduated from here a little over three months ago."

That story could wait. Carmen already had enough questions about the people she could see. Her gossipy brain would go on overload if she wasn't careful. "So what's her story?" Carmen tipped her head at the sad Goth girl.

"No one knows for sure." Kira's eyes clouded. "She won't talk to anyone. She's been here for about a month and does nothing but what you've already seen."

"You mean she won't tell her story? Or she won't talk at all?" Tricia shook her head. "She doesn't speak at all."

"Ben allows that?" Carmen would have thought he'd require more interaction.

"Sure. She does nothing wrong. She shows up to everything

on time. She seems to listen to the teachers and even participates in her own way in prayer times." Kira shrugged. "So I guess Ben believes she'll come around in time."

Another one for the mystery book.

"Speaking of Ben, here he comes with Donna." Tricia scooted her chair over to make room at the table.

Who was Donna? A blonde who looked like a fitness guru approached the table. What was it with all these gorgeous and perfectly fit women around here? Almost enough to make Carmen diet. And Carmen never dieted.

"Hi there, ladies. Mind if we join you for a minute?" Ben grabbed an empty chair from a nearby table and pulled it over for Donna, who perched on the end of it. He yanked one over for himself and straddled it backward. "Carmen, I'd like you to meet Donna. Donna, Carmen. You'll be spending a lot of time together during the coming months, so I hope you'll find some time to get acquainted before your first counseling session on Monday."

Oh. Ben had mentioned that Carmen would have a counselor. Would she be expected to, like, open up to her or what? How could she meet someone and then no more than a few days later get all personal with her? That would be weird.

"Leila, your counselor will be Tammy. She's away for the weekend, so you'll meet her on Monday."

Leila shrugged. "Sounds good."

Were those the first words Leila had spoken since they sat down to eat? Carmen would have to make sure she drew her out more. Though that probably wasn't her job. Maybe she should worry more about herself and less about everyone else's problems.

Nah. It was way more fun to meddle.

ᔕ

"Time to get up for prayer." Tricia's syrupy voice grated on Carmen's last nerve.

"It's seven thirty in the morning. There's no way I'm getting up to go pray." Leave her toasty covers and her soft pillow in exchange for a stone-cold floor in a cavernous house? How could they expect her to do that? Why would they even want to? If Carmen ran this place, she'd make everyone sleep in and start the day at noon. And then she would, too.

"You have to. It's required." Kira stretched the neck of her sweatshirt to fit over her ponytail.

"What happens if I don't go?" She didn't even claim to know God. Who would she pray to anyway?

"I'm not sure." Kira seemed to think it over. "I don't think anyone's actually tried that one."

"Watch me. What can they do to me? I'm the new girl." Carmen rolled over and pulled a pillow down over her face. She lay huddled in her bed, clutching her blankets while the other three got ready and left for the prayer room.

Right on time, the door clicked into place, and the room grew silent.

Now that was what Carmen was talking about. Peace and quiet. Privacy. She flopped onto her belly and pulled her covers over her head. Sleep. Blessed sleep.

Voices. Laughter.

Carmen strained to make out the sounds. She rubbed her eyes. How long had she slept, and who was in the room? Were they back from prayer time already? That was the problem with sleeping—it was impossible to enjoy while in the middle of doing it. Then it was over.

"Hey, sleepyhead." Tricia's voice came through the blanket. "You'd better get up. They're coming for you."

Chapter 24

Who's *they*?" Her eyes didn't want to open. More sleep.

"Donna, probably. They weren't at all happy you didn't show up to prayer." Kira chuckled. "You should have seen their faces. I don't think they've been that blatantly blown off before."

"I didn't blow anyone off. I just slept." All right, all right. Sleep time over. "What can they do to me, really?" Carmen pulled herself up and jumped down from her bed then reached up and smoothed the covers. They'd like that she made her bed. Should she open her Bible on the desk and pretend she'd been having her own private study time? No, they'd see right through her. And Kira, Tricia, and Leila would know she lied.

Carmen moved toward the bathroom—what if she stayed in there for a while? Would they eventually tire of waiting for her to come out? Or better yet, maybe they'd think she was sick. She stepped up to the left sink beside Kira, who stared in the mirror applying makeup. "So, be honest. Was it awful?"

Kira's eyebrows furrowed. "Was what awful?"

"You know. Quiet time. Prayer time. Whatever they call it here." Carmen put toothpaste on her toothbrush.

"There's nothing horrible about it at all. It's a wonderful way to start the day. You'll see." Kira smiled.

Right. That's what they wanted her to say. No teenager

would welcome that early call to prayer. Unless they lived in India.

"Actually, I used to feel the same way about it as you do. I used to try to find ways to doze. It was fine until I started snoring." She laughed. "I'll never forget the time I was out like a light and woke up to find every single person in the room staring at me."

"Did you get in trouble for nodding off?"

"Not really. I mean, it's not condoned, but it happens sometimes. I guess the goal is that eventually each girl will have a deep-enough relationship with God that she'll naturally want the time for communicating with Him, and that desire will keep her awake."

"But what if I'm not ready for that? If I don't have that relationship or want that communication? Why can't I sleep in?" She spoke around the toothbrush in her mouth.

"Excuse me." Donna stood in the doorway. "I don't mean to interrupt."

Right. Of course she didn't. How much had she heard? Carmen spit into the sink.

"What you just described—you know, the state of your relationship with God—makes this the worst time to skip out on prayer time. Which we know you'd do—anyone would—if given the choice, which is why we don't give you the option."

That didn't make a bit of sense. It would be like showing up to meet a friend for breakfast at a restaurant with no previous agreement and no actual friend. She'd be eating alone. Sleep was better. "I don't get it."

"Here it is. The reason you can't sleep in and skip prayer times when you don't have that personal relationship with Him yet is because we want to make sure you're in the path of receiving it. Ever hear the phrase 'Fake it till you make it'?"

Carmen nodded. What did that have to do with God?

"It's kind of like that." Donna's eyes seemed heavy, almost sad. "But, you know, that's not the point today. Today you blatantly disregarded a rule that's in place for you to uphold whether you like it and agree with it or not. That's a choice you made, and it carries consequences. So come with me."

Carmen rinsed out her toothbrush and put it back in her drawer, dried her hands, and sighed. "Let's go." She followed Donna from the room then turned back to shoot a wink at her roommates. All eyes were on them as they made their way down to the main level. Carmen felt some disapproving stares and noticed a few that were simply quizzical. Those girls probably wondered what was going to happen to Carmen so they could decide if it was worth it to skip prayer time. Maybe Carmen had launched a revolution simply by pressing the proverbial snooze button a few too many times. Wars had been started over less.

But now wasn't the time to be cocky. "I didn't mean anything bad, Donna." Maybe Carmen should have gone with the program and stayed under the radar. "I just wanted to sleep in."

"I understand. But that's part of why you're here at Diamond Estates in the first place. When people react to things or make choices simply based on what they want to do, there are often consequences. Today is no different." Donna pursed her lips. "You made the choice, and now you have to face the results."

Uh-oh. If only Carmen could crawl back in bed and have a redo of the morning.

They stood outside the open door to Ben's office. Donna stepped forward. "Ben? We're here."

He turned his swivel chair and smiled at them. "Well, well. Come on in. Have a seat." A pleasant-looking woman with twinkling eyes and two of the deepest dimples Carmen had ever seen stood right behind him. "Carmen, this lovely lady is my wife, Alicia. She's been dying to meet you."

She just bet. Carmen put out her hand for a shake.

Alicia rushed around to the other side of the desk and pulled Carmen into a smothering embrace. "I'm so glad to meet you, dear."

Carmen mumbled something about being happy to know her, too, then sank into one of the red chairs in front of Ben's desk and stared at her hands in her lap. How embarrassing to meet someone at the moment she was about to hear her sentence.

"So let's make this easy for everyone. I'm confused, Carmen." Ben leaned forward on his elbows. "I don't understand why you would pick something so basic to rebel against and on your very first day. Why?"

She shrugged. "I was tired. I wanted to sleep in."

Ben scrutinized Carmen's face then shook his head. "I don't think this has much, if anything, to do with sleep. I think there's a deeper issue at hand." He stood and paced to the window. "Until you prove me wrong, I'm going to have to assume you're a boundary tester and someone who doesn't appreciate authority and rules. It signals that there might be trouble as we try to break through the bondage you've been under."

Wow. Cue the *Twilight Zone* music. Ben read into things a little too deeply—maybe a lot too deeply. Carmen had made a mistake. She should have gone to prayer, and she wouldn't skip it again. But all this talk of bondage was taking it too far. "I'm not going to be a troublemaker. I promise."

"Well, do you see that you've got some hurdles to jump to prove that now?" Ben lifted one shoulder. "This is really our one and only experience with you, the first time we've seen you faced with a choice. . .and it's ending in negative consequences. That's not good. But so be it."

Consequences? She was already grounded in a figurative sense. What was left to do to her? It wasn't like he could take away her birthday. Carmen shrugged. "If it's worth anything, I'm really sorry."

"That's good to hear, and it's always worth something." Ben smiled.

"Definitely." Alicia rubbed Carmen's shoulder. She flinched away, trying not to let it show.

Ben cleared his throat. "Now, rather than getting your first taste of the activity center, you'll be spending the day in the kitchen with Marilyn. She has plenty to keep you busy, and I expect you to stick it out until she releases you. Any questions?"

Carmen shook her head. She'd been looking forward to free time. The girls had said there were movies, exercise equipment, games, and all sorts of fun things to do during free time. Guess that would have to wait until next time.

"I assume we'll see you in prayer tomorrow?"

"I'll be there. Am I excused?" Carmen stood.

"Go straight on to the kitchen. Marilyn's expecting you."

Carmen left the room and practically skipped to her destination. Did they think cooking was a punishment? Hah. Carmen rounded the corner and pushed on the swinging door. She stepped into the kitchen, where Marilyn stood beside a huge pile of potatoes, holding out a potato peeler.

Uh-oh.

"Let me guess. You want me to peel all of these?" Carmen surveyed the pile. There had to be one hundred potatoes.

"Yeppers. Peel 'em. Chunk 'em. Boil 'em. Mash 'em." Marilyn wiped her reddened hands on her apron.

"I don't see what this has to do with what I did. I mean, is it really that big of a deal?" Maybe she'd find a compassionate coconspirator in Marilyn. Maybe Marilyn didn't buy into all the

God and prayer stuff either.

"Is what a big deal? Missing prayer time or breaking the rules on purpose? The way I see it, those are two separate things."

Huh? "What do you mean?"

"Well, missing prayer time in itself isn't a huge deal. God is with you everywhere. He knows your heart—which can be a good thing or a bad thing, depending on what's in there." Marilyn patted her ample chest.

"Yeah. I agree. And He doesn't care what time people pray, does He?"

"No, of course not."

See. Carmen knew Marilyn would be on her side.

"But God does care an awful lot about obedience and respect. He also loves when we're disciplined enough to set aside time for Him. It's like a friendship. If you don't make time for your friends, the relationship kinda gets stale."

"But what if I don't have a relationship with Him? I mean, isn't it kind of pointless to pray if I don't even know if He's there?"

"Pointless? No." Marilyn shrugged. "I can't explain it all to you with the Bible verses and fancy words like Ben and the others. But I can tell you what I know in my heart to be true because it's been true for me since I was a little girl on my mama's knee." She pointed up. "He's there. He hears. And He answers. Whether you believe in Him or not. You let Him, and He'll prove Himself true to you, too."

Oh. She was a sneaky one, that Marilyn. Went around the back door with the same message as everyone else. Carmen hadn't even seen it coming.

"But whether you like it or not, rules are rules. Prayer time is a big one 'round here. You pulled a silly stunt, girl. You need to learn to just go with the flow and not draw negative attention to yourself."

Carmen nodded. Enough lectures. She stepped up to the mound of potatoes. It would take all day to get them peeled.

"Okay. 'Nuff said. I'm sure you got an earful already. I'm going to read for a while. I'll be back to check on you in a few hours." Marilyn patted Carmen on the back. "You'll be okay once you get your pride broken a bit." She waddled away, turning sideways through the swinging door.

"This is ridiculous," Carmen muttered. "What do potatoes have to do with prayer time? And who are they to tell me when I have to pray anyway? And why am I talking to potatoes?"

Chapter 25

The van bounced down the mountain road as it spiraled away from the center on its way to church. Carmen felt nauseous for the first time since the baby. . . . She tried not to think about it. So painful to realize that she was a mother who would never hold her baby.

"You should be glad you're going to church here now." Kira's supercharged excitement bubbled over and interrupted Carmen's thoughts. "As recently as a few months ago, there was no Sunday morning youth service, and we had to stay in the main auditorium with the adults. Now we have our own space, even our own worship team. It's awesome. You'll love it."

Just shoot me now. Carmen slid down the seat with her head resting on the headrest and closed her eyes. She pulled her denim-clad legs up to her chest and curled up to take a nap. With no special dress code for church, Carmen hadn't been about to dress up like Leila had. A floral dress in November over a white turtleneck? Really? No thanks. Carmen would wear her favorite comfy jeans every chance she got. How strange that a few short weeks ago they hadn't fit her because there'd been a baby growing inside her.

"Hey. What's wrong?" Tricia leaned over and nudged Carmen.

"Nothing's wrong. I'm just tired." *And bored. And angry. And lonely. Any other questions?*

"You sure do like your sleep." Tricia laughed.

Teenagers were supposed to sleep a lot. Guess Ben Bradley hadn't gotten that memo. Carmen had read that it was perfectly normal for a teenager to require twelve hours of sleep. She should print that out for him.

No, that would backfire. He'd tell her to go to bed earlier.

Ben and Alicia had a son? Poor kid. Bet they drove him crazy with rules and constant church. He was probably a total nerd who got up with the sun, prayed for an hour, then did chores. Bet he wore overalls.

The van loped over a set of speed bumps as they pulled into the church parking lot. The place was huge. Did that mean God approved of the people at this church more than others since they got to have a building like that? Whatever. Didn't impress her. God must be more easily impressed than she was.

Carmen walked between Tricia and Kira at the back of the pack as they sauntered through the parking lot. Where had Leila gone? Carmen searched the group. Oh, there she was. Trailing behind Ben and Alicia like a puppy dog lapping up any bit of attention they might throw her way. Except they didn't seem to notice her. Leila often had that effect on people.

The group passed through the side entrance into a small vestibule. Alicia gave a little wave then grabbed Ben's hand, and they went down the hall to the right toward the sound of music.

Donna stepped into the center of the Diamond Estates group. "You girls know the rules. No leaving the youth room without a chaperone. Stick together. Pay attention. Be respectful. Got it?"

Most of the girls nodded.

"I'll be in the back of the room as usual, so don't try anything funny." She laughed and wagged her finger at them then looked straight at Carmen.

I get it. I get it. One little mistake and now they'd be all over her for everything.

The group began its migration down the hall like a herd of buffalo. Where were they going? Probably the youth service Kira had been prattling on about. Oh goody.

As they approached a set of double doors, the floor vibrated with strains of bass and a heavy drumbeat. At least the music sounded like it might be cool. They called it "worship." But what did that mean? Probably like the church back home. They had a segment of the service called "praise and worship" at Mom's church. There was even a line item for that in the bulletin. How awkward. Was it really something to be scheduled, or should it be more organic, spontaneous? Not that she'd participate even then.

Donna pushed open the doors and stood back to let the girls pass into the dimly lit room.

There had to be close to two hundred teens in there, with more than ten percent coming straight from Diamond Estates, but it was too dark to make out faces any farther than two feet. The girls filed to some empty rows and filled three of them, but Carmen hung back in the aisle and watched the band for a moment. The music was as good as any rock concert she'd been to. She stepped over to an empty end seat beside Tricia.

Who was the gorgeous guy behind the mic with that clear, almost sultry voice? His wavy brown hair fell in front of his eyes, but his eyes were closed, and he didn't seem to notice. She'd always had such a thing for singers.

Some of the girls, like Tricia and Kira, launched right into it. Hands waving in the air and the whole bit. Some of the others held back, more reserved. Goth girl sat down on her seat, leaned her head back on her chair, and closed her eyes. Was she napping? Was that okay to do? If so. . .

But first things first. Carmen had to go to the bathroom. . .

bad. "Hey, T, where's the restroom?"

Tricia's eyes popped open, and she jerked her head toward the back right corner of the room. "Out those doors. But make sure you tell Donna where you're going."

Why? There was no way Donna could see them in the dark. How long would it stay dim in there? Maybe Carmen could go explore a little. She chuckled as memories of her recent expedition and a secret passageway haunted her mind.

Carmen stepped through the doors out into the empty lobby, which had been bustling with people when they'd entered the youth hall only a few minutes prior. Three teenagers—one girl, two boys—dressed like they'd just stepped out of a music video were practically running down the hall away from the worship service. Who were those kids, and where were they going? Carmen couldn't help but follow them to some unknown place that had to be better than what was happening back in church.

One of the boys grabbed the waistband of his sagging gray pants as he ducked through an open fire-exit door and then under a set of stairs that didn't seem to get much use. The girl and other boy followed. Carmen stayed back, peeking around the corner to see what they were up to. She heard a lot of shuffling and then a zipper from something big like a backpack.

A match struck.

Within seconds the sweet smell of pot wafted from under the stairs and tickled Carmen's nostrils. She'd never smoked marijuana, but if they offered it to her in that moment, she'd do it in a heartbeat. She needed something to get through another day at Diamond Estates.

"Hey. We know you're out there." A male voice intruded her thoughts. "Join us."

Was he talking to her? Carmen stepped into the stairwell.

"I. . .uh. . .I'd love to. But I can't really."

"We know. You're with Diamond Estates, right?" He was hidden in the shadows, but his voice sounded kind, almost sympathetic. "You're a new kid." Carmen nodded. Strange that they could see her, but she couldn't see them. Would they tell someone she'd left the service? Unlikely. They didn't seem like the type who would rat her out. Plus, they were out there smoking.

"Have you drunk the Kool-Aid yet?"

She snorted. "That's what I've been saying about everyone there."

"Ah. Then you're a smart one. My sister went there; she wasn't so lucky." His voice trailed off. "But that's a story for another day."

Carmen didn't know what to say. Awkward.

"Hey, if that place ever gets old, here's my number. We'll help you out." A wadded up piece of scrap paper landed at Carmen's feet.

She snatched it and shoved it deep into her pocket. "Thanks. I gotta get back before the lights come on."

So much for rule number twenty-two.

⟳

The dining room bustled with activity. People Carmen had never seen before milled around and gabbed with the girls who were setting the tables for Sunday dinner.

Gasp.

There he was leaning against the window. The singer with the long hair from church. Did he plan the halo effect of the sunlight streaming through his hair, or was that an accident? He could be a model. A star.

"That's Ben and Alicia's son, Justin," Tricia whispered.

"You scared me. Don't do that." Carmen fanned her face. "*He's* their son. Him? That guy over there from church?" Tricia couldn't be serious. It was impossible that Ben and Alicia had produced such a godlike specimen.

"Don't worry. Justin has that effect on everyone. He's definitely a special dude. But he's taken. More than taken actually."

"What do you mean? Is he married. . .or gay?" Carmen couldn't take her eyes off his wide smile.

"Ga—what? You're crazy." Tricia pointed across the room as a cute girl with long dark waves and dark eyes stepped up beside Justin. "That's Olivia. She's his girlfriend."

"*The* Olivia? The one you guys keep promising to tell me about but never do? We're having that talk tonight." Carmen needed to get that story for her mystery book. Speaking of that, who did she need to see to actually get her hands on an empty notebook?

"Come on. I'll introduce you." Tricia clasped Carmen's hand.

Carmen pulled back. "No. It's okay. There's no need to bother them." How embarrassing.

Tricia tugged harder. "Come on. They won't bite. I promise." She marched Carmen over to the cluster of people where Justin held court.

"Hey guys. Carmen is one of our new girls. She's from New York."

No way was Carmen going to correct Tricia and admit she was from New Jersey, let alone Hackensack. New York wasn't a lie because she hadn't said it herself, right? Plus it was her dad's address. She could have mail sent there if she wanted to.

"This is Ginny Mansfield and her daughter Olivia."

Carmen shook their outstretched hands. Next she'd have to shake Justin's. Would it be too obvious if she wiped hers on her jeans before touching him? Because she wouldn't be wiping them on anything afterward. Ever.

"This is Justin, Ben and Alicia's son."

"Pleased to meet you." Yep. That was the voice from the stage at church that morning.

Carmen averted her eyes as the flush crept up her neck. At least he hadn't reached for her clammy hand.

"And this is Mark Stapleton. He and Ginny are the ones getting married here at Diamond Estates in a few weeks."

Mark pumped Carmen's hand.

"Congratulations." Couldn't she just go back to her seat? Meeting people was such an awkward experience. The moment of that first meeting was when people sized each other up. It was when first impressions were locked in and the bias toward a person became either positive or negative. How stressful to shake someone's hand knowing that was happening at that very moment.

"Where are Skye and Ju-Ju today? I didn't see them at church." Tricia's eyebrows furrowed.

"Skye had to work at the mall, and Ju-Ju's home sick with the flu. I'm supposed to take her a doggie bag. And a Ding Dong." Olivia laughed. "You know Ju-Ju. No surprise there."

It couldn't get any more embarrassing than just standing there while they all talked about stuff that had nothing to do with Carmen. "It was nice to meet you all." Carmen slunk away to her table where Leila sat alone.

"Hey. Where've you been all day?" Had she been sitting there when they stepped away for introductions? If so, why hadn't she joined them?

"Nowhere. Here. I don't know." Leila shrugged.

She seemed fine, but did Leila feel left out? She never jumped in or made her opinion known about anything. She went with the flow, but only if someone singled her out and asked her to participate. Was that how she liked it? Or maybe she felt insecure. Carmen would have to find out sometime.

With Leila, she couldn't come right out and ask her something personal like that. At least not in that setting.

How about something with less pressure? "What do you like to do with your free time?"

Leila smiled. "My free time? I don't know. I like to listen to music, and I babysit. Oh, I like gardening. It's probably my favorite hobby."

"That's cool. Like flowers and stuff?"

"No, I mean vegetables, herbs, that sort of thing."

Carmen sat forward in her chair. "I've always wanted to do that. I want to be a chef, you know. Fresh ingredients are always the best. You'll have to give me some tips."

"I'd love to. Maybe we can even plant some things in the spring."

The spring? They would still be at Diamond Estates then. Even long enough to plant something and wait for it to grow. Her baby would have been close to being born around that time. The enormity of her commitment to be at Diamond Estates hadn't quite registered with Carmen until that very moment. Could she last that long?

Chapter 26

"Y"ou getting up for prayer this time, sleepyhead?" Kira stood on Leila's bed railing and peered over the edge at Carmen.

"You think I should?" Carmen smirked and threw back the covers. "Is the bathroom open?"

"Yep. But you've only got twelve minutes. I'd leave in ten. We'll meet you down there."

Carmen padded across the empty room and used her ten minutes to wash her face and brush her teeth. A shower would have to wait. At least the place was all girls—no one to impress. Unless she counted Ben. Which she didn't.

The warm washcloth comforted her tired eyes. Carmen stared into the mirror. *You can do this. Fake it till you make it.*

Dressed in Juicy sweats and ready to go, Carmen had two minutes to get down to the prayer room. She couldn't be late. It wasn't an option. That would be like thumbing her nose at the rules—Ben would not be happy with her, and he'd make a huge deal out of it. Carmen jogged down the stairs, taking them two at a time. She skidded to a stop just in time to enter the foyer before the grandfather clock began its countdown to six o'clock.

Deep breath.

Carmen smoothed her sweatshirt and entered the prayer room at the fifth gong.

"Welcome, Carmen. We're glad you could join us." Ben smiled.

"Was there ever a doubt?" Carmen looked around the room. What was she supposed to do? Join her roommates in their cluster? Or was she supposed to pray alone until she earned the right to commiserate with her buddies?

Ben held out an arm and gestured to the room. "Feel free to find a quiet place by yourself or join a cluster. I want to encourage you, Carmen, to open your mind and heart. Let down your guard and see what happens. You never know what might happen. Be open to anything."

"I'll try." Yeah. Probably wasn't going to happen. But she could pretend with the best of them. She selected a spot near the window depicting the Last Supper and huddled on a floor pillow. If she sat with others, they might pray out loud, or worse, expect her to.

Carmen surveyed the space. How many of the girls were praying for real, and how many were totally blowing it off? Some had to be sleeping. That was actually a pretty good idea. But Ben would be watching her closely this first week. She should be on her best behavior.

Here goes. Carmen closed her eyes. She opened one no more than a slit and saw that many people were speaking in whispers or at least moving their lips. Carmen's mouth formed the words of a pretend prayer. "I pledge allegiance to the flag. . ."

⑤

Prayer out of the way, now she had to deal with school. That would be interesting. How would classes work in a house with twenty-five girls? Carmen stood at her dresser and looked at her options. Stay in her sweats or actually put something decent on? At least jeans.

Pulling on her favorite pair, Carmen strained to hear the conversation in the bathroom. Tricia spoke softly to Leila about how the day would go. Breakfast then straight to school.

Carmen's stomach rumbled at the thought of food. "You guys almost ready?"

"Coming now." Tricia came out of the bathroom looking like she'd been pulled off the pages of *Cosmo*. A gorgeous pumpkin-colored sweater fit snugly over a lace cami. The orange brought out the rich tones of her black skin. Her hair, usually straightened, had been left curly and wild.

Carmen would have never thought that raspberry lipstick would look right with the sweater, but it was actually the perfect complement, and it showed off her bright smile. The dark jeans and camel boots finished off the perfect look. "Do you do this every day?" Carmen gestured at Tricia's body.

"This? You mean get dressed?"

"Right. Next you're going to say, 'What, this old thing?' " Carmen laughed and turned to Leila. "You ready?"

"Guess so." Leila exhaled and slung her backpack over her shoulder.

They paraded silently to the library, which was another room they'd skipped on the tour. One she'd been eager to see.

They stepped inside to a world of books. The walls were lined with sagging shelves from floor to ceiling. Ladders hung on rails on each wall, giving access to the volumes above. A big picture window overlooked the pasture. Plush seats near the windows offered a comfy spot to curl up with a good book. Carmen could kill some hours in here for sure.

"Have a seat, girls," Tammy signed and spoke in her broken dialect. "Welcome to your first day of school here at Diamond Estates."

Wait. Was she deaf? "Thanks," Carmen mumbled as she chose the seat beside Tricia and across from Kira at a table. They worked at tables? Carmen hadn't done that since Mr. Wersal's third-grade class. The fourth seat at the table remained empty.

Where was Leila? Carmen craned her neck to look behind her. Oh, for Pete's sake. Leila stood back by the window. What was she waiting for? A personal invite?

Carmen motioned to the empty seat. Leila beamed and scurried to fill it.

"Tricia, would you please show Carmen and Leila around the classroom and give them an overview on how we do our work?"

Carmen stared at Tammy's fingers as they flew in sign language. How could a deaf teacher work with twenty-four girls who didn't know sign language? That would be interesting.

"Happy to." Tricia jumped up and crooked a finger. "C'mon with me."

They approached a countertop with bins labeled with the various subjects. Tricia slid the one marked MATH over to herself. "Here's the way it works. You pull out the workbook that corresponds with your lesson plan—Tammy will help you figure out what that is." Tricia flipped the book open. "You do the work then take the test. That's it."

"What do you mean, 'do the work'?" Carmen flipped through the pages.

"Actually do the lessons in the workbook. That's classwork."

"Where's the test, and when is it?" Carmen hated tests, but she usually rocked them. At least it didn't sound like there would be that much work involved.

"You have to request it from that day's teacher, and then you take it at your desk."

Sounded easy enough.

Leila set her workbook down. "What if I need help with something?"

"That's what the teacher is here for. Some days it's Donna, other days Tammy. If they don't know the answer, they'll know how to find out what it is." Tricia smiled and waited. "No more questions?" She turned toward the front of the classroom. "Tammy? We're ready for you to evaluate them for a starting point."

"Great. Come on over, girls. Have a seat at your table." Tammy laid down two packets. "This is a standardized test. This isn't scored for a grade—it's only a placement test. Do the best you can, but don't guess. We need to get an accurate assessment of your skills."

Like she knew she would, Carmen placed well above grade level. Kind of awkward to see that Leila, a year younger than Carmen, was about a year behind where she should be. How had that happened? She seemed smart enough. Though how could one really tell algebra skills or geography knowledge from friendly conversations? No one else really noticed though. And Carmen sure didn't want to draw attention to it.

As the day drew to a close, Carmen stretched her back and cracked her knuckles. She had to admit, schooling this way was pretty awesome. She got to work at her own pace and see immediate accomplishment. It was like the system was made for her. She worked through two entire workbooks that first day and passed the tests to move on to the next one. At that rate, she'd finish high school on schedule without a bit of trouble. Thank heaven for small favors.

Tammy walked up to Carmen's side. "Great job today." She laid a memo on top of Carmen's papers.

Immediately following school, please report to Donna's office for your first counseling session.

Blessings, Ben

Chapter 27

Carmen peeked into the window that ran up the side of Donna's office door. Was she in there? Oh, there she was. Kneeling at her chair. Was she praying? Probably for Carmen and their first counseling session. Or maybe there was something else that Donna needed to pray about. Was there a Mr. Donna? A boyfriend? An ex? Carmen would have to dig a little to find some details to add to the mystery book she intended to compile as soon as she could get her hands on a notebook.

"I'm here, Donna."

"Hey there." She stood up from her crouch, her knees popping and cracking. "Feel like walking? I'm sick of being inside, and pretty soon the snow is going to start piling up— not like this inch or two we have now."

Fresh air sounded good—and a more casual counseling session even better. "Can I go get my coat?"

"Yep. Meet me at the back door in five minutes. Okay?"

Carmen scurried back to her room, found her winter coat and gloves in the pile on the floor of her closet, then reversed her path to go meet Donna.

Of the three counselors at Diamond Estates, why had Ben assigned her to Donna? Maybe the choice was purely random, or maybe there was some reason that he expected them to relate well. If only she could figure that out so she could play into that a bit when they had this first meeting.

Or she could try being herself. No lies. No pretenses.

Nah.

She huffed a steam patch on the back door and traced a heart through it. Nate. She'd tried to keep him from her thoughts since leaving home, but every once in a while she had an unsuccessful moment, and thoughts of him crept in. Where was he? What was he doing? Did he have a new girlfriend already? Did he hate Carmen?

Carmen watched the horses run through the snowy pasture. Freedom.

No matter how Nate felt about her, in a weird way Carmen felt bound to him. They created life together. Sure, the way Carmen had gone about it was treacherous. And yes, she deserved to be hated. But that didn't change the fact that the life had existed. Their DNA was linked for eternity—if there was a God and a heaven.

Carmen's heart skipped a beat. Would she have to face her baby one day and explain what had happened? Tell her or him why they never met in this life? She hadn't meant for the baby to die. But she had definitely made stupid choices that led up to the miscarriage.

How about Nate? Would that mean they were linked in some weird way in heaven—if they both made it there. If it was real. If they were both married to other people, yet they shared a child, how would that work? She'd have to get some of those questions answered before she'd ever be able to believe in God again. Too many unknowns and impossibilities.

"There you are." Donna looked so cool in her purple ski jacket with the white cap pulled down over her head, her long blond hair escaping the bottom and flowing down her back.

There had to be a Mr. Donna.

"So, you married?" Nothing like subtleties.

Donna coughed. "I. . .I was."

"What happened?" He must have died. No one would divorce Donna.

"We're divorced. Have been for three years." Donna pulled on purple and white ski gloves and held the door open for Carmen.

"Wow. That's awful. Do you date?"

Donna laughed. "You're a sneaky one. Making this about me so the focus is off you? No. I don't date at this time. Someday maybe, when I feel like God has released me from my commitment to my husband. But that time hasn't come yet." She faced up the mountain and began to walk.

Oh, this was going to be a real walk? Like exercise and everything? Was Carmen's body ready for that? She'd find out soon enough.

"Now, how about you? Tell me about yourself. What do you love to do?"

At least she hadn't opened with the bad stuff. "I love to cook. I really, really love to make gourmet dishes and try out new things. I hope to go to culinary school one day."

"Oh? Well, in that case, we can be sure to give you the opportunity to practice. We like to encourage you all in your individual passions." Donna stepped over a fallen log. "What else?"

"I don't really have any other hobbies." Unless Carmen counted playing tennis, but she may never set foot on a court again. "Oh, well I do love to read, and lately I've been thinking that I might like to write, like maybe even a book someday."

"Very cool. What can we do to support you in that? You've seen the library, right?"

"Yeah, it's epic. I'll be using it a lot, I'm sure. As for writing

. . .I assume a laptop is out of the question?" Can't blame a girl for trying.

Donna laughed. "Yeah, I'm pretty sure that's outside the range of my genie abilities."

"Then how about a few blank notebooks?"

"Now *that* I can do." Donna's eyes narrowed. "Tell me this, give me one or two words to describe what it is that has brought you to this place in your life. I don't need the details of events yet, just want to know how you would see it."

One or two words to sum up all that she'd done? Carmen searched her mind. "Betrayal and extreme selfishness."

"On the part of others toward you?"

"No. Me toward them." Where was all this honesty coming from?

"Them being. . . ?"

"Everyone." Carmen hung her head as she trudged along the snowy path. What must Donna think of her?

"You're a pretty self-aware young lady." Donna squinted against the sun.

Carmen shrugged. "To be honest, I was afraid I was a sociopath. Did a little reading about it to see if I fit the description, but now I don't think so. I mean, I have a lot of regrets, and I do care that I hurt people. But I can't seem to stop."

"Well right there you know you're not a sociopath." Donna kept her tone casual as she lifted her face to the sun. "Hmm. Let me ask you this. The things you've done that have really hurt people you care about—you know, the biggies. . ."

Carmen nodded. Those events were never far from her mind.

"Is it more often that you've done them to achieve or gain something you want or more often to avoid some sort of pain or negativity in your life?"

Good question. "I'm not sure. I might have to give that

some thought. Can I ask you why that distinction is important? I mean, if someone else gets hurt, who cares what the reason was?"

"One signals an inflated sense of self-worth. The other simply identifies a lack of faith in God to handle the tough parts of life."

Wow. That made perfect sense. Now Carmen had to figure out where she fell on that spectrum.

"I tell you what. I'd like to explore those extremes a bit more. Let's make that the subject of tomorrow's session. Sound okay?"

Carmen heard herself agreeing to ponder the ideas until they met again. How had Donna gotten into her head so easily? Carmen had thought she was smarter than that. Yet there she was. Affected.

"Knock. Knock." Why did people say they were knocking instead of just doing it? Annoying. Carmen laid her novel across her chest. "Come in."

Donna breezed into the room. "Hey. I have two quick things or so. One: here are some notebooks for you. Will these do?"

Carmen reached a hand down to accept three spiral-bound books. "These are perfect."

"I also brought you this." She handed up a faux leather satchel. "It locks with a combination right here. That way you can feel comfortable writing whatever your heart desires without fear of someone else reading it."

Unless they steal it and break it open. But it was better than nothing. "Thanks a lot, Donna. That's awesome." Wow. She was way cooler than Carmen had ever expected. "Thanks for remembering and getting this stuff so fast."

"The other thing is about the cooking. You know we're hosting a wedding here in two weeks, right?"

Carmen nodded. Where was this going?

"How would you like to handle all of the appetizers yourself?"

She has got to be kidding. It was a dream come true. "You mean I can create and choose the selections *and* cook them?"

"That's exactly what I mean. We'll need a grocery list from you so we can make sure we have everything you need. There will be around one hundred guests plus all of us. It's a week before Christmas, so it's a holiday-themed wedding. Mark and Ginny need you to keep your budget for the appetizers around five hundred dollars. Can it be done?"

Carmen jumped to the floor. "You're telling me that I get to create an *hors d'oeuvres* menu for one hundred and forty people with a budget of five hundred bucks—no restraints at all?" She couldn't be serious.

"You mean you want to do it?"

"Of course." Carmen grabbed one of her notebooks from her bed and sat hard on the desk chair. "I'm going to get started right away. This is going to be awesome."

Donna grinned and moved toward the door. "Have fun with it. Just remember not to stay up too late. You don't want to miss prayer time."

Carmen looked up from her paper. "Hey Donna, thanks."

Hand on the door frame, Donna winked. "You bet."

〜

Dear Nellie,

I'm back! I have so much to tell you. First of all, you should see this place. It's like a horror movie set. I've gotten myself in a little trouble exploring, but nothing major.

Ben Bradley. He's a piece of work. I think he means well, but he's so intense all the time. He needs to lighten up and have a little fun. Turns out he got his girlfriend pregnant when they were in high school. They're still married, though.

That should have been me and Nate. They never had any
more kids, and from the look on Ben's face when I asked,
there's a story there. I wonder if his wife was never able.
Maybe that's why they do this Diamond Estates stuff.

Justin—He is so hot. Nuff said.

Olivia—doesn't deserve him.

Leila—she's got issues. I wish she'd just get a little more
confident. It's annoying to have to drag her everywhere
like a little child. And her last name is Wong. She must be
adopted by that perfect family in the picture. How must she
feel to be an oddball among such perfection?

Tammy is deaf? How'd that happen?

Donna—she's pretty cool. But what's the story about
her divorce?

Oh, Nellie. . .we've got so much to talk about now.

Love,
Carmen

ⓢ

Now that was a getup Carmen had never seen before. Leila stood
in front of the bathroom mirror with a towel wrapped around
her lower half, held by a clip since the ends barely met, and a Vail
sweatshirt on top. "Aren't you hot? It's steamy in here."

Leila shook her head. "Nah. I'm never hot."

Then why was her forehead glistening? And weren't all
overweight people usually sweaty?

Carmen went back to her bed, reached under the mattress,
and pulled out her satchel. She spun the little dials, and the lock
popped open. Flipping the notebook open to Leila's page with
one hand, she plucked the pen cap off with her teeth.

Dear Nellie,
This has to be quick because she'll be right back.

Leila always wears long sleeves, even in a hot and steamy bathroom right after a shower. She says she's never hot. But she says that even while sweat drips down her face. Is she hiding something under that shirt, or is she just trying to cover her body as much as she can?

Also, why is she so elusive? She's never around. Just when I think she's disappeared, she shows up somewhere, and then I wonder if she was really there all along.

And why is she always in the bathroom?

Love,
Carmen

Carmen recapped the pen and shoved the book into her bag, spun the lock, and tucked it under her mattress as Leila entered the room. "Can we talk?"

Leila's face registered surprise. "Uh, sure."

"Are you happy here?" Carmen cocked her head in concern.

"Happy? I'm not sure that's the goal. I'm satisfied. I think I needed to be here. I wish. . . Oh, never mind."

"No. Tell me. You wish what?"

"I wish I fit in with the girls more. I'm always the outsider . . .but that's nothing new." Leila shrugged and turned her back.

"Why do you feel like you don't fit in?"

"Well, look at the two of us. We got here on the same day just over a week ago. You have tons of friends; I have none. Well, except for the sympathy friendships like yours, Tricia's, and Kira's."

"You have friends—and more than only sympathy ones."

"Not the way I see it."

"Can I speak frankly?"

Leila shrugged again. "Go for it."

"You really can't blame other people for you not fitting

in. You haven't done your part. You need to get in there and mingle. Talk to people. Put yourself out there so they can respond. They aren't going to come hunt you down—you have to go where they are and then make yourself noticeable when you do." It probably was more natural for Carmen—she realized that. And she didn't carry the baggage of being self-conscious like Leila did, but still. Leila needed to make an effort.

"Easy for you to say." Leila scowled. "You can't possibly know what it's like to be from a perfect family like mine. They're so beautiful and thin. People always know right away that I'm adopted. I hate the moment when I see the realization dawn on their face. It brings up the truth of who I am. An embarrassment. I bet my family wishes they'd never adopted me."

What could she say to that? She hardly knew Leila and certainly didn't know her parents. "I'm sure that's not true. Your family loves you. I'm saying that if you don't reach out, you can't really blame other people. That's all I meant."

"Then there's school. It comes so easily to you—and to the others. I have to fight so hard to keep up. And yet I fall behind more and more. . ."

Carmen opened her mouth to offer reassurance, but what could she say to that? It was all kind of true.

"I'll be fine. I'm just feeling bummed out, but I'll get over it."

Leila tugged her sleeves down past her wrists and disappeared into the bathroom. Again.

Chapter 28

A billow of clouds entered the dining room.

What on earth was that? Carmen nudged Tricia. "I think our lunch is being invaded by a Charmin commercial."

White fabric swirled and waved as it pressed forward. "Oh look, it has feet." Carmen pointed at four legs sticking out from beneath the poufs.

Ben and Donna rushed over to the intruders and helped rescue them from their tangled mess.

"It's Olivia and Justin." Tricia beamed.

Carmen choked on her chocolate milk. Justin was there? In the same room? Thank the good Lord she'd had enough sense to dress nice for school lately. Not that it mattered—Justin only had eyes for Olivia. But still, it wasn't often there was a male in the house other than Ben. And he didn't count. Handsome, sure, but icky.

Should Carmen go help them? It would give her a chance to interact with Justin. No. Probably best she stay far away. What was all that fabric for, anyway?

Ginny staggered into the dining room carrying a long, shallow box with centerpieces standing tall enough to block her face.

Ah. Wedding decorations. It was still more than a week away, though. Why were they bringing it all now? Were they going to set it up already?

Ben opened the large storage closet next to the kitchen and rolled out an empty cart they used for clearing dishes. Gross. Hopefully he washed it off.

Carmen wanted to stop watching, but she couldn't tear her eyes off Justin's forearms as he loaded the centerpieces onto the top of the cart and then stuffed the fabric into a box on the bottom. He pushed it toward the closet, his hair falling forward to cover one eye.

Ginny gasped. "Hold it a second. You can't shove that in there, silly."

"What do you mean?" Justin crouched down and peered into the box. "What'd I do?" His ears reddened like a little boy with his hand caught in a pack of Oreos.

Olivia laughed. "It's all going to be a wrinkled mess, hon. Here, let me help." She pulled all the fabric out and began to fold it, and fold it, and fold it. Might have been easier if she'd rolled it. Justin watched his girlfriend like she was from outer space. He'd probably have been fine with the wrinkled decorations.

Carmen grinned.

As her eyes moved away from him, they locked with Olivia. She didn't look too happy. Uh-oh. Carmen had better be careful. She wasn't a threat to Olivia, obviously, but try telling that to a girl in love.

ᔐ

Dear Nellie,

What's up with Olivia? She's got the man. No need to be jealous or shoot daggers with her eyes. Justin clearly had no interest in anyone else. Then again, it wasn't Justin Olivia was glaring at. It was me. I guess I'd better lay off a little.

Leila is a little bit of all kinds of crazy. She thinks she has no friends, but does nothing to make new ones. We're all her friends—or we would be if she'd open up, even just a little. There's a big story there. What's the deal with her education? Is she not that bright, or is there a reason she's behind? I'm going to go with a little of both and see what further investigation unfolds.

Still on the hunt to find out more about Goth girl. The fact that no one seems to know makes me desperate to find out.

Love,
Carmen

Now there was work to do. Carmen slipped Nellie back into her safe pouch and spun the combo locks. She opened her newly named cooking notebook and turned to page one. Wedding Appetizers. She wanted to make five things. Three were too few, and an even number was a faux pas.

Mini lobster quiche. Chicken teriyaki skewers. Prime rib sliders with horseradish sauce. Bleu-cheese-and-spinach-stuffed mushroom caps in case there were any vegetarians. One more. . . She needed one more, and it had to be a good one.

She'd have to come back to that in a little while. For now Carmen needed to work on her grocery list. If she figured one hundred and fifty people eating two of each appetizer, that meant she needed three hundred of each one.

Uh-oh.

That five-hundred-dollar budget was flying out the window. Or maybe that was her lobster.

⟳

"How are you feeling about things this week, Carmen?" Donna settled into the sofa beside Carmen.

"Pretty good. I mean, I'm having a blast cooking. I hope it all turns out okay."

"Well, Marilyn's been keeping an eye on your progress, and

she thinks the appetizers are going to far outshine the main course. So that should tell you something."

Carmen laughed. Marilyn was probably right. Family style mostaccioli, Caesar salad, and garlic bread? Not too hard to top that.

"What else? How about your thoughts? What have you been thinking or feeling lately?"

She probably expected Carmen to be honest, but Donna wouldn't like what she'd hear if Carmen totally opened up. "I'm doing okay."

"Define okay." Donna narrowed her eyes.

"Well, I'm not as angry at life. I guess that's progress. I feel sort of hopeful that I'll make it—not even here at Diamond Estates. . .that's not what I mean. Just in life, I guess. With or without God."

"You said, 'With or without God.' Can you explain that?"

"Well, I've made it this far in life without Him. I messed up pretty badly on my own, so I thought that maybe, just maybe, I'd have to let Him take over in order to live a good life." Carmen shivered and pulled a crocheted afghan over her body. "But that's hard to do if I'm not even sure He's real. So I'm glad to see that I can have growth and do good things in my life on my own— because that might be all there is. Just me." She shrugged.

Donna frowned. "I feel like we're missing the mark. I'm not sure how we get from daily counseling and prayer, church and youth group attendance, and ultra-Christian surroundings to you feeling like it's okay not to have God in your life." She closed her eyes for a moment, lips moving. "You know, I wonder if that's how you want it to be. And no matter how circumstances and experiences prove otherwise, until the Holy Spirit gets ahold of your heart, you won't seek Him."

"Maybe you're right. . . . I don't know. I don't feel closed off. I just don't feel anything."

Chapter 29

Do you, Mark Edward Stapleton, take this woman, Virginia Elizabeth Mansfield, to be your lawfully wedded wife. . ." Ben's voice droned on and on. It was impossible to pay attention with the scenery Carmen had in front of her. Justin in a tuxedo? That was almost too much to bear. She'd never seen Nate in a tux. She would have on their wedding day, though.

Nate.

The regret cascaded over Carmen's body like a waterfall, dousing any thought of Justin. Which was a good thing. She and Nate were supposed to be standing up there like that. Would she have made as beautiful a bride as Ginny did? What kind of dress would Carmen have worn? Surely she'd have gone with an actual wedding dress—not like Ginny's, which looked more like an ivory cocktail dress. Or would they have gotten married on the beach after the baby came? So many possibilities. Not anymore.

Justin moved forward to hand the ring to Mark as he brushed the hair out of his eyes. He was even more gorgeous than Nate, which until recently, Carmen wouldn't have thought possible.

Eyes off Justin. Focus on the wedding. Carmen dragged her gaze from the unreachable Justin and examined the bridesmaids' dresses. Tricia, Skye, and Ju-Ju wore beautiful burgundy crushed-velvet mermaid gowns. Olivia wore the same style in a rich emerald green. Carmen let her gaze travel from Olivia's strappy crystal shoes, up her body, which looked like it had been sewn into the dress—the fit was so perfect—to her elegant updo. Then to her radiant eyes. She truly was a picture of class and style. And a force to be reckoned with.

Carmen could hold her own in a fashion show. Olivia really did look an awful lot like Carmen in many ways. Coloring, hair, body type. But guys didn't like the meek and mild type, and Olivia, well, she just wasn't very worldly. Even though they were almost the same age, Carmen had a womanly way about her that Olivia just didn't possess yet. But it would take something more important than physical appearance to win Justin away from Olivia. If it were even possible.

Pretty soon he would find out how well Carmen could cook. They always said that the way to a man's heart was through his stomach, right? That probably wouldn't do it with him, though. From the looks of things, Justin spent more time in the gym than in the kitchen. What else? What did she have to offer him that Olivia didn't have?

She shouldn't forget the power of a story. If Carmen had something on Olivia. If she could get a minute alone with Justin and tell him everything about some awful secret Olivia had been keeping from him, maybe he'd see her as his rescuer and fall into her arms. But she didn't know anything bad about Olivia. There probably *was* nothing scandalous in her past. At least in the past since he'd known her.

What could she tell him?

It didn't have to be true. He just had to believe it was true.

No. No. Carmen was trying to leave the life of deception behind. She needed to do things right if she wanted any hope of being normal. Justin was happy with Olivia. Carmen would leave them alone. She had no business interfering, especially if it had to be based on lies.

Mark and Ginny approached the unity candle. Each held their own taper and joined them together to light the main candle. Here's where they blow out their own light. Stupid move. No woman should ever extinguish herself for any man. *Look what happened to Mom.*

"Mark and Ginny have elected to leave their individual candles burning bright lest they lose their own gifts, talents, and callings. They choose to support each other in the beauty of their uniqueness and let the light of God shine through them as they unite as one with the Lord in the fullness of their individuality. May the three become one, yet remain distinctly three."

Okay, Carmen had to admit, that was awesome. That's what she would want if she were to get married.

Speaking of what she would want. . . Justin took the microphone from the stand, and music began to play. He closed his eyes and opened his mouth to sing.

Oh yeah. Forget that earlier promise she made to leave manipulations out of it. All bets were off. Olivia was on her own.

Olivia was toast.

🌀

"Where are my servers?"

Leila, Kira, Bridget, and Ami lined up facing Carmen. Good choices.

"Great. Let's check you out." Carmen walked past each girl as they stood at attention for inspection. Bridget and Ami were brand-new as of that week, so having a part in the wedding gave them something to get excited about. Carmen knew firsthand how important that was. But Bridget, coming off a cocaine addiction, needed to be watched closely. Ami wouldn't be any problem. Carmen couldn't wait to find out her story, though.

"Hair is pulled back, good. Black pants and shoes, great. White shirts, perfect." Except. . . Carmen grabbed Lelia's sleeve and yanked it up past her elbow. "You're going to want to roll your sleeves up, or they'll be a mess by the time you're through. . . ." Were those cut marks all up and down Leila's arm? Some looked fresh. Had anyone else seen?

Leila jerked her sleeve down to her wrist. "I'll be fine. I'm cold." Leila looked away, shutting off any further conversation about her sleeves.

That's it. Carmen was going to find out the truth about Leila. But it would have to wait until after the reception.

"Okay. Here's how it's going to work. You will each take one tray at a time. They each contain a mix of the offerings, some serving utensils, and plenty of napkins. All you have to do is mingle and offer the food to people until your tray is empty. When that happens, just return to the kitchen for a new one." Carmen smiled. "Any questions?"

"Do we get a taste?" Bridget eyed the trays.

"Oh yes. You should definitely taste the item you're serving so you can offer descriptions to guests or answer questions."

Leila wasted no time in reaching for a chicken skewer and taking a bite. "This is amazing." She grabbed a mushroom cap.

Kira mumbled around a mouthful of prime rib. "This is the best thing I've ever tasted." She examined the tray. "I thought there were going to be five different items. I only see four."

"That was the plan." Carmen scoffed. "I ran out of money. It was either quality or quantity. I obviously went for the good stuff."

"And I'm so glad you did." Bridget devoured a lobster quiche.

"Okay. It's time. Make sure you mingle, and get to everyone in the crowd. They should all have the opportunity to sample everything at least once."

"What if someone wants more than one of something?"

"That's totally fine. There will be some who pass completely and others who eat a dozen. It'll all balance out. Running out is okay, too. These are appetizers, not the main course."

"So what do we do when our trays are empty?" Bridget popped a mushroom in her mouth.

Hadn't she been listening? "Just come on back here for a new one. I'll keep checking back here, supervising the distribution to make sure the timing is right." Carmen grinned. "All you need to do is meander through the people and offer them food. Easy enough, right?"

Carmen grabbed her tray and went through the swinging door into the decorated dining room. Find the bride. For where the bride is, there her daughter will be. And where Olivia is, Justin would be hovering. Besides, it would be proper to make sure the bride and groom got to hit the appetizers first.

Hoisting her tray above the heads of the mass of people, Carmen wrangled her way back to the bride's table, where Ginny and Mark stood with their arms around each other. Ginny looked up at Mark; then he kissed her on the nose.

"Care for an hors d'oeuvre?" Carmen lowered the tray.

Ginny leaned over the tray, holding her ivory satin close to her body, and peered at the selection. "Oh my. These look fabulous. I'm going to take one of each." She picked up a lobster quiche with french-manicured acrylics and set it on a napkin then reached for the slider.

Carmen searched the room. Where was Justin? Olivia stood talking with Tricia and Skye. Justin had disappeared. Carmen waited for Mark and Ginny to fill their napkins then hurried away to find her target.

Noise crackled through the speaker system. Apparently someone was trying to get the music to pipe into the dining room. Justin. Carmen set her tray down on a nearby table, filled a napkin with some food, hiked up her skirt so she could move easily, then took off for the media room.

Don't run. Don't draw attention. Move gracefully and quickly like a panther. Carmen arrived at her destination in a matter of moments.

Deep breath. *Don't let him see you flustered.*

Pretend you just heard a good joke. Carmen gave a little laugh and wiped at her eyes as she rounded the corner and entered the media room. There he stood, peering into a laptop screen with a media player open. Perfect. "Oh. You scared me. I didn't know anyone was in here." Carmen fanned herself.

Justin turned piercing blue eyes onto her face. "Sorry. Didn't mean to frighten you. . .Carmen, is it?"

He remembered her name. Carmen wanted to squeal like the president of his fan club. She set down the bulging napkin and pretended to riffle through some papers on the desk.

"Are you looking for the music playlist, too? I can't seem to find it anywhere." Justin ran his fingers through his waves, pulling them back from his face for one blissful moment.

The bump to the right of the bridge of his nose gave away the childhood secret of a once-broken nose. Had it happened during sports? Or maybe a school-yard scuffle?

"Yeah. It seems to have disappeared." Carmen shrugged. "Guess we'll have to wing it." Oh, the food. "Hey, want a snack?" She tipped her head toward the napkin. "They're all yours if you want them."

Justin's eyes lit up. "I'm starving. Thanks so much." He took a bite of the stuffed mushroom, and his eyebrows went sky high. "This is amazing. I don't think I've ever tasted anything like this." He raised a hand to cover his lips as he spoke through the food in his mouth.

"Thank you." Nate loved her mushrooms, too.

"I heard you want to be a chef. Is that true?"

"I think so. It's really competitive, but I'll give it a try." Carmen shrugged.

"I definitely think you should."

Well, it's settled then.

"And then I want to know where your restaurant is so I can have more of these one day."

"I'll keep you posted." Now or never. But how could she hurt Justin? He was such a good soul. But Carmen needed to look out for herself and not worry about Olivia. The girl had never even given her the time of day. "So, Justin. Can we talk for a minute?"

His eyes narrowed. "Sure. . . . What's up?"

His hesitation gave Carmen pause. He was probably predisposed not to trust Carmen because of her background. She'd have to tread lightly. "This is kind of hard to say. . . . I'm a firm believer in just spitting out the bad stuff. . .like ripping off a Band-Aid."

Justin smiled. "All evidence to the contrary." His hair fell forward to cover his eye.

Swoon. "Okay." Deep breath. "I heard something the other day, and I thought you should know about it." Act nervous. Justin needed to believe that it was difficult for Carmen to tell him the bad news. If she spoke confidently, he'd be more likely to question her motives.

"Okay. Can we try to get to the point? I'm kind of expected back."

"It's Olivia."

Justin's eyes narrowed. "Go on."

"Well, I met these people at church, and apparently she's been. . .uh. . .hooking up with one of the guys." Carmen averted her eyes as though she were embarrassed. Was he buying it? If he did, then it would mean he didn't trust Olivia deep down. If he didn't trust her, then Olivia must have done something to make him doubt. If that was the case, then their relationship was already rocky, and Carmen was just giving it a little push.

"What are you talking about?" His eyes flamed.

Uh-oh. He sounded angry. "Look, don't shoot the messenger. I'm just passing along information I think you should know."

"This is quite an accusation. I don't believe it for a minute. I'm going to need a name so I can have a few words with this jerk."

Was that smoke coming from his ears? "I can't give you a name. In fact, I don't even know the dude. I'm just telling you what I heard."

"Okay, I'm sorry I snapped at you. Thank you, I guess, for telling me this, however ridiculous it is. Just keep it to yourself, okay?"

"Of course I will." *Just between you and me, baby.*

Justin moved to leave the room, shaking his head. "Ridiculous."

Had that been a statement or a question? "Hey, Justin, if you ever need to talk. . ."

Chapter 30

"I will dance. . .for my King. . . ," the worship team belted. Rows and rows of teenagers began to gallop around the youth room like a herd of wild horses, shouting the words to the song. What were they doing?

"That's it, you guys." Justin spoke into the microphone as he strummed his guitar and the drums beat a raucous cadence. "Let go. Be undignified for God. Show the world, like King David did, you don't care what people think."

". . .even more undignified than this." The running teenagers shouted the words to the song.

Undignified? Well at least they got something right. Carmen couldn't take it any longer. And while the herd was on the move, she was out of there.

Maneuvering among the mass of teens, Carmen scooted to the door and sneaked through just before the music trickled down to a ballad. Phew. Perfect timing.

Without a moment's hesitation, she zipped over to the stairwell where she'd met up with those three her first week there. Maybe they wouldn't be there, but it was worth a shot. Ah. The familiar smell reached her senses before the sound of their giggling did.

"Hey. Mind if I join you guys?"

"Hey look. It's our buddy from Diamond Estates." The

apparent leader of the group scooted his superstretch, green skinny jeans over to make room for Carmen. "Have a seat."

A girl with two pitch-black pigtails, thick black eyeliner, and bright-red lipstick moved over to make room. "I'm Kansas. Like the band."

"I'm Carmen." She looked at the two boys.

"I'm Billy. He's my brother Sam." Billy jerked his head back at the slouchy boy with the saggy jeans.

"Hey."

He gave a nod toward Carmen.

Sam didn't talk? Why so dark and unhappy?

"So why do you keep sneaking out of church?" The girl flipped her hair out of her eyes.

Kansas? Was that really her name? "I just can't take it in there. I would never, ever jump around and wave my hands like they do. I don't get it at all." Were they going to share the marijuana with Carmen? Did she even want them to?

Billy nodded.

"I feel the same way." Kansas rolled her eyes. "I can see acting like a crazed fan if you're high at an epic rock concert. But church? Totally sober? No thanks. And it seems like they all want to outdo each other with how nutso they get."

Kansas held the joint out to Carmen. "Want a hit off this?"

Yes. She wanted to feel normal even if only for a moment. "I don't know. I could get in a lot of trouble." But how much did she care?

"We could all get in trouble. Sometimes you just have to take some chances." Billy bumped knuckles with Sam.

Carmen knew all about taking chances; she'd been the master of risk taking her whole life. But she would be in huge trouble just for sneaking out of church. Imagine if they caught her smoking dope. How bad would it be if she got caught leaving the youth room, hanging out with undesirables like those three, *and* smoking pot? Her time at Diamond Estates would likely be over—Ben might even call the cops. But maybe Carmen just didn't care enough to stay out of trouble. Didn't seem like life was all that different at Diamond Estates than anywhere else.

People were the same everywhere. She could keep rules, break rules, miss Nate, and hate herself all from the comforts of home. If Mom would let her. Carmen just didn't sense any big life-changing epiphany about to come over her.

One hit couldn't affect her too much, but it might be just enough. She pinched the stick between her thumb and forefinger and brought it to her lips. Sucking in the heady air, Carmen filled her lungs until they were on fire. She held the smoke for as long as she could stand it then released the air along with much of her tension.

Ahh. Carmen leaned her head back on the wall and closed her eyes as the waves of peace flooded her body. "Now that's what I'm talking about."

Everyone lost in a private experience, no one said a word until Carmen couldn't stand the silence any longer. "So you two are brothers?"

Billy nodded. "He's the baby."

Sam slugged him in the arm.

"So your parents make you come to church?" Carmen took another drag as the marijuana came around the tight circle.

Billy chuckled. "Yeah. You could say that."

What did he mean? Carmen shot a quizzical glance at Kansas.

"His dad's the main pastor here."

Their father? "Really? That must be weird." Mommy and Daddy must be so proud.

"Yeah. Me and Sam are kind of stuck coming to church. But it doesn't mean we have to like it."

Sam snorted. "Not for long."

So he did speak. "What do you mean not for long?"

Kansas flashed a bright smile as she handed the joint to Billy. "We're moving into an apartment together. All three of us."

"Do your parents know?"

"We're not telling them until we move out."

"Um, yeah. I tried the same approach. It didn't work all that well, just FYI." Would things have gone very differently if Carmen had waited only a few more days to give her mom the time to get used to the idea of Carmen living with Nate? She'd have never been out on the street that night. She might never have been kidnapped by Marco. Diego might not have gotten hurt, at least that time or in her defense.

And she might still be with Nate. Pregnant with his baby. Planning a wedding.

Wasn't marijuana supposed to put people in a good mood? Carmen needed to change the subject. "Are you and Billy dating?" She looked at Kansas.

Kansas coughed. "Me and Billy? That's too funny. No, me and Sam are a thing. I don't know if you call it dating." She nudged Sam, and they both laughed. "Might be more of a friend with bennies kind of thing."

Gross.

Billy nudged Carmen with his shoulder. "I'm right here. If you're trying to ask me out, feel free. You don't have to go through Kansas."

"Ha. Like I could go out with anyone. . .let alone someone like you." Or would want to. Cute and, according to his name brands and who his dad was, he was obviously rolling in the bank. But even so, that whole Hollister, metrosexual vibe was a bit out there for Carmen.

"They'd let you go out with me. Remember, I'm the PK."

"Yeah, not gonna happen." At least not now. But who knew what could happen if Justin shot her down.

The minutes rolled by, and the last thing Carmen wanted to do was go back to the church service, but she had no choice. "I have to go. Wish I could hang out with you guys, though. Maybe next week?"

"You still have my number?" Billy lifted his cell phone. "You might need it."

"I've got it hidden away for safekeeping." Never know.

※

"How about a Sunday afternoon horseback ride to burn off all that pasta?" Tricia rubbed her nonexistent belly as she rinsed a dish and put it in the tray to run though the industrial-sized dishwasher.

"No one said you had to eat it all." Not horses. Anything but horses.

"Well, there's so much left over from the wedding yesterday because everyone filled up on your appetizers. Any chance you could take over the cooking in this place?"

"Hey. I heard that." Marilyn put her hands on her hips and scowled at Tricia.

Did Marilyn have supersonic hearing? Carmen covered her mouth to suppress a giggle.

Tricia strode across the room and patted Marilyn's arm. "I didn't mean any offense, but come on. Did you taste that stuff she made?" Tricia jerked her head toward Carmen.

"Yeah, yeah. She had weeks to plan her little finger sandwiches. Try three meals a day, every single day. Then come talk to me about taking over." Marilyn crossed her arms on her bosom. A smile tugged at the corners of her mouth.

Hard to tell if she was kidding or serious. Probably a little of both.

Tricia laughed. "Someone's jealous." She winked. "Anyway, back to this afternoon. Want to saddle up some horses and go for a ride?"

Oh no. Carmen thought she'd managed to avoid the question. She'd done a pretty good job of steering clear of the horses in the weeks she'd been at Diamond Estates. Whenever the other girls wanted to ride, she claimed a headache or something, but no one would believe illness had crept up on her all of a sudden.

"We need to sneak in a good run before the trail disappears completely until spring."

Which is exactly what Carmen had hoped would happen. "I don't know, T. Kinda in the mood for a book and a nap."

"Oh please. You're always in the mood for bed. It's a gorgeous day out there. Let's get outside."

"Why don't you ask Kira? Or Leila?" Although Leila might hurt the horse.

Tricia shook her head. "Nope. I want you to come. We're going. No more discussion. I'll go get permission from someone."

"Great." What a nightmare. Visions of her last ride pelted Carmen's memory. At nine years old a family friend had invited them over for a ride. They put Carmen on top of the sweetest old horse. They said she was even too old to run very fast. But as soon as Carmen settled on her back, she took off bucking and jumping around like crazy. It didn't take much for that manic animal to toss Carmen high into the air.

She shuddered as she remembered being airborne, knowing she would hit the ground and likely be trampled by a horse. Carmen shook her head to clear the trauma. There had been way too many moments of lucid thought as she flew through the air and then landed on the hard ground. Should she roll or stay still? Should she scream or remain calm? Those horse hooves had danced all around her head, but they never touched her.

Marilyn cleared her throat. "Um. You never know. You might like it."

"I doubt it."

Marilyn bustled away. "But hey, enough about horses. Would you teach me how to make that lobster stuff you served yesterday?" Marilyn busied herself.

Ha. Marilyn was trying to be nonchalant? "Oh? You liked my food?"

"Well, you know. It was different." Marilyn blushed.

"Don't worry—your secret is safe with me."

⑤

Dear Nellie,

Kind of in a hurry, not that I want to rush, but I needed to get this off my chest first.

What am I going to do about Leila's arms? I should tell someone else and then back out of it. It's too freaky for me to imagine she's been spending all that time in the bathroom cutting on her own body. I'm positive that's what it is because some of the scars are old, some are only healing, and some are very fresh. Why do people do that?

The cutting explains the long sleeves and the disappearing. But it doesn't answer why. Why is she like that? What's been so bad in her past?

Now I'm supposed to meet Tricia at the stables to go riding. I'm not a fan of the idea. If anything should happen to me, give all of my possessions to my mom.

Love,
Carmen

⑤

"I've got us a riding buddy." Tricia approached from around the front of the barn with Goth girl at her side wearing all black. Her silver chains tinkled as she walked. She stared at the ground even as she approached. Carmen knew she'd be uncomfortable, too, if she were dragged out to be a third wheel on a horseback ride.

But Goth girl? Where had she come from, and why would Tricia befriend her now, all of a sudden? Tammy must have counseled her about reaching out more. "I don't think we've actually met. I'm Carmen."

"Good to meet you. I'm Roxy." Her voice sounded raspy. From lack of use? She looked down at her feet, never making eye contact. How did she know who she was speaking to? She must have eyes in the top of her head. Did her earlobes hurt stretched to the size of a dime? And how about those tattoos that peeked out the neckline of her shirt? Those had to hurt.

"Roxy has been here for a couple of months, and I thought it was past time we got to know each other a little bit." Tricia approached a gelding from the side and rubbed its neck.

"Good plan." But now with Roxy there, how could Carmen ever admit to Tricia that she was terrified of horses? She knew how to ride—that wasn't the problem. Carmen had done it a lot when she was little, but that one throw had been all it took to turn her off the animal completely. But she was stuck unless she wanted to admit she was scared. Hopefully the Diamond Estates horses were mild and well behaved. But they'd said the same thing about that other monster, too.

"So, T, how do I pick a horse?" Carmen looked up and down the stalls. Two were snorting and pacing. No way she would get on one of those.

"You seem a tad skittish. You should probably go with Cinnamon." Tricia inspected both sides of Cinnamon's saddle blanket and then laid it across the horse's back. She heaved the saddle onto Cinnamon and tightened the cinch.

The horse didn't fuss or snort at the weight of the saddle. So far, so good.

Tricia held Cinnamon's head up and made soothing shushing noises. "Go ahead and put your left foot in the stirrup and swing your right leg over. Super easy."

Carmen grabbed the saddle and pulled, trying to swing her leg over. Three tries later, in not quite the graceful elegance demonstrated by Tricia, Carmen sat atop her horse. Something she had once vowed never to do again.

Where had Roxy gone? Carmen spied her through the barn door, walking her mare in the barnyard.

"Tricia," Carmen whispered. "What made you invite *her*? She's not your usual type."

Tricia shrugged. "She's pretty cool. She's always alone here, but I heard she had tons of friends at her school. I think she has kind of pulled back to avoid rejection. Plus, Tammy has been talking to me. . .and I'm sort of convicted lately about being too cliquish. Does that make sense?"

"Sure. I guess that's great. I've been meaning to talk to her a little bit, too." So she could write about her.

Their horses pranced anxiously, breath floating in smoky pools around their noses. Carmen pulled on one rein and turned Cinnamon toward the pasture. The horse followed the direction perfectly. At least Cinnamon knew what she was doing.

"So where are we headed, ladies? I have the walkie-talkie." Tricia pulled it out of her jacket pocket and confirmed that it was on. "Full battery."

Roxy gazed up the tree line. "We can't really go up the mountain—the fresh snow is too deep and would be dangerous for the horses. We can go around on the mountain pass and come back the same way. Not as exciting probably, but safer."

That was the most Carmen had ever heard Roxy talk. "Safer works for me."

What an unlikely trio they made.

"I'm going to let Starlight go for a minute. She's dying for some exercise." Tricia patted Starlight's neck then clicked her heels and moved the reins. Starlight wasted no time and trotted off through the snowy meadow.

Awkward.

Carmen clicked her heels, and Cinnamon moved forward at a slow walk. Roxy held her eager horse back to match Cinnamon's gait. This was Carmen's chance. "So, if you don't mind my asking. . .why are you here at Diamond Estates? You sure don't seem like the type. And you don't seem to be that interested in what's going on with the program." Goth girl, er, Roxy, shrugged. "I needed out of town. It was this or jail."

"But I thought they wouldn't take someone who didn't want to be here."

Roxy eyed Carmen for a moment. "I'm a good actor. Same as you." She clicked her heels, and the horse took off.

Roxy had a point. But how had she known?

Chapter 31

"Merry Christmas."

Carmen's eyes blinked against the light flooding the room. She rolled over. "Leave me alone. It's a holiday—we get to sleep in." She pulled her pillow over the back of her head.

"You did sleep in, silly. It's way past time to get up." Kira spoke near Carmen's ear.

"Go away." Carmen pulled the covers over her head and gripped them tight.

With a whoosh, her body was exposed to the cold air, and her eyes stared into the light. Carmen might have to kill someone. She rose up on her elbow.

Kira stood triumphantly with Carmen's blankets in her hands like a trophy. "Trust me. You want to get up for this."

"For what? What's going on?" Whatever it was, it had better be good.

"They always do something big here on Christmas. I don't know what it is this year, but we're supposed to be in the dining room in twenty minutes."

A fancy breakfast or something? "What time is it?"

"It's ten forty. C'mon. Get up." Kira tugged on Carmen's arm.

"Okay. Okay. Clear the way to the bathroom." Luckily Carmen showered the night before or Kira might come unglued having to wait.

Twenty minutes later, Tricia and Kira ushered Carmen and Leila down the hall and down the stairs toward the dining room.

"What should we expect? What happened last year?" Leila grinned like a little kid.

"We'll explain that later. No time now. Just believe us when we tell you it was awesome. I can't imagine how they could top it this year." Tricia peeked in the hall mirror and smoothed down the flyaways from her wiry straightened hair.

The dining room door was already open, so Carmen stepped over the threshold into a long-ago world. Maybe England? Carmen's ankles wobbled on the cobblestone floor as she moved to a table in the center of town square.

Carmen leaned over to Tricia. "How is it so huge in here?"

"The divider's been pulled. You're actually in the library."

"No way." Carmen spun around to see all sides. That meant the clock-maker's shop behind them actually blocked the reference section, and across the room, fiction was hidden by a bakery. Where had they gotten the fresh flowers that lined the walkways and hung from corners of storefronts and the lampposts that lit the room?

"What do you suppose is going to happen?" Leila turned in every direction before she sat down.

A bead of sweat dripped down Carmen's back as the fire in the center of town roared. The patio doors were flung open to let in the brisk air. Snow fluttered into the space.

The seats were filled with Diamond girls, staff, and even some people she'd never seen. "Hey, Kira, who are all the strangers?"

"Just a sec." Kira nodded toward the wooden bridge along the far wall. Ben stood in the center holding a microphone in one hand with his other arm around Alicia's back.

"Merry Christmas." He smiled out at the crowd as a chorus

of Merry Christmases soared back to him. "Welcome girls, staff, and guests. Some of you are visiting family members; others are locals who have been a part of Diamond Estates in some way this year. And what a year it's been. God has done some amazing things."

Like what? Why didn't he say what was so amazing? Ben always said stuff like that but never explained. Like when he talked sometimes about the movement of the Holy Spirit. What did that mean? Were they just supposed to know?

"We love to sit back on Christmas and celebrate who He is and what He's done. Usually we do something with a representation of the nativity, but this year, as you can tell, we've decided to go somewhere different with our celebrations. Last we heard, Christ was not born in nineteenth-century England. . . so something else must be afoot." His eyes twinkled.

"You'll be served your brunch in a family-style manner as our program opens with the award-winning choral group from St. Anthony's. Following that. . .well, you'll just have to wait and see." Ben grinned and stepped off the bridge then turned to help Alicia navigate the cobblestones.

The kitchen doors swung open, and a dozen servers dressed in period clothes pushed tottery wooden carts into the dining room. Bread towered on one of them. . .wheat, rye, pumpernickel, bagels of every variety, doughnuts, scones. A recovering carb addict's nightmare.

The man pushing the fruit cart leaned to his right as he attempted to steer his heavy burden. What would happen if those oranges, pomegranates, peaches, and apples avalanched off the cart and slid across the room? Justin jumped up to help him.

Justin? How had Carmen not seen him yet that morning? He looked amazing in that rich-chocolate sweater and a pair of slick khakis. It hadn't even occurred to her that he'd be there.

Her hands shook as she selected a steaming pumpkin scone and a dollop of almond butter.

Carmen considered the offerings of the next cart. "Ham for me, please." The roast beef looked too rare for her taste, and she wasn't a big fan of salmon. A huge serving bowl of scrambled eggs, one of hash brown potatoes, and another of gravy appeared on their table. A biscuit basket came next, followed by a tray of bacon.

Tricia looked a little uneasy as she broke a biscuit in half, leaving one half in the bowl. She drizzled a teaspoon of gravy on top.

Leila grabbed two biscuits and about six pieces of bacon, scooped a mound of eggs to the side, then ladled gravy on top of the whole feast. Looked good, if it weren't so deadly.

Carmen nibbled on her scone as she surveyed the room. Families chattering at full tables, girls alone at others. Justin and Olivia toasting some private secret. Had he told her what Carmen had said at the wedding? Even if he had, Olivia wouldn't assume Carmen made it up, would she? It was possible that someone at church actually said that about Olivia, wasn't it?

Wearing layers of drab clothing and long, bright scarves, the choir filed through the library door and lined up three deep on the bridge. They sang Christmas carols and holiday songs as everyone enjoyed the decadent brunch. It wasn't Christmas morning at home, but it was so special Carmen almost forgot about home. Which was probably Ben's goal.

"I'm stuffed." Carmen leaned back in her chair and puffed out her cheeks.

"Me, too." Kira groaned. "I could use a nap now."

"I wonder what happens when they're done singing." Leila buttered another cranberry scone.

As they waited for the song to end and something new to

happen, Carmen felt a presence near her right ear. A folded slip of paper dropped down the front of her shirt. What? She whipped around to see Roxy slumping back to her seat with her head down.

Had anyone else seen her pass Carmen the note? Was it safe to open here, or should she go to the restroom?

Carmen slipped the note from her shirt and smoothed it on her pant leg. When she was sure no one was looking, she peeked.

> *Carmen,*
>
> *Talk with me during free time tonight. Tell the others we're playing Battleship so they can't ask to join us. Please.*
>
> *Roxy*

The final bars of "Silent Night" echoed through the room. The lights went out, and drapes were dropped in front of the windows to darken the room. The ornate iron lampposts blinked on and illuminated the room with the help of fire.

What on earth did Roxy want? That had to be the most random note Carmen had ever gotten. Unless she counted the text message from Hillary McConnell.

A hunched figure in ritzy period clothes, carrying a bag of coins, stepped up to the bank.

"A merry Christmas, Uncle! God save you!" came from inside.

"Bah humbug!" the tottery old man shouted.

"*A Christmas Carol.* They're performing Dickens." Carmen settled back with a grin to watch Ebenezer Scrooge come face-to-face with his past, present, and future. Would she have to do that one day? Would the spirits make her face up to all she'd done to the people she cared about? Maybe that would be the day she'd make a change, just like Scrooge.

ᔕ

"We need to talk." Olivia leaned against the sink counter in the ladies' room.

Carmen whipped her head in every direction. They were alone. She looked Olivia up and down. They were about the same size, but Carmen was much scrappier. She could take Olivia any day.

"I'm not going to hurt you." Olivia rolled her eyes. "Though I might like to."

"I have to get back to the brunch or someone will come looking for me. I don't want to disturb their Christmas morning by making them miss the play. Can we talk another time?"

"No." Olivia held Carmen's gaze. "What were you thinking?"

Deny. Deny. Deny. The first rule of treachery. "What are you talking about?"

"You know exactly what I'm talking about."

Olivia stared at Carmen.

Carmen returned the steely gaze. How long would the face-off last? She could go all day.

"Keep away from Justin." Olivia jabbed a finger at Carmen.

"Hah. I want nothing to do with Justin. He's not my type." That might even be too big a lie for Carmen.

"Right. Then why did you tell him I was hooking up with some other guy?" Olivia's eyes flashed with anger.

"Well, aren't you?" Carmen shrugged. "It's kind of common knowledge."

Olivia's jaw dropped. "No. Of course I'm not. Justin is the love of my life. He's my best friend. There's no one out there I'd ever risk what I have with Justin for." She drew her brows together. "Wait. Did you say common knowledge? What are you talking about?"

"Oh, you know. Just that I heard it from more than one

source." Carmen wanted to laugh at the absurdity.

Olivia sank into a chair. "Are you telling the truth?"

Carmen offered an apologetic look. "Sorry to say, but yeah."

"I'm going to need names." Olivia put her head in her hands. "I have to prove nothing happened."

"Did Justin believe the rumor?" Carmen felt the briefest fluttering of hope that the answer would be no. The girl who stood in front of her, while irritating at best, probably didn't deserve what Carmen had done to her.

"He said he didn't. But his eyes gave away his doubt." Tears flowed from Olivia eyes. "What am I going to do?"

Really? "Are you sure you read him right?" Carmen grimaced. "Because if he really did doubt your innocence, is he the right guy for you?"

෨

"What do you guys want to do for free time?" Tricia led the way to the activity room. Leila shrugged. "Whatever you guys want to do."

"Oh, I'm going to hang out with Roxy tonight. We're going to play Battleship and talk."

"Really? You two are friends now?" Kira looked stunned.

"I have no idea. She just asked me to hang out with her, and I said yes." Carmen shrugged.

"I don't know why that's funny, but it is." Kira laughed. "You and Roxy playing Battleship together. How bizarre."

"I don't know. I think it's good for you both to make friends." Leila coughed.

Tricia pulled the door to the activity room open and let the others pass.

Carmen spied Roxy on the other side, facing the window with her back to the room. The game was spread out in front of her as she waited for her partner. Carmen crossed the room, past the group watching *Facing the Giants* on the big-screen TV, past the health nuts on the treadmill, and past the reading corner to slide into the seat across from Roxy. Carmen smiled. "I'm glad you've called this meeting."

Roxy didn't smile.

Was she okay? "What's up? Seriously. Is something wrong?"

"I need to get out of here. You have to help me." Roxy glanced to both sides. "Word is you know a secret passageway."

"What?" How did word spread like that? Who would have told? It had to be Tricia or Kira. Or maybe Leila overheard them talking. But who did Leila confide in? She had no friends. Maybe she used the info to try to make friends.

"You know what I'm talking about. Don't play dumb. It just wastes everyone's time."

No point in denying, but that didn't mean she had to give up the info. "I'm going to have to think about it. Meet me back here, same time, same place on Wednesday. I'll know by then."

Chapter 32

"It has come to our attention you left the youth room during service last week and didn't come back until it was almost time to leave." Ben leaned back in his chair with his hands clasped behind his head and shot a glance at Donna in the chair beside Carmen. "Care to explain?"

Carmen's body turned to ice. She'd been caught. Who told? And why had they waited almost a whole week? "I'm sorry."

Ben did not look happy. Way less understanding than he had been the first time she messed up. He rocked in his chair and stared at her face like he was reading the newspaper. "There's a difference between being sorry and regretting an action simply because you got caught. But that doesn't answer my question. I'd like an explanation of where you were and why you left."

Donna looked at Carmen but remained silent. Her face an unreadable mask. Was she the one who told Ben? Then who told her? Had anyone seen her under the stairs? Carmen chewed on her lower lip. She didn't want to give away any information, but she didn't want to be caught in a lie either. Somewhere in the middle would be safe.

"I had to go to the bathroom really bad, and everyone was in the middle of that really cool song. They were running around the room, and it was really loud. I couldn't find anyone, but I couldn't wait. When ya gotta go, ya gotta go." Carmen shrugged. Who could argue with that?

"That would explain where you were for the duration of that song, but what about the next forty-five minutes before you returned to your seat?" Ben rubbed his eyes. "You might as well be honest with me."

"I went to the bathroom. That took about ten minutes— do you want a play-by-play on that? I must warn you, it isn't pretty." Carmen smiled. Come on, Ben. Laugh. That was funny.

He stared at her.

Okay. Tough crowd.

"Coming back from the restroom, I bumped into some people who wanted to know what Diamond Estates was like. I talked to them for about ten minutes and then returned to the service. I hung out in the back so I wouldn't disturb anyone."

Ben glanced at Donna.

Donna shrugged.

Ah-ha! They couldn't prove that wasn't what happened.

"Then tell me, Carmen, what was the message about?"

Carmen cringed. "I didn't exactly pay attention. I have no idea." There, that sealed it. She appeared completely honest.

Ben nodded. "Okay. Well, at this point I can't prove otherwise, so we'll go with your story. For future reference, you may not leave the worship service for any reason. You find someone who can give you permission or sit tight until you do."

"I promise it won't happen again." That was far easier than she'd expected. Carmen rose to leave.

"We're not quite through here." Ben gestured to the chair.

Oh great. What now? Carmen slumped into the seat.

"What can we do for you?" Ben lifted one shoulder. "I'm at a loss. I must admit, I thought you'd be very receptive to the program and to the Lord because you called us for help and you sounded so eager."

"Do you not want to be here?" Donna's words were so quiet Carmen had to strain to hear them.

Did she want to be there? Not particularly. But what was the alternative? Dad's house wouldn't be that bad, but it would only be a short-term solution. What about the rest of her life?

Did Carmen want to be this person forever? Did she have the power to change the ending? Those two questions were the ones that kept her rooted to her seat. And the possible answers were the ones that gave her chills at night.

"I guess. . . I don't know. I guess I just. . . I want to have been here. I want to be on the other side to see how it came out in the end." Carmen's eyes watered. She blinked a dozen times. She would not cry. No way. "How am I supposed to give myself over to something and trust that the results will happen or that they'll even be what I want for my life?"

"Faith." Ben leaned forward, elbows on his desk. "Discovering it and putting it to use are two of the most difficult aspects of a relationship with God. It's like a roadblock. You have to decide if you're going to plow through it to keep going on your journey or if you're going to let it force you to turn around and go back."

Donna took Carmen's hand. "You have to decide."

"How long do I have?" Were they going to kick her out?

Ben's eyebrows narrowed. "What do you mean?"

"You're asking if you're going to get sent home if you can't get this figured out?" Donna shook her head. "No. No. That's not how it works. You could get kicked out for behavior, but not for matters of the heart, faith issues. That's between you and God—it's His timing. We can't legislate the Holy Spirit by a set of rules."

That made perfect sense. Carmen gazed out the window

beside Ben's desk. "Okay. Just give me some time then. I'll try to get it together."

"Great." Ben leaned forward. "Now let's pray."

Oh goody.

ⓢ

"Hey, Mom. It's me." Carmen plopped on the sofa in the phone room for her weekly call home. Carmen wanted out of there, and the only way was to get through to Mom.

"Carmen! It's great to hear your voice. I'm so glad you caught me. I was about to go out for a Mary Kay meeting."

Shocker. "How's business going?"

"You're never going to believe it. I'm getting the car. I earned a car from Mary Kay. I get the award tonight."

Carmen pulled herself up. "Seriously? Mom, that's awesome. You must be working really hard."

"Yeah. I am. I'll have to keep working just as hard now, if not harder, because I'll have to qualify with my business every month in order to keep the car. But I can do it."

"I know you can. I'm really proud of you." Carmen eye's stung as she fought back tears. She never cried, but that was twice in two days. What was the deal?

"Mom? Do you think I can come home?"

"You mean for a visit?" Her voice sounded guarded.

"I mean I want to move home."

"No."

"What do you mean no?" Seriously?

"I mean, all the reasons why you're there still exist. Nothing has changed except for a very little bit of time. You haven't even been there a full six weeks."

Carmen's own mother wasn't going to let her come home. "What if this place burned down? Then what would you say?"

"I don't want to have one of these ridiculous conversations.

If it burns down, give me a call, and we'll talk." Mom sighed. "Look, you're my daughter, and I love you very much. I miss you more than you could know—so do your sisters. But I love you too much to let you quit."

That sounded rehearsed. Someone had been coaching her. Would Mom tell Ben that Carmen had tried to leave Diamond Estates? Did Carmen even care at this point?

"There are tons of people praying for you, Carmen. Just let go."

Whatever. "I have to go." Thanks for nothing.

Carmen hung up the phone and spun from the room. She stormed into the hallway and crashed into Ben. Had he been listening in? How rude. "I suppose you heard all of that?" Was nothing sacred? Not even phone calls home? She crossed her arms on her chest and waited.

"So you want to go home?" Ben smiled.

Carmen shrugged. "Wouldn't you?"

"It's a good sign, you know."

What was he talking about? The man so rarely made sense. "What do you mean?"

"I mean this usually comes right before a breakthrough. Those feelings of wanting to give up and go back to where it was easier, where you were in control, they're natural. You only have to be strong in the face of them and not give in. You'll see the reward when you move past the struggle."

What did he know about her struggle?

⟳

"That's it. I'm so done." Carmen pulled her pillow over her face.

Kira pried the corner of the pillow up and looked at Carmen. "Hey. What's wrong? Why are you crying?"

"I can't do it. I just can't do this anymore. These people are crazy." Sobs wracked Carmen's body, and her throat constricted. She needed air.

"Who's crazy, honey? What's going on?" Kira stroked the hair away from Carmen's eyes.

The tears kept coming. Carmen hated crying. How weak and childish. If only she could get ahold of herself. Yet the weeping continued.

"It's going to be okay."

"Okay? You can't be serious," Carmen wailed as she raised herself up on her elbows. "You've heard the rumors around here, I'm sure. You know what I've done. How I've hurt everyone close to me. I'll never get over what I've done. Never." She gulped.

"I tricked my boyfriend and got pregnant, convinced him to marry me, then lost the baby. And it's not like that kind of deception has stopped since I got here. I'm right in the thick of it again. And this stupid farce of prayer time and church. . . I'm such a hypocrite." But she couldn't see any other way. She'd never be what these people wanted her to be. And she'd never come to terms with who she really was.

Kira nodded. "Yes. I've heard the stories. I know your past. At least some of it. So what?"

"How can you say 'so what'?"

"Because I did it, too."

Carmen's breath caught in her throat. "What do you mean?"

"When I first got here, I found out I was pregnant. I didn't want to have a baby by myself, so I decided to try to pin it on Justin." Kira whipped her head from side to side as if disgusted with the memory. "I went after him hard. He was around a lot in those days—not so much now that Olivia is keeping him busy."

Kira was being serious? Justin? She obviously hadn't been successful, but what if he'd fallen for it? What if he'd actually gotten trapped in that kind of deception for the rest of his life?

Like Nate almost did.

"Anyway, I tried to seduce Justin so I could blame him for the pregnancy. If he would have had sex with me, he'd never have questioned the legitimacy of the pregnancy. But he wouldn't have any part of it. He shot me down every time. And believe me, I gave it all I had." Kira shook her head. "I have to admit, that was painful. I don't think I'd ever been rejected before."

She probably hadn't been. That little gymnastics body, long blond hair, cute little face. Carmen shuddered at the thought of what could have happened. "Then what?"

"Then I lost the baby." Kira shook her head. "Some people said that was divine providence. But it was such a mess. I never thought I'd get over it."

Whoa. That even rivaled Carmen's situation in nastiness because Justin had been a stranger to Kira. At least Carmen and Nate had been in love. For whatever that was worth. "Why are you telling me this now?"

"Because you're at a crossroads. You're reaching a tipping point where you'll fall to one side or the other. You mentioned it all being a farce, that you're a hypocrite, that these people are crazy." Kira offered a soft smile. "I felt the same way. I hated myself for what I'd done, but I put my failures off on everyone else. As if I raised myself above them in some way, then I didn't have to answer to them. If I could pretend that God had no interest in me, you know, wasn't trying to get ahold of me, I wouldn't have to face my past and make changes."

Wow. It was like she could read Carmen's mind. Did Carmen's thoughts really go that far though? Kira's story seemed a little extreme.

"Sound familiar?" Carmen shrugged. "I mean, yeah. Some of it. I don't know."

"Okay. I'm not going to push. I know when people pushed

me, I shut down. Just think about it, okay?"

They had way more in common than Carmen had ever imagined. She nodded.

Kira winked. "Maybe pray about things if you're feeling adventurous."

If she heard the word *pray* one more time, she would have to punch someone. Maybe it would be Kira.

ॐ

Dear Nellie,

It has come to my attention that everyone is crazy. Certifiable. Nutso. Even Kira. You'll never believe what she did. Well, it was pretty much what I did, but a little worse because she wasn't even dating the guy. And guess who the boy was? You guessed it, clever Nellie. Justin.

Why could Kira get herself all figured out, but it doesn't seem like I have any hope of that at all? How can I stick around here and watch all these people have success at something that I can't even grasp?

Something had better change in a hurry.

Love,
Carmen

Carmen jolted when she heard voices at the door. So far no one even knew Nellie existed, and Carmen would much prefer to keep it that way. She jumped from the bunk and shoved the notebook deep under her mattress just seconds before the door opened.

ॐ

"Marilyn, can I please have a glass of milk?" Maybe that would settle her stomach.

"Sure, doll. You okay?"

Carmen nodded. "Yeah, I'm fine, I guess. Just having one of those days."

Marilyn handed her a tall glass. "You okay if I go? I was headed to my room just before you came in."

"Of course. I think I'd rather be alone anyway. Thanks for the milk." Carmen licked off her milk moustache. The door opened behind her as Marilyn left the kitchen.

"Ahem."

Carmen squealed and knocked her milk into the sink. She twirled around to face the intruder.

She gasped.

Justin.

Judging by his reddened ears and the deep lines around his eyes, Justin hadn't come to find her for a friendly visit. Uh-oh. Act natural. "Hey, Justin. What's up?"

"You know what's up. Why did you lie to me about Olivia?" He looked like talking to Carmen disgusted him about as much as cleaning up vomit.

"Because I'm a liar. The better question would be, why did you believe me?"

"I didn't believe you, but that's not the point here. When are you going to get real with yourself? When are you going to own up to the choices you make? You want to blame everyone else. . .even now, with this stupid stunt you pulled." Justin shook his head.

"What do you know about me?" Did Daddy run home and talk about secrets? Or did Justin have some kind of ESP?

"It doesn't take a rocket scientist to figure out that you're on the run."

"On the run? What are you talking about?"

"You're running from help. Running from God. Running from yourself." Justin shrugged. "Until you decide to be still, you'll keep hurting other people and yourself. Until you stop running, there's no hope for you."

Chapter 33

W hat had Carmen done with that crumpled piece of paper Billy had thrown at her? She had wadded it up and shoved it in the pocket of her jeans. They hadn't been through the wash lately, had they? Maybe she could look him up by his last name. But that wouldn't give her his cell phone number, and there's no way his parents would just give it out. Besides, pastors of that huge church, they probably had an unlisted number to keep the crazies at bay.

What could she do? She had to get away from Diamond Estates before she lost her mind. Too much touchy-feely. Too much internal stuff. And then Justin, of all people, telling her there was no hope for her. Talk about a final straw.

Carmen had never felt so bad about herself in her life, but she didn't know how to fix it. She would be much happier surrounded by people who *got* her. Who didn't make her feel like a failure. Who didn't tell her she needed to pray all the time.

Ah. She found the wadded paper shoved in the back corner of her drawer. Carmen smoothed it open on the desk. How had she forgotten she'd put it there?

Now, to get out of the house without being noticed. If she carried a stuffed backpack through the halls, someone would get suspicious. If she got permission to go for a walk or a ride, she'd be required to take someone with her. That would never work.

She'd have to walk out with not much more than the clothes on her back. She could at least add a few more layers of those.

Carmen pulled off her shirt and jeans. She layered five pair of panties and tugged on two pairs of yoga pants then stepped back into her favorite jeans. She added two sweatshirts over a few graphic tees then shoved a pair of gloves in her pocket and grabbed her pouch of private papers and musings. She sure didn't want to leave Nellie behind for other people to read.

With everyone up in the activity room thinking Carmen had another one of her bad headaches, she had a good hour to get far enough away before they started asking questions.

She crept down the hall toward the stairs. Wait a second. Carmen needed to act confident. If she bumped into anyone, she didn't want to raise any suspicions or even draw their attention. She was walking down the hall. Nothing more.

Her hand traced over the graffiti. She'd miss that actually. Carmen had even hoped to be able to add her piece to the wall one day. She had her spot all picked out. No idea what she'd put there, but she'd hoped it would come to her at the right time. Oh well. She could probably find a bridge or an abandoned store to deface if she really wanted to. But this symbolic artwork wasn't just graffiti for the fun of it. It had a point.

Carmen didn't.

She reached the bottom and turned right. Picking up the pace, she made it to the far end where the coat closet hid the secret door. She stepped through the coats like Lucy Pevensie scouting through the wardrobe and felt for the handle.

There.

She gave it a slight turn, and it popped open, just like before. Now she could hurry. Carmen ran down the stairs to the next door, not bothering with the light, and into the passageway that led outside. Crouching down, she felt sweat pool in the small of her back, and the earth all around her seemed to close in. Carmen had to get outside. She scurried as best she could.

Her hand reached out and opened the door that would release her from her prison. Finally. Carmen breathed the crisp mountain air and gazed at the twinkling stars.

Roxy had been desperate to know the way out. Maybe Carmen should have left her a note. But it was too late now. Every woman for herself.

She pulled on her gloves but didn't have much time before the sweatshirts and underclothes proved ill efficient at keeping out the cold. Now, where to go? The church might be her best bet. She'd noticed an old pay phone still hung on the gymnasium wall, reminiscent of the days before cell phones—she could use that to call Billy. Plus the pastor's family, and therefore Billy, wouldn't live far away from the church.

Oh, unless Billy, Sam, and Kansas had moved into their new place already. Which Carmen hoped they had. If so, she'd figure that out once she got to the pay phone and called Billy. She set off for the foot of the mountain.

What would she do for money? Hopefully they'd help her out until she got a job. She could waitress, cashier, clean. Whatever. As long as it paid enough to keep her from having to run back to Mom or Dad for help.

The mid-January cold filtered through her layers and clawed at her skin as the snow fell hard, the biting wind whipping the flakes against her exposed cheeks. Maybe Carmen should have checked the weather reports before barreling out into the elements. But no matter what, she couldn't turn back now. She'd have to make it down the mountain before she had any hope of getting warm.

One foot in front of the other, the snow crunched beneath her feet. The steep descent brought her to lower elevation with each step, the snow pelting her face as its intensity grew. Carmen squinted to see if she could get a better view through the falling blanket. What if she couldn't get down the mountain? She'd freeze up here. But if she kept moving forward and down the mountain, she'd make it eventually.

Carmen leaned into the wind and closed her eyes against the icy snow that pelted her face. Should she go back? It had been at least an hour since she'd left. How far had she managed to travel? Without the weather slowing her down, she'd still be at least an hour from her destination. With the storm, she might be three hours away. Could she last that long in the middle of a snowstorm and freezing temps?

It had to pass or at least lighten up soon. Maybe she should huddle up somewhere to keep from getting slammed. But what if she got so cold she passed out? People died like that. No, probably best to keep moving.

Carmen pulled the neck of her shirt over her face to trap the warm air she breathed against her body and plodded on. If only she had her cell phone. At least she could press hard down the mountain whenever the raging snow let up for moments at a time. She'd make it. She had to.

The black night closed in around her, and the snow pressing in on all sides felt like walls. Did bears hide at times like this, or were they on the prowl even though the weather raged? Carmen guessed they didn't want to be out in this either. But how could she know for sure? Another way research might have helped this situation. Mom had always said her impulsiveness would get her in trouble one day. Carmen didn't have enough fingers and toes to count the times that statement had been dead-on. Now let's hope none of those fingers or toes froze off.

Finally, with no warning, the snowy curtain parted, and the sky shone through. The snowfall continued at the higher elevation, but Carmen had broken through. Her spirit soared as she picked up the pace.

She marched down as fast as she could, her mind blank and her energy depleted. Thirty minutes later, Carmen stumbled onto the church parking lot. Would they look for her there? The thought sent her hurtling into the bushes. But they wouldn't be able to drive the van down the mountain in the storm Carmen had just walked through. They'd have to wait until the roads were cleared.

In his twisted logic, the church would be the most likely place for Ben to look for her since it's the only place she'd been other than the center. She'd have to hurry.

The snow covered the unplowed parking lot, and Carmen's footprints would give her away. She'd be long gone before anyone saw the prints, but any searchers would know she'd used the phone. If it even worked—it looked ancient. Would the police be able to trace the call? Probably not if she kept it short enough.

Carmen dug the phone number out of her pocket and dropped two quarters into the slot. That should more than cover it. She pressed the numbers and waited.

"Yo."

"Oh thank goodness, Billy. Can you come pick me up?"

"Is this my Diamond Estates girl? What was your name? Cameron?"

"Carmen. Yep, it's me. Can you come get me?" *Please say yes.*

"You bet. Where?"

Oh thank goodness. What would she have done if he'd said no? "At the church? That okay?"

"Yep. Be out back behind the gym. I'll be there in no more than five minutes."

The line went dead. Carmen huddled behind the building

and waited, shivering, until the tires crunched on the snow. She poked her head around the corner. *Please don't be Ben. . .or the cops.*

A rusted-out Corolla pulled as close to the gym as it could get. Billy leaned over and popped open the door for Carmen to climb in. "Where's your stuff?"

Phew. She'd reached the home stretch. "I only took what I could carry." Carmen rubbed her hands together and held them in front of the heat wafting from the dashboard vents.

Billy's jaw dropped. "You mean you walked all the way down from Diamond Estates? No coat, no boots?" He pulled away from the church.

"Yep. Had no choice. If I'd had any of that stuff with me, someone would have known something was up."

"How'd you get out?"

"I found a secret passageway, like in some scary movie."

Billy nodded, his eyes clouded. "My sister used to sneak out through there all the time. I'd pick her up, and we'd go to a party or something. As long as she made it back to her bed by prayer time, her roommates didn't care." He pulled into a parking spot in front of an apartment building.

Carmen laughed. "Cool roomies. When did she graduate the program?"

"Naomi left Diamond Estates about eighteen months ago. But it wasn't by graduating. It was in the back of a hearse."

Chapter 34

A hearse?" Carmen clambered up the back steps to Billy's third-floor apartment. Was there an elevator somewhere? He unlocked the door then the deadbolt and swung it open.

Carmen rushed in and sank onto the sofa. She pulled a blanket over her shivering body. His sister died? That must have been horrible. "What happened?"

"Naomi hung herself in her bedroom." Billy punched out the words then looked away and took a few deep breaths.

"How awful. I'm really sorry, Billy." That was probably when he'd turned against the church and started smoking pot. . .and who knew what else. His poor family.

Billy moved to the kitchenette and nuked some mugs of milk.

"How did your family take it?" Dumb question.

Billy eyed her then shrugged. "You know. Everyone crumbled. There's a lot of guilt involved when someone kills herself." He poured a packet of hot cocoa mix into the cups and stirred. "The board forced my dad to take a leave of absence. Sam has barely spoken since."

He shook his head. "I can't believe you haven't heard about it at Diamond Estates. A house full of two dozen girls, you'd think someone would be yapping."

Carmen accepted the steaming mug of hot chocolate and let it warm her frigid hands. Was it spiked? She let a taste touch her tongue. Hot cocoa straight up. "Most of the girls who are there now wouldn't have been there then. And mostly it's only my roommates who talk to me. I haven't made a ton of other friends." Carmen stared at the bobbing marshmallows.

"I guess I can understand that."

"What?" Carmen laughed. "You can understand why I don't have many friends?"

"Yeah. You're like me. Not really the type for BFFs."

Billy was right, but Carmen hadn't thought of it that way before. She'd never had any really good best girlfriends. She'd either been alone or in a relationship with a boy. Why was that? Did girls avoid her, or did she push them away? When she lived in upstate New York, the girls didn't like her much because of her Mexican descent. She would have been open to friendships like that, but they just never developed.

"So how's this going to work? I mean. . .can I stay here like you guys offered?"

" 'Course you can. We'll figure out the stuff like rent and chores or whatever—Kansas handles all of that. She just tells us what to do, and we do it."

Not sure that arrangement would work for Carmen, but she'd give it a try. "I'll have to get a job."

"Yeah, we're easy though. We'll float you for a little bit as long as you're looking for something."

Carmen leaned back on the sofa and exhaled. Relaxed for the first time in months.

Wait a sec. "What about sleeping arrangements?"

"That's how you're going to earn your rent, baby." Billy wiggled his eyebrows. "Just kidding. Kansas and Sam have the back bedroom. This one over on the right is mine. You can either sleep in my room with me or sleep on the couch. I don't bite, and I won't touch you. . .much. But it's your call."

"Thanks, I think I'll take the couch." For now. "But do you think I could take a hot shower and wash my clothes? My body is chilled to the bone, and these clothes are soaked through to the bottom layer."

"Sure. You live here now. You don't have to ask. Want to borrow a sweatshirt or something?"

"Perfect." What a nice guy. She could get used to hanging out with Billy. Maybe he wouldn't make a bad boyfriend after all.

Carmen entered the beach-themed bathroom complete with a seashell soap dish and starfish switch plates. Bet that stuff was handed down from someone's mom who redid a bathroom. She couldn't see Billy or Sam, or even Kansas, buying the shower curtain with the sandy beach and dolphins swimming in the distance. She chuckled as she turned the hot water on and stepped in.

The water cascaded over her tense muscles and caressed her frozen skin. She might never get out.

Warmed, scrubbed, and pruned, Carmen turned off the water and toweled dry. Billy had left her a nice thick Broncos sweatshirt and a pair of sweats folded on the toilet. They swallowed her as she stepped into them, but they were warm and smelled good. Why didn't she feel weird that he'd come into the bathroom while she showered naked? She felt safe with him for some reason. Hopefully her intuition served her well for once.

Was there a hair dryer somewhere? Carmen opened the vanity door. Nope. Toilet paper and Mr. Clean. How about there? She opened the closet. Ah. Bingo. But she'd let her thick hair air dry for a while first or she'd be standing there for an hour blowing it dry.

Towel draped over her shoulders to catch the drips, Carmen returned to the family room. "Hey, Sam. Didn't know you were here."

He nodded.

"Hope it's okay I stay here for a while." What if he hated the idea? Or hated her?

"Works for me. We needed a fourth roomie to cut the costs. And I heard you can cook."

"That I can—"

The doorbell buzzed.

"Who could that be?" Billy looked at Carmen. "You don't think?"

"Nah. How could they know I'm with you? And how would they know where you live?"

Billy pressed the intercom button. "Who is it?"

"Ben Bradley from Diamond Estates. Can we talk for just a minute?"

Oh no. Carmen's heart sank as she locked eyes with Billy. They had found her already. What should she do? Why did Billy look so unconcerned? Was he high? That certainly wouldn't help matters at all.

"Uh. Hi, Ben. Come on up. Third floor." Billy pressed the entry button for a few seconds then released it.

"What am I going to do?" Carmen's eyes searched the corners of the two-bedroom apartment.

"Listen. He's not going to search the place. At least not while I'm here. So hide somewhere." Billy shrugged.

Easy for him to be so casual. His whole life didn't hang in the balance.

Carmen raced to the bathroom and stepped into the tub. Wait. What if Ben had to use the restroom and then found her there? Or worse, what if he *did* go to the bathroom and *didn't* find her there. Eww. She stepped out of the tub and dove for the bedroom across the hall just as a knock sounded on the front door. Carmen scrambled to the other side of the bed and collapsed between it and the wall.

The front door squeaked open. "Hi, Ben. This is a surprise. Come on in."

"Thank you." Ben's voice.

The door closed. Carmen strained to catch every word, every nuance.

"Listen, before you tell me why you're here, let me just save you the trouble."

Was he about to turn her in? *No. Don't do it, Billy*. Carmen clutched the quilt on the bed.

"I'm sure my parents sent you here to talk some sense into me and Sam, right? I'm not interested in sense right now. In fact, I probably have more than my share of it."

Smart. He was deflecting completely so Ben wouldn't suspect a thing.

"I agree. We're doing fine," Sam chimed in. "Our parents didn't need to send out the troops to round us up."

Way to go, guys.

"Actually, that's not why I'm here. I'm looking for a girl—"

"Aren't we all?" Billy laughed too hard at his own joke.

"Here, just take a look at her picture. Have you seen her?"

"Hmm. No. Can't say as I have. . ."

"Well, I was given your names by some of the girls. Apparently Carmen has been witnessed with you three on more than one occasion. It was a natural assumption to think she'd be here."

Carmen could picture his eyes scanning every square inch of the room as he spoke, hoping for clues of some kind.

"Let me remind you, Billy. Carmen is seventeen, and you are nineteen. That makes her a minor and you an adult. Don't do anything stupid."

"Wait. Let me see that picture again."

No! Billy, don't rat me out.

"Nope, I'm sure I haven't seen her. That's a face I would have remembered."

⑨

"Hey guys. I'm home, and I brought the party." Kansas breezed through the door holding a case of beer.

Where had she bought that? She was around the same age as Carmen. Wasn't she?

Kansas set the case on the counter and swiveled toward the family room. "So, we have a guest. . .or a roomie?"

"I'm staying, if that's okay." Carmen shrugged.

"Great. It's perfect. We needed a fourth, and I like you." Kansas put her hand up to her mouth and pretended to whisper. "And Billy needs a girlfriend."

"Hey. Would you cut that out?"

"Our pal Billy. . .well, he's still the big V."

What was she talking about?

"Kansas. I'm going to kill you," Billy shouted from the bedroom.

"Oh, have a smoke and a beer. You'll get over it." Kansas winked at Carmen.

Did big V mean what she thought it did? Billy? Wow. If that were true. . .well, Carmen hardly knew anyone who was still a virgin. Except maybe Justin, if his girlfriend's attitude was any indication.

Kansas popped open a beer and took a long swig then suppressed a belch with her hand. "Excuse me."

Gross.

"Okay. Let's just set down some ground rules so we can get right to living together." She handed Carmen a beer.

Not Carmen's first, of course, but it had been awhile. She popped the top and took several swigs. "Ground rules?" This should be good.

"I figure you'll need a few weeks to get on your feet, get a job, that sort of thing. So we'll take care of everything this month. We'll share food and beverage, maybe even some weed now and then."

"Don't go crazy over there, Kansas," Billy joked from the bedroom. Or at least half joked.

"In a month, you need to be pulling your own weight. You'll pay a quarter of the rent and all household bills and put fifty dollars into the kitchen every week. We share everything. Sound okay?"

"Sounds great. Thanks for the help. I'll pay you back for this month." Somehow.

"Naw. Don't worry about that. It's our contribution to rescuing you from that place. . .from a life of zombiedom."

※

Make it stop. No matter how hard she begged, the marching band continued to trample all over Carmen's brain. She rolled gingerly onto her stomach, careful not to shake the bed, and pulled a pillow down over her ears. They still rang. The room had stopped spinning at least—after she'd thrown up for the second time.

The banging in her head seemed audible. Could other people in the apartment hear it? Or were they listening to their own drumbeat?

Clearly Billy's was a party house. Carmen would have to watch out. She didn't want to spend all of her days feeling like she'd rather be dead.

Water. Must get water. She pried herself up from the mattress. The room started wobbling ever so slightly. The kitchen was so far away. . . . She flopped back onto the bed. She'd try again in a few minutes. If someone brought her water, she'd be a personal slave forever.

"Knock, knock." Billy pushed the door open a crack.

Another one who says "knock" in place of actually knocking. Weird. "Ugh. You don't want to see me like this. Really." Carmen's eyes flew open. "Why am I in your bed?"

"You mean you don't remember?" Billy grinned, flashing two dimples. Where had those been hiding?

"Very funny. Seriously though. . . ?"

"You had a little too much fun last night, and I thought you might stand a better chance of waking up feeling human if you slept in a real bed." He sat on the edge. "Been awhile since you partied, huh?"

"Oh no. Don't talk about it. It makes me want to throw up again."

"Sorry." Billy reached under her head and lifted. "Here, drink some cold water."

Her hero. Carmen gulped it like she'd been in the Sahara for a week without fluid. It soothed her throat and calmed her stomach a bit. It even helped her headache while actually drinking it, but the throbbing returned as soon as she stopped swallowing. "Got anything for a raging headache? Anything legal?"

"Well, you sure didn't make that *legal* qualifier last night." Billy laughed.

"I know, I know. I'm just feeling a little guilty for acting like I did."

"Oh, don't worry. You'll get over the guilt in no time."

That's what she was afraid of.

Chapter 35

"Hey, Nater. It's me." *Please don't hang up.*

"Carmen?" He sighed. "What do you want?"

Ouch. "I just want to talk to you. I have to know how you are."

"I'm fine. Was that all you wanted?"

"Nate, come on. Give me a chance. Talk to me."

"A chance for what?"

"No pressure or anything, just a conversation. I need to know how your life is going. If you're. . .you know. . .if you're okay."

"I don't know if I'll ever be okay. But that's fine. I'm going through the motions. School. Work. Home. Whatever."

He had a job already? So many changes. She'd done this to him. This was her fault. Why was she dragging him through the pain of this conversation, too? Just because she wanted to talk to him? Again, her wishes were overriding everyone else's needs. "Would it be better if I let you go?"

"It would have been better if you hadn't called. But now that the scab has been torn off, we might as well talk."

"How's school?"

"Is this really about school?"

Of course not. "Not really. Tell me you're okay."

"I'm okay. Really. What did you expect?"

What had she expected? That he'd become a hermit

mourning for her? That he'd gone on a hunger strike or stayed in bed all day and night pining away? No, probably more that he'd gotten married to someone else already. "I don't know. I guess I'm just sorry."

"Well there's a start. Maybe you should have opened with that."

"Probably." What was there to say?

"How are you calling me? I thought you couldn't call anyone but family."

Oh man. Nate wasn't going to like this at all. "I'm actually not at Diamond Estates anymore." Points for telling the truth?

"Did you finish? Are you home in New Jersey?"

Did she hear a slight lilt of hope in his voice? "No, I'm actually in Denver living with some friends temporarily."

"You ran away?" Disappointment singed the phone. "Some things never change, do they?"

Carmen searched her brain for something witty to say or some way to spin the situation. She came up empty. The silence went on.

"Well, thanks for calling. Take care of yourself. And. . .um. . . Carmen?"

"Yes?" Carmen croaked.

"Don't call again. I'm not up for more of the same."

The connection died.

ॐ

"So what have you got that will make me forget everything?" Carmen lay on the family room floor watching the ceiling fan rotate. A few moments of relief from the regret. A little time to forget about Nate. An hour or two to not think about the baby and all she'd lost in the past year. And even to forget about Diamond Estates and what she'd given up in running away. She didn't regret it. Well, not much. If only she could have seen what it looked like on the other side before she had to jump in.

"Hmm. Well, I do have some good stuff. But we'd have to use it while Billy's out. He'd kill me if he knew I had it and again if he found out I gave you some." Kansas checked her phone. "He leaves for work in fifteen minutes."

The shower turned off as if on cue.

"What do you have?"

"You'll have to wait and see." She nudged her head toward the bathroom door.

Kansas went into her bedroom and rummaged through her drawer. Carmen could hear her muttering to herself.

What could it be? It had to be hard drugs, or she wouldn't mind showing Billy. He drew the line at marijuana, huh? Carmen thought she had, too. But things change as life changed. She needed an escape, and if Kansas had it, Carmen would take it.

"Bye, girls. I'm going to work. See you about eleven." Billy went through the door in his blue factory shirt and gray pants.

"Bye." Carmen sat up. If she knew Kansas like she thought she did, that girl would be out there in a flash.

Right on cue, Kansas bustled into the room, crossed her legs on the couch and pulled the coffee table close to her knees. She set down a mirror and took out a packet of white powder. "Up for some of the real stuff?"

"What will it do to me? I don't want to lose control or hallucinate. That totally freaks me out."

"Oh, snorting coke doesn't cause that. You'll feel like you're on top of the world. You'll be invincible, successful, awesome. You'll forget about any negativity, and everything will be great."

"That's what I'm talking about. Let's do it."

§

Carmen stuck her head into Billy's room where he slept. "Mind if I use your computer for a sec?" It had been almost two months since she'd checked e-mail. The day she'd gotten on the plane for Diamond Estates. She'd been tempted to ask Billy for access since she arrived at his apartment two weeks ago, but it felt like too big an intrusion. She couldn't hold back anymore, though. Besides, they were getting closer. He wouldn't mind.

"Sure. Help yourself." Billy rolled over and pulled his covers with him.

She logged in to her e-mail account. One hundred eleven unread messages? Start with the most important. Nate. Nope. The search revealed not a single message from him. Then again, he'd known she wouldn't be able to e-mail from Diamond Estates, so maybe she shouldn't read too much into that. Oh, who was she kidding? Nate was through with her. Rightfully so.

How about Diego? He'd be another one disappointed in her. Especially about the drugs. She really needed to stop doing that. It seemed like Kansas was up for anything all the time, and each time it went further. Carmen would stick to some beer and maybe a little weed now and then. But the coke—that had to go.

She did a search for Diego's name. Nothing from him, but Theresa's name popped up. Hopefully with information about Diego.

Dear Carmen,

I hope ur doing good at that place. We pray for you at home all the time. Diego is fine, at least physically. He's in jail waiting for his trial. He'll prolly go to prison for a while.

I'm sorry about all you went through here. It didn't have to be so hard. Most of us Hackensackers are good people. I'm also sorry that you lost the baby. I wish you'd have talked to me about it. I wanted to be your friend.

I also wanted to let you know that I'm comin there in a

*few weeks for a mission trip with my church. We're going to
be helping with the start of some building project. Should
be fun. I'm looking forward to seeing u. Let me know if u
want me to bring you anything special.*

*Love,
Theresa*

Cool. Almost like a real friend. Carmen should have let a
relationship develop there. Theresa might have helped her figure
things out without all the Diego drama. Now it was too late to
be friends. Or was it? Two problems, though. Carmen was no
longer at Diamond Estates—at least not at the moment. And
she had no intention of moving home to New Jersey. Now or
ever. Maybe. Okay, so her choices weren't set in stone. Never
really known for decisiveness, that was for sure.

She could at least return the e-mail and then see what
developed.

Dear Theresa,
*Sorry I'm just now replying. We don't get much
computer access at Diamond Estates. Thanks so much
for writing and telling me about Diego. I've been really
worried. If you get to talk to him somehow, tell him I said
hi and that I miss him.*
*That's cool you're coming to Diamond Estates! I hope I
get to see you.*

Should Carmen tell her she'd left the program? No, anything
could change between now and then. No sense upsetting her.

Mission trips sound like so much fun.
Thanks for what you said about the baby. It does help

to talk about it rather than pretend it never happened like
a lot of people seem to want to do. I think about it every
day and wish things had turned out differently.

Anyway, write again soon.

Best,
Carmen

"Okay. There's only so much a man can take." Billy barged into his bedroom.

"What?" Carmen sat up. "You said I could nap on your bed. Did I sleep too long?"

"No, silly. I'm talking about that pot on the stove. What is in there, and when can I eat it?"

"That's what this is about?" Carmen threw a pillow at Billy.

"Well, you're going to share, aren't you?"

"Of course I will. It's almost done."

"That pot's been simmering for two days. What's in it?"

Carmen wiggled her eyebrows. "You're in for a pot of the greatest award-winning chili known to man."

"Mmm. I'm such a chili fan. I've been waiting to taste some of that awesome cooking I've been hearing about."

Speaking of the chili, it was time to stir. "Come on." Carmen led the way to the kitchen. She backed up to the counter and hopped up onto it, her piggy slippers dangling. She took the lid off the stockpot and stirred the simmering brew, breathing in the heady aroma of chili powder, cinnamon, cloves, and red pepper. To die for.

Carmen blew on a spoonful. "Here. Taste."

Billy leaned forward and slurped the chili from the spoon. He closed his eyes and rolled his tongue around his mouth. "I think that's the best chili I've ever tasted. It's amazing."

"Thanks." She ladled a big scoop into a bowl, dumped

oyster crackers on top, sprinkled some shredded cheese, and added a dollop of sour cream. "Now that is a bowl of chili." She handed it to Billy and then made one for herself.

Billy sat at the dinette with his untouched food.

"Go ahead. Eat."

"This will sound weird, but I can't eat without praying. Do you mind?" He took her hand and began to pray.

"Heavenly Father. . ."

Carmen guessed she didn't mind, but how strange. Billy sure didn't seem to be living like someone who prayed over every meal.

§

Dear Nellie,

Where are you? I remember shoving you deep under my mattress when I was in a hurry the other day, but I can't believe I ran off without you. I hope no one finds you until I can find a way to get you back.

I don't understand Billy at all. He's a cute guy, lots going for him. Grieving over his sister, he's kind of throwing everything away   at least as it looks on the outside. But then in private moments, I wonder if he's really the bad boy he wants people to think he is. He's an interesting dude. Definitely going to be keeping my eye on him.

Love,
Carmen

Chapter 36

"U h. . .Carmen? You have a visitor." Billy spoke through the bathroom door.

Carmen squeezed water from her hair. "Who is it?" It had better not be Ben. He couldn't do a thing to force her back to Diamond Estates, but she really didn't want to talk to him face-to-face. He'd be all spiritual, and that's the last thing she needed. She was confused enough as it was.

"I think you just need to come out here." Billy's voice sounded broken. Hesitant.

Was he pulling some kind of prank? "Should I come out naked, or can I have a minute?"

"No. I suggest you put on some clothes."

Great. Just what she needed. A job interview in two hours and now this. Who could it be, and why was Billy being so weird about it?

Carmen pulled on a clean pair of yoga pants and a tank top. The interview clothes could wait. She twisted her hair back into a clip, willing it to dry wavy and flowy. A swipe of deodorant under each arm and a mist of perfume. Carmen was ready to face her mysterious visitor.

She opened the bathroom door and stepped into the family room when her heartbeat came to a crashing halt.

Nate.

He stood at the front door with his hands in his jeans pockets. Looking down at the floor.

Billy sat on the couch and stared at him.

Why didn't Billy invite Nate in? Why was Nate there? He must've come to get back together. There'd be no other reason to make such a long trip.

Nate's eyes rose and locked with Carmen's. The corners turned down, and the lids were heavy. Why was he so sad?

Billy cleared his throat.

Oh no. Nate must think. . .Billy? What should she deal with first? "Nate. Why didn't you tell me you were coming? I'd have been so excited."

"Tell you? So you could hide your *friend*?"

"Billy's not that kind of friend. Nothing has ever happened between us. Trust me."

"Trust you? That's a pretty tall order."

Carmen had that coming to her.

"Well, I guess I'll leave you two lovebirds to your catching up. I'll be in my room if you need me." Billy slunk away and closed his door softly.

Poor Billy. It was clear he had feelings for her. She might have entertained the idea if circumstances had been different. As things stood though, she had to figure out what was happening with Nate and even with Justin before she could move on with someone else.

How to start this conversation? She had no idea what Nate was there to say. Why didn't he just get it over with so they could go from there?

Nate leaned back against the walk beside the front door and stared at Carmen's face. His steely eyes gave away nothing.

If he wasn't going to speak, she'd start with small talk. "How did you know where I was?"

"Reverse phone lookup. Got the address from there. Took a chance." Nate shrugged like he did that sort of detective work every day.

"If you'd have asked, I'd have given you the address. But I'm super glad you're here. Will you come in and sit on the couch with me?" Carmen perched on the edge and patted the worn fabric beside her.

Nate sat down but kept his jacket on. He looked like a squirrel, ready to bolt at the slightest wrong move.

"Talk to me. What have you come to say?" He certainly hadn't come all that way for nothing. Unless he was like her and had no idea what he wanted. Was his soul as empty as hers?

"I miss you. I love you. I feel like we're soul mates. . ."

Carmen's heart soared.

". . .but—"

"But what? What else matters than that?" That word erased everything that came before it. *Take it back.*

"But I can't get back together with the old you. I just can't. I was hoping a new, improved, mature, confident version of you would return home after awhile apart, and we'd get back together and live happily ever after." Nate took her hand.

"That can still happen." *Please say it can.*

"We've been through a lot. I don't want to start over with someone else. A stranger. Someone who doesn't know me for who I am."

Carmen nodded.

"I was willing to wait for you when you left for Diamond Estates. I still am. But only if I think there's hope. When I heard you'd run away and quit the program—" Nate's voice caught.

Leave it to Carmen. She'd blown it again. When would she learn? Would she ever take the hard road and do something right? "I know. I've sort of been regretting that decision now and then. I sort of wish I'd given it more time. I'll go back. If what you say is true. . .if you really mean it, I'll go back."

"No. I mean what I said, but that won't work. I don't want you to go back there for me—just to get me back. It's not real then." Nate let go of her hand. "And it won't last."

But she meant it. It wasn't just for him. But now he'd never believe that. Like apologizing for someone after getting caught—it didn't feel genuine. "I'm serious. I've regretted my choice and have considered calling them to come get me. I've been thinking about it, even before you came. Please believe me. It's different this time."

Nate's sad gaze pierced her heart. He wasn't buying it.

"Have you talked to your mom since you left Diamond Estates?"

What did that have to do with anything? Why was he changing the subject? "No. Why?"

"Because she loves you, and she's so worried about you." Nate shook his head. "Your sisters, your dad. . . It doesn't make any sense to me how you could just avoid them like you are."

Humiliation. Regret. "I don't know, Nate. I guess I'm just running. . .or hiding. Whatever. I know it's wrong. I can imagine they're pretty hurt." Carmen gulped back a sob. She refused to cry.

"That's an understatement." Nate took her hand again. "Will you contact them? For me?"

"Anything. Yes. I'll do it today." Carmen sounded desperate, but she couldn't help it. She *was* desperate. What did she ever do to deserve someone like Nate? "I'll go back."

"Think about it—pray about it—before you make promises. Make sure you're ready."

Did he say pray about it? When had he started pushing prayer? Had he found what she'd been unable to?

"I'm leaving for the airport in an hour." Her stomach clenched. They needed more time. "An hour? Why so soon? You just got here." *Don't go. Please.*

"It has to be this way. I wanted to make sure I wasn't tempted to stay here holed up in this place with you. But listen. If you can find the will to go back to Diamond Estates, dive into the program, and let it change your heart, I'm here. . .waiting for you."

If. If. If. Even though Carmen bristled at the ultimatum, she knew he was right. In the end, he deserved someone who had her act together. Thankfully he wanted that someone to be her. Could she do it? She could sure try.

But what if she failed?

Billy entered the family room humming "My Boyfriend's Back." He stopped abruptly. "What are you doing sitting here all alone in the dark?"

Carmen shrugged.

"How long have you been like that?" Billy sat beside her and touched her leg. "You're freezing." He covered her with a blanket. "Have you not moved since Nate left? I laid down for a nap hours ago."

"If I move, I have to do something. This way I can prolong the inevitable." Even Carmen heard the despair in her voice.

"What are you talking about, Carmen? Talk to me."

"I can never be what Nate wants me to be—what he deserves." Carmen put her head in her hands.

"You should never let another person try to change you. You should always be yourself."

"No. It's not like that. I'm talking about the basics. Honesty. Trust. Loyalty. Respect. Commitment. He'd like to see some of those qualities in me. I guess I would, too. But the harder I try, the more I just want to give up."

Billy nodded.

"I mean, I promised Nate that I'd go back to Diamond Estates, talk to my family, get it together. But I kind of wonder if it's even worth trying. Maybe I should just tell him I went back and pretend all is well. But that would be just another deception in a long history of lies."

"You don't want that." Billy's voice dropped, and he looked away.

"Then there's you." Carmen shrugged. "I think maybe we could have had something with each other if my life wasn't such a big mess. But I feel like I owe it to the old me—the one who hurt everyone I loved—to fix things." *If that's possible.*

"Making things right is great, but be sure you don't try to resurrect a relationship just because you think you owe it to someone."

Carmen nodded. Add Billy to the list of people she'd hurt. "I'm sorry you got bruised along the way."

"Oh, don't worry about me. Besides, we have no idea how God is going to end this story."

"You really think He is involved in what happens? You really think He cares?"

"Yes, very much so. Do you believe in God?"

"I—I think so." Carmen looked up. "I don't know. But if you really do, then why. . . Why the partying and rebelling? Why the drugs?"

Billy nodded. "I know. It makes no sense. But truth is, I'm just like you. It got tough for me when Naomi died. I just figured I'd never be able to make it on the Christian journey with the rage I had in my heart. So rather than try, I just let go. Really pathetic when you think about it." He grimaced.

"Any regrets?"

"All day, every day."

Chapter 37

"Uh. . .Carmen? Someone's here for you!" Billy shouted through the bathroom door.

Seriously? This showing up unannounced while she was in the shower needed to stop. Carmen turned off the faucet and twisted her hair and let the water drip off. Who could it be this time?

Maybe Nate.

Carmen rubbed the towel over her body and absorbed most of the moisture then threw on her clothes, which mopped up the rest. She ran a comb through her hair and twisted it back in a clip.

When did people stop calling to say they were coming by? Too bad she couldn't have retrieved her cell phone from Ben's stash before she'd ducked out.

Ready as she could get, Carmen plastered a smile on her face and threw the door open. *Please be Nate.*

Olivia. And she wasn't smiling.

Carmen's stomach lurched as her archenemy strode toward her.

Would Olivia hit her? But Carmen hadn't spoken to Justin even once since the whole lie thing. She'd given up on the possibility of Justin. It was just a stupid game. Olivia wouldn't see it that way though.

As she walked across the room, Olivia's face softened. Her

lips turned up into a smile, and she reached out her arms,
pulling Carmen into a stiff hug.

What? In some time warp, Carmen was being hugged
by Olivia. It couldn't be real. Or if it was, the girl was crazy.
What should Carmen do? She couldn't hug Olivia back. How
weird. Maybe she was high? With her face pressed over Olivia's
shoulder, Carmen could smell the scent of strawberry in her
hair. And, oh look. A vibrant purple streak ran down from
the top of Olivia's head. Had she always had that? How had
Carmen missed it before?

Finally Olivia's grip loosened, and Carmen stepped back.
"Um. . .care to fill me in on what this is all about?" Carmen
smoothed her hair and straightened her clothes.

"Sure. I just wanted to tell you I forgive you."

"Uh. Okay. Thanks?" Didn't people usually have to
apologize before they were forgiven? It was probably step forty-
seven in the Diamond Estates program to forgive everyone who
hurt you. But come on. Wasn't that pushing things a bit?

"I understand where you're at and why you did what you
did. I'd like to put it behind us so we can be friends."

Maybe she did understand. She'd been in a similar place in
her own life. But was it a trick? "Friends, like real friends? Or is
this a keep-your-friends-close-and-your-enemies-closer kind of
thing?" Probably the latter.

"Definitely real. I don't have time for games in my life. I've
been praying for you, and I feel like this is what God wants for
all of us." Olivia put out her hand. "Friends?"

It's worth a shot. Carmen shook Olivia's hand. "Friends."

"Now the other reason I'm here. . ." Olivia glanced around
her. "I know it's going to be hard to leave all this. . ."

"Hey. This is an awesome place," Billy called from the kitchen.

"No offense meant to the voice behind the curtain." Olivia

gestured at the apartment and shook her head. "We can do better than this. What's it going to take for you to let me take you back to Diamond Estates?"

"Will you go in with me to talk to Ben?" He'd never forgive her. Not like Olivia had.

"Easy one. Let's go."

Chapter 38

"So. Here we are." Ben sat in his desk chair in his favorite pose with his hands behind his head. "Back where we started."

He didn't look angry. More like blank with a touch of disappointment. Carmen rubbed her palms on her jeans until the friction warmed them. What could she say to him? There was no explanation or excuse that sounded even remotely plausible. Anything she said would come off as defensiveness. Suppose she could start with an apology.

Carmen took a deep breath and raised her eyes to lock with Ben's. "I'm *really* sorry." Emphasis on the really. And not just because she wanted to come back. Though Ben might think so.

Ben nodded. "I appreciate your apology."

What was he waiting for? He didn't try very hard to make stuff like this easy, did he? What else did he want from her? If only there were some magic formula. She could try honesty. "Is it okay if I come back? I want to come back."

"Why?"

A good question. With no simple answer. "I want to stop running. I want to raise the white flag and give up the control. I want to stop lying and manipulating everyone. I want to be someone people can be proud of. . .someone I can be proud of." Was that enough? Because she had more if he wanted to hear it.

"Those are great things. How do you think coming back to

Diamond Estates will help you achieve them?"

He was full of the hard questions. "Um. I just. . . I guess I need training. I need you guys to help me know God personally and stick to my commitments until they become a real part of me."

Ben dropped his hands and rocked forward, his chair squeaking and bouncing. He jabbed a finger at Carmen. "That's it. Right there. That's what we're talking about here. Knowing God and making commitments that become part of who you are. Is that really what you want, or are those just pretty words because you know what I want to hear? Really think about that."

Carmen searched her inner thoughts. Was there any deception there? Was she running yet again, this time back to safety? Was she doing this only to get Nate back? No. No. No. She meant what she said.

"That's really what I want." *Desperately*.

"Then welcome home."

⑨

Carmen knocked gently on the door to her old room. Ben had promised she still had a home waiting for her in there, but she'd believe it when she saw it. The door squeaked open a few inches, so she peeked in. "Anyone home?"

"Hey! You're back." Tricia grinned from her bunk and laid that month's *Vogue* on her chest.

Kira jumped up and pulled Carmen into a hug. "We were so happy when we found out you'd be home today."

Happy? Carmen expected reluctant but amenable at best. "I see you saved my spot." Carmen looked over her things. "I was gone for three weeks. What if I hadn't come back? How long would they have kept this all here?"

Tricia shrugged. "I doubt there's any set amount of time. I think they just always knew this was part of your journey, and you'd have your fill and return."

Carmen nodded. Smart people.

Her eyes traveled from her bunk to the one below it. A black blanket with black sheets and a black throw pillow covered Leila's bunk. Had she gotten new bedding? That somber look didn't seem like something she'd choose for herself. "So where's Leila?"

Tricia looked at Kira and groaned. "I really don't want to tell you this." She closed her eyes.

Had something happened to Leila? Why were they making such a big deal out of it? "What happened? Just tell me."

"Roxy sleeps there now. Leila went home a few days ago. She left the program."

"Oh man. She was nowhere near ready for that." What about the cuts on her arm? Carmen had never told anyone or done anything to help her. What would happen to her now?

Tricia and Kira shared another strained look. There was something they weren't telling Carmen.

"What else? Come on. Tell me."

"She left because. . .because she found your journal and read it. I guess there was a lot in there about her. You'd know better than we would." Kira gave Carmen a sympathetic pat on the shoulder.

No. The air squeezed from Carmen's lungs like they were in a vice grip. She leaned against the wall and slid to the floor. She could see Leila opening the book in curiosity then little by little feeling her world crumble around her. The words she'd written about Leila ran through Carmen's brain like the news tickers on Times Square.

. . .unattractive. . .mousy. . .if the horse would hold her. . . never been kissed. . .never would be kissed. . .cutting. . .what a dumb thing to do. . .

"I can't believe this. It's horrible." Carmen put her head in her hands. "What did she say?"

"Nothing to us. I guess she took the book to Donna so no one else would find it and then asked to go home." Kira looked away. "Ben doesn't give up easily when a girl wants to leave. She must have been pretty convincing."

"What happens now? I have to do something."

"Welcome back," Donna spoke from the doorway.

Carmen looked up from where she slumped on the floor. Donna's frown revealed she'd been listening long enough to know the subject.

"What am I going to do? I have to fix this." Carmen's careless words had destroyed an already-messed-up girl.

"Sometimes there's no possible repair for actions, Carmen." Donna offered a gentle smile. "Forgiveness is available from God, of course. And you can reach out to Leila by writing a letter or calling. But you can't be guaranteed she'll accept your apology. And even if she did, some of the words she read will leave lasting scars."

Carmen sighed. "Just what Leila needed. More scars." This time she let the tears come.

Donna crouched down. "What do you mean by that?"

"Her arms. Didn't you ever wonder why she always wore long sleeves?" *Come on, Donna, think.* Wait a minute. "Didn't you read my journal when Leila gave it to you guys?"

"Yes. But there were pages torn out before I got it."

Leila probably destroyed the important parts. Carmen jumped up. "Donna. Leila cuts herself. And I mean all the time. She goes in the bathroom and slices up her arms."

"Oh, dear Jesus." Donna's face turned white.

"She's in danger, isn't she?"

Tricia jumped off the bunk. "Is that true?"

Carmen looked into her eyes and nodded.

"Then why on earth didn't you say something to someone?" Tricia shook Carmen's shoulders.

"I didn't. . .I don't know. . ." Carmen withered under Tricia's glare. She deserved it.

Donna held up a hand. "That's not important now. I need to get Ben involved and talk to her parents right away." She took off toward the stairs.

The room remained so quiet, Carmen was sure they could hear her heart pounding. What had she done? She asked herself that question a lot, didn't she? Well, she left a lot of terror in her wake. But this time. . .

"Why didn't you tell anyone? Even us?" Tricia's eyes drooped. "I don't get it."

"I'm not going to lie and tell you that it was because I was protecting her privacy or keeping her secret. Though the thought did cross my mind." Carmen took a deep breath. "The honest truth about why I let the poor girl deal with her pain her own way is because I didn't really care. I was too selfish to let her problems affect me as anything more than fodder for gossip."

Kira nodded. "I've been there."

"This is all my fault, and I will fix it."

᠖

"So how do you feel about a new roommate?" Roxy hesitated in the bedroom doorway.

Carmen motioned her in. "You? You're a super cool roomie. I just don't like how this happened. You know." Carmen shrugged. "I'm sure you know the story."

Roxy crossed her legs and sat on the floor beside Carmen, leaning against the bottom bunk. She hung her head, the newly dyed band of bright-red hair fell in front of her eyes. "Yeah.

Um, I was wondering. What did you say about me in that book of yours? I mean, it's weird to know it exists somewhere but not be able to read it."

Carmen sighed and plucked at strands of carpet. "I wish I'd never started that thing. No good can come of it. It's nothing but a catalog of people's faults." Like she didn't have any of her own. "You know what I'd say about me if I were writing in it?"

Roxy lifted her bright-blue eyes. "No, but now you've got me curious."

"I'd write: 'Dear Nellie, Carmen Castillo is a big loser. She makes fun of other people because she hates herself. She lies and manipulates people because she doesn't believe she's worthy of their love without her deception. She is the most negative, ugly hearted person I know. She has no friends, and I can see why. And her clothes? How about a new pair of jeans? Love, Carmen.' "

Roxy nodded. "That was pretty honest. Brutal, but honest." She grimaced. "Was mine that bad?"

"No. I didn't spend enough time with you, so my entry about you was mostly questions. Why is she here? Where did she come from? Why is she so quiet? You know, that sort of thing."

"Want answers?"

Carmen nodded.

"I'm here because I beat up my mom's boyfriend after he beat her up. I come from Madison, Wisconsin. I'm quiet because people usually don't listen when I talk anyway. And, like you, I don't have any friends." Roxy looked down at her checkerboard Converse.

"Maybe we could be friends."

"Really?" Roxy offered the first hint of a smile.

"As long as you never, ever say 'BFF' in my presence. That makes me want to hurl."

***

Dear Nellie,
Roxy is pretty cool.
Love,
Carmen

Chapter 39

B en put a hand on Carmen's shoulder as they walked from the prayer room toward his office. "I've arranged a conference call via Skype with your family." He stopped, put his hands on her shoulders, and looked her in the eyes. "Are you ready?"

Was she ready? Well, who knew? She couldn't answer that unless she knew what the outcome of the conversations would be. Was she ready for any potential outcome? No. Was she strong enough to do her part and hope for the best? Probably.

"I'm ready."

"Good. It's necessary that you settle some of those relationships."

Carmen took a shuddering breath. What would they say to her? What would Mom say? After three weeks of no communication, would it be awkward?

"First you'll have a few minutes to talk with your mom without the others on the line." Ben held the door open for her to enter. The computer was all set up with the flat-screen monitor facing the guest chairs. Ben took one and waited for Carmen to sit in the other. He was going to stay and listen? That could get awkward. Maybe he'd leave once it got going.

Ben moved the mouse around and clicked on some buttons. The screen came to life. He typed in some numbers, selected a few boxes, then pressed CALL.

Connecting. . .

So Mom would show up right there in that little box? How strange to talk to her like that. Could she see Carmen on the other end?

Connected. . .

Carmen gasped. "Hi, Mom. You look fantastic." She didn't look a day past thirty. Her makeup was perfect, and her wrinkles had all but disappeared. Had she had a face-lift? No way she'd spend money on that.

"Thanks. It's great to see your face." Her smile was bright. Teeth whitener?

Enough of the inspection. Time to get serious. Carmen looked right into the webcam. "Mom, I'm so sorry for everything I've done. I've messed up so bad. I've lied to you, and I know I've hurt you deeply. I'm. . .just really sorry. Can you forgive me?"

"I already forgave you, Carmen. The day you were born you became my daughter, and nothing you do will ever change that fact. I'll admit, I haven't been thrilled with your choices lately, but I've never stopped loving you."

Hmm. "Ben says that's how God is. Do you think that, too?"

"That's exactly the way God loves you. I'm so glad to see you're starting to figure that out." She seemed to be selecting her words. "You know, even though I have loved you since birth, the God who created you has loved you since the beginning of time. He is passionate about you. And He's already forgiven you—you only need to accept it."

Carmen nodded and exhaled for what felt like the first time all day. "I think I get that." Carmen turned to Ben. "How do I do that?"

"I think your mom is doing an excellent job of explaining.

I'm going to let her continue." Ben nodded at the camera.

"Sweetie, I can understand you turning to Ben for spiritual leadership. I haven't been very strong in that area. But that's all going to change. Can you trust me?"

Carmen nodded. This was a side of Mom she'd never seen before.

"Accepting Christ requires you to humble yourself, admitting to God that you're a sinner—we all are—and that you need His gift of grace. Then you have to live in faith that even though you're a work in progress, the forgiveness is complete." Mom leaned forward. "Do you want to do that right now?"

Carmen nodded. "It's scary, but I believe it's real."

"It's okay to be scared about turning your life upside down. But it won't be like that. You'll see." Mom reached a hand out as though touching Carmen.

Ben laid a hand on her shoulder.

Mom cleared her throat. "Repeat this prayer after me, but consider the words. Make them your own."

Carmen gulped then nodded. "Okay."

"Father God, I stand before You with a broken and sinful heart."

Oh boy. Here goes. "God, I stand before You with a broken and sinful heart."

"Please forgive me for my sins. I accept Your gift of grace."

"Please forgive me for my sins, and I accept Your grace." It wasn't so hard to pray. Why had she fought it so long?

"I want to live my life in relationship with You from this day forward."

Carmen nodded. "I want to be in a relationship with You from now on."

"And I surrender my life to You. Amen."

"And I surrender my life to You. Thank You for loving me,

Jesus. Amen." Where had that last part come from? Carmen hadn't meant to add that on, but neither could she stop herself.

She opened her eyes. "Is that it?"

"That's it." Mom grinned. "How do you feel?"

How did she feel? Carmen took inventory on her emotions. "I feel like me. Only clearer. At peace. Forgiven."

"Ahh. Blissful, isn't it?"

"It really is." If only that moment didn't have to end. Carmen had so much repair work to do. But at least now she didn't have to do it alone.

Ben coughed. "I have to say, that was one of the most touching moments I've had since I've been here." He wiped his eyes with a hanky. "Carmen, is it okay if your dad joins us now?"

"Daddy's there?" What was he doing at Mom's apartment in New Jersey?

Mom shook her head. "No, no. I think Ben is going to conference him in. Is that right, Ben?"

"Yes. Just give me a moment to bring him into the call. If we get disconnected, we'll call you right back."

Carmen fidgeted in her seat and stared out the window while Ben's body blocked her view of the screen. Carmen missed her daddy. The old him—not the newly divorced, single-father edition. What would Dad say to her? He'd always been more liberal than Mom, but what if Carmen's actions had pushed him over the edge? And what would he say about her new commitment to Christ?

Ben sat down in his chair beside Carmen. "I think that did it."

Connecting. . .

"Carmen? Is that my girl?" Dad's smile spread across his webcam box beside Mom's.

"It's me, Daddy. It's good to see you."

"You, too, baby. How are you?"

"Dad? First I want to tell you that I'm sorry for everything. I didn't mean to hurt you guys. . .or anyone. But I did some dumb things. I'm really sorry."

"Thanks, but I'm the one who should be apologizing to you. I haven't been a great dad this year, and I've allowed some things I never should have. I'm sorry for not protecting your innocence and for not being there for you."

Carmen wiped her eyes. She refused to cry. "I love you, Daddy."

"I love you, too." He took a deep breath.

"I want to tell you something." Carmen squared her shoulders. "I'm a Christian now. I've accepted Jesus as my Savior." Wow. Saying it out loud for the first time was really cool.

Daddy gasped. "That's wonderful, angel. I'm so proud of you."

Where had that come from? "You are? But you don't get into all that God stuff. You never have."

"Well, I never have, but I'll look into it if it's something important to you. I should have a long time ago. It's probably what made your mom such a better person than I am."

Carmen couldn't help but steal a glance at Mom's face in her video box.

Mom's teeth clamped down hard on her lip. Smart woman.

"I'm glad to hear that, Dad. I figured you'd laugh it off as a crutch or just the next phase I'd go through."

He shook his head. "No. This is different. My baby is growing up." He smiled. "Hey, how about we start going to church together when you move home?"

"I'd love that so much."

"Now I have some news for you."

Oh boy. He and Tiffany are getting married. "What is it?" It would be okay. She could handle it.

"Tiff and I broke up."

"What?" Carmen forced her voice lower than the shout she wanted to release. "You broke up? Why?" She sure hadn't seen that one coming.

"We wanted different things out of life, and I didn't like who I'd become to my family. So I'm going to focus on my girls for a while and not worry about dating." Dad smiled. "Does that sound okay to you?"

"Yeah, totally. I mean, Tiffany had some good qualities. She turned out not to be as horrible as I thought. But she wasn't a mom. She wasn't Mom." Carmen glanced to the webcam vignette just to the right of Dad's face.

"Mom, does this mean. . . ? Are you and Dad. . .you know?"

"No. Not right now. Who knows what the future holds? But we're taking it all one day at a time. With our hearts and minds on you girls most of all."

Carmen let that thought wash over her. Bliss.

"Speaking of girls, I have two sitting outside the door to this room who are desperate to talk to their big sis."

"Bring 'em on."

Mom stepped out of the frame. A few moments later two grinning girls took her place.

Carmen's heart swelled. "Kim. Harper. I missed you both so much."

Harper looked at Kim. "Ready? One. Two. Three."

"WE MISS YOU!"

The computer crackled as it strained to cope with the decibels coming from her sisters' lungs. Carmen laughed. "Wow. Thanks, guys."

She focused her stare on Kim. "Are you keeping it together? Remembering your promise to me?"

"Yeah. I guess." Kim averted her eyes.

What did that mean? "Kim. Look at me." She waited until Kim looked into the camera. "You're scaring me. Tell me what's happening."

Mom and Dad grew strangely quiet as if waiting for a verdict to be handed down.

"No. I mean, I'm good. I just wish you'd been here to help me through some things lately. I thought that was what big sisters were for."

Carmen nodded. "It is. And I will be soon. Please keep hanging in there and doing the right thing. Please. Promise?"

"I promise." Kim smiled. "I'll make you proud of me."

"I am proud." Carmen ached for her annoying little sisters. As much as they bugged her sometimes, they were family.

"When are you coming home?" Harper whined. "It's been too long."

"I agree. Way too long. But I still don't know when I'll be home. How about we make it a goal that I get there for your birthday in August? I can't promise anything, but I'll do my very best." Carmen held up a fist. "Deal?"

Harper pretended to bump knuckles. "Deal."

☙

Dearest Nellie,

You've been a good friend to me. A sounding board, a listening ear. But just knowing you were there kept me looking for the worst in people so I had something to report back to my best friend. But the time has come that we must part ways. Look, I have to move on. I've decided to change the way I approach life. I want to be bias positive rather than bias negative about everything and everyone. I want to love people, embrace their good qualities, and be intrigued by their uniqueness.

This feels like a breakup. In many ways I guess it is. Thanks for all the laughs.

Love,
Carmen

Chapter 40

Well hello there, stranger." Theresa dusted off her jeans as she rose from her seat on the foyer stairs just as prayer time ended.

Carmen gasped. Wow. She pulled Theresa close for a hug. "It's awesome to see a familiar face from home." Not that Hackensack was home. . .or was it?

Theresa let her gaze travel up and down Carmen's body. "You look good. Softer. Happier, maybe. I can't tell what's different."

"Yeah, thanks. That's how I feel." Carmen examined Theresa. "You look exactly the same." High hair, tight clothes, lots of makeup and accessories. "Jersey couture."

"Hey." Theresa's bottom lip poked out in a pretend pout.

"I'm just teasing, T." Carmen nodded toward the dining hall. "You hungry?"

"Famished."

"You're going to love breakfast here." Carmen ushered her toward the smell of bacon. "How long are you staying?"

"We're here for two weeks."

"What about school? Can you miss that much?"

"Believe it or not, I'm sort of homeschooling now. My mom and dad started up a charter school at my church, and a bunch of us are going there." Theresa smiled. "They're doing all they can to keep us out of trouble so we can go to college."

"Is that like a private school?"

"Yep. We even have private schools in the slums of New Jersey." Theresa winked.

Wonder if Kimberley could go there instead of public school. Carmen would have to ask Mom the next time they spoke. "So how did you get hooked up to come here?" Carmen grabbed a tray and two cartons of orange juice.

"It's missions work, which is part of our schooling." Theresa shrugged. "It's a construction project, so I expect they'll keep me pretty busy. But that's okay—that's what I'm here for."

"Construction on what?" Carmen motioned for Theresa to grab a tray and slide it along the steel bars while she selected her food.

"I think Ben's going to announce it soon. They're doing something with that empty building out back. I'm not sure what." She shrugged. "Dad said Ben's been talking about it for years. Whatever it is."

"Cool." Carmen led her to the table with Kira, Tricia, and Roxy then pulled up an extra chair. "Have a seat. Let me introduce you to my friends."

The introductions went around the table. How neat to be able to call each of these people a real friend. She felt. . .rich.

But one question still niggled at Carmen. "Hey, Theresa, can I ask you something else?"

Theresa nodded. "Sure."

"Back a couple of months when we went out that night with Diego, remember that night?"

"Sure."

"Who was that dude in the backseat by you? Diego wouldn't tell me. He called him a ghost."

Theresa sighed. "I knew you were going to ask about him. He was bad news. A local drug dealer and a pimp."

A pimp? Right there in the car with her? How scary.

Theresa eyed Carmen. "He wanted you. Diego had to buy him off with drugs, or he was gonna have you one way or another."

Could that be true? That would explain why Diego ran in the house without her. To think she'd come so close to such danger. "Typical New Jersey." Carmen shook her head.

Theresa's eyes narrowed. "Um. The dude was from Queens."

"You're kidding." So Carmen left upstate New York to move to New Jersey, where she expected gang violence and drugs. But one of her biggest threats had come from New York?

"Yeah, girl, you gotta get off New Jersey's back. Especially Hackensack. Just because people don't have as much money as they do upstate, and just because their houses aren't as big— though Jersey has some mansions, too—don't make them killers or bangers. People are people."

People are people. Hadn't Carmen used those exact words in retaliation against Nate's mom when her prejudice became so glaringly clear? This was different, though. Right?

Carmen raised a finger. "Hold on. If the dude from Queens was after me, why did Diego have me in the car with him?"

"Yeah, it was awkward. Diego didn't find out until we were waiting for you to change your clothes and come out." Theresa picked at her food. "I was afraid for you even then. But Diego took care of it. You never did hear from that dude, did you?"

"No. Diego took care of it." Hopefully his solution wasn't a *permanent* one.

ॐ

Oh, catch her before she leaves. "Donna, can we talk?" Carmen blocked her exit out the back door.

"Sure. I'm just going for a little walk. Want to come?" Donna zipped her red parka. "I can wait for you out there if you want to grab your coat."

"Okay. I'll be right back." Carmen raced up to her room. The last thing she wanted was anything to do with a cold and snowy mountain after the stormy hike she took in arctic January. But it was worth it if Donna could help her figure some things out. She slipped her jacket over her arms as she rushed back to the door where Donna said she'd be waiting.

"Ready?" Donna shouted from the pasture when she saw Carmen step out. "Come on, I want to show you something." She set off in a direction Carmen had never walked before.

It didn't even look like there was a path. Hope Donna knew the way.

"So what's up?" Donna grinned, her cheeks already pink from the crisp wind.

"How do you define *prejudice*?"

Donna's head jerked back in surprise. "Hmm. Good question. To me, prejudice is making a value judgment or setting an expectation on someone based on irrelevant factors like race, sex, body type, income, geographic location. . .stuff like that. Does that make sense?"

Carmen wanted to throw up. She was just as guilty as Hillary McConnell. "I am what I've accused others of being." How had she missed it?

"Ah. I see." Donna smiled. "Another layer of self-realization, huh?"

"Yeah. That stupid book I've been writing. The things I said about and thought about Leila because of her weight and appearance." Carmen shook her head. "Oh no. All that I've thought about Hackensack and New Jersey—and the people who live there." How could she be exactly like the person she hated most?

"And the light dawns." Donna smiled.

"You know, it's funny. I've been blasting Hackensack, but it was there that I met two of the best people I know. Theresa and Diego. True friends."

Carmen's voice caught as she tried to catch her breath. "You know, Briarcliff Manor and Ossining has something ridiculous like three percent Mexican, and most of those were probably hired help. I was the subject of prejudice there, and then I turned around and handed it down. I even thought I was above Nate's Mexican maid because I lived in that town and she only worked there."

Donna nodded.

"What can I do about this?" There had to be a way to fix it.

"Okay. Here's where I'll step in." Donna paused and closed her eyes for a moment. "Life is full of mistakes. We each make them every single day. We're all flawed individuals. The best thing we can do for ourselves and for the Kingdom of God is to be open for growth. Open to hear from God and receive conviction from the Holy Spirit."

Carmen nodded. "I think that's what I'm going through right now."

"Right. There's a story in the Bible about a woman caught in adultery. Jesus forgave her and told her to go and sin no more. He didn't send her back to fix the problem because some things just can't be fixed. You can't go make amends with an entire town or state. You can't change people's thinking, and you can't undo what's done."

"But that sounds so hopeless." Carmen kicked at the snow.

"Well, what you can do is pray that you'd have the opportunity to right any wrongs that are possible. That God would lead you to individuals who are ready to hear or receive an apology. Start there." Donna took Carmen's hand. "And like Jesus said to the adulteress, go and sin no more."

ॐ

"What did he say? Just come outside—no explanation?"

Carmen pulled her parka on then shoved her hands into her gloves.

Tricia shrugged. "You know Ben, always after the drama."

"I think it's about the building project." Theresa stepped in line with the other two on their way to the stable. "I mean, my group's been here for a couple of hours—we kind of need to know what we're going to be doing."

Made perfect sense. They rounded the corner past the barn doors and then stepped up to a clearing where Ben stood atop a tree stump.

"Why are we here?" Carmen shielded her eyes from the sun.

"Gather around, folks. I have an announcement."

Carmen surveyed the crowd. Olivia smiled and waved. Justin averted his eyes. Not quite over the whole situation apparently. Should Carmen approach him? Try to fix it? Or let it go and give it time? Well, she'd never actually apologized directly to him—only to Olivia. She'd have to find a moment to talk with him later.

There were Ginny and Mark Stapleton standing beside Ben and Alicia. Mark held a gleaming pair of scissors near a long yellow ribbon that ran the length of the building behind them.

Ben clapped his hands for attention. "Ladies and gentlemen, I have an exciting announcement. Through much prayer and counsel with the Diamond Estates executive board. . ."

There was an executive board?

". . .we've decided to move ahead with the expansion of Diamond Estates. Construction will begin today to turn this dilapidated outbuilding in front of you into a fortress for hurting girls."

That pile of rubble? It would take a miracle.

"It will be a spiritual boot camp of sorts. A first stop on the way into the heart of Diamond Estates for a very select group of needs."

Ben ran his hand through his hair. "Over the years we've seen the importance of the more spiritually mature girls pouring into the lives of the newer girls as sort of mentors; in fact we train them to do that."

Like the day Tricia brought Roxy horseback riding. She must have been on assignment. Carmen glanced at Tricia and smiled.

"But we have to be sensitive to some of the more intense needs that the big house, for lack of a better term, can't handle."

Kira's hand shot up in the air.

"Yes?" Ben nodded in her direction.

"What types of things can't be handled at the main center? What kinds of problems will send girls there?" She tipped her head at the rundown structure.

"Let me explain." Ben smiled. "One step at a time. This building behind me was once a medical facility, a dispensary, if you will. That means it's already divided up into small rooms and has water and electricity. It has a solid foundation, and it's basically intact. It simply needs love. That's what our team from New Jersey has come to help with. Between all of us, we believe we can have it sparkling in two weeks."

Carmen nudged Theresa. "Looks like we'll all be helping." She laughed. At one time she'd have resented Ben's assumption. Carmen warmed at the evidence of core change within her heart. It was happening right before her eyes.

"As for the types of girls, we're talking drug addicts, people with severe depression, suicidal girls, even girls with strong spiritual strongholds in activities like witchcraft." Ben ticked the list off on his fingers. "Anyone who needs some time of intense spiritual, mental, or physical help before entering the mainstream Diamond Estates program." He surveyed the crowd. "Now what do you think?"

This was a good move. Smart. Carmen lifted her hands and began to clap. Several joined in. Others followed. Carmen raised her hand. "But who will run that part of things?"

"Good thinking, Carmen. It will clearly need to have its own staff and an even smaller staff-to-teen ratio. The director of the Diamond Intensive Program will be Mark Stapleton, and the medical manager will be his wife, Ginny, who is a now a nurse practitioner. She will oversee the medical needs of the entire campus."

He paused and grinned. "And I have one more announcement that makes me especially grateful. My lovely wife"—he held up Alicia's hand—"will be joining us full-time here. We tried to go with only myself and two other counselors after Patty left us last year. But it's just not enough, especially with all the changes coming."

Donna and Tammy clapped. Everyone laughed.

Ben grinned and pulled his wife close. "So, Alicia is leaving her job at the hospital as of next week and will come on as a counselor/nurse. She'll be the Donna-Tammy to the Intensive center and available for any medical needs that arise."

Alicia beamed. "My heart has been here with you girls all this time. I'm so grateful to God that He's blessed us and this ministry enough for me to be able to leave my outside job and come here to serve beside my husband and love you all."

The group broke into applause. It would be so great to have Alicia around all the time.

"Any other questions?" Ben gazed around the group.

Carmen shrugged. "Where's a shovel?"

Chapter 41

H ey, Nater." Carmen sat on the floor outside Ben's office. She leaned on the wall and closed her eyes.

"Hey, C. It's so good to hear your voice. How are you calling me, though? You didn't run away again, did you?"

Carmen almost forgot to listen to the words as she reveled in the sound of Nate's familiar voice. Therein lay the problem. Too familiar. "No. I didn't leave. Things here are going really well."

"That's great. I wish I were there."

So did Carmen.

"But how are you calling me?" Nate's pep transformed into doubt.

"I got special permission to make this one call. So we could talk." Carmen waited for Nate to realize the reason. He was too smart not to.

"I see." Silence. "They wouldn't give out privileges for no reason. There would have to be a point to the call other than catching up. So what's up?"

Like walking into the dentist's office, knowing there would be drilling that day. Submitting to pain for the greater good. How could Carmen take that first step? How could she hurt Nate and in the process hurt herself when all she'd like to do is curl up in his arms and fall asleep?

"Nater. . .I think you know why I'm calling." *Please say you do. Please don't make me say the words.*

"You're not coming back?" Fear laced his words.

Why did he love her so much—even after all she did to him? "I don't know about geographically, but I'm not coming back emotionally." There. It was finished.

"Why? Don't you love me anymore?" Nate croaked. "I don't understand. After I forgave you and waited for you for so long. . . I supported you."

"The fact that you're going to get hurt in the process of my growth and healing stings me to the core, but I can't go back. I just can't."

"We won't go back. We'll just move forward."

If only it were that easy. "Being with you is going back. I can't live my life trapped under the memories of my actions. It will darken our path forever."

"So you're telling me you messed up, and even though I'm willing to forgive and let go, you're going to hold *your* actions against *me* and punish me for them? That makes absolutely no sense."

"It's not quite like that. But it's time for me to make wise choices for my life. You'll thank me someday. You need a fresh start with someone who will put you first from the very beginning." *Please say you understand. Please don't hate me.*

"I guess I get it. I don't like it though."

"I have to go now." Carmen choked back a sob. "I'll always love you, Nater."

ᔐ

Dear Leila,

I'm so sorry. I can't possibly express enough how truly sorry I am. You've been through so much. . . . The last thing I wanted to do was heap more onto your shoulders. I hope you can forgive me, though I know that doesn't erase anything. . . . If I could have one wish, I'd go back in time and never write in that stupid journal. Or I'd write only good things like this:

I miss Leila. I miss her smile and her easygoing attitude. I miss her because she was always so easy to be around. I think she's someone I could talk to and even be friends with. I wish she'd come back.

Would you maybe consider coming back? We have a garden to plant.

Love, your friend,
Carmen

☙

The music swelled and brought Carmen's spirit with it. Justin leading and the worship team providing perfect harmonies, the musicians pounding out their parts, and the youth congregation on their feet praising their God.

She got it. Carmen felt the same pull to worship that she mocked in others before. It rose up from within her in response to what she'd been given. She couldn't stay in her seat and observe for anything. Compelled to stand, Carmen reveled in the music and responded as her body guided. Slowly her hands lifted in praise to her Creator, and her heart joined in.

Someone slipped in the empty seat next to her, but Carmen was too enraptured to look. Eventually the music quieted as Justin led the group in prayer. He prayed for unity, justice, mercy, and grace. Beautiful words—but they'd become more than just words; they were gifts.

As the prayer ended and they were directed to take their seats, Carmen stole a quick peek at the seat beside her.

Billy.

She gasped and threw her arms around his neck for a quick hug. Oops. She wasn't supposed to do that. She pulled back and settled into her seat. "I'm so glad you're here. What's going on?" she whispered. He looked so cute in regular jeans and a polo shirt. None of that goofy stuff he'd been wearing lately.

"You went back, so I went back." Billy lifted his chin.

"I'm so glad." Carmen sighed. "You're back at your parents'?"

He nodded. "For a little over a week."

"How about Sam?"

He shook his head. "Not yet."

"Kansas?"

"No."

"I'll be praying for them." For once, Carmen meant it.

She sat back and enjoyed Billy's nearness through the message. Such a good friend. . .if only. . . The service ended way too soon, and the pastor was calling them to stand for prayer. Couldn't they do one more song or have some more preaching just so she could sit next to him longer? It felt too much like good-bye.

". . .Amen." The youth pastor looked up and smiled. "Have a wonderful week. Love each other. You're dismissed."

Carmen stood. Billy grabbed her hand and pulled her back down.

"Is everything okay?" Where was Donna or Tammy? Carmen didn't want to get in trouble. After all, Billy was the one she ran away with. They might not like her talking to him.

"I know you have to go. I just need to know. Are you back with that one guy, or is there a chance of something between us?"

How did she answer that? She didn't want to hurt him. She simply didn't know. Carmen opened her mouth.

Billy held up a hand. "Wait. So you know, that's not why I'm back here—not at all. But it sure is on my mind a lot. I get the feeling that you don't feel quite the same way, though."

"I'm not back with Nate, and I do love you so much, Billy—as a friend and a brother." Carmen smiled. "I could easily have seen something happening between us under different circumstances or maybe even in the future. But right now I have a date with God—I need some time alone in my life so He can teach me stuff. You know?" *Please understand.*

Billy cocked his head to one side. "You know, that's the best let-him-down-easy approach I've ever heard." He laughed. "Seriously, though, I can't argue with that. And if, someday, God wants us to be together, I'll be a very lucky man because you took this time alone."

Chapter 42

K nock, knock." Carmen chuckled.

"Come on in." Donna looked up from her desk and smiled. "Have a seat. You've been a busy girl these past couple of weeks. In one word, tell me, how do you feel?"

"Hmm." Carmen gazed out the window at the pasture, where the horses were nibbling at the grass poking up through the snow. One word? Forgiven. Peaceful. Blessed. "I know." Carmen inhaled deeply and closed her eyes. "I feel free."

"Ah. Freedom. Free from guilt?"

"Yes, but more than that."

"Free from shame?"

"Well, I'm working on that one. Might take awhile."

Donna smiled. "Fair enough. Free from what then?"

"Mostly I feel free *from* myself and free to *be* myself."

"That's a very good way to put it. I'm writing that down." Donna scrawled on a notepad. "I think you're in a good place. Do you have any concerns?"

This was one of those moments when, in the past, she'd have told Donna exactly what she wanted to hear. "I don't want to fake it anymore. I want to be authentic. So I'll be honest about this." Carmen sighed. "I'm terrified."

Donna nodded. "About what exactly?"

"I'm so afraid none of these changes will last when it comes time for me to go home and reenter real life."

"That's a very common fear at this stage of your walk, and there are two things I want to say to that. Number one, we won't send you off from here until you feel ready, until you're equipped to stand strong and maintain your commitment to Christ. But more importantly, you need to know that you aren't strong enough, and you never will be."

Well that was a lovely thought. How could she say that? "Um. I don't feel very encouraged."

"No. Look here. You'll see what I mean." Donna opened her Bible. "Second Corinthians twelve tells us that it's only when we are weakest we see the fullness of His strength. Those weak moments in our lives are when He can rise up and show Himself strong and faithful to us."

Carmen nodded. Made sense in a backward sort of way. Which was consistent with much of what she had learned about God. He didn't always do what she expected. But yet it held true.

"And, Carmen, realize that you're a work in progress. You're not going to be perfect as long as you walk this earth. So give yourself a bit of a break. Not a license to sin, but freedom to live. Rest in your forgiveness. Savor it. Don't let your desire to earn it suck the joy right out of it. You can't earn it. Thankfully, it's already paid for."

Ah. There it was. Carmen let those words roll over her.

"So what does someone have to do to add to the graffiti wall? Do I have to wait until I graduate?"

"Oh no. It's just whenever someone has something they'd like to indelibly imprint on the walls of this place as an Ebenezer."

"A what?" Carmen just wanted to go crazy with some spray paint and make a symbol of what she'd learned.

Donna nodded. "Yeah. It's a great story. Israel went through a lot of trouble because of their own disobedience."

"I can already see the connection." Carmen smirked.

"Hold on. It gets better." Donna grinned. "Samuel became the priest and judge, and Israel repented. After that God kept them safe. Samuel wanted a way to remind the people of how when they turned their hearts toward God, He poured blessings and safety into their lives; so he put up a large stone in the place where they began their surrender. And that Ebenezer stone remained there to remind the people of their fresh start and God's covenant with them."

"Wow. That is pretty cool. So can I have my turn?"

"You're ready?"

"Yep." Carmen stood up. "Where's the paint? You have red, right?"

"We have every color. You're going to do this now?"

"Why not?"

"Okay. Follow me." Donna led her to the electronics room and closed the door. There on the wall behind the door were shelves packed with all kinds of spray paints, brushes, markers, and whatever she might need to create her art.

"Take whatever you need, and then have at it. I'll leave you to your ponderings so I don't get in the way of your creative energy."

"Thanks." Carmen dropped to the floor by the metallic paint and selected ResplendentRed Glitter. Six other flat colors, and she had what she needed. She put everything in an empty cardboard box and pulled the door closed.

Should she sketch it out first? Or just go for it? As she climbed the stairs, she looked in detail at some of the others. She'd be just fine without sketching it. It would be more abstract.

She selected the wall section to the right of their bedroom door. How much room was that? Best guess. . .about two feet to the corner. Perfect.

First the cross. Carmen made a gradient yellow sunburst in

the center of the wall canvas then added a brown slash from the floor up about four feet. Next came the cross beam from the edge of the door frame across to the corner. How did that look? She stepped back.

Good, except for. . . Carmen added some darker brown shading and shadows to the edges of the cross. The cross with the sun shining through it, symbolic of Christ's love for her and her awakening to new life. Perfect.

Now for the other important lesson. Carmen stared at the wall. *Come on, inspiration.* What did she want to say with this part? People are people. At the cross there's no color or status. That's it. Unity.

Just below the cross beam, she used peach paint to spray a hand reaching out toward the cross. Then from the other door frame, she used her darkest brown to spray another hand the same way. From the bottom up, a light-brown hand. And from the top, yet another shade of brown. In the center of them all, right on top of the cross, Carmen sprayed a heart.

That's awesome. Carmen stepped back, proud of the work, but even more proud of the internal work it took to have the right to paint that graffiti for all to see.

But she wasn't finished yet. She grabbed the red-diamond glitter paint and added a pair of ruby slippers at the foot of the cross.

"There's no place like home."

Discussion Questions

1. Describe the various ways Carmen faced loss in the early chapters of this book. How did she handle it?

2. What prejudice does Carmen experience that is directed toward her? Does she see it clearly?

3. How did she land on a slippery slope of sin? What happened?

4. Once she realized what she was doing, how could she have stopped it? Would it have been better to prevent it completely? How could she have done that?

5. What was the final event or catalyst that led her to seek help at Diamond Estates? Do you think that was the right choice at that time? Why or why not?

6. In her first few weeks there, was Carmen open to the guidance she received at Diamond Estates? How do you know?

7. What led her to run away? What was she seeking?

8. When she ran away, was she farther from God than before she arrived at Diamond Estates or closer?

9. During the course of the entire book, what prejudices does Carmen direct toward others? How does she come to face the truth about herself?

10. How many ways can you identify prejudice in *The Embittered Ruby*? How about in your own life?

11. What does God say about His love for people of different ethnicities, social statuses, body types, and income levels?

12. What is the overarching message of *The Embittered Ruby*?

Chapter-by-Chapter
Discussion Guide

CHAPTER 1

1. Describe Carmen's attitude about the move. Is she justified in feeling like she does? How would you feel in the exact same situation?
2. What does Carmen assume Nate's family thinks about her? Why do you think she assumes what she does? Is there evidence in the story to support that?
3. Describe the faith element in Carmen's family.
4. How do you feel about teenagers being on birth control? Why?

CHAPTER 2

1. What signs, if any, do you see that indicate Carmen's relationship with Nate is inappropriate or sinful?
2. Why do you think Carmen is concerned about two missed pills?
3. Is it right that Carmen's dad knows she's on birth control but her mom doesn't?

CHAPTER 3

1. Who's Nellie, and what's her role in Carmen's life?
2. Describe the different behaviors of the three sisters.
3. Is there something Carmen could do to help her sisters through the divorce? Or is she the only one hurting?

CHAPTER 4

1. How does Carmen feel about Tiffany?
2. What makes that relationship so strained?
3. Who's more at fault? Carmen's mom, dad, Tiffany, or Carmen herself? Why?

4. Is there evidence in the story that proves Tiffany is the one who got Carmen kicked out of the club?
5. How would you describe Carmen's treatment of her dad at the end of this chapter? Is it fair or not?

CHAPTER 5

1. Do you think Diego is really looking out for Carmen? Or does he have ulterior motives?
2. What do you think the chances are that Carmen could be successful in getting her parents back together? Do you think it's a wise plan?
3. Was her father truly clueless about what was going on between Tiffany and his daughter, or did he just want to ignore it and hope the situation would fix itself?
4. How did Tiffany undermine Carmen's role in her dad's life?
5. What plot does Carmen devise to force Nate to marry her?

CHAPTER 6

1. Describe the perceived differences between Carmen's new school and her old school.
2. How would you have handled Marco?
3. How do you feel about Carmen's plan?
4. Would it ever be fair, even if the couple were married, to do something like that behind someone's back?
5. How important is honesty and trust in a relationship?

CHAPTER 7

1. If Hillary McConnell knows Spanish, why does she ask Carmen to communicate with Consuelo for her?
2. Compare Hillary's prejudices with Carmen's.

Chapter 8

1. Describe Carmen's general feelings about church.
2. How important is appearance to you? Compare that to Tricia's situation and how physical expectations drove her to take drastic measures.
3. How can unbelief control your life?

Chapter 9

1. Between Theresa and Kayla, who was closer to the mark when trying to figure Carmen out?
2. Carmen was nervous about Nate's reaction to her new home. Is there anything in your life you're ashamed to let your friends see? Something material, or even something internal?
3. Is it your hang-up, or is it something your friends have caused?
4. Carmen does a lot of sneaking around behind her mom's back, and now even in her own home. How do you feel about her sneaking out to the couch where Nate was sleeping?

Chapter 10

1. Describe Carmen's thoughts during the wait for the pregnancy test results.
2. Is it logical that she felt some twinges of doubt and regret? Or do you think she should deal with it because she brought it on herself?
3. At this point, before you know the outcome, how do you think Nate will respond to the baby news?

CHAPTER 11

1. How do you feel about abortion?
2. How does God feel about abortion? See Psalm 137 and 139.
3. What about adoption? What are your thoughts on that? What do you think about the conclusion Nate and Carmen arrive at when they touch on the possibility of adoption?
4. What do you think the chances are of this marriage working?

CHAPTER 12

1. Is it okay for Carmen to be hanging out with Diego without knowing the full story of his past?
2. Do you think her "friendship" with Diego is inappropriate considering Nate has no idea he exists?
3. What do you think about Tiffany's reaction to the baby? Does it alter your impressions of her at all?

CHAPTER 13

1. Did Nate's parents react the way Carmen expected them to?
2. Why do you think Nate doesn't see the truth about his mom?
3. Do you think this situation might open his eyes a little?
4. Does the commandment to honor your father and mother extend to things like what Hillary is doing?

CHAPTER 14

1. What did you think Hillary wanted to see Carmen about?
2. Is it smart or unfair for Carmen to plan to record the meeting?
3. What do you think about Hillary's offer? What is motivating her to behave that way?
4. Should Carmen have taken the money?

Chapter 15

1. Tiffany took Carmen to the doctor. Was that cool of her or intrusive?
2. When in this whole process would you have involved your mom?

Chapter 16

1. Do you think Carmen has any right to worry about what Kim is up to? Should she just leave her alone?
2. Is it really necessary for Carmen to pretend Diego is her boyfriend? If so, why? If not, why do you think she continues?
3. Diego calls the stranger in the car a ghost. Who do you think he is?

Chapter 17

1. Hillary has photos, Carmen has a recording. Who was right? Who was wrong?
2. Do you think it was okay for Carmen to talk to Nate's mom like she did?
3. How do you think Nate should handle this situation?
4. Nate finds out about Diego. What do you think of his reaction?
5. Why did Carmen and Nate go to her dad rather than her mom to get permission to marry? Was that sneaky or perfectly fine?
6. How might she have handled things with Mom a little better?

Chapter 18

1. Carmen is in a pretty tough situation with Marco and his buddies. What's the first thing you'd do under the same circumstances?

2. When she gets out of there, what does she do? What should she do?
3. If Diego died, would it be her fault?
4. Should she have told Nate what happened? Why or why not?
5. What about the blood? Should she have told him that?

CHAPTER 19

1. Do you think it's safe for Carmen to play tennis?
2. Was it her fault she lost the baby?
3. Do you think Nate would forgive her if she told him everything right away?
4. Do you think it was worse for her because of how he actually found out?

CHAPTER 20

1. Is Carmen's mom's tough-love approach a good thing or a bad thing? Why?
2. Why is she handling it that way?
3. How does Carmen feel about Diamond Estates in general?
4. How does she feel about going there herself?

CHAPTER 21

1. Ben tells of a teenage pregnancy in his past. Is Carmen able to apply his and Alicia's success at moving past their bad choices to her own life yet?
2. What are Carmen's thoughts about Leila?
3. In what ways do they compare to Hillary's thoughts about Carmen?
4. Carmen acts tough, even in her thoughts, but how do you think she's really feeling about checking in to Diamond Estates?
5. What evidence is there to support your opinion?

CHAPTER 22

1. What did Ben mean by the idea of free will?
2. How did it relate to what Carmen had said?
3. What did Ju-Ju's graffiti represent?
4. Would you have walked into the secret passageway?

CHAPTER 23

1. What would you do if faced with Carmen's current predicament of being locked out?
2. What do you think Leila's story might be at this point?

CHAPTER 24

1. Do you think the phrase "fake it till you make it" applies in any real way to Christianity?
2. Is it fair to punish Carmen for missing prayer time when she is admittedly not a Christian?
3. Was the punishment fair?
4. Why did Carmen say Marilyn was a sneaky one?

CHAPTER 25

1. How does Carmen feel about worship in general?
2. How does she describe the worshippers in the youth service on her first Sunday at church?
3. Do you think Carmen will last at Diamond Estates until spring?

CHAPTER 26

1. How do you think God feels about Carmen at this stage of her journey? See Luke 19.

CHAPTER 27

1. Carmen wondered if she'd have to face her baby one day

and explain what had happened. What do you think about that?

2. Donna asks Carmen to choose one or two words to describe her actions. What words does she choose?

3. What two words would you choose to describe yourself?

4. What is one way Carmen shows prejudice in her own thoughts in this chapter?

CHAPTER 28

1. Have you read book one, *The Wishing Pearl*? If so, does Carmen have an accurate impression of Olivia? Why or why not?

2. Describe how Olivia feels about God's presence in her life.

3. If she were a friend of yours and said those things to you, how would you respond?

CHAPTER 29

1. What do you think about the unity candle service at the wedding? Should the individual candles be blown out as the two become one, or should they leave them lit as a symbol of individuality?

2. What scheme does Carmen devise to split up Olivia and Justin?

3. Will it work?

CHAPTER 30

1. What does it mean to be undignified before God? Read about King David in 2 Samuel 6:21–22.

2. Why would Carmen take so many chances, like hanging out with Billy, Sam, and Kansas under the stairwell and smoking pot?

3. What's Billy's story?

CHAPTER 31

1. If Carmen were visited by the ghosts of Christmas future, what do you think she'd learn about herself if she doesn't surrender to God? What if she does?
2. How many lies did Carmen tell Olivia in the bathroom?
3. Should Carmen help Roxy?

CHAPTER 32

1. How can we tell that Carmen has truly mastered the art of deception?
2. Why does she want to go home already?
3. Why did Ben say Carmen's feelings of hopelessness were a good sign?

CHAPTER 33

1. Considering all of her internal dialogue as well as the actual events, what do you think are the real reasons Carmen runs away?

CHAPTER 34

1. Do you think Billy is acting out in response to grief? In what ways?
2. Is there evidence that suggests Billy isn't the big party animal Carmen had once assumed?
3. What about Kansas? How is she different from Billy?

CHAPTER 35

1. Was it fair for Carmen to call Nate, or should she have left him alone?
2. What did he get upset with her about?
3. Why does Carmen turn to drugs?

CHAPTER 36

1. What are the two main things Nate wants to see from Carmen?
2. What more do we learn about Billy?

CHAPTER 37

1. Why does Olivia offer forgiveness to Carmen even though Carmen didn't ask for it?
2. Why is Carmen ready for friendship now when she wasn't ever before?

CHAPTER 38

1. How many times will Ben forgive Carmen and let her come back? How many times will God?
2. Donna says that forgiveness is always available, but that sometimes there's no possible repair for actions. Do you think that's true?
3. How has gossip caused damage to innocent people in this story?

CHAPTER 39

1. How did the phone call with her family go?
2. Summarize what Carmen's mom said about receiving God's forgiveness.
3. Is it good that Carmen says good-bye to Nellie? Why?

CHAPTER 40

1. What does Carmen discover about herself when she learns the truth about the stranger in the car?
2. She digs a little deeper with Donna on the subject of prejudice. What does she learn?

CHAPTER 41

1. Do you think Carmen was fair to Nate? Why did he think she wasn't?

2. Can you think of anything else Carmen could have done to try to fix things with Leila?

3. Why is Nate having such a hard time letting go even though Carmen did horrible things to him? Is it out of love or fear of being alone?

4. What reason does Carmen give Billy for not wanting a relationship with him at that time?

5. Could you consider choosing God over a boy?

CHAPTER 42

1. What did Carmen mean by this statement: "I feel free *from* myself and free to *be* myself"?

2. Describe the symbolism behind Carmen's graffiti.

THE SHADOWED ONYX

·········· Chapter 1 ··········

A re there any spirits in this room with us?"
Joy Christianson stared at Raven, her face glowing in
the candlelight from the black tapers to either side of the game
board on the floor between them. Raven's eyes drifted shut,
and her fingers danced atop the same wooden triangle that lay
motionless beneath Joy's.

The tallest candle flickered, casting a somber spotlight,
illuminating the letters that would spell messages from beyond.
The flame bent to the left as though a birthday child begged for
a wish.

Peeling her gaze from the candle, Joy followed her new friend's
instructions and squeezed her eyes shut, leaning back against the
bed. It was Raven's house after all. Her house, her rules.

The game piece—that's all it was, right?—trembled and
then slithered across the Ouija board. Joy's eyes snapped open,
and she jerked back. "Very funny, Raven." Joy inched away as
though gnarled fingers would reach from underneath, grab her
ankles, and pull her to the great beyond. "I don't even believe in
this stuff." She slid her hands under her legs. No way she'd put
them back on that thing.

Raven raised one eyebrow and cocked her head. "Oh? You
don't, huh? Then I don't suppose that's your heartbeat I can
practically hear all the way over here? What about the rapid

breathing and"—she yanked on Joy's arm and inspected her hand—"sweaty palms?" She returned to the ready position and waited. "People aren't usually scared of things they don't believe in."

Something was out there. Beyond reality. Joy could feel it in her bones. But did she want to communicate with whatever—whoever—it was? "I don't know Ray. I. . .I might not be ready for something like this. Besides, it's just a game."

"It is so not just a game." Raven shrugged. "You can think that if you want to. But then you might as well play if it's only for fun."

Okay, now what? Joy could play along and pretend she didn't believe in it, or she could admit her terror and leave Raven's house immediately. The whole Ouija board thing was probably totally fake, but then why the shivers, and most importantly, why did that thing move?

Perfectly explainable. The shivers were simply a product of her own nervousness, and the triangle thingy moved because Raven pushed it on purpose.

Raven flipped her dark brown hair behind her shoulder, though the top layers fell in front of her pale face like a dark curtain. She placed her fingers on the triangle's wooden edge and tipped her chin toward Joy. "Come on. What are you waiting for? There's activity here, and I'm going to prove it to you."

"What are you saying? You think there are ghosts or. . .what?"

One corner of Raven's mouth curled up. "Or something like that. Let's go."

Joy pushed the sleeves of her fuzzy pink sweater up to her elbows and gathered her long hair into a ponytail, rolling a hair tie from her wrist to secure it out of her face.

Deep breath. Only a game.

Reaching her hands toward Raven's, Joy barely let her fingertips rest in position. Her bright pink nails glared a contrast to Raven's black ones just inches away. The candle teased the big black stone in Raven's skull ring with glints of light.

Joy trembled.

"Oh great sprit here tonight, will you identify yourself to us, please?" Raven slowly opened her eyes and gazed into the dancing candle flame nearest the door.

Joy begged her muscles to lift her fingers from the game, but she couldn't move. What if something were there? What if—

Joy's fingers jerked an inch and then gently glided along the game board as the triangle headed toward a letter. Raven, again? Or did something more sinister propel it? She stared at the fingertips across from hers. They didn't appear to be applying any pressure to the planchette at all. Yet it continued to move.

"We mean no harm. Who is with us here?" Raven's voice sounded strange. Calm. Gravelly.

The bedroom door stood open only a few feet away, letting a bit of a glow into the dark room from a nightlight near the hallway bathroom. Joy could make a mad dash, but she'd have to jump over the candles and the game to get to the door. And then what? She'd be out in the strange, empty house with all the worked up spirits while Raven stayed back and made friends with the nice ones? No thanks.

The glass part of the triangle stopped over a letter.

"M," Raven whispered.

Was it okay to talk out loud? The thing continued moving after a brief pause. It paused over the letter *E*. "Me? Is that what it's saying? What does that mean?" Joy shook her head, blond wisps sticking to her lip gloss. "I'm done. Seriously this time." She stood and reached over Raven's head to flip on the light.

"For now." Raven licked both thumbs and forefingers and squeezed the flames, extinguishing them with a sizzle.

"No, for good. I'm done messing with this stuff. It freaks me out." Joy shivered and pulled her sweater tight around her body.

Raven shrugged as she folded the board and slid it under her bed. "There's not a lot you can do about it now. You've had a taste, and you'll want more."

⑥

"Hey! Joy's back." Coach Templeton waved from the other side of the volleyball court.

Several players stepped aside as Joy jogged toward her trying not to inhale the familiar gym aroma so she wouldn't totally lose it. What was it about smells that stimulated emotions more than the other senses?

"Good to have you back." Heather patted Joy's shoulder.

"Yeah. Glad you're here."

"Right. Me too."

Joy nodded, but kept her eye on Coach. It was the only way she'd get through the practice. She ducked under the net and met Coach mid-court.

"How you holding up, kiddo?"

Way to go right for the jugular. Joy's eyelids were humming-bird wings as she fought back the ever-present tears. "I'm good, I guess. I mean, look at me." She gestured the length of her body. "I'm perfect. But Melanie. . .well, she's another story." The tears rolled down Joy's cheeks. She could do nothing to hold them back.

Coach slipped an arm across Joy's shoulders and steered her toward her office. "Go on in and have a seat. I'll be right in." She turned toward the team stretching on the court. "Lauren, you're the. . .um. . .new captain. . .so put everyone through some drills. I'll be right out."

New captain. Melanie's position. She'd loved that the team

had thought so highly of her to vote her as captain. Well, why not? Mel was the best person Joy ever knew. And Melanie felt the same about Joy. They'd sure told each other plenty of times. Until two weeks ago.

Coach Templeton closed the door, sealing out the sound of bouncing balls and shoes squeaking on the gymnasium floor. Noises that reverberated until they blended into one perfect sound called volleyball. Would Joy ever love the game again? Could she let herself love anything again?

"So. How are you, really?"

Dead inside. Alone. "I don't know. What you'd expect, I guess."

"I can imagine how hard this must be."

Joy nodded. Coach couldn't possibly imagine. Not unless her best friend had committed suicide. Not unless she had been the one to find her dead and then have to break the news to her best friend's parents? No. Probably not. That stuff only happened in Lifetime movies. Or Joy's life.

"Are you seeing anyone?" Coach almost whispered.

Joy recoiled. "You mean like dating?" What kind of question was that? Like Joy would ever date again.

Coach shook her head. "No, no. I mean like a counselor."

Joy shrugged. "My parents offered. But the pastor said it's nothing we can't handle with God. Thinks I don't need counseling."

"God is great, but even He talked about getting counsel from wise people and all that good stuff. You should really consider it." Coach peered into Joy's eyes. "I think you have what's called survivor's guilt. It's normal. But it stinks."

You think? Joy nodded. "I'll talk to my mom about it."

"That's all I ask. Now. You ready to play some V-ball?"

The thought of stepping out onto that court among her friends—Melanie's friends—without her there, made the bile rise to Joy's throat. She whipped her head side to side. "I can't. Not yet." She searched the room for an escape. Great. One way in, one way out.

"That's fine, kiddo. Baby steps. You'll play next time." Coach stood. "Come on, I'll walk you out so you don't get a barrage of questions on your way."

If only there were answers.

꩜

Joy sat on a pillow in the center of Raven's candle-lit room. Why had she agreed to do this again? "Um. What, exactly, do we hope happens here tonight?"

Lucas plopped down to the ground and gave his signature grin—the same sneer he'd had since second grade. "We are reaching out to the spirit who tried to talk to you guys the other night." He opened the Ouija board and placed it in the center of their human triangle. The glass piece in place, he settled his hands in position and waited.

Raven reached her fingers to the board, and laid them beside Luc's, barely touching his pinkie.

Oh please.

Joy cracked her knuckles and settled her hands in place. Just get it over with.

"Spirit friend, we know you're with us. We'd like to know who you are. Will you please tell us?" Lucas looked into the flame.

Joy felt movement as her arm was pulled along the board until the glass stopped over a letter.

M

Here we go again. Joy lifted some of the weight off her fingertips. She sure didn't want to be the cause of where the planchette moved. She glanced at Raven who stared at Lucas, as usual. When he was around, no one else existed. If they only knew. Joy's stomach churned. Never again would she care about a boy that much. Ever.

Lucas cleared his throat. "Do you feel that?" He spoke in even tones and looked at Raven. "There's like a low rumble, a hum maybe, in the room."

Yeah. Probably the furnace, you idiot.

"I do feel it." Raven closed her eyes and lifted her face.

Oh please. What did she want? A ghostly kiss on the cheek? In better times, Joy would have giggled at the thought of playing a trick on her. But not today. . .maybe never. Just too much effort.

The triangle continued its path on the board.

E

"See, Luc? That's what it said last time. *Me*. What is it trying to tell us?"

"Shh." Lucas shook his head. "It's not finished, yet." He closed his eyes. "Are you still identifying yourself to us?"

With force Joy hadn't been expecting, the glass eye slid to the *Yes*.

What had just happened? It sure seemed real. . .it had to be Lucas or Raven making that thing move. It had to be. But it sure didn't seem like it. Joy searched her friends' eyes for a clue to the truth.

Raven chewed on her lower lip. Was she nervous?

"Okay. It's getting irritated. Feels interrupted." Lucas sat up straighter. "We're listening, spirit. Tell us who you are."

Back to the normal speed of death, their hands eased along until they revealed another letter.

L

What if it was real? Pastor Joel talked about the spirit world sometimes. It made sense that if God existed like she'd always believed, the dark side would too. Joy watched in fascination as her hands were drawn to the next letter.

A

It paused for only a few seconds and dropped to the letter below.

N

Wait just a second. Was this some kind of sick joke? Joy looked from Raven to Lucas. Were they in on this together? How undeniably cruel to make that thing spell out. . . "Come on—"

"Shh," Lucas hissed, his eyes trained on the space above his gnawed fingernails.

I

Joy would never speak to them again. Simple as that. But then why didn't she just leave? Why let them finish out their ruse at her expense?

Lucas nodded at Raven and lifted his hands. He reached across the table and lifted Joy's fingers as Raven removed hers.

The planchette moved a few inches.

All. By. Itself.

Horror filled the pit of Joy's stomach. Everything she ever believed about life, death, God, and heaven crumbled into purgatory as a game claimed her faith.

E